THE END OF
THE PIER SHOW

Jeremy Carrad

Dear Paul and Peggy,

With my love,

Jeremy

CCL Books

Published by CCL Books, PO Box 112, Bristol BS20 8XQ, England.

A CIP catalogue record for this book is available from the British Library.

ISBN 0-9546188-0-7

Cover design and illustration by Mike Kendall
Typeset by Academic + Technical, Bristol
Printed and bound in Great Britain
by Antony Rowe Ltd, Chippenham, Wiltshire

AUTHOR'S NOTE

Whilst the characters and the storyline in this book are completely fictional, the framework around which it is created is based on the facts of the time.

Work on the development of the atomic bomb had been progressing, albeit slowly, through the thirties and, in 1940, the race was on, principally between England, America, Germany and Japan, to be the first to 'harness the atom' and thereby control the destiny of the world.

My one and only deliberate distortion of these facts has been to make the leading physicist in this work on nuclear fission a Polish Professor and this I do with great delight as my own very small dedication to that nation so cruelly served over the past two hundred-or-so years.

Every thought, word, dot and comma on these pages is dedicated to my dearest wife, Jean without whom – it wouldn't be…

ACKNOWLEDGEMENTS

My grateful thanks to Rosemary Elms for her tireless typing of the many drafts of the book.

I also want to thank a group of people who have been foremost in my mind as I committed their characters to print.

THE END OF THE PIER SHOW started life in a somewhat simpler form as a stage play and was first performed in January 1999. Here I salute the brave actors and back-stage team of THE WIG PLAYERS from Weston in Gordano in North Somerset who submitted themselves, almost willingly, to my direction during the months of rehearsal and achieved such justifiable acclaim at the performances.

Jean Carrad – Nell Masters
Gill Stringer – Vi Ulthwaite
Ann Bridges – Pat Baker
Angela Borland – Peggy Baker
Alma Youde – Elaine Price
Sue Broadway – Rita Rogers
Emma Massey – Rena Rogers
David Lewis – Tad Stevens
Jeremy Carrad – Belvedere Galbraith
Ian Borland – Norman Jackson
Geoff Mitchell – George Noble
John Bridges – The Great Marvo
Stuart Redway – Ludovic Henschel
Chris Stringer – Freddy Crisciak
Don Pearce – Don Preace

and Ann and Patrick Chavasse, May Harris, Ann Redway and Ross Merrifield – who made a splendid Winston Churchill!

Others who appeared – or didn't quite – were Paul Smith, Steve Rogers, Mike Challenor and someone without whom we would have been in serious trouble, our 'prompt', Liz Matthews!

P.S.
It isn't often that an author acknowledges himself – but what the heck…

PROLOGUE

June 4th 1940. 338,226 British and French troops have been evacuated from the beaches of Dunkirk. The massed forces of the German Wehrmacht are poised to follow them across the Channel. An invasion of the British Isles is considered imminent.

Belvedere Galbraith sneezed. The explosion was mighty and caused a thin cloud of briefly inhaled snuff to roll like the morning mist towards those squashed with him into the small lounge of Flaxton-on-Sea's Station Hotel. It was easy to tell which of them knew him and which did not share that honour.

His colleagues, Nell Masters and Pat Baker, without a blink between them, continued to stare with a mixture of awe and disbelief at their distinguished visitor who had arrived from London and, at the start of his tour of the inadequate anti-invasion defences dotted along the east coast, had astounded his high-ranking entourage by demanding to meet two members of the town's seaside theatre troupe!

To those present who were unacquainted with Belvedere the suddenness of the explosive sneeze caused two distinct reactions. The forefingers of the two Royal Marines guarding the closed door involuntarily whitened as they tightened them around the triggers of their sub-machine guns. They eyed Belvedere with a malevolence normally reserved for any member of the Armed Forces other than fellow Marines. In contrast the blue-suited and Service-Dressed members of the Prime Minister's team found various different parts of themselves clenching in anticipation of what might follow this damp, slightly perfumed salvo from this extraordinary man.

Belvedere, blissfully unaware of any of this, selected another pinch of his Royal Angus Mix, placed it with precision into the hollow between thumb and first finger of his left hand and raised it to his right nostril. Marines and entourage, as far apart in class and social standing as could be, tensed and clenched as one, as he noisily inhaled the powder into his breathing tubes. They waited. Nothing happened. Belvedere smiled benignly at them.

"Would any of you care for a pinch?" he boomed, waving the small silver box in their approximate direction. Discipline had taught the Marines to refuse; etiquette, the others. No-one moved.

Winston Churchill was aware of none of this. The thick plume of smoke from his Havana cigar had been more than a match for the snuff barrage and, anyway, his mind had been concentrated totally on the bizarre set of circumstances that had turned a troupe of small-time music-hall artistes into what he, in his flowing rhetoric, described as 'saviours of the free world'.

Through the blue haze he viewed as unlikely a trio of heroes as he would meet throughout the course of the entire war – which he, unlike almost all other leaders in the conflict at this darkest time, intended would last as long as it took to beat the Hun.

First there was this tiny woman sitting uncomfortably on the edge of an armchair. His briefing notes identified her as Nell Masters, the owner of the Pier Theatre Company. She was dressed in a man's enormous dark blue overcoat and had perched on top of her bun of hair a rather tired felt hat with an ostrich feather, which had obviously experienced a long hard life, poking vertically into the stale air above it. The Prime Minister, with a meticulous eye for such detail, noted that it had remained stiffly erect, unwavering, despite being within a few inches of the violent eruption of the large man standing alongside her.

Churchill drew deeply on his cigar releasing another vast cloud of smoke into the already fetid atmosphere and swivelled his gaze to this large man. Belvedere Galbraith, tragedian. That's all the notes said.

As with most plump men Churchill was surprised how plump the other man was – and he was tall, certainly six feet and maybe an inch or two more. This large frame was draped with a wild array of snuff-stained Edwardian clothes, some too small and stretched like a corset, others too large hanging loosely from him. With Belvedere it depended only on what the second-hand clothes shops had to offer at a very reasonable price.

Standing a little away from the two was a young girl, probably, Churchill thought, in her late twenties or early thirties. There was nothing stunning about her but she had delicate, pretty features, auburn hair around her shoulders and, he didn't doubt, a sunny smile. She must be Pat Baker, the closest friend of the person who had been at the heart of this drama, Peggy Ashbourne, Countess Margaret Crisciak.

He wished she would smile; he needed smiles just now, but he understood. He had read the briefing notes in the car on the way down from London and was well aware of what they had all been through. Looking through their tense expressions, he could see the steel in all their eyes. He knew better than anyone that the nation would need toughness and resolve to match theirs in the months and years to come.

The sneeze had hardly ended and the particles of snuff settled before he rumbled out a series of Churchillian phrases regarding the struggle ahead which, long afterwards, they were able to repeat, word for word, to the many who listened to their extraordinary tale; "…averting a vast, indefinite butchery – laying healing hands on a tortured people – creating a miracle of deliverance." And then he came forward and took Nell's hands in his.

"You have driven home one of the first rivets in the making of the machine which will ultimately bring us victory."

"Indistractable," said Nell firmly, "that's what this country is," and her ostrich feather inclined in agreement.

Before Pat could put right the malapropism, inevitable from Nell in times of emotion, Belvedere stole the limelight, not this time with a sneeze, but rather with a contribution from his beloved Bard.

"All's well that ends well" he boomed causing more whitening of trigger fingers.

"But it isn't, hasn't, Bel" Nell jumped up with startling agility sending her distinguished visitors including their leader hastily back a pace. Her ostrich feather scythed vertically within a whisker of Belvedere's nose.

"It hasn't. It's been an unmedicated disaster for us from…" she hunted for the phrase.

Pat broke in quickly, "start to finish." She couldn't risk an exchange of first letters that Nell was prone to make when flustered.

"The time, Sir." A Service-Dress with red braided cap leant forward towards his master's ear. The General feared more fervently than ever for the safety of the country if even a minuscule part of it rested in the hands of such extraordinary people. The expressions on the faces of his blue-suited colleagues suggested that they obviously endorsed his view.

Churchill had no such thoughts. He liked these people and their idiosyncratic ways. More of it, he mused, and the Hun, should he ever gain British soil, would be dumbfounded, confounded and floundering. They were a ready-made secret weapon.

His genial face broke into a boyish grin; anything that obviously riled his high-ranking entourage delighted him. He stuffed his Homburg hat firmly on his head, stuck his cigar into his mouth, and lifted his ebony cane in salute to them.

Contrary to protocol he impatiently ushered his entourage out of the room ahead of him as Belvedere and the sentries, almost as one, pulled themselves to attention. Last to leave, he turned at the door.

"You have rendered a great service." His voice was strangely quiet and sad. "You have fought your war. Now I must go and fight mine."

And he was gone.

CHAPTER ONE

Early April 1940. In just seven months Hitler has exterminated all but three per cent of the intelligentsia in Poland. The country is now divided between Germany and the USSR.

In England nothing of a warlike nature has occurred.

Charles Turville sat uncomfortably on the hard wooden chair in Miss Gilbert's office on the top floor of the Headquarters of the Special Investigation Service in central London. He hated being here, not because of the forthcoming interview with his chief, Sir Philip Southern – he always enjoyed meeting the old man – but rather because he felt vulnerable in confined spaces. He also had a fear of one day being retired from active service into a pen-pushing desk job in this very building; the fate of so many over-the-hill secret agents.

"C will see you now." Miss Gilbert, known to Sir Philip – but to *no-one* else – as 'Gilly', captured two real and a few imaginary stray hairs, pushed them up into her tightly pinned bun, sniffed – delicately – and resumed her secretarial seat with an elaborate smoothing of her severe frock beneath her well proportioned person.

Miss Gilbert didn't approve of visitors, whether summoned or craving an audience of her beloved master. They made the place untidy and disturbed the well-ordered functioning of her – their – office. The fact that Sir Philip spent much of his life summoning, or being craved an audience by, all manner of people left her in a state of perpetual disapproval which she displayed to everyone, whether high or low, who sat patiently on the three deliberately uncomfortable chairs in her office.

But although she would never – ever – wish it to be known, Charles Turville was an exception, not only due to his status as the most senior MI6 agent in the Service, but also because he did strange things to her – in a manner of speaking. In his presence she found herself somewhat breathless, a little hot – she would suggest 'glowing' – and a trifle wobbly around the knees. Why, her severe upbringing had ensured, she didn't really know. But it was quite nice.

Having received her command Charles Turville now unfolded himself from the planned discomfort of one of the chairs until the top of his head was its full six foot four inches above the carpet and moved towards the large oak double doors. He bowed very slightly to Miss Gilbert as he passed her desk and, despite herself, she felt her heart briefly flutter as she looked up into a pair of blue eyes which, though usually without expression, were now twinkling.

"As ever, Miss Gilbert, it has been a pleasure making your brief acquaintance." And through the door he went.

The flutter was still there but, Miss Gilbert reassured herself, it was a mere shadow of the one which frequently enveloped her when she was anywhere near Sir Philip. It was, however, sufficient to prevent her catching the innuendo of the word 'brief' in Charles Turville's remark and, hurriedly tidying her already immaculately tidy desk, she returned to her Imperial typewriter.

As Head of the SIS – the Secret Intelligence Service – Sir Philip, following in the tradition of its founder near the start of the century, Sir Mansfield Cumming, was known to everyone who was allowed to know him as 'C'. As Turville entered he was sitting behind his immense oak desk set in the corner of his equally immense office. In fact everything in the once opulent, but now rather threadbare room – settees, armchairs, coffee tables, drapes, pictures and Sir Philip himself – was immense. Two walls were punctured with floor to distant ceiling windows looking out onto a grey and grimy London. Little of it could be seen due partly to the dullness of this April morning but also to the criss-crossed white tape stuck diagonally over most of the glass surface to, it was hoped, prevent it shattering into lethal splinters in the event of a bomb blast.

"Good morning C." Turville raised a hand and started the long walk to the desk. Sir Philip looked up from his writing.

"Morning, Charles. Sit you down over there and read the notes." He indicated with his large gold fountain pen a pile of buff files on a low table fifteen or so yards away from him. "Then we'll talk."

His voice had the soft lilt of the genteel Edinburgh from whence he had set forth forty years before to seek steady, gainful employment and found instead the excitement of a Secret Service career. Now desk-bound and gammy-legged as a result of his greatest escape of all from the yawning barrels of a firing squad he had groomed Charles Turville to carry on where he'd left off. A natural successor; the son he'd never had.

"You've had some tea?" Miss Gilbert had taught him to say that. Only the high and mighty would dare say "no"; others muttered "yes" through parched lips. Charles Turville said nothing; he knew the two of them too well...

Turville changed direction to the suite of deep armchairs and settees and, settling into one, picked up the files and started to wade through the mass of papers, all stamped 'Most Secret'. Sir Philip, meanwhile, continued scratching his pen, filled with the green ink traditionally used by the head of MI6, over countless sheets of paper, occasionally adding counterpoint to the rhythm of his work by noisily wielding his desk blotter to dry the results.

The top file had just one word, other than the familiar 'Most Secret', typed in capitals on its buff surface:

OMEGA

Turville opened it. The first page was startling in its blankness. There was just one inscription:

PROJECT OMEGA

Omega: The last word. The end – or final development

For some reason he couldn't define he found that he was holding his breath. He felt the familiar tingle of anticipation, a mixture of so many emotions from excitement to dread, that accompanied him through the many extreme moments of his mad life.

Omega – the end?

Another word flashed through his mind. Armageddon – the final battle – the end of the world.

He was shocked to find his hand shaking as he turned to the next page. As he read the unfolding story the contents were so beyond belief that nothing could have distracted him. Before his disbelieving eyes science fiction was becoming reality.

He began with the background and the incredulity of it all washed over him almost from the first words that he read. The race was on between, principally at this stage, America, Britain and Germany to produce the most fearsome weapon of destruction the world had ever known – or could ever envisage. Since the turn of the century scientists had evidently been aware of the vast energy locked inside an atom and, mainly through scientific curiosity, had devoted their lives and careers to solving the mass of complex obstacles that kept the quest a dream rather than a reality. Nuclear Physics, a totally new branch of science, was born.

In the past few years some of these physicists had turned their attention, at the behest of their governments, to harnessing this unbelievable but, as yet, unreleased energy for destructive purposes. The challenge was this: could that energy be used to create an explosion which, they guessed, would equal untold millions of tons of TNT? If so, could it be contained in a cylinder small enough to be carried in a large aeroplane? This device would be no ordinary bomb; it would be an *atomic bomb*.

Turville paused and looked, unseeing, at the ceiling. Untold millions of tons of TNT? In one bomb? Impossible. But if it *were* possible... He went back to the file...

The undisputed leader amongst this group of scientists was a Polish nuclear physicist, Professor F.D. Crisciak. To solve language problems he was known to his friends and colleagues around the world as 'Freddy', a sound adaptation of his initials. He was not belligerent by nature – in fact he was very much the opposite – but he firmly believed that possession of such a weapon would stop the world's tyrants from waging war.

In the thirties, the Poles probably had more reason than anyone for pursuing such an aim and Freddy Crisciak saw this as a way of saving his beloved Poland from yet another humiliation at the hands of its historical enemies – and immediate neighbours – Germany now in the control of Hitler's Third Reich, and Stalin's Russia.

Turville paused in his reading again. And if the Germans or the Russians got hold of the man? Almost certainly Armageddon. And a messy one at that. He sighed and, looking up, saw that Sir

Philip was still industriously scribbling with his scratchy pen. He noted that he was being given more time than usual to digest this amazing information and turned to another part of the file.

After the background there was a section on his assignment. Professor Crisciak was stuck in Nazi-occupied Poland and, if he was still alive, it would be his job to get him spirited away from under the noses of the Gestapo to England. To help him achieve this almost impossible task he would have the full co-operation of the exiled Polish military leaders in London who were in close contact with the partisan army in Poland, the Armia Krajowa, and a support SIS agent to, as the notes put it, 'act as liaison'. How easy it all seemed in print. He chuckled to himself, a habit which often unnerved those around him.

There was, as the notes baldly stated, an added complication – Turville reckoned there always was – their quarry, the eminent Professor, would only agree to come to, and subsequently work in, the country where his wife, Peggy, was living. Although now in his forties he had been married for just over a year and she had become, as he had often told his friends, the only reason for his existence. To have the full services of his unique brain he would need her alongside him.

Turville groaned – again out loud. He didn't believe in women becoming involved in SIS activities: to him it suggested unnecessary complications often leading to disaster. No-one had yet had the temerity to suggest that his concern was far more to do with his fear of women. With another sigh he read on…

The part Peggy was to play wasn't only as a lure to secure the services of the Professor for Britain. As the Germans advanced through Poland he had decided to send her to safety on a boat to Norway and had entrusted into her safe keeping five notebooks, for the years 1935 to 1939, which contained all his scientific calculations which would be essential to the continuation and successful completion of his amazing work. She had them – somewhere – and without them the development of an atomic bomb could not happen – unless he started again from scratch and then the race would certainly be lost.

So Crisciak's wife – Peggy – was, at this stage, the pivot on which the mission succeeded or failed. Surveillance work had already established that she was somewhere on the East Coast, last seen in a small seaside town called Flaxton-on-Sea. The first task was to find her. She was the magnet that would draw their quarry to them.

Again the briefing notes stressed the same unequivocal message: time was short. If Britain didn't get the Professor others would – probably the Third Reich. Whoever got him first would end the war the winner. As simple as that.

Turville paused to consider this. How unbelievably foolhardy this man with evidently one of the world's most brilliant brains was proving to be. To put his life's work into the hands of a slip of a girl and send her off into the unknown? There must be more to it than that. He sat back, closed his eyes and considered the implications of all that he had read so far.

Sir Philip looked up and, seeing that Turville had finished his scanning of the files, rose from his desk and limped towards him pausing on the way to open the door.

"No disturbance of any sort if you please Gilly unless, of course it's one of them up there," he indicated with a long bony finger towards the heavens. "Charles and I will be a little time."

The door closed and he sat heavily, filling with his considerable bulk one of the massive armchairs alongside Turville.

"I noticed from the chuckles, sighs and groans that you've got the gist of the story. What do you make of it all?"

"Extraordinary, unlikely, science fiction and, to cap it all, we'll have to cope with a sentimental scientist. They're the thoughts that first come to mind." His educated, clipped English was in stark contrast to his Chief's Scottish drawl.

Sir Philip began the painstaking process of filling his pipe from a very old, cracked leather tobacco pouch. He indicated to Turville to do the same and they both busied themselves with the rubbing of the tobacco in the palms of their hands, tamping it into the burnt bowls of their pipes and, at last, passing lit matches over the surface of their respective mixtures. Whilst Sir Philip did all this ritualistically, Turville's movements were automatic, his thoughts being totally absorbed by the incredible information he'd gleaned from the files.

"How's your Polish?" Sir Philip's voice came through a thick cloud of smoke.

Turville grinned, "After my Italian on the last assignment it will be a blessed relief. I went through every excuse to say as little as possible – sore throat, lost voice, bad tooth. Thank heavens Henshaw spoke it perfectly. He got us out of many a scrape. I take it he'll be with me here?"

The tobacco smoke couldn't disguise from Turville the slight tensing of Sir Philip's face.

"You've taught him too well. He's earned his own assignment. More use for his Italian."

It was a disappointment but understandable and he felt that Peter Henshaw was ready now to lead rather than follow. But why the tenseness?

"I'm giving you Henschel."

So that was it. The agent with the biggest chip, surliest manner and most vicious nature of the lot of them. Ludovic Henschel's reputation was all too well known throughout the corridors of MI6: born Polish, naturalised British, and a turbulent career behind him; a man of no subtlety whose one redeeming feature was his undoubted bravery. A good hatchet-man – literally – but surely that doubtful skill wouldn't be wanted here?

"Why Henschel? The importance of this assignment should rule out any unnecessary risks."

Sir Philip leant forward and tapped the stem of his pipe on the pile of documents. He didn't like to be told what he already knew.

"Be in no doubt whatever..." his voice was harder now, "there will be no unnecessary risks. I have selected him for a number of reasons. One..." his pipe stem banged out the numerals, "he knows Poland better than any of us ever will. Two, he is known to most of the exiled Polish Army leaders in London who are working with the Armia Krajowa in Poland and this should ease our liaison with Warsaw and, three, I know you of all people can handle him. GILLY, TEA PLEASE. FOR TWO."

The last sentence was shouted with a force Turville had never experienced in his Chief before and it suggested to him that Sir Philip's unaccustomed anger was more an expression of guilt than frustration with him.

Miss Gilbert stood at the door.

"I heard what I took to be a shout, Sir Philip. I trust it was not directed at me." The tone would have cowed most men and, on this occasion, Sir Philip was no exception.

"Certainly not, Miss Gilbert. What an idea. We men just had something to shout about."

It was a lame finish but the best he could do at the time and past experience had taught him that much of the pleasure of life tended to disappear for long periods of time if Miss Gilbert was angry with him. Now she fixed him with a disapproving stare, turned slowly and began to leave.

Sir Philip, overcorrecting to a cloying degree, purred at her, "Would a pot of tea be in order, do you feel? For Mr Turville and myself?"

The sniff could have meant anything as, without looking back at them, she left, silently closing the door.

"I must apologise, Charles, and try to explain my frustration just now. I had not felt it fair or right to burden you with unnecessary detail but it may help, if help is needed, to impress upon you the enormous importance of the success of this assignment. I don't believe the English language has words to describe its degree of importance, although Winston Churchill called upon a vast wealth of his extraordinary vocabulary when he briefed me this morning."

Turville looked up.

"Yes," Sir Philip saw that the name of the First Lord of the Admiralty had hit home. "A personal briefing. Why Winston is involved heaven knows, but he has a finger in many pies these days and frankly I shan't be surprised if, now appeasement is out of the window, he doesn't take the helm soon. He's the warrior the country needs now, not Chamberlain for all his diplomacy — or Halifax. That would never do."

Miss Gilbert arrived with a silver tray bearing a silver teapot, milk jug and sugar basin and two fine bone china cups. Turville sprang up and took it from her, earning a thin flicker of a smile through her pursed lips that was wiped away as she glanced at Sir Philip. Then she was gone.

"A fine woman. She makes an old bachelor like me feel sorry that he never..." He noisily knocked the burnt tobacco out his pipe into the large glass ashtray and set about the task of relighting it.

"She insists on doing my tea herself, do you know. Doesn't want the trolley ladies near me."

He disappeared behind another cloud of smoke.

Turville was becoming impatient. He longed to be away and into action but it struck him that Sir Philip didn't want him to go. Was the man lonely? What an extraordinary thought. He looked up at his chief. Through the smoke he saw a tired sadness which, after a lifetime of danger and adventure, of hair-raising feats and numerous encounters with wild, wild women, now had left, if the rumours were correct, only the occasional excitements of a mild flirtation with the formidable Miss Gilbert.

But emotions and fine feelings were only fleeting experiences for Charles Turville and he certainly wouldn't let them interfere with assignment briefings.

"These notes suggest that Crisciak will only come to where his wife", he glanced at the notes, "Peggy is. And that's" another glance, "a place called Flaxton-on-Sea."

Sir Philip had now completely resumed his composure, angry with himself for his lapse.

"I want you to base yourself in and around this place Flaxton and keep a close eye on the girl. Never forget, she is the *only* reason the Professor will put his unique skills in the service of Britain rather than, God forbid, America or some other neutral State. Henschel can work on the Poles in London and set in motion the repatriation of the Professor and then he can settle down and build us this, according to Churchill, war-winning bomb."

It was Turville's turn to be riled now but wisely he decided not to let his anger show. As the undisputed top agent in the SIS he was not used to being told how he would deploy his forces. He would appraise the situation and formulate his own plan. He saw Sir Philip's input as unnecessarily interfering but he decided to let it pass and then take what he considered to be the right course once he was free of the smoke-laden, depressing atmosphere of this huge office.

He gathered up the files and put them carefully in his despatch case which he then locked. The gesture did the trick and both men stood up, Sir Philip making his heavy way towards his desk. He didn't look back.

"Daily reports, as usual. Code book procedure. Good luck, Charles. Something we all need just now." And then he was back to his green-inked fountain pen.

Turville collected his mackintosh from the coat stand in the outer office and, putting his trilby hat on, tipped it at Miss Gilbert. Before she could respond in any way he was gone. It was amazing, she thought, how such a big man could evidently move so languidly and yet, in fact, so fast. And those blue eyes…

Turville escaped from the building as quickly as he could. Women who gave him that certain look flustered him.

A quick call at his flat for a few essential items and then on to the railway station. There was no time to lose…

*

The dull, disinterested voice of the station announcer droned out the departure of the eleven fifteen train for Norwich stopping at Chelmsford, Colchester and Ipswich. Despite his training few could hear what he said in the vast echoing chamber that was London's Liverpool Street Station and, frankly, few cared.

On this early April wartime day the station resembled a giant glass-roofed army camp – only much dirtier. The vast concourse teamed with khaki uniforms and tiny brush-strokes of colour provided by the coats and hats of wives, mothers and girl-friends, some only an hour or two into that last category, seeing their young and middle-aged men off to the giant garrison town of Colchester.

No-one seemed to be in a hurry. The pace of Britain had slowed down again to its normal, unrushed calm. The frenzy of seven months ago, when Chamberlain in his sombre tones had announced that "…consequently this country is at war with Germany" had cooled and there were many who felt that it had all been a fuss about nothing. The liquidation of Poland, the first graphic example of Nazi obscenity, wasn't known to this population. It was all so far away and, anyway, the news in the papers and on the wireless was sketchy having gone through editorial cleansing before it was read so as not to unnecessarily alarm the readers and listeners.

So there were no emotional farewells on this sunny Spring morning; regular periods of leave ensured that parting would not be for long. Many of the younger soldiers on their way back to the spit-and-polish of army barrack life envied their mates in the British Expeditionary Force on the continent. Out there they might well be fighting for their lives and these youngsters believed, in their ignorance, that firing a rifle was infinitely preferable to constantly cleaning and polishing it. The older soldiers knew differently; most had fathers or other close relations who had fought in Flanders only twenty or so years before, and some had been there themselves. Uprooted from steady peacetime lives they resented this interruption to their marriages and careers.

The train would be late leaving. To fill it with reluctant passengers was a long process and the more the porters and station staff tried to rush them the slower it all became.

The heavy locomotive stood snorting and steaming at the head of the long line of carriages, its driver and fireman leaning out looking back at the still open doors and crowded platform. The driver took out his watch and checked it against the giant station clock. Eleven twenty-two. It was going to be difficult to make up time with this load to pull.

Charles Turville sat in the relative calm of a first-class compartment and closed his eyes, but it wasn't sleep that made him unaware of the frustrations and petulance going on around him on the station platforms. His mind was still reeling from the experience of the extraordinary assignment he had been given that morning.

*

As his colleague started his journey to Flaxton-on-Sea another Secret Service agent had already arrived on the outskirts of the town.

Ludovic Henschel was in his usual bad mood. He'd arrived that morning in the back of an army truck at a hutted camp hastily built on Flaxton's golf course. His mood would have been infinitely worse if he had known how his fellow agent had spent *his* morning; personal briefings by Sir Philip Southern and reserved seats in First Class railway compartments!

Henschel was born, the middle of five children, in 1909 in a small town to the west of Warsaw in what was then the Central Province of Prussian Poland. His parents were poor but, like so many others around them, fiercely patriotic and it was probably his early years witnessing the fierce struggles of the First World War and the emergence of Poland as a Republic in its own right that forged the steel in the man adding, as extra ingredients, stubbornness, pride and a vicious ruthlessness which sometimes, according to his SIS assessors, made him 'leap before he looked'. He was rather proud that these traits were carefully listed in his confidential file but he acknowledged that it was undoubtedly the reason why he was to be, on this mission, subordinate to Charles Turville.

Despite these blemishes his background ideally suited this job. He had taken British citizenship in 1937 and, after rigorous examination, had been accepted into the Secret Service. His knowledge of Poland was, of course, second to none and before he left his mother country he had already met many of the exiled Polish leaders now in London with whom the SIS would be liaising in their bid to evacuate Freddy Crisciak to England.

Henschel had been told that his cover for this assignment would be that of a refugee which, being born Polish, was simple and effective.

Refugees fleeing to England were mainly the intelligentsia of Eastern Europe who, Hitler had vowed, would be exterminated; simple as that. The Führer was expanding Germany's boundaries to provide more land for the Aryan race on which to multiply and prosper and those within the conquered countries who were not easily converted to slaves and who might, with their intelligence, ferment and lead unrest were best destroyed. Hitler had proved the efficiency of his extermination squads by doing just that to all but three percent of these gifted people in Poland, his first major conquest – and all within a few weeks.

Amongst that tiny percentage was Professor Crisciak who, according to Winston Churchill, could win the war – for either side.

Henschel knew of only one way to work – and stay alive – and that was to do any job thoroughly. He had insisted on blending into the role of a refugee by being smuggled onto a boat-load of these poor bewildered souls in Dover where their escape into relative safety had landed them. Single men, a few single women and whole families, or parts of families, now stood on the dockside, their brains numbed by the sudden turn of events that had changed their lives from comfortable affluence into those of gypsies wandering, homeless, with their worldly possessions packed into one bundle or suitcase.

Henschel's masquerade was made easier by the lack of any inquisitiveness between them. No-one asked questions; in fact other than brief words of discipline within families, no-one talked at all. Their deep, hollow, fearful eyes said everything: they were literally struck dumb. And yet, thought Henschel, a week or so ago they had been successful people – industrialists, lawyers, schoolteachers, bankers, doctors and the like. He wondered how they'd feel if they knew that they now had a Secret Service agent amongst them! But the thought didn't make him smile; very little made Ludovic Henschel smile...

He had made sure that he was in the group bound for the camp at Flaxton-on-Sea and after an interminable and totally unnecessary wait they were packed into the back of canvas-topped lorries and driven up through Southern England, around London and into East Anglia. Twice they stopped at village community halls where local people and the WVS provided hot soup, bread and tea. This was the first kindness they had received since their terror started and many broke down in tears. They wouldn't have realized that, as the anaesthetic of the trauma they'd experienced wore off, there would be many days of weeping ahead.

Now, half a day later, Henschel stood in the compound of Flaxton-on-Sea's hutted refugee camp on the outskirts of the town. Even he saw the stupid incongruity of a war where two groups of those involved – on the *same* side – could be separated by a fence of barbed wire and, even more bizarre, could have one of the groups, whose members had just escaped butchery with little more than their lives, watching the other group playing golf!

After an unnecessary lengthy and rather pompous pep-talk from the Commandant – a long-retired Colonel much pleased to don his uniform again even if it was only to command a camp full of foreigners – the lorry loads of dejected souls were documented and assigned to barrack huts – single men, single women and families.

As soon as he had dropped his bundle on his bunk Henschel made his way to the Commandant's office. He was informed by a clerk that the Colonel would not see him but that he could report the next morning at 'O-nine-hundred-hours'. With a flash of his renowned impetuosity Henschel nodded curtly and strode straight into the great man's office. The clerk and the Colonel exploded simultaneously. Henschel ejected the clerk with one push to the chest and closed the door.

The noise from the office reduced from shouting to murmuring within a matter of moments and then the clerk heard the telephone being used. Within five minutes Henschel reappeared and, without a sideways glance, strode out of the office hut.

A moment later the Colonel, white faced, informed his clerk that Mr Ludovic Henschel was to be allowed to leave the camp as and when he wished and to issue him with a pass to that effect. He then re-entered his office and slammed the door.

It wouldn't be long before that pass was needed. Henschel had a meeting to attend in a small bedroom at Flaxton's Station Hotel. The itinerary of his assignment ordered him to report there to meet Mr Charles Turville at fifteen hundred hours – 3 p.m. – precisely.

*

Turville chuckled. The others crowding around him in the train compartment stared at him and, despite the crush, instinctively squeezed together giving him more space. They were all army officers and eyed with distrust this handsome, athletic man sitting almost primly with his despatch case held apparently casually on his knees. Why wasn't he in uniform? They knew all about those who clung to the so-called 'reserved occupations' to avoid call-up. Turville made no eye contact with them; his thoughts were elsewhere. His first task was to find the girl, then he could construct his plan. He chuckled a second time. He would enjoy this one. Nothing had been so big before and probably never would be again...

The guard, to vent his frustration at the delayed departure of his train, blew two long blasts on his whistle. The engine driver, equally fed-up, responded with a loud steam-driven hoot and with a mighty jerk the train pulled out of the platform. The locomotive's big driving wheels spun on the track as it fought to gain adhesion to pull the heavy twelve carriages away from London and towards the flat, friendly countryside of East Anglia.

Turville checked the hastily typed itinerary which he had drawn from his despatch case. It told him to change at Ipswich onto a branch line which would hug the coast and take him to this place called Flaxton-on-Sea.

He had never heard of Flaxton but then, having rarely taken a holiday of any kind, it's doubtful he would have. The girl he was to find had been followed to the railway station in the centre of the town and then to a house in Clarence Road. To illustrate that even the SIS could, if it tried hard enough, be stupid, the lowly agent charged with tailing her had then been ordered to return to base. It had all seemed a pointless assignment anyway, far beneath the skills of the Secret Service and his superior had better things for the man to do.

The train rocked and jolted through the grimy, damp London suburbs and clattered its way slowly north east into Essex. The unsteady vibrations made reading difficult but Turville had some catching-up to do.

He got the notes from his briefcase, lit his pipe and, in the heavy, smoky atmosphere of the compartment, settled down to learn a little about his destination, this out-of-the-way town on the Suffolk coast. Opening the brochure he read:

Flaxton-on-Sea is about half-way up the East Anglian coast between Felixstowe and Lowestoft. Like so many small fishing villages it has grown in the past two hundred years or so into a popular seaside resort. The town – for that is what it now is – has spread inland as its popularity and prosperity has grown, but its expansion over the low-lying fertile hinterland is as much due to the chronic erosion of the soft, sandy coastline. So much has the sea reclaimed that its old sixteenth century Moot Hall which was built originally in the town centre now sits alongside the Promenade! Jutting out into the sea, almost at this very point is the central feature of the town, the Pier...

On one of the pages of the brochure was a hand-drawn map showing the pier, and a date, 1867, but what caught his attention more than any other feature of the town was a blob at the end of their nineteenth century pride-and-joy. It was labelled 'Pier Theatre'.

Turville drummed his fingers on the glossy page. The briefing notes said that the girl – Peggy – had been a stage performer, an artiste, and added that she had been a soubrette. He knitted his brow. Why did the fools in the research department assume that an agent would know theatrical terms. 'A soubrette in Ivor Novello musicals'. Well, at least he knew who Ivor Novello was; a cousin had dragged him to one of his shows. He didn't think much of it. So, if her career had been on the stage would she not gravitate to the town theatre? It would be his first port of call.

The train juddered to a halt. "Chelmsford. This is Chelmsford." It was a similarly disinterested voice drifting through the steam that billowed up around the compartment door. Two officers dragged their cases out onto the platform and Turville, amused, watched them waving their canes in the air demanding attention. He was strangely pleased that no-one responded and they had to lug their luggage out of his view.

Another mighty jolt and the train was off again. Smoke and grit filled the compartment even though the window was shut. It was unbearably hot and he could feel the under-seat pipes pumping heat against his legs.

He rubbed at the steamed-up window with his handkerchief leaving it black with dirt. Looking through the smeared glass he noted that the countryside was flat and dull with concrete pill-boxes set in scars in the landscape. He hoped that if, as seemed likely, the mighty Wehrmacht arrived, some camouflage might be used to at least slightly conceal them; they'd be enough of a death-trap for their occupants without pointing themselves out to the enemy.

The train bounced on, slowly. He went back to his briefing notes and became so absorbed that he was only startled back to awareness of the world around him by the train jolting to a halt in Colchester station. His fellow passengers stirred themselves from their sleep and hurriedly grabbed their belongings. They smoothed down their uniforms, rebuckled their Sam Browne belts, set their peaked caps carefully on their heads, nodded at him and left the carriage. Turville smiled at them. He hoped they'd be quicker off the mark when they met the enemy.

A glance at his watch showed that there was still thirty minutes to go if the train arrived at Ipswich on time – which he very much doubted. In the peace of the empty compartment he decided on some more light reading and went back to the Flaxton-on-Sea brochure.

First and foremost Flaxton still sees itself as a farming and fishing community and for centuries has relied on its farmers to till the soil and its fishermen, in their small, frail craft, to brave the cruelty of the North Sea. But nowadays the start of May is traditionally the time when seaside resorts start to sit up and, with a gleeful rubbing of hands, realize that another summer season is on the horizon. Easter comes and goes with a flurry of activity as holiday-makers descend for a short break and provide welcome revenue giving the townspeople a chance to have a dummy run at the summer season. In May the days get longer, the weather – usually – gets better and the sun lifts the spirits, brightens the paintwork and brings the smiles back to winter-gloomy faces. Flaxton is no exception to this metamorphosis and eagerly looks forward to the days ahead when it will gather in the bulk of its annual revenue from its 'catch' of holidaymakers who provide the income needed for survival.

Some hope, he grimly thought. No longer. The East coast was a prime spot for a German invasion force to land and Flaxton seemed to be sitting right in the centre of it. They were only just over a hundred miles from Rotterdam and in Turville's informed view there was little to stop the highly trained German army, supported by the might of Goering's Luftwaffe, from reaching Holland. Then a fairly effortless hop across a small lump of water.

That set him thinking again of the task ahead. Speed was essential. Obviously everything would have to be achieved *before* any invasion took place. What a place for the girl to go to. Could she be moved? Maybe only by force…

Whilst the train rocked its way slowly up the line towards Ipswich he planned the reconnaissance schedule ahead of him. If they continued at this snail's pace he'd only just be in time for the briefing session with Ludovic Henschel which he'd fixed for fifteen hundred hours. After that he planned to explore Flaxton and, if possible, trace the girl Peggy who appeared to be the linchpin of this mission. He could then carry back to London tomorrow a more detailed assessment of her than could be gained from the blurred snap-shot in the briefing folder.

It was the meeting with Henschel that occupied most of his thoughts now. He lit a cigarette and glanced again through the notes he had been given on the man. He skimmed through the first page which tabulated his assignments in the SIS to date but it was the paragraph detailing Henschel's character that made him frown. His previous Controllers had obviously experienced considerable frustration handling this impetuous and aggressive man who brought such cold viciousness to his work. Ideal in battle, thought Turville, but this coming assignment called for surveillance and protection, tact and diplomacy and these were attributes singularly lacking in the man's character.

They were now bumping and jolting through the outskirts of a town: Ipswich. He put his files carefully away amongst the underwear and washing bag in his despatch case. He wasn't aware of the fact but, even before he met him, Henschel had put him in a bad mood. He was now finding this journey by train irksome and wasn't looking forward to the trundle down the single branch line to Flaxton.

At Ipswich, with little help from the uncommunicative station staff, he grumbled his way to the branch line bay platform where his opinion of trains was not improved by finding two elderly matrons occupying the only first-class compartment in the single coach, each clutching a yapping dog. He doffed his hat to them and settled next door in third-class.

It was a no-corridor coach and he was pleased that he had the twelve seat spaces to himself. That would do nicely.

The guard blew his whistle and almost as the train started the door was flung open and two cardboard boxes followed by a garishly dressed man tumbled in. Turville jumped up and closed the door. There were angry shouts from the platform.

"Thanks, squire," gasped this strange apparition, trying to get his breath back and dust himself down at the same time. Having lifted the boxes onto the seat each side of him he looked across the aisle into the eyes of Turville and smiled a wide, crinkly smile. Turville returned the gesture with a civil nod and felt it best to immerse himself in something.

He opened his despatch case on the seat beside him. Its contents, including his spare vest and underpants, were in full view but it was of no matter, they were both men and there was no cause for either to be embarrassed.

"You in it as well? Know what I mean?" The strange double question was followed by a lick of all the finger tips on his left hand in quick succession.

"Pardon?" Turville was getting out his file of notes. The man pointed to the underwear in his despatch case.

"Clothes. Selling. Cheap. Not room for us both in this area, squire. My patch, you see."

Turville wondered if there was an East Anglian syntax of the English language with which he was not acquainted – and yet this extraordinary man sounded more like East London.

He closed his case and smiled in an attempt to terminate this impossible dialogue. Opening the file, the brochure on Flaxton fell to the floor.

"Oh dear Lordy no." The strange man bent and picked it up. "Certainly no room in Flaxton old man. Clothes and knick-knacks are my department. Know what I mean?" Another flick of the fingers. Turville bent over his papers.

"Jolly good."

The man sat forwards and tapped him on the knee. "Better push off back then."

Turville lowered his notes and eyed this extraordinary person with a look that had reduced many an adversary to jelly. It worked.

"Sorry squire. Just checking. Know what I mean?" Again the fingers.

Somehow the grotesqueness of the gesture went with the outfit, a strangely tartanned sports jacket, yellow flannel trousers, a wide garish tie and brown and white brogue shoes, all topped with a brown trilby hat at a rakish angle.

A hand shot out from somewhere in the sea of tartan. Turville was about to take it, swing it in a half circle and deposit its owner on the floor of the carriage with his foot crushing the back of his neck but just in time he realized that the hand was being offered to shake! Gingerly he took it.

"Tad Stevens." It was a perfunctory shake.

"How do you do. John Smith. And I am not in clothes and knick-knacks I assure you, Mr Stevens."

"Thank gawd for that, John. Call me Tad, everyone does. Know what I mean?" Another lick.

"Thank you Ted. Now if you'll excuse me I must concentrate..."

"Tad."

"Pardon?"

"Tad. That's me."

Turville buried himself in his notes and, uncharacteristically, Tad Stevens took the hint but in a most infuriating way. Looking out of the window at the slowly passing countryside he murmured a very doubtful setting of a well-known army song whilst, at the same time, tapping the fingers of each hand on the adjacent cardboard boxes as if they were side-drums.

The one-man band stopped its performance in mid-bar.

"What's your business then?"

Turville used that look again. "Private."

Tad, who had started to search through his boxes, looked up.

"Come again, John?"

"My business is private, Mr Stevens. Let's just leave it at that."

Tad started to lay out a strange array of clothing, bottles and small containers from his boxes. "All right by me, squire. Know what I mean?"

Turville wondered what he had done to deserve this and, not for the first time, considered the extreme contrasts happening in the world around him. This morning he had been briefed by the Head of the Secret Service who himself had just been briefed by no less a person than Winston Churchill and now, a few hours later, he was having to experience the antics of a madman!

He tried not to notice but he found himself gazing in amazement as the long seat opposite him was rapidly converted into a market stall. There were bottles of scent, medicaments, handkerchiefs, ladies manicure sets, hair brushes, brooches and bangles and, with a final flourish, a dozen or so pairs of white lace knickers. Tad noticed Turville's curiosity.

"Mostly for the refugees old man."

Quickly this strange character counted everything. Mental arithmetic was obviously a strong point. He was multiplying in pounds, shillings and pence using his well licked fingers as beads on an abacus. He seemed well pleased with the result and started to pack everything away again. When, finally, he got to the knickers he held up a pair for Turville's inspection.

"Two and a tanner to you, squire. For your little lady." To add insult to injury he tapped the side of his nose.

In any other situation Turville might have found these antics mildly amusing but here he could only see sadness and, anyway, the sort of morning he'd had was no prelude to such crassness. He disappointed himself with a show of pomposity.

"Thank you, no. I do not have a little lady."

Tad, to whom all comment was literal and whose friendliness missed even the most obvious put-downs came straight back.

"Any sizes, John. Any sizes. Give me her size and I'll fit her out all snug for the summer. Know what I mean?"

As the fingers were licked again the train mercifully stopped with a jolt and a hiss of escaping steam. "Flaxton-on-Sea. Flaxton-on-Sea." Such had been Tad's performance that, uncharacteristically, Charles Turville had lost all sense of time and place; he could have been wiped out by anyone. No-one before had ever achieved that with him.

Tad threw everything back into the boxes, dropped the window and opened the door.

"See you again, squire."

Turville watched him saunter down the platform greeting everyone and evidently having to sign small books to get himself out of the station.

"I do rather hope not" said Turville to himself but, as on the train, he was no match for Tad Stevens. He'd see him again. Very soon.

CHAPTER TWO

Early April 1940. *In Germany Hitler orders the expulsion of 300,000 Polish Jews and 1,200,000 Slavs from their homeland. For them no alternative accommodation is provided.*

In Britain the National Ploughing Campaign is well under-way. 1,900,000 extra acres of land are now under the plough.

The pier had been a feature of Flaxton-on-Sea since Victorian times; a solid planked deck supported by sturdy oak piles designed to withstand the North Sea at its fiercest. The theatre would have looked magnificent at the time of its opening in the latter half of the last century but even then it was a bit of a sham. You couldn't build a solid, ornate Victorian theatre on a platform resting on the sea bed so, like all pier structures it was, in essence, a wooden shed covered, like a Christmas or wedding cake, in thick layers of decoration. Plaster was moulded and fashioned everywhere with, it would seem, little heed for its condition in eighty-or-so years time. Now, like the town – like so much of the British Isles – it looked old and tired, run down and sad, its two tall flag poles standing naked, flagless.

The pier's one expression of belligerence – other than itself daring to poke out from the shore straight across the sea to the threatened continent of Europe – sat at its farthest end beyond the theatre and out of view to most of the town. It was a Bofors rapid-firing, dual-purpose, forty millimetre gun capable of taking on aircraft and landing-craft alike.

The theatre was, in fact, closed in the early months of the war as were all places of entertainment but the government quickly realised that the damage to the nation's morale far outweighed any other consideration and, with relief from a beleaguered and nearly destitute Theatre Company echoed in communities throughout the country, the Flaxton-on-Sea Pier Theatre opened its doors again.

And in they flocked, a population with little to do out of working hours than to visit the dance hall, the cinema or the theatre. Most evenings a couple of army truck-loads of refugees would turn up from the camp on the outskirts of the town. Whilst most of them, being from Europe's educated classes, knew at least a smattering of English, few could understand the humour, but they didn't seem to care; the theatre was warm, friendly and jolly, three commodities in very short supply since the upheaval in their ordered lives.

Alongside them in the audience, in the faded, rather rickety theatre seats, sat the people of Flaxton. They were a kindly lot, helping the refugees where they could even though the deprivations of war were starting to bite them too. Instead of the freedom the British had enjoyed through the twenties and thirties they now found themselves in a policed state with rules, regulations and laws that were multiplying with bewildering rapidity, and the penalties for breaking them were harsh and summary. The towns-people were not used to this and, coupled with the fear of the unknown that lay ahead, they banded together for strength and courage.

The more informed amongst them knew that with the news of the rapid success of the German army in Europe their future could well be inside a similar but far less hospitable camp than that occupied by their foreign guests!

The third and most vociferous group in the audience was the Armed Forces. There were a few sailors, home on leave, but mainly it was the soldiers and airmen and the fast growing women's services from the camps and airfields which were now being crowded into the flat East Anglian countryside. For them the Pier Theatre provided one of the main and cheapest forms of escapism.

*

For a man who had sought and experienced far more than his fair share of mental and physical assaults in his life Charles Turville was, to his own surprise, strangely disturbed by his erstwhile travelling companion Tad Stevens. He would have been only slightly mollified to know that such was the man's effect on pretty well everyone he met!

In a tetchy frame of mind he walked the few yards from the train and booked into a single room in the Station Hotel where he washed off the considerable grime deposited on him by the London and North Eastern Railway.

The room was dusty and airless and its atmosphere, coupled with the noisy, jolting train journey and the forced inoculation into his system of a dose of Tad Stevens made him feel unusually tired. He lay down on the hard, narrow bed and instantly fell into a disturbed sleep plagued by visions of Miss Gilbert, unmentionable items of lace underwear and Sir Philip smoking his large green-inked fountain-pen...

A persistent knocking on the door started in his dream as Tad's percussion work on his cardboard boxes.

He awoke to hear the hotel manager half-whispering through the thin wood. "There's a man downstairs to see you Mr. Smithers." Then with distinct disapproval in his voice he added "I believe he's from the camp."

Five minutes later, in the cramped confines of his tiny room, Turville and Ludovic Henschel were facing each other for the first time.

Henschel had hardly set foot inside the door before, ignoring his superior's outstretched hand, he launched into a headstrong attack on the subordinate role he was required to adopt on this mission.

Turville sat down and propped his chin in his hands. He only partly heard the man's tirade, preferring to spend the time continuing to plan the first stages of the assignment but this was frequently interrupted by phrases such as "...infinitely more qualified to lead", "...only in charge because you are the golden boy", "...man of the moment".

Henschel suddenly realised that Turville wasn't listening to him and was so surprised at this unusual response to his aggressive attack that he paused in mid-sentence.

Turville lowered his hands and laid them, palms down, on the table. The tone of his voice – all his movements – were in sharp contrast to his colleague's agitation. He leant across to him and his voice dropped to little above a whisper.

"The package – that is how we will refer to him from now onwards – has scientific knowledge stored in his head and his notebooks that will, in the right hands, save the world from Nazi tyranny. This, I am assured, is no exaggeration. We both have details of the man in our briefing notes. You will know the workings of the Polish mind better than any of us. Tell me, my friend, how will he be reacting to his life as a fugitive?"

Henschel felt slightly better now. His expertise was needed. He had information which Turville lacked. He pulled his chair back and crossed one leg over the other in a gesture of relaxed authority.

"We know he is hiding somewhere in the north of Poland. Our agents had traced him back to Warsaw after his foolish efforts to be a foot soldier but then the cretins lost him."

It was now Turville's turn to be angry.

"You call those who are fighting underground – the Armia Krajowa – cretins? I imagine you know what unspeakable forms of death they face if they are captured? You would do well to keep to yourself your opinions of those who have stayed in their country to fight the barbarians occupying it. The refugee camp in which you are now billeted contains many who would plant a knife between your shoulder-blades for such an insult."

He fixed Henschel with a cold stare and then abruptly averted his eyes towards the window. He was annoyed and surprised that he had shown his anger; it suggested a lack of control and that was reprehensible.

Neither man wished to catch the other's eye at this moment and they sat motionless, Henschel looking down at the ring-stained table and Turville gazing unseeing at the view over the flat countryside. The slow eddying of suspended particles of dust in the bright rays of sunlight was the only movement in the small room. Finally Turville stirred. He looked at Henschel forcing the man to meet his gaze and noted the flicker of fury in his eyes. His voice was quietly calm again, totally controlled.

"Now tell me what I do *not* know about this man."

The reference to those who had stayed in Poland had not been lost on Henschel. He now pulled himself back from the table, his knuckles white with fury, but he knew better than to let his temper master him this time. Sullenly, in his near perfect English, he went on.

"He does indeed have a brilliant mind. All his peers defer to him. They say that, at this time, he is the leading nuclear physicist in the world." He banged the table. "It was a criminal act to stay. He should have been forced to leave with his wife and mother when he could. Abducted if necessary."

Turville sighed. Could he ever work with this man? The conversation was getting nowhere. Impatiently he tried again.

"Why do you think he did not leave?"

Henschel shook his head in disbelief. "He had this patriotic thing. He was so protected as a child. I am told that he sometimes, in the long winter evenings at the camp on the Baltic coast, spoke of his privileged childhood to his colleagues. His villa – that's what he arrogantly called his big country house – his acres of land, his unearned title." Again he brought down his clenched fist onto the rickety table top. "I fought in the backstreets in my youth and had the patriotic stuff beaten out of me. *His* adolescence came late, in his forties" he added quietly "...the fool."

They were both silent again for a moment. Henschel had relaxed, his mind far away in the battered streets of Warsaw. Turville spoke softly.

"So the man with a brain that could save the world went off as a foot-soldier to fight the might of Hitler's Wehrmacht."

Henschel nodded.

Turville leant forward. "And, you understand, we have to get him safely out of the country *if* he's still alive and *if* he can be found. That is our mission."

He knew that the words, though punctuated clearly and slowly, could not begin to express the enormity of the task ahead.

Turville took out his cigarette case and offered one to Henschel. They eyed each other through the haze of smoke.

"Will he stand up to torture?"

The question was asked as if it were an inquiry about the departure time of a train. The answer from Henschel was swift.

"No," he paused, "no-one eventually stands up to torture." He couldn't resist adding "Not even you."

To his surprise Turville laughed. "A fair point, my friend. Not even me. That means that we must move quickly. The package *must* be found and spirited out of Poland *before* he becomes a guest of the Third Reich."

The period of calm between them was short-lived. To Turville's annoyance Henschel yet again banged his fist on the table.

"It's ridiculous. A waste of time. The package is in no position to lay down conditions. He must be found and forced to leave. Arrest him. Drug him. Let him wake up in London. Job done."

The silence following the outburst was telling. Henschel knew that he had gone too far but for a second time he was surprised by Turville who, drawing deeply on his cigarette, asked him, quietly,

"And his brain?"

Henschel had no answer; Turville knew that he wouldn't have; such subtlety was beyond the man.

"The only value of the package being in our hands is if he is willing – I stress – *willing* to use the unique powers of his brain in Britain's cause. No-one – I stress again – *no-one* can make his brain operate other than him. *We*, my friend, are in *his* hands. All we can do is to provide the means of his escape and hope that he accepts them. Do I make myself clear?"

The last sentence was less of a question than a cold, uncompromising directive. Henschel didn't reply. All he could manage was a nod. Inwardly he was still shaking with anger but he didn't let it show.

Turville took the file of notes from his case.

"We know that he will come, willingly, to wherever his wife is. In our notes that point is stressed." He glanced into his file. "Peggy. And where, my friend, is Peggy?" He didn't wait for a reply. "Here, in Flaxton, somewhere. She must be found, tailed *and.*" he leant forward within a few inches of Henschel and stared into his eyes, "*protected.*"

This word contained such menace that even Henschel reacted. He blinked, breaking the gaze between them and sat back.

Turville rammed home the point.

"If, of course, she were to suggest that she had been harassed in any way when, as we must all hope, she and the package are reunited, it is doubtful that he will put his services at the disposal of Britain. You will see how careful we must be."

This was said slowly, Turville's eyes never wavering from Henschel's cold stare. He stood up to stretch his legs in the cramped, small room and looked out over the station platform

31

with its one railway track leading off into the distant Suffolk countryside. He turned.

"And then there is the matter of the notebooks."

Henschel had carefully read this section of the briefing notes. It interested him far more than the feelings and concerns of one human being for another. He still felt that brutal force would get either the package or his wife Peggy to do anything they were ordered to do. Pain was a wonderful persuader and had never, in his experience, been known to fail. But the notebooks were a different matter. To use the girl, unwittingly, to get the man was one thing, to get her to surrender the books would undoubtedly be far more difficult particularly if, as was likely, she had promised to hand them only to him when – if – they next met.

Again, thought Henschel, force could be used but that would, as he grudgingly admitted to himself and as Turville had stressed to him, mean a cut-off of any future collaboration with the Professor. This was going to prove a far more difficult mission than he had first thought because it would undoubtedly require large quantities of finesse, an ingredient in his armoury that was in very short supply.

"We must suggest she hands them over to us," was the best that he could do.

Turville turned to him. "No action on that for the moment. I need to work things out before we make any move. For the time being I want you to handle the first stages of the retrieval of the package through liaison with the Polish exiles in London whilst I undertake the surveillance of the wife, Peggy. I will issue detailed orders later. You get settled in the refugee camp, I shall take a look at Flaxton. I'll be in touch tomorrow."

Turville's body language clearly indicated that the meeting was over. Henschel nodded briefly and stood up.

"I have little time for these partisans in London but I will do my best." He knew that such a dismissive statement would anger Turville but so be it, it was the truth and he felt it needed to be said. He gave a curt bow, nothing more than a slight inclination of the head, turned on his heel and left.

There was no shaking of hands, no sign of comrades parting. This mission was strictly business of a totally impersonal nature.

*

Charles Turville carried out a last, thorough search of his bedroom; it was as routine to him as brushing his teeth. Even when he was to be absent only for a short while he left nothing behind; his belongings travelled with him, hence the sparseness of personal effects all of which could be carried in his despatch case. In this self-contained way his identity was totally secure, available to no-one else, as were the secret documents he frequently had to carry with him.

From the hotel he strode downhill towards the sea. To any onlooker he was obviously a businessman on the last lap of his evening journey home. He glanced at his watch. Just after five o'clock. Seventeen hundred hours.

For a while his thoughts were on Ludovic Henschel. The devil take Sir Philip for inflicting on him this cold, soulless agent to help him in this delicate mission. But he acknowledged the sense behind it. Henschel, he reasoned to himself, obviously knew the Polish better than anyone. They were, after all, his kith and kin. He *should* be able to negotiate with the exiles in London. Somehow the doubt in his mind made him quicken his pace.

If necessary, whatever Sir Philip had said, he could always reverse the roles and leave Henschel to protect the girl here in Flaxton. Henschel protecting? Subtle diplomacy? Heaven forbid...Turville fervently hoped it wouldn't come to that. There was, though, one thing very much in the man's favour; he was known to be totally reliable in any crisis and there were likely to be plenty of them before – if – the mission was successfully accomplished.

He cleared his mind of unfruitful speculation and decided instead to concentrate on getting the feel of the unlikely centre of this operation, Flaxton-on-Sea.

It was a pleasant, brisk walk into the town from the Station Hotel and an early April sun warmed the back of Turville's neck lifting his spirits away from the aggravations caused by the meeting with Henschel.

He didn't think that it would be hard to find where Peggy worked. Stage people would, he felt, gravitate to their own kind and if there was a theatre operating in Flaxton she would probably have at least some connection with it.

There was no need for a map to find the pier; from some distance away you could sense the sea. He crossed roads running parallel with the coast, the last but one, he noted, being the High Street, and came out on a grassed area beside which stood a small ancient building hardly two storeys high. It would be the sixteenth century Moot Hall mentioned in the brochure. Incongruously set alongside it was a twentieth century emergency water tank, full to the brim, with a man painting EWS – emergency water supply – in large letters on its steel sides.

But although he took in all this detail in a flash, it was what lay ahead that caused a frisson of excitement to run through him: the pier and at its end, large and very imposing, the Pier Theatre.

Now he could get down to work. He glanced around as if looking for a friend. Where, before the outbreak of war, there would have been milling throngs of cheerful, holidaymakers arriving for the Easter break, now there were just a few townspeople going about their business. They were used to strangers these days; officials from the plethora of government departments springing up to help – many would say impede – the nation in its preparation for the all-out warfare that would surely engulf it. Here, apparently, was just another of them, snooping.

He strolled up to the pier and along its length towards the theatre accompanied by a screaming army of inquisitive seagulls. Above the entrance was an impressive banner –

The Nell Masters Concert Party presents BY THE SEASIDE

Nightly performances, it said, started at 7.30. Turville looked at his watch. 6 p.m.

On the walls each side of the doors were the playbills with the names of the artistes in large black and red lettering. His eyes scanned the cast of the show; a couple of comedians: dear Lord, a tragedian: a singing duo calling themselves 'The Welsh Nightingales' and in the bottom right hand corner 'Flaxton's Answer to Elsie and Doris Waters – Pat and Peggy Baker'. It was a very long shot but it *could* be her and he felt he should certainly investigate further.

Peggy Baker? He turned away and leant on the balustrade looking down at the sea swirling in and out over the heavy shingle. She'd be unlikely to use her Polish married name or her maiden name, Ashbourn, and stage artistes usually adopted stage names so this might well be the woman they were looking for. If so, here she was, back in the theatre in the relative safety of a performing troupe of players. He admired her tactics – supposing it *was* her. Much wiser to blend in rather than try to come to terms with the drama she'd just lived through on her own.

He looked again at the playbill: comedians, a tragedian and a pair of singers. In the light of his briefing this morning by Sir Philip Southern the triviality of it all took his breath away.

He turned back to the theatre entrance and, apparently casually, surveyed it again focusing now on the sturdy entrance doors. Totally relaxed he tried a handle. They were locked. He looked around him but apart from the curious seagulls he was alone. Feeling in his pocket he brought out a set of metal probes with small hooks on the ends and within thirty seconds he was inside the foyer with the door re-locked.

He could hear voices coming from what was obviously the auditorium. At lightning speed his eyes assessed the layout of the foyer. It was semi-dark but he could see to his right an archway with stairs leading up beyond it and, across the arch, a chain with a 'No Entry' sign hanging from it. Such an instruction *had* to be challenged. Grabbing a programme from the box-office shelf he silently climbed the dusty stairs brushing away the cobwebs that enveloped his head as he moved up towards the dim light.

At the top he found a disused Dress Circle, tiered with dilapidated seats. From almost total darkness he looked out across the dimly-lit auditorium to the empty stage lit by weak emergency lighting. Somewhere behind it was the murmur of voices blending with the sound of the sea beneath the floor of the theatre. He felt his way along the rear row of tip-up seats, picked the middle one and sat in the deep shadows to await developments. He was in no hurry, surveillance was a prerequisite of undercover work demanding patience and considerable skill and he had an abundance of both.

But there was no need for the time to be wasted. His eyes were now getting used to the low light so, muffling even the slightest sounds, he got out the briefing notes from his case and settled down to some more research.

*

Only a few yards away from Charles Turville, across the auditorium and through the stage to the murky nether regions of the theatre, Pat and Peggy Baker, '*Flaxton's answer to Elsie and Doris Waters*', sat in their dressing room relaxing before the evening's performance. The heady mix of tobacco smoke, alcohol and perspiring bodies, very much the atmosphere of any back-stage theatre area, wasn't totally absent here but was thinner and somewhat sweetened by the added aroma of nail varnish and cheap scent.

Both women were in their early thirties, brought up not too far from Suffolk on the eastern outskirts of London. They had formed themselves into a double-act some three months before when Peggy had arrived at the theatre seeking work. Pat's 'stand-up' comedy act hadn't been doing too well – women comediennes on their own were a new phenomenon – and it was clear from the start that they'd work splendidly together.

They had based their stage act on the women who lived further into London, struggling to make ends meet, into it the crowded terraces of the East End; those who proudly called themselves 'the real Londoners'. Pat and Peggy's voices were strong and they had the eastern England twang. But the dialect was nowhere near as marked as the one they had adopted in their act.

Pat had asked Alice Banbury at the Post Office, where she already lodged, if Peggy could have the other spare room and into it she had moved. It was a happy environment for her, Alice, very much the mother figure, Pat, Mountjoy the black Labrador and Harriet the tabby cat. But as she got to know her Pat noticed that Peggy had two extreme moods: on stage bubbling with fun and yet in her everyday life, very withdrawn. Something traumatic was troubling her but Alice cautioned Pat to let her find her own time and place to talk about it.

Now the two of them, in varying stages of undress, sat with their feet up in their dressing room, clutching mugs of strong sweet tea. They were reading the Daily Mail split between the two of them – and the news from Europe was grim.

With a shudder Pat drew deeply on her cigarette and stubbed it out in the cheap tin ashtray. She lowered the page, "I can't read any more of this just now. How can we go on fooling around on the stage when this carnage is happening over there? First Poland, and soon they'll be here! All in, what, about seven months"

Peggy's pages dropped to the floor as she jumped up and went to the washbasin and then, to Pat's surprise, she burst into tears. Dabbing her eyes with her flannel she whispered in a strained voice, "Pat love, there's something I've got to tell you…"

All the dressing rooms were filling up now as the artistes – the troupe – prepared for this evening's performance. The next door room to Pat and Peggy's was occupied by Elaine Price, the prettier half of *'the Welsh Nightingales – Songs to Suit Everyone'* who, with George Noble, provided the tasteful musical part of the show. Not for them the raucous ballads and barrack room ditties used to end some of the other acts.

Elaine and George were somewhat upset at not being permitted by Nell Masters, the owner of the Theatre Company, to share a dressing room. "We could practise", they argued. "Practise what luvvie?" retorted Nell with apparent innocence. 1940 was not the time for such behaviour. "What you get up to away from the theatre is your respectability," she said. "But there'll be no panky-hanky here."

Elaine was always seeking perfection in her looks and turn-out. Now, in a delicate silk petticoat in pale ivory – George's favourite colour – her face was lost in an expensive mud-pack which she could ill afford – and soon wouldn't be able to buy anyway. Tad Stevens, the resident comic who managed on a regular basis to get on everybody's nerves, suggested that she'd do better to drill a hole in her dressing room floor, lower a bucket, and fill it from the banks of mud that lay beneath the pier when the tide was out!

Squeezed into the dressing room with Elaine were Rita and Rena Rogers, the twenty year old twins. It was fortunate that the two of them were so petite because they were sharing a space already overflowing with every type of outer and underwear, boxes of make-up in tubs and tubes, piles of shoes, and sheets of music!

Rita and Rena were identical twins and were on stage for the pure fun of it. You could tell them apart only because Rena wore glasses and her hair in plaits. She was an hour younger than her twin and was treated by everyone as very much the junior of the two. They had come to Nell willing to do anything in the show and such was their enthusiasm that she took them on to help Don Preace, the stage manager, but in no time they were assisting anyone who needed a stooge in their act and taking it in turns, in spangly leotards and tights to appear in front of the curtains with boards announcing the next artistes. They lodged with Nell, which was company for her and Vi and which provided a motherly eye and care for them.

Between the male and female dressing-rooms was Nell's office. To this inner sanctum people entered by invitation only. When they did they found themselves transported to another world far removed from the tawdriness of a seaside theatre trying to make ends meet in the early months of a terrible war. The contrast – and the heavy scent – made visitors catch their breath.

There was a feeling of the Orient about it, with a touch of India and a dash of a Cairo bordello thrown in – not that anything which would shock the daughter of a Scottish Presbyterian minister would ever take place there! There were drapes on the walls hiding the shoddy wooden planks; materials of every colour and weave culled from a plethora of productions over the years, stage jewellery hanging haphazardly from nails, pins and hooks – and a lampshade, a Victorian monster of tasselled fabric containing, incongruously, a small forty watt bulb.

Pictures of nearly every past production covered the draped walls with, in pride of place, a rather faded, soft focused photograph of a heavily moustached and side-burned Frank Masters. It was to this photograph of her beloved husband 'Masters' that Nell, so many times each day, would defer. He had been dead many years now but, through her, he still ran the Theatre Company he had founded in the twenties.

Nell was well into her sixties. Short and now 'well filled', as only her sister would dare to describe her, she was known, and much loved, for the generous sprinklings of malapropisms and spoonerisms which, unknown to her often adorned her speech.

The beauty which had won the heart of her beloved Masters so very many years ago was still there to be seen. Her features were strong and striking, those of a Highland lass from a family whose lineage went straight back to Robert the Bruce, although it must be said that her various chins worked hard now whenever she spoke! Firm but fair, she held the respect of everyone with whom she came into contact.

Masters had done his own bit of moulding and she had, through him, acquired that indefinable sense of theatre, an artistry far deeper than mere stage performance and production. It flowed in her blood.

She now sat in her office wrapped up in one of her husband's enormous overcoats with a bright woolly scarf and a wide brimmed hat, worn at a rakish angle topped with a rather tired ostrich feather. This was her 'uniform' when off stage. The feather seemed, by appearance, to lead a rather tough life and was to everyone in the troupe an indicator of her mood at any one time. Behind her stood her long-time help, confidante and friend, Vi Ulthwaite. Nell was struggling to fill in a very official looking form.

"Astrophe," she sighed. "I never know whether it should be before or after an S."

Vi peered over her shoulder. "Apostrophe, dear. And I don't think it really matters to ENSA. If they want to disband us and send us to France to entertain the troops, they will. Apostrophe or no apostrophe."

Nell sighed even more deeply. "It might even be a blessing in disguise. Masters left me the Concert Party and a fair bit of cash," she whispered, "in pillow-cases in the loft – but it won't last for ever."

"I know, dear, but I'm sure it would be safer in the cellar, away from the bombs." Vi was always practical.

Nell shuddered. Would it really come to that?

Vi, aware of the faintest of signals in Nell's demeanour, fetched a glass from the wash stand, poured a thimbleful of whisky from a bottle kept for emergencies in a desk drawer and handed it to her. Nell drained it in one gulp.

"If ENSA inquisition us…"

"requisition" whispered Vi.

Nell apparently didn't hear her, "the Pier Theatre Company that Masters, my dear old husband, formed twenty years ago will be no more. Dessicated."

"Devastated, dear" breathed Vi gently lifting the form from the desk. "Let me finish it for you."

Nell stood and surveyed her cluttered desk. "Unnecessary clatter" she hissed and swept it all into and around her wicker waste paper basket.

The boys' dressing room – Nell insisted on calling them that even though they were aged between forty and the upper sixties – was always cluttered. Four of them shared it, Tad, Belvedere, George and Norman.

Tad Stevens was very much a law unto himself. Despite clear orders to the contrary he would arrive at the last minute, throw on his costume for the opening number, barge his way through the rest of the infuriated artistes who had been poised for three or four minutes awaiting their entrances, and glide on stage precisely on cue!

As well as being a very successful con-man, wide-boy and spiv, Tad wrote and delivered good material with machine-gun rapidity. He had moulded himself on the king of stand-up comics of the time, Max Miller. Much of his material was risqué but its rudeness was quite beyond Nell and if the audience laughed she was only too pleased.

One of the things that really annoyed the others was that Tad just didn't know when to stop; it was the same rapid-fire delivery to all and sundry. To him, all the world was a stage and therefore it was logical to perform in the same way whether he was physically on one or not, and it was common knowledge that he kept some of his best performances for Pru, the barmaid at The Anchor, long after the rest of the troupe had gone to their own beds! So the fact that his visits to the dressing room before and after the show were brief, was a blessing for his fellow inmates. The briefer the better!

Accepting that Tad's dressing table would stay unoccupied until just before the show, the empty space was adequately compensated for by the considerable bulk of Belvedere Galbraith. He had a personal hatred of everything to do with war. Whilst most of the rest of the troupe were children during the 1914–18 conflict, he had fought on the battlefields of the Somme. As if this wasn't enough, he'd discovered on his return to the stage that his chances were gone. The promising young actor now found it hard to get work; others had taken his rung on the ladder and there was no room for the likes of him. Since then bitterness had turned to melancholy and, now in his late sixties, he trod these boards, rather pathetically, as a 'Tragedian' reciting with elaborate gestures famous tracts of verse, the Agincourt speech and Hamlet's 'dagger' soliloquy being his favourites.

Belvedere spent his time off-stage, fuelled by large quantities of snuff, regaling those around him with his much enhanced memories of those pre-first world war days. "When I was with Johnny at His Majesty's Theatre," he would bellow at them and, out of respect, they would listen. It was hardly surprising that he had little time for Tad Stevens or Tad for him.

Now Belvedere sat at his small dressing table and slapped on make-up as he had done for as long as he could remember. To his left stood a flask of whisky incongruously nudging an ever-full glass of fizzing Eno's Liver Salts. He felt that taking them together created a neutralising effect on his battered digestive system and he had no-one to tell him what nonsense this was. Having gulped from each he took an enormous pinch of his snuff, dropping a fair quantity of it onto his vest and, sneezing an equal amount over those around him, railed at the absent Tad.

"Those poor refugees," he boomed in his deep bass-baritone voice, "as if being displaced from their homes because the enemy has taken all they had isn't enough, they have to listen to our brave comrade Tad Stevens tell disgusting jokes – and fend him off as he tries to sell them contraband goods at inflated prices. As a comedian he makes a good spiv, and vice versa. As Lord Byron so aptly put it..."

The door burst open. "Who's for a bit of hows-yer-father down at the Anchor tonight?" Tad had arrived! He slapped Belvedere on the back at the moment when lipstick was being applied to lips and the result was, of course, catastrophic. With a bellow the tragedian rose and grabbed at Tad.

"Cut your mouth, Belly, old mate?" There would have been carnage if George Price, the other half of the *'Welsh Nightingales'* hadn't quickly stepped between them. He looked like one of those pint-sized referees who were specially chosen to keep heavyweight boxers in order but it worked. It was just the heat of the moment and, anyway, neither wanted to fight the other. Nerves were taut now – there was the show to do.

"You're back early, Tad" said George, looking up many inches at the underside of his chin, "a full hour before curtain-up."

Tad sighed noisily and flopped onto his dressing-table chair.

"Had to scarper, didn't I? Know what I mean?" He licked the ends of his fingers. "There I was offering a glimpse of the good life..." – he winked and tapped his suitcase which they all knew was full of black-market goods – "to a people subjected by us to a life that we wouldn't force on our mother-in-laws," he reflected, "well, not force, perhaps try and persuade," fingers were licked again, "and there were the plod-ders. At least four of our own, our very own, coppers. And they less than politely asked me to leave. So I did – scarper – fast."

The others either laughed, sighed or clicked their teeth. They didn't quite know whether to love or detest Tad, nothing in between seemed to work. Belvedere, pulling white flannel trousers over his white cotton long-johns, passed sentence.

"I hope they take you away and put you in the stocks overnight. It'll save the audience having to tolerate your disgraceful patter." He dropped exhausted onto his chair and, seeing him reach for his snuff box, they all retreated from the inevitable sneeze.

George, who liked to see the dark side, paused in the act of rubbing rouge into his already ruddy cheeks.

"Without Tad we probably wouldn't be here," he somehow made his light Welsh tenor voice sound mournful. "Eighteen of our thirty-strong house yesterday evening were from the refugee camp. Most of them come for the contraband he sells them afterwards."

Tad, now changed into the opening number outfit – white trousers, striped blazer and boater – looked up from applying the minimum of make-up.

"Here, what d'you mean, without me? Tad Stevens, my friends, is a fixture here."

Norman Jackson, 'Over the Garden Wall', was the fourth occupant of the dressing room. He turned to them from his dressing table and made his usual mistake of asking a question.

"Why Tad? What's it stand for?"

"Terence Arthur Desmond," said Tad licking his fingers. "The three chaps who could have been my father."

There was a stunned silence. Then Norman, embarrassed, turned back to the mirror mumbling the words of his act which went rather wrong yesterday.

Norman had been born and bred in Halifax and had deeply shocked his father by deciding to try his luck on the stage rather than extend the family tradition of mill worker. At the start it had seemed easier, healthier and a lot better paid but now, in his early thirties, he wasn't so sure.

Norman was gaunt. You would have thought, looking at him, that food rationing wouldn't worry him over much but, in fact, like so many apparently emaciated figures, he ate like a horse. He'd been hungry since rationing started last January and he'd stay hungry for the duration!

*

The stage lighting suddenly flooded the theatre to full brilliance. Charles Turville blinked, put down the file of briefing notes which had been totally absorbing him and, easing further back into the shadows, pulled across his coat lapels to cover his white shirt.

A man with a severe limp was checking the scenery and the various stage props. Turville looked at his watch. He'd been reading for over half an hour. Now the adrenalin pumped up his system. Eavesdropping – or as the Secret Service would prefer to have it called – undercover surveillance always excited him. To see when you weren't seen, hear when you couldn't be heard had always been for him the essence of power, one over another. His father, a retired Admiral, and his mother had argued long about the impropriety of such behaviour but he merely accepted that they, and probably most other people, wouldn't understand the need for it. "Wars aren't won by bullets and bombs alone" he had told them – but they weren't convinced.

He looked at the programme and identified the stage crew as they carried out their pre-show tasks. Don Preace, the stage manager, was overseeing the preparation and helping Reg Prentice and Bob Bennett, the stage hands, to set the opening scene which would resemble Flaxton's own sea front. The backdrop showed a painting of the pier receding into the distance with gates through which the cast would dance – or in the case of most of the men, stagger – onto the stage dressed in sailor outfits and singing seaside and patriotic songs.

Checking the lighting was 'sparks', Bill Colbourn. He wandered around the stage looking up at his rows of battens and then coming down into the audience to check the effect. He was wearing a pair of old woolly gloves without which he would never touch the plugs and switches which fizzed and sparked in his cubicle. His wife insisted on it. Nell had remarked that "if they avoided his electrification it was a worthwhile pretension."

Many evenings the heady cocktail of tobacco smoke and sweat wafting from the auditorium would be augmented by the smell of singeing as Bill rubbed the burning ends of ropes, scenery or drapes which had come into contact with the red-hot faders.

Turville shook his head. How incongruous this all was. Atomic bombs and seaside follies…He found the mix extraordinary but tantalising.

He went back to the notes. They confirmed yet again that, whilst shadowing Peggy was vitally important as she was the only reason why Freddy Crisciak would allow himself to be spirited to England, finding the notebooks had equal priority. Although he had made the point firmly to Henschel, he felt it would need to be made to the impulsive man time and time again.

At seven o'clock, half-an-hour before 'curtain-up', the auditorium lights came on and the stage curtains were closed. Turville could now see the interior of the big hall and, despite himself, it relaxed him with its gaily coloured plaster ornamentation, crimson lamp shades and the lit crimson stage curtain, bright at the bottom nearest the footlights and receding to near darkness at the top, creating an air of excitement and expectancy; it took him back to pantomimes as a child.

In the centre of the proscenium arch two naked cherubs were holding a scroll which said: **THE FLAXTON PIE THEATRE**. This caused several sorts of mirth amongst the audience. One rude soldier had suggested to Nell that she had trouble with her Rs. The vulgarity was naturally lost on her.

In the half hour before the start the audience arrived – and the fug set in! The combination of fifty or so chain-smokers, thick, occasionally washed, serge military uniforms on as rarely washed bodies, scent on the ladies and Brylcreem on the men made for a heady cocktail in this confined space. But it was what everyone expected, and no-one mentioned it except the actors who were always taken by surprise when the curtain opened at the start of the show and the full force of the fetid atmosphere hit them like a gas cloud. Now it was making itself very evident to Charles Turville as it rose and invaded the darkened seats in the disused Dress Circle.

Turville couldn't see the seats in the auditorium, but he sensed by the babble of raucous laughter and shouted vulgarities followed by scandalized 'shushing' that there was a good mixture of the military and civilians in the audience that evening.

The lights dimmed and he settled back into his seat dreading what was to come but as the show swung along he was, in fact, surprised at what fun it was. He marvelled at the way in which the British, more than any other nation, got pleasure from laughing at themselves.

They were certainly a professional group and the stand-up comedian, Tad Stevens, had the audience in the palm of his hand. Turville had almost cried out when the dreadful man had first appeared and he recognised him as his travelling tormentor. He cringed back in his seat fearing that Tad would reach out and, for a second time, perform directly to him but the gales of laughter from below acted as an effective barrier between them.

Turville had to wait some time before the reason for this furtive viewing revealed itself. He had taken Peggy's photograph from the briefing file and knew her as soon as she came on stage. She and Pat were both dressed as charladies in cheap cotton frocks topped with old coats and felt hats set at rakish angles on their auburn curls. They strolled to the centre of the stage cheerfully greeting each other.

PEGGY   "My Charlie tried to join up but they turned him down.
PAT   Why? They need all the men they can get.

45

PEGGY	They said his eyesight's poor, he's pigeon-toed and his hearing's defective.
PAT	You'd have known that, being married to him.
PEGGY	Not really, I've had no-one to compare him with. They found a job for him though.
PAT	What? Poor eyesight? Pigeon-toed? Defective hearing?
PEGGY	Oh yes, no problem. They're going to make him an officer."

In those dark days of enforced mobilisation any joke at the expense of the Officer class caused hoots of merriment and howls of derision amongst the audience.

Whilst they were continuing the dialogue, Charles Turville mentally assessed the woman who seemed to be at the centre of the delicate job ahead. It amazed him that this girl who, from what he had read in his notes, should be on the edge of madness and grief was cheerfully exchanging banter with her friend on a brightly lit stage. Peggy must be a very accomplished actress. He heard a chord on the piano and the girls, arms around each other's waist, launched into their end-of-act song.

> "If you want to help our gallant lads
> Who fight across the sea
> Bang the drum – Victory.
>
> If you've had enough of Adolf
> And his brand of tyranny
> Bang the drum – Victory.
>
> If your thoughts are for the millions
> Who are bowed beneath his yoke;
> All the mothers and the children
> Who have lost their loved menfolk,
> As they scramble through the ruins,
> And through dust and rubble choke,
> Bang the drum – Victory.

But if all seems lost and helpless
And our nerves are jagged raw,
We'll show Hitler that our sticking power
Is equal to before.
We'll turn back the clock just two decades
And win this ruddy war
Bang the drum – Victory."

There was loud applause and a discordant emission of wolf-whistles as the girls walked off each side of the stage. Charles Turville would dearly have loved to join in and he clapped silently, not so much because of the quality of the material but more in recognition of another smooth operator.

As the troupe took their bows and received some good-humoured banter from the audience he descended the stairs and, checking that the foyer was still empty, left the theatre as silently as he had come making his way back down the pier into the town.

After dark the strict blackout laws tended to keep people indoors and although it was not yet nine o'clock the town seemed to be already deserted. He climbed the hill to the railway station lighting his pipe as he went and took stock of his day. Even accounting for some very strange adventures in his Secret Service career, this had been one of the more unusual starts to a mission.

What really interested him was the enormous contrast this assignment was already throwing up: the creation of a bomb of such mass destruction that one detonation would almost certainly end the war, the rescuing from enemy occupied territory of the man who could make this possible and the protection of a girl clowning her way through comedy sketches in a seaside Concert Party without whom the whole enterprise would be lost!

He sighed. What ludicrous contrasts – and yet it seemed to him that they typified the condition of the world, precariously balanced as it was between two far more dangerous extremes: the mediaeval barbarism he knew was being perpetrated in Poland in the Third Reich's first major conquest of the war, and the apparent sleepy air of calm – 'business as usual' – that had settled after seven months of the phoney war on Flaxton and, probably, most of the rest of Britain.

He wondered how long it would be before these extremes merged, as he was sure they certainly would, and which would be forced to give way to the other? He feared he might know the answer: before calmness could return there would be appalling savagery inflicted on many more millions of innocent people.

Such weighty thoughts had carried him at a quick pace up the hill towards the station. He glanced at his watch. He'd need to keep up the speed if he was to put into effect a sudden change of plan. He'd seen all he needed to on this first visit and would book out of his hotel room without disturbing the bed-clothes and catch the last train to Ipswich, then on to London and the spartan comforts of his own flat. He could spend the journey planning the next move regarding Peggy, the notebooks and the handling of that cantankerous devil, Henschel. The decision made, he strode on.

Turville rushed onto the station platform aware that he was probably the only passenger on the last journey for the day. Judging by the smoke and steam the train was about to leave. The guard was at the rear standing by an open door looking up the length of the single carriage towards the steaming engine. He blew his whistle, held up his lamp and the driver disappeared from view to set the train in motion. Turville pushed past the guard and threw himself into an empty rear compartment. The door slammed as the engine whistle let out one short blast and the train jolted forward and pulled out of the platform.

It was the signalman, going off duty, who found the guard on the deserted platform. He was lying on his back, his whistle in his hand and his paraffin lamp lying shattered beside him. The signalman bent down in the dim light.

"Come on, mate. You've missed your own last train."

It was then that he saw the neat hole in the man's forehead. It was tinged with blue and oozing a little blood. He would have died instantly.

*   *   *

In the back of a Mercedes staff car, Count Freddy Crisciak sat between two black uniformed soldiers. The SS insignia on their jackets was all that could be seen in the pitch darkness of that Polish April night.

Crisciak was huddled in a heavy overcoat, a fur hat pulled down over his forehead, his face a blank, white mask. His eyes showed the fear that was gripping him.

The car sped through the night, eastwards towards Warsaw, towards Gestapo Headquarters.

'The Package' was quickly slipping out of Britain's reach.

CHAPTER THREE

Early April 1940. Hitler invades Denmark and Norway. Denmark quickly capitulates. Norway fights on. "House-cleaning" by the SS in Poland continues.

In Britain a Leicestershire clergyman writes in his Parish magazine of his concern that women ARP wardens are wearing trousers.

It was just as well that the paralysing fear that was gripping Freddy Crisciak prevented his brain from dwelling for any time on a single aspect of the terrible danger he was in. He felt ice cold, numb, even though the car heater was full on. Something about this gnawed at him but he couldn't place it; rational thinking was impossible.

Through the windows of the staff car the blackness of this April night in 1940, in which he had been hustled from his villa, was giving way to a grey dawn. Faint outlines of buildings showed against a dark sky. There was no life out there; not a single light to suggest that anything was alive in this apparently God forsaken country. Poland had died and its ashes were scattered over the desolate land. He closed his eyes. If he was approaching the end his last thoughts would be of happier times...

*

Freddy had first seen Peggy on a working visit to England in 1938. On his last night he went to the theatre. It was a musical comedy. He saw her at a distance, he in the centre stalls, she on stage singing, dancing and acting her way through the role of a young, love-struck girl. Everything about her was vibrant and gay. Her movements were light, her voice enchanting. To him she stood out a mile from those around her. He was spellbound.

Nöel Coward and Ivor Novello were filling the London theatres at this time with light, cheerful plays and musicals, and the audiences flocked to them unconsciously or, in some cases, consciously anaesthetising themselves against the pain that was spreading through Europe towards the very coast of England.

Freddy was all too aware of this pain, was even experiencing it in his own beloved Poland, but for this one brief moment in a London theatre he, too, could forget.

But, of course, the gaiety was false; a cover for the fears and anxieties gnawing at those who knew that Churchill and his cronies were right – and had been so through most of the decade. And many who accused them of 'scare mongering' knew in their hearts that all this carefree living couldn't, wouldn't, last.

Freddy Crisciak was born in 1905 into a Polish noble family. His father was a member of the diplomatic corps serving both the 'old' and 'new' Poland, the Second Republic, in Embassies around the world. In his early life the boy had trailed along with his mother and father in this nomad existence becoming world-wise and, in the process, a multi-linguist. After school in Switzerland he came to England, gaining a First Class Honours Degree at Cambridge University in Physical Chemistry.

In 1935 his father died and Freddy assumed the title of 'Count' and with it a thousand acres of farming land, the family villa and a town house in Warsaw. He was, by this time, an established and highly respected physicist: a professor at Crakow University and, at thirty, one of the youngest to hold such a position. The choice between career or wealthy landowner was an easy one to make: on succeeding to the title he put the running of his estate into the hands of his mother and its very efficient manager.

But to the amazement of his colleagues and many friends – his reputation had by now spread to other parts of the world – he suddenly, in 1936, resigned his post at Crakow, and with it a fine and much envied lifestyle, and apparently disappeared into oblivion. He left his grand house and severed himself from the carefree world he had always known to live in the austerity of a government research establishment on the Baltic coast; a collection of wooden huts thrown together in a bleak, cold wilderness.

His friends looked for an explanation. A scandal? Unlikely. He was a highly eligible bachelor. His shyness forced on him an almost monastic life and, despite his good looks and noble bearing, an unfortunate affair was most unlikely. Financial ruin? Surely not. Funds were always available to pay his household staff and the farms made good profits. He was, his bankers let slip, very wealthy and spent little. A mental breakdown? Impossible. The government did not recruit scientists with mental breakdowns to work in their secret research establishments – whatever that work might be.

Speculation turned to that very subject. What was going on? Why had the government gathered in the scientific elite of the nation and put them to work, as they would prisoners, in closely guarded, secret compounds far from the main centres of habitation?

No-one, of course, knew the answer to this except a very small core of people at the centre of government. For the ordinary scientists working in the camp life was, indeed, like that of an internee. They lived a communal existence in wooden huts, ate in wooden mess-halls and worked in wooden laboratories. Around the perimeter was a barbed-wire fence punctured at intervals by watch towers. This was, they were assured, to keep the outside world out rather than them in, but it was hardly reassuring because none of them were, in fact, allowed to leave!

For the elite amongst them – the half dozen or so eminent scientists like Freddy Crisciak – life was somewhat easier. Their living huts were divided into separate bedrooms and their work less regimented. They, in fact, ran the establishment with the other scientists and the administrative staff working to them. That is not to say that they were free agents; they were continually harried by government officials who asked the impossible and would not take 'no', 'wait' or 'later' for an answer.

One of the great advantages of his position was that Freddy was, on occasions, required to travel. Work on Project Omega took him to world centres of physical chemistry to compare research, share findings and explore new theories. All this was carried out in conditions of the utmost secrecy. Freddy always travelled with a government 'minder' who shadowed his every move. He met the world leaders of scientific development in the thirties, amongst them Willstatter, Franck, Schroedinger and Einstein himself. Many were to become refugees, hounded from their native countries and soon, it seemed, Freddy now accepted as an equal of theirs, might suffer an even worse fate.

In 1938 his travels polarised on America and England; secrets could no longer be safely shared with the rest of Europe. It was at this time, in April 1938, that Freddy, attending a top secret conference dealing with Project Omega at a research centre in the Hertfordshire countryside, visited London with, of course, his minder. After a splendid meal bringing back memories of his old, rather than his present lifestyle in Poland, they adjourned to the Palace Theatre in Cambridge Circus for a matinée performance of Ivor Novello's 'Careless Rapture'.

Freddy's mind was many miles away. Tucked into his private notebook, which never left him, were detailed notes from the conference, but such was the ability of his brain that most of the content of the two days' intensive discussions was clearly tabulated in his memory. Now he had time to review it. There were formulae and equations to consider, re-construct, reject, interpret in different ways. All the time he was searching for answers. There *must* be a way. There *had* to be a way…

He didn't know when his senses started to shift to the performance on the theatre stage. First it was his eyes that focused on the young girl dancing and singing her way through a jaunty number, then his ears picked up the dialogue and, in a flash, his brain transferred to the scene. He was transfixed.

Later he wouldn't be able to explain to Peggy exactly why she, of everyone on stage, focused his attention; there was just something magical about her. In the near darkness he snatched the programme from the hand of his minder who, asleep, jerked to life letting out an explicit Polish oath. The shushing of the audience around them would have been rather more admonishing if they'd known what the word meant in English!

Freddy peered at the cast list. There was a choice of three or four characters who could have been this beautiful girl, but then, as he read, he heard her role revealed by name. There it was, written in front of him. The part was played by a Miss Peggy Ashbourn.

She was so alive and, somehow, more prominent than the others on stage. He glanced up behind him but there were no spot-lights following the action at this time. It must have been a combination of her vitality and that strange 'something' that clicks between two people and brings them together, inseparable for the rest of their lives.

Having had little other distraction in his first thirty-three years other than his work he was now totally besotted by this girl whom he had only seen, so far, in stage costume across the footlights!

He knew nothing about her other than her stage personality in 'Careless Rapture', and he knew what a fool he might be making of himself but this didn't deter him. Much to his minder's annoyance, as soon as the curtain fell, he insisted they rush around to the stage door. There the two of them stood in light but penetrating Spring rain watching the comings and goings of this busy London theatre and waiting for the emergence of Peggy.

Three times he approached a group of happy, chattering girls leaving in a rush, hats pulled down and coat collars up to keep out the wet. Three times they laughed friendlily and said Peggy Ashbourn was still inside. He asked the doorman to contact her but he firmly refused; such goings-on were to be discouraged and it was his duty, he said, "to protect the morals of his charges". Freddy, untypically angry, felt that this was a rather high-handed approach for a stage-door man and said so. He was suitably put in his place.

He didn't see her that time. There was a train to catch to Harwich and his minder, aware of his responsibilities to deliver him back to the Baltic coast at the scheduled time, had to order him to the railway station. They travelled through the night and the next day, by train, ship, train again and car, he in a childish sulk and the minder perplexed at how one of the greatest scientific brains in the world could behave in such an irrational way.

But there were to be other visits. Two months later he was back in Hertfordshire sharing new scientific developments concerning Project Omega with British physicists. Such was his inborn discipline that despite his infatuation for the girl he was able to devote all his prodigious mental powers to this complex work. But the moment he was free he dragged his unwilling minder to London, booked them into a smart hotel and prepared himself for another visit to 'Careless Rapture'. The reaction of his minder, on hearing that he had to sit through the same inexplicable musical play yet again, can be imagined. He was a very unwilling accomplice!

Whilst settling themselves in their seats, Freddy was considering another urgent matter. It was at the end of the meeting that afternoon in Hertfordshire, over sherry in the Principal Scientific Officer's room, that it had been suggested to him that he might be willing to leave Poland and settle here amongst his English colleagues until, at some time in the distant future, Project Omega was completed. The temptation to do this and so be near the woman he had yet to meet but already loved was enormous but, even before the lights dimmed and the curtain rose on the brightly lit stage, he had decided that it was out of the question. It was no use agonising over it: as tension grew in Poland he knew that his place was there and that, despite everything, he would fight to the death for his country.

That night they met. He had planned it carefully. In her dressing room was a long letter from him asking for nothing more at the first meeting than an opportunity to see whether there was any mutual attraction between them. With the letter was a single red rose. This was very different from the usual, hastily written, gushing notes from 'stage-door johnnies' promising 'eternal love' and similar empty phrases, whilst what was actually on offer was far more strenuous! The usual bouquets of flowers, too, were more cosmetic than genuine, personal gifts.

Peggy held the single rose. She was intrigued. Why not? She decided to meet this unusual but obviously sincere admirer and sent a note to the stage doorman. He, having opened it and read it as stage doormen tend to do 'to protect the morals of their charges', sniffed, stuffed it back in its envelope and, when Freddy turned up at his cubby-hole just inside the stage door immediately after the show, sniffed again and handed it to him.

So it was that, in a state of some shyness, a party of four, Peggy, her dressing room sharer and best friend Jane, Freddy and the ever-present minder sat down to a meal in a small French restaurant off Shaftesbury Avenue.

The two of them knew at once that they were right for each other. From the first moment they met they were in love and, through the coming months this love developed and strengthened.

Communication between the two of them was difficult and spasmodic. Messages were passed via visiting scientists and government officials. They had to be short and cryptic. Everything was by word-of-mouth, such was the level of security on Project Omega.

But then, in August 1938, came a heaven-sent breakthrough. Even though he wouldn't countenance a permanent transfer to England Freddy was pressed – amazingly by his own government – to accept a six month secondment to Hertfordshire. He was on the next boat! Free from his minder he at last could pursue his life on his own and, whilst nothing detracted him from his vital work, he saw Peggy almost every day and their love blossomed.

As an artiste's special guest he spent his evenings in the wings of the theatre never tiring of her performance which always had, for him, the same magical touch that had first attracted him.

It was through one of those strange coincidences in life that, one evening, he shared the cramped dark corner of the stage with a small, vibrant woman in a large hat topped by a rather tired ostrich feather who was obviously very much at home in the theatre. She and her colleague, the theatre's manager, had frequent whispered conversations. No-one hushed them. No-one would. Nell Masters, owner of the Flaxton-on-Sea Pier Theatre Company was here as a guest of the manager who had been a close friend of both Nell, and her husband Frank, in their London days.

It was to be another eighteen months before Nell and Freddy would meet again in very different circumstances.

The news from Poland grew darker. Freddy's time in England was coming to an end. Neither he nor Peggy could see a way forward other than parting, probably forever, but neither would consider such an impossible event happening. It became their only topic of conversation blighting their happiness and causing unfamiliar friction between them.

His position was impossible: how could he measure his loyalty to his country, its Second Republic only twenty years old, with his love for his beloved Peggy? This man of formulae and equations, possessing one of the sharpest scientific brains in the world, had no answer.

It was noticed by his colleagues that Freddy's dilemma was affecting his work; he became irritable and intolerant with those around him. But the Head of the Research Centre in Hertfordshire, a wise and elderly retired Professor of Chemistry had seen it all before. Decades of handling students and their tangled love lives came to the rescue with the simplest solution of all: marriage. He summoned Freddy to his office and over the obligatory sherry outlined the plan to him. Freddy was sceptical. Somehow marriage had always seemed impossible and too difficult in these uncertain times and, however much he yearned for it, he felt it unfair to ask Peggy and thereby cause her to make the decision; it would seem as if he was passing the problem to her to solve. The Professor would have none of it. If Freddy felt he couldn't take the lead he was pretty sure he knew someone who would!

It was simple. A little detective work and he was soon speaking to Peggy on the theatre telephone. It was a bizarre scene. She was called to the 'phone by the ever-protective stage doorman just before the evening performance. She stood in the draughty, ill-lit corridor, paint peeling from the brick walls, in her opening-scene costume with people squeezing and bustling past her, listening to an elderly man whom she'd never met quietly telling her, almost ordering her, to marry Freddy Crisciak *now*.

The bizarreness of the situation was amplified because, due to the quietness of his voice and the poor quality of the telephone connection set against the loudness of the orchestra striking up the National Anthem in the auditorium, she had to shout at him to repeat much of the message.

"Shush dear" whispered the doorman, "They'll arrest you for treason. Not even His Majesty would shout during his own National Anthem."

She went through the performance in a dream. It was, of course, the simple, obvious solution. Due to a late meeting Freddy for once missed the performance but as soon as they were settled at their favourite table in the French restaurant where they had first met Peggy asked for Freddy's hand in marriage! It was an unheard of breach of etiquette which delighted them both and led to a long examination of the facts as intense as any Freddy conducted on Project Omega.

As his scientific training had taught him so thoroughly and successfully, they created a formula. They would marry the next day, have a brief honeymoon, he would finish his secondment in two weeks time, she would give two weeks notice and they would sail together for Poland where she would be installed in the family villa to the delight of his mother and all the army of Crisciak retainers. He would – somehow – leave the Research Establishment on the Baltic coast and continue his work on Project Omega at home.

Who says that love is blind? The formula, unlike no others that Freddy had created in his illustrious career, was flawed. But it all began according to plan. On the first of February 1939 Freddy embarked on the steamer at Harwich with his new wife, Countess Margaret Crisciak.

*

All that had been so long ago: an eternity. Now, fifteen months later, on a dull April morning in 1940, the big staff car threaded its way along the highway from Poznan to Warsaw. The term 'highway' scarcely applied any more. Even seven months after the invasion the road was still pock-marked with shell and bomb craters and littered with the shattered carcasses of cars and lorries, guns, tanks and the pathetic remains of carts and wagons that had, until they and their human cargoes were annihilated by the Luftwaffe and the Wehrmacht, been all that could escape from the Nazi onslaught.

The Germans on each side of him wiped the condensation from the windows. They rarely escaped into the countryside, being only used to the mountains of rubble that had once been Warsaw, and were duly impressed at the destruction around them. Even the trees and hedgerows were shattered, farms, hamlets, barns, every type of structure gutted or demolished; nothing had been allowed to escape the whirlwind advance of the Wehrmacht.

A mist hung in the air: a mixture of dust from the shattered soil and smoke that, like a pall, never seemed to clear. Freddy sat back between his guards and huddled down into his overcoat so that the upturned collar enveloped most of his head. With his hat brim pulled down over his forehead he again closed his eyes shutting out the bleak world around him.

He forced himself to think; to try to stabilize his brain which had, to his shame, dislodged itself from the smooth-running axis on which it usually functioned. He knew he had a sharp mind capable of feats of memory and deduction way beyond average mental powers and if ever it needed to be operating at its very best it was now.

"It is hot". The SS guard on his left undid his overcoat. In such a confined space this caused a great amount of buffeting with his elbows into Freddy who, in turn, pushed into the other guard.

"Relax Pieter", the man grunted and leaning forward tapped the driver heavily on the shoulder. "Driver, reduce the heat".

It was a simple demand but said in the way Freddy would expect the SS to behave – abrupt, cold, no compromise.

"Jawohl, Herr Oberst". The driver adjusted the buttons on the dash panel. The sound of the fan reduced.

Freddy's eyes flashed open. Herr Oberst? Colonel? It clicked. It was so obvious and yet in the drama and fear of the moment Freddy had missed it. How could he? He was amazed and angry with himself for letting fear paralyse his brain. The car was the first clue. Why such a grand car? Wouldn't he be dragged to prison and the torture chamber trussed up like a chicken in the back of a truck? And the heater? It was that, as much as anything, that had struck his brain as odd. If he was to be treated as a criminal why cart him off in a car grand enough to have a heater? Staff cars sporting such luxuries were for senior officers only and were therefore few and far between. It seemed that the Third Reich wanted him alive and well...

Waves of relief washed over him and, with that comforting thought, he settled back and retraced the events that had led to his arrest by the Gestapo.

*

Throughout the first half of 1939 at the camp on the Baltic coast Freddy had been constantly urged to leave Poland; ordered to leave. Messages bombarded him. The Government insisted that he, of all people in Poland, must be saved from the Nazis; his brain and his copious notes carried what might well be salvation for the world. The wireless room hummed with messages "For the attention of Professor F. Crisciak".

In the safe days the transmissions had been in open speech via a radio-telephone system and then, as the situation worsened, secret material was sent in government code by teleprinter. But as the end approached the only contact with the outside world was by a special 'unbreakable' code, altered according to the day of the week. By the time he had unravelled all the messages they said nearly the same thing, "You are ordered to leave Poland **now** by the northern route. Report to our Embassy in Norway."

He didn't, wouldn't, couldn't. It may have been his upbringing as the son of a senior diplomat, a man so proud of his country that he talked of little else. Right from his earliest years this loyalty had seeped into Freddy's soul to such an extent that it blotted out reason.

And so it was a strangely easy decision for him; he would rather stay and fight – and die – as a foot-soldier than take his unique scientific knowledge to safety where it could be used to defeat the enemy. Nothing anyone could do would change his mind.

But he did follow orders as far as his mother and Peggy were concerned. On the third of September 1939 he put them, much against their will, on one of the last boats to leave Poland heading for neutral Norway. They left in a fishing boat from the quay of a tiny fishing village near the town of Uska and Peggy, his beloved Peggy, carried with her a small brown-paper package, heavily sealing-waxed, which, in the right hands, could mean the survival of the free world.

The Baltic looked grey and menacing. They all knew that it was almost certainly patrolled by enemy warships and submarines. In truth Freddy doubted they would survive; that he would ever see them again, but the alternative was German captivity which, for most Poles, was a contradiction in terms. In abject misery he sat on a wet stone wall on the quayside in the pouring rain and wept bitter, uncontrollable tears.

For Peggy that moment of parting had been equally painful. In the cold drizzling rain Freddy had handed her and his mother down the slippery steps into the small rocking fishing boat. He had brought down their suitcases and then embraced them both. She had held him tightly, dreading the moment when he would have to break away from her.

They had kissed, gently and then fiercely before pulling their heads back and looking pleadingly into each other's eyes. They were both crying now, each believing but not being willing to accept that this could well be the last moment that they would ever set eyes upon each other.

Then he was gone. So fast. Up the steps and away. She and Anya just stood there trying to keep their balance as the boatload of numbed, crying refugees were torn from their homeland and those they loved…

*　　*　　*

Now, six months later, it was Peggy's turn to sit on a low stone wall looking out to sea. She had walked away from Flaxton, out along the narrow shingle spit of land that ran southwards from the town dividing the estuary of the river Flax from the sea. She needed to get away and have some space. The members of the Theatre Company were all so kind and caring, each in his or her own way, wanting to help her come to terms with the desolation that she felt but their kindness could be smothering.

She knew that she was one amongst thousands, tens, hundreds of thousands experiencing the pain of sudden separation, but it didn't make the feeling of desolation any better. She was in limbo, in a vacuum; she couldn't find the right words to describe the state of mind that she was in. She didn't know if Freddy was alive or dead but she could guess at the destruction of the country he had been determined to stay and defend.

There had long been talk about the future for Poland if it again fell into German hands. It was fortunate that few actually knew the scale of the reign of terror that had engulfed the nation, but it would have made little difference to Peggy in the state of mind she was in. She feared for Freddy if he was alive and desperately mourned for him if he was already dead.

Although the morning was pleasantly warm, the sun shining down from above the calm sea, she pulled her coat around her and shivered. She found the sound of the gentle waves pulling on the shingle comforting.

Being alone suited her; it had been like that for much of her early life. She thought back now, as she so often did, to that moment at school when, in the middle of an arithmetic lesson, she had been called out to go to the headmaster's room. She was thirteen; 1921. A policeman was with this stern man whom she had only ever seen but never spoken to who now, to her horror, put his arm around her shoulder. The news hardly registered at first. Her parents had died in a fire at their house.

What really hurt her was that she had left that morning without saying goodbye; the noise of their bickering in the bedroom upstairs had so distressed her that she'd rushed out slamming the door behind her.

The anger transmitted itself to her now all those years later. She picked up a handful of pebbles from the shingle around her and threw them, one by one, into the sea. Her early life annoyed her and, although she knew it was unfair, she blamed her parents for the mess it had turned out to be. Perhaps some brothers and sisters would have helped to dilute the pressure she had always experienced but, as an only child – even then her mother had told her she had been a mistake – she had borne the brunt of their constant displeasure and handled alone their interminable fighting.

She had always wanted to be lost in the crowd, a follower rather than a leader and was a shy, introverted girl; so much so that it's doubtful if any of those early teachers would even remember her.

"Look at me now," she whispered. "Whatever happened to Peggy Ashbourn?"

A dog bounded up to her, breaking away from its owners who were strolling along the coiled, barbed-wire barrier which was the nearest anyone could get to the sea edge. The dog thought that Peggy was calling to it and fussed around, smelling Mountjoy, Alice Banbury's labrador, on her and delighting in some serious sniffing of her coat and shoes. She patted it and off it rushed following other scents along the edge of the wall.

She shielded her eyes against the bright sparkle of the sea. She could see the outline of naval vessels on the horizon but her gaze went far beyond them, eight hundred miles or so through Holland and Nazi Germany into Poland. She knew that she *had* to believe that Freddy was still alive, otherwise there was no point in any of this, no point in anything. And what of the notebooks? Freddy's unique scientific calculations? What should she do with them if...

She stood up and turned away from the sea. It was too painful to look and not find him there. She walked on, away from the town, towards the Martello tower at the end of the spit where she could just make out the snout of the Bofors gun which had been sited alongside the squat, nineteenth century fortress. To her right was the placid estuary of the Flax with dinghies and sailing boats still lying at anchor, their owners engulfed now in more serious tests than navigating them through the channels between the reed beds.

It had really started with the fire. She had stood in the room in her scruffy navy blue school gymslip with the headmaster's arm around her shoulders feeling more embarrassed than shocked. The news of the catastrophe hadn't yet sunk in but this totally new experience of being comforted by this stranger certainly had! She had prised herself away and sat heavily on a chair and just stared ahead of her. It was, she remembered, the first time that she had experienced that strange, detached feeling of numbness, weightlessness, that she had felt so often since then and felt again with such intensity now.

She had left that school there and then with, literally, the clothes she was wearing as her only remaining possessions – and she could trace her emergence from the crowd to that moment. For three years she lived with an elderly aunt in Surrey and attended a girls-only grammar school having, to her amazement, passed the entrance exam and, from the start, Peggy Ashbourn blossomed, not so much academically but via the arts. She developed a love for the stage, dancing and acting her way through school plays and in the local amateur dramatic society. She won singing, dancing and drama prizes and there was no doubt in her mind about the career she would choose. The stage called...

Her nagging guilt was that she knew that this euphoria and sense of well-being just wasn't right. It had really all emerged as a result of the tragic deaths of her parents and, in all honesty, she had never felt the grief she knew she should have. Instead there was a strong sense of relief that all the shouting, anger and tears were over. And she was free.

Free! What a strange word to contemplate now, twenty or so years later.

To her surprise she'd now walked as far as the barbed wire around the gun emplacement would let her, totally unaware of doing so. The gun crew eyed her hoping for a suggestion that would lift the boredom of their lonely morning, but one look told them that the previous hour or so spent watching her through binoculars that should have been trained on the sea searching for the first signs of landing craft had been a fruitless waste of time.

She smiled at them and turned looking back towards the town. Free? Inland, barrage balloons ducked and weaved in the gentle breeze and the beach, now on her right, was a mass of anti-invasion defences. The price of freedom, she felt with a shudder, was going to be a high one.

She shouted to the gun crew to come to the Show when they were off duty, vaguely pointing to the distant smudge of the theatre at the end of the pier and then, waving goodbye, started to trudge back along the narrow spit of shingle.

It had taken her a dozen or so years to reach a fair degree of stardom on the London stage. She'd followed the accepted path of provincial repertory, rising from odd-job girl and then assistant stage-manager, to walk-on roles until she reached the dizzy heights of 'young female lead', a soubrette. Her accomplished singing and dancing lifted her through the barrier that so many artistes found impenetrable, from the provinces into London. She thought of her excitement in passing the audition for Ivor Novello's 'Careless Rapture' and then that strange moment when she knew that the single rose and its accompanying modest letter were different to the countless others – and very special.

Her descent into this fearful vacuum in which she now found herself could well be measured from that point onwards, but she knew that her decision to meet Freddy after that night's performance had been, by a very long way, the best decision that she had ever made in the thirty-or-so years of her turbulent life.

CHAPTER FOUR

Early April 1940. SS Reichsführer Heinrich Himmler appoints Odilo Globocnik as Police Chief of Poland's Lublin province. He is known to be a murderer and sadist.

In England a leaflet, 'If the Invader Comes', tells people to decline German requests for food, bicycles and maps!

In the German staff car Freddy could see that they were approaching Warsaw. The number of buildings dotted about the barren landscape was increasing and all, he noted, were ruined shells. It seemed that nothing had been allowed to survive the systematic wanton destruction of the Polish nation. Ruined machinery, dead animals, dead people all lay jumbled together, none given precedence over the other because, as Freddy knew, in the diseased minds of their victors, none took precedence. He closed his eyes again in an attempt to blot out the present – and what he knew would be the future.

*

The flight from the Research Establishment had been dramatic. The whole place had been torched. It was done so cruelly and in such a pathetic panic. The government sent a hand-picked squad, trained in sabotage. They arrived on the evening of September the fifth, five days after the Nazi invasion started. Everyone was given two hours to clear their few possessions from the huts and then the precious scientific instruments were shattered with pick-axes and heavy mallets.

The ordinary workers were told to scatter, go to their homes, find their loved ones, but for obvious reasons the top scientists were offered – ordered – to escape by boat across the Baltic to neutral Norway. As it turned out most of the camp turned to the sea as their only means of escape aware that the news they were receiving suggested that there was nothing left in Poland for them. They were resigned for death anyway; they knew that if the vicious Baltic didn't claim them enemy sea patrols or the Luftwaffe almost certainly would – and both would be preferable to the treatment they could expect at the hands of the invaders.

The Germans were advancing at such great speed from the West and the hated and feared Russians from the East that the destruction of the camp, so complete that nothing other than ash and twisted metal remained, was nearly the last act of the Polish Government. Poland was, for the fourth time in its recent history, being squeezed out of existence.

*

"You will now be blindfolded, Herr Professor. It is decided."

Freddy jerked into awareness. This wouldn't do. The past was gone. Concentrate on now and the future.

"There seems no need, Herr Oberst," commented the officer on his left. "He travels with his eyes shut". He chuckled. "Perhaps he is praying. His God has not helped him so far."

Freddy turned his head and stared into the man's eyes.

"Please do"

He hadn't spoken for some time and was surprised how quiet and calm his voice was. He sighed. "I have seen Warsaw when it was so very beautiful, I would rather not see it now." He sat forward to make the task easier.

The two Germans were confused and angry; prisoners did not invite them to carry out their duties.

"You will do as you are told." The Colonel fixed him with cold, dispassionate eyes. "Fix it tightly, Herr Hauptmann." He barked the order as if the tightness was a further punishment.

A black scarf was tied around his head and Freddy re-closed his eyes. So be it. He was surprised to find the blindfold an unwelcome encumbrance; an invasion of his liberty. Frightening. He had an urge to rip it off but knew it would be foolish, they would then manacle his hands.

"It is necessary that you are unaware of our headquarters." The Colonel's voice had lost its roughness as if he was trying to calm the situation. He was no fool: a guest of SS General Friedrich Streyer must not be in a position where he complained of his treatment.

The most senior Nazi in Poland was feared as much by his own people as his enemies.

Freddy sank back again. Was it now time for the end? If it was, then so be it. The secrets would die with him. He had planned to take his life – but when? It had to be when there was absolutely no chance of survival. The ampoule of potassium cyanide had been expertly inserted in a tooth by the dentist at the Research Centre. All the top scientists had been equipped this way, many against their will. Freddy shuddered. He certainly hadn't seen this as part of the baggage he would carry through life in return for a First Class Honours Cambridge degree!

He would bide his time. He closed his eyes behind the blindfold and his mind drifted back to the one episode in this tragedy that plagued him more than any other through the long fearful days and sleepless nights since the heart-breaking parting from Peggy.

*

He couldn't remember how long he had sat on the stone wall in that small fishing village looking out over the grey, angry Baltic sea. It was a bleak early September day, more like winter. There was no discernible horizon; the sea merged with the sky.

He watched through his tears the tiny fishing boat simply fade away. There was no waving, no contact of any kind. All three of them were in a state of extreme shock; they seemed to be silently pleading with each other to end the nightmare…

It had only been eight months since he and Peggy had arrived at the villa. They had been met by his mother, Countess Anya Crisciak. She delighted in this young, vivacious and very beautiful wife that her shy, bachelor son had taken. To celebrate the marriage she had secretly arranged a sumptuous Estate party. Everyone was there; every member of every family on the Crisciak thousand acres of land attended. It was rather like an Indian durbar with Freddy cast as the sultan. To such a shy person the obeisance was uncomfortable but, for his mother's – and Peggy's sake – he endured it happily.

They received wedding gifts. Everyone had provided something; silver and porcelain from the senior estate workers down to hand-made ornaments from the farm workers and children. They were enchanted and consumed a vast meal, drank a fair corner of his father's wine cellar and danced until dawn.

Although, on this February day in 1939, dark rumblings in Germany were already disturbing the minds of those Poles who were aware of the paranoid hatred their Russian and German neighbours had for them, this night all could be forgotten.

Freddy and Peggy were hopelessly in love and entered their kingdom. They danced closely, and closely went to their bed.

*

The car stopped. Freddy's eyes jerked open and, in a moment of panic he thought he had lost his sight. It was the blindfold, of course, but his panic wasn't eased by the fury erupting around him.

The Colonel had lost control and was screaming through the driver's open window. He and the Captain were sitting forward shouting orders to the soldiers manning the road block.

Freddy suddenly felt space. He hadn't realised how cramped he had been between them in the back and it made him realize why he had felt so much a captive. Had they arranged themselves, one in the front and the other beside him in the back, it would have seemed like any other car journey but here they were crowding him, preventing any movement. There could be no escape, he was under their total control. He shuddered. They felt him do so and smiled in satisfaction. They needed fear in their captives; to most it instantly swamped them. This man had proved to be more difficult.

The car cleared the check point. Freddy felt the cobbled street and knew that they were entering Warsaw. He was glad for the blindfold. He didn't want to see this proud city gutted and ravaged as it now was, a landscape of gaunt ruins covering an area that had housed one-and-a-third million people and provided work for many more. Most of them had now been driven out and in their place was a brutal, sadistic enemy.

He guessed that army bulldozers would have cleared paths through the rubble where the streets had been and these they were negotiating slowly and with care.

"You are too slow, driver. You shall be reported for your performance today." The Colonel was feeling stiff and cramped. "Hauptmann Fengel, you will speak with his Feldwebel."

From his left he heard the Captain. "Jawohl Herr Oberst." It seemed to be one of his stock phrases.

Freddy felt like joining in. How was it that only a moment ago he was considering biting the ampoule in his tooth and now he felt strangely light-headed? Fear did strange things to a person, and it was mounting as they neared the end of this unpleasant journey. He wanted to say that the driver was doing his best in very difficult conditions, that his negotiation of the shell and bomb craters was nothing short of masterly and that his patience in keeping quiet whilst two over-inflated buffoons with giant egos ranted at him was nothing short of heroic.

But he said nothing. He and the driver were in enough trouble as it was. Again he did his disappearing act into his overcoat and tried to imagine where they were in the city that was no more.

*

He had last been in Warsaw in September. Seven months ago, September the fourth. The Third Reich had been on Polish soil for only two days but had already covered an amazing distance against very little resistance.

In the pouring rain he had, at last, left the wall in the fishing village and started the trek south. He moved very slowly at first, desperately aware that every step he took lengthened the distance between him and Peggy. He was lucky, a lorry carrying fish stopped for this lone figure carrying two heavy suitcases trudging along the verge of the road and he gratefully clambered over the tail gate. In the back were vast vats of fish layered with ice.

It was freezing cold lying between the vats and the stench made him want to gag but none of that mattered; the lorry was going to Warsaw and that was where Freddy planned to join the fight.

The journey lasted through the night. Along the way the driver picked up a dozen other zealots eager to bear arms against the invaders. They all lay amongst the vats huddled together to keep warm and cursed at their luck in flagging down a lorry laden with ice and fish.

But amazingly they were cheerful and Freddy joined in the patriotic songs they sang and smiled sadly at their extravagant boasts of victory over the hated Germans. They saw a fierce contest ahead but, without doubt, they assured him, they would win; the Third Reich would be no match for the highly trained, well equipped Polish Army.

Freddy wanted to share their childlike optimism but what he had seen when he had attended scientific meetings in Germany in the early thirties was seared on his mind. He knew that it would not be an easy victory and, in his heart, he acknowledged that there would be no victory at all.

The fish lorry deposited them in Warsaw in a small bomb-damaged square by the fast flowing grey-brown waters of the Wista.

They stood, gazing wildly around them. This wasn't what they had been expecting at all. Instead of a dazed, demoralised population there seemed to be an eerie carnival spirit.

In a seedy bar in an atmosphere of excited drunkenness they were told that Great Britain had declared war on Germany. They and France had honoured their promise to fight for Poland if it was invaded. Now the Poles had a clear goal: to hold out until their allies arrived to help them or, more likely, using their renowned diplomatic skills, force Germany to withdraw its forces from Polish soil.

The citizens of Warsaw manned the barricades. Many were given weapons – mostly the old nineteenth century French Lebelle rifles – and a clip of ammunition.

Others converged on the British and French embassies, full of relief and hope that their armies would come to defend them. "Long live our Allies," they shouted. "Now we can defeat Hitler." Such was their faith.

Freddy deposited his suitcases in the office of his old friend, the Professor of Applied Physics at the University, who accepted this intrusion somewhat gracelessly. He greatly admired Freddy as a scientist but doubted the man's sanity on hearing that he was here to fight. Also, in a city already pervaded with unpleasant smells, he found the addition of fish odour in his office too much to take! He requested Freddy to retire, wash and change his clothes. Wash he could, change his clothes he could not.

He opened his suitcases and the Professor was in no way surprised to see that they were filled with his reference books from the doomed Research Centre. Jumbled in amongst them, as if to provide protection, was a change of underwear and some socks, the only clothes he had brought with him! Still smelling of fish Freddy went out into a calm autumnal day to hitch a lift eastwards to the fast approaching front line and, in all probability, to die.

Two weeks later Warsaw was a beleaguered fortress in an occupied land. That is all the time it took for Germany to occupy the west half of the country and, most cruel of all, for Russia to occupy the eastern half. The Polish state was no more.

Freddy was one of the lucky ones not to be killed or, worse, captured; execution was the easiest, most efficient way to handle Polish prisoners. He made his way back into Warsaw exhausted and, like all those around him, totally demoralised. Now it would be the final battle, on the barricades of their beloved capital city. A battle to the death.

The Polish Army had been almost totally destroyed and a new dark age had descended over the land. The invaders saw this wanton rape and pillage as just retribution for their humiliation, twenty years before, when the Versailles Treaty pushed back their frontiers to create the Polish Second Republic. Now they were back – and there would be no mercy.

Warsaw held out for a further two weeks and then, bombed and shelled into a mound of rubble, it died. On September the twenty-third came what was to be the final bombardment. Every day, all day, the Polish National Anthem blared out, non-stop, to the invaders. On the twenty-seventh the loud-speakers fell silent.

Freddy had already left. He had to be forced, almost at gun-point, to leave. He wanted to join the Armia Krajowa, the underground resistance army, but it was the Professor at the University who finally made him see sense. There was nothing left to fight for anyway but far more important than that was what Freddy had stored in his head.

"You owe it to mankind. It's as simple as that," the professor had said. "Your dead body in a Warsaw street means nothing alongside the thousands of others."

He handed Freddy a sherry – still, in this shattered building, there was a decanter filled with sherry – and they raised their crystal glasses.

"To our beloved country. God save us."

"No-one else seems bothered to," Freddy replied dryly. "To Poland." They drank, and were silent.

The Professor went to the window. Around him his room appeared to be dead, the bookcases lining the walls condemning him for letting such barbarism supplant the quiet academic life they represented. The furniture, dark and heavy, was covered in thick dust and a curtain had fallen in an untidy heap amongst shards of shattered glass which lay in sharp fragments on the damaged carpet. The sound of heavy guns invaded the peace of his sanctuary and shook its very foundations.

"You must go." The Professor was talking quietly, looking out on the scene of desolation. He turned and put his hand gently on Freddy's shoulder. "The peace of the world depends on it. That is not a trite statement my friend. I'm not given to uttering banalities. It is true. You know it. Your duty must take you away from here and, please God, somehow to safety."

A violent explosion raised the dust into a cloud around them.

An hour later Freddy, weighed down with his suitcases, was on the road north out of Warsaw heading towards the only refuge he could think of: his villa.

He went back to the villa because there was really no other place to go. As he approached it up the long drive on a grey September day he knew that it would not have escaped the vengeance of the German invaders. Nor had it. It stood grey and dead in the bleak countryside and even from a distance he sensed – could feel – that it had been ransacked.

He made his way slowly along the curving drive, dragging his heavy suitcases and, without thought, climbed the steps under the entrance portico and approached the big front doors.

Was he surprised that it wasn't flung open be a footman? Surely not. He shook his head in disgust at himself and his stupidity. Why was his brain so numbed that it could so often these days drop from the present into the past? It was at times like this that he despaired of it ever functioning sufficiently well again for him to be able to resume his work on the project. Of course all the staff would have gone – dead, or scattered to the four winds. It was yet something else that didn't bear thinking about...

He leant on the doors expecting them to give easily but they were firmly fastened: the ransackers had evidently entered and left from the back.

The kitchen door gave easily. He dropped his suitcases and stared around him at the familiar room but this time he was ready for his brain's attempt to carry him into the past and, with a shudder, he set out to discover what havoc the Wehrmacht had wrought.

As he toured the house his spirits slowly rose. He saw that the damage to the interior was more an act of spite than calculated destruction. The rooms had been roughly treated and the furniture and most of their possessions either broken beyond repair or stolen. In the library – to Freddy the most important room in the house – whilst the shelves had all been torn out and carted away, probably for firewood, the books, strewn in heaps around the floor, were more or less undamaged.

He decided that until he could work out a plan for the future he'd live in the big kitchen. He closed the shutters. No-one must see that the house was occupied. He knew he couldn't live indefinitely in this one room, but there was food in the storerooms to last one person, on meagre rations, indefinitely and, ironically, enough wine in the cellar, lovingly laid down by his father, to see him drunk into eternity!

But what was the point? The army he had stayed to serve had disintegrated even before he'd reached Warsaw from the Baltic camp. He couldn't believe or understand how a fighting force, supposedly well aware of the strength of the enemy lined up against them could be so taken by surprise. He could only guess that the politicians, who had so interfered with his scientific work at the Research Centre, had got it terribly wrong again. How many wars were started by politicians and ended by soldiers? He shook his head angrily. Most of them.

On his third day, holed-up in the kitchen of the villa, he heard a baby cry. He heard it quite distinctly and his spine chilled, irrational fear making him shake. He'd been alone too long; talked to no-one; heard nothing.

Now he heard it again. A quiet contented cry.

Creeping silently he followed the sound and came to the cellar steps leading to an enormous labyrinth of store rooms, boiler room and wood store, covering the whole area of the house. Moving down the steps he heard the wail again and now a gentle shushing and a girl's voice whispering a lullaby.

He was at the door. He knew that to open it would create a panic, maybe injury, so instead he called softly through the wood. He found himself saying, ridiculously pompously, "This is Count Freddy Crisciak here. May I come in?"

All sound stopped.

He imagined a hand pressed over the baby's mouth. There was whispering and then a man's tremulous voice, "What is your mother's first name?"

It was his Estate Manager. There was no doubt.

"Anya" he replied. "Is that you, Jan?"

A pause, and then the door opened to a crack. An eye appeared, and then it was flung open.

The room was furnished as a comfortable bed-sitting room with a small kitchen curtained off at one side. All they needed they had carried down from the house. Jan, his wife and baby had planned to stay there until some form of normal life resumed in the countryside, or they decided to join the stream of refugees roaming Europe searching for somewhere, anywhere, safe to settle.

For the next six months Freddy, living and working in the villa kitchen, was cared for by Jan and his wife. They remained vigilant but being well away from any other homes there was no real need; the Germans had no use for the barren, scarred countryside. The little group had no contact with the outside world. It was as if they were on another planet.

With all his reference books still intact in the dusty library Freddy worked daily at Project Omega but decided that nothing must be in writing. No more notebooks. Far too dangerous. His only storehouse would be his brain and now, with no other distractions, he put it into over-drive.

The way towards nuclear fission, splitting the atomic nucleus, which he had been evolving for over four years was starting to materialize.

In early April, this weird twilit world ended as suddenly as it had begun. The banging on the big front door of the villa was insistent.

He jerked awake. His watch said one o'clock. It was a little early to be making an arrest; they usually left it to three or four in the morning, 'lowest ebb' time.

He got up and padded through the deserted hall. He knew he was going to die but the act of doing so meant very little to him. His beloved Peggy and his mother were safe, or dead. Whichever, there was little chance that he would ever see them again.

What frightened him was that the Gestapo would torture the secrets out of him. He wasn't a coward but had often been reminded in recent months that you didn't have to be one to fear torture and he didn't need reminding that those secrets, stored in his brain, would almost certainly decide who would win the war that was escalating rapidly through Europe. His tongue sought the cyanide ampoule...

*

The car swerving to the right brought him back to the present. It bounced over paving stones and loose rubble throwing the three occupants in the back this way and that and then came violently to a halt. The driver was angry. For six hours he had steered the vehicle through obstacles of every shape and size. Now he was to be reported to his sergeant and would probably lose this prized job of driver of the SS General's Staff Car and find himself back on patrol.

Freddy, his mind jerked back to the present, sensed the others getting out. A hand touched his shoulder and he was roughly pulled out, banging his head on the car roof. He heard a laugh. The hand cupped itself under his elbow.

The Captain's voice was harsh. "This way."

The Colonel added "Please."

Please? Was this the lull before the storm? There was something very fearful about being moved around blindfolded. Even in normal circumstances he felt that it must be unnerving but when each step may be leading towards swift, or worse, slow execution he found the experience unbearable.

His reluctance to move transmitted itself to the Captain who urged him along.

"Move faster. We don't have all day."

Freddy had all day – and more if possible.

"Do not rush the Herr Professor, Hauptmann." The Colonel's voice was oily smooth. "We must present him in the best possible condition for General Streyer." This was said with obvious sarcasm. The duties of SS officers did not usually include arresting and escorting an enemy of the Third Reich and delivering him in one piece and unharmed to, not a prison cell, but the Headquarters of the SS in Poland.

Freddy felt himself being led across an echoing space with, evidently a tiled floor.

"Welcome to the Hotel Bristol." The Captain's tone was mocking, unaware that he had provided Freddy with everything he needed to know and, at a stroke, made the blindfold superfluous.

Freddy knew the Hotel Bristol well; he had delivered speeches and lectures here on so many occasions in the past occupying, as an honoured guest, the Presidential Suite on the top floor. The irony of it would be laughable if he wasn't now in such mortal danger. He imagined the hotel manager last time he was here saying to him as he greeted him at the entrance, so obsequiously "Welcome Herr Professor. The next time you enter my hotel you will be blindfolded and facing execution." Why did the mind flit to such foolish things at times like this?

He was stopped and he heard the sound of clanking machinery: the lift. He wondered if all the staff he knew were gone; dead probably, most would have manned the barricades. The lift gate squeaked open and he was roughly pushed inside by the Captain who couldn't comply with his orders to be gentle. Hitler described the Poles as 'worms'. You did not treat worms gently.

Freddy was squashed in the lift with the Colonel and Captain and, pushed tightly against him, a fourth person who must be, he deduced, the lift operator. For a moment of panic he thought the lift was descending. Deprivation of sight confused the senses. If they were going down it would be to the cellars. What went on in the cellars of SS headquarters? He could guess.

But no, he now felt the weight on his feet as the clanking lift slowly clawed its way *upwards*.

"Can't you make this wreck move faster? I dislike confined spaces."

Freddy's mind again saw humour when it was least appropriate. The Colonel, an officer in one of the most brutal services ever conceived, had a fear of small spaces!

"No, Herr Oberst. Four is too many," the attendant whined, adding proudly "but we are the only lift still working in Warsaw."

Eventually they clanked to a halt, the gate opened and Freddy was led over thick carpet to a door. It was unlocked and he was pushed inside.

Now the blindfold was mercifully removed. At first the brightness was so intense that he was dazzled, but his eyes quickly adjusted. He saw that he was in what had once been a principal bedroom in the hotel, so grand that it had, in one corner, a small bathroom.

"You are dismissed, Hauptmann. You may resume your duties." The Colonel loosely waved his hand towards the door. There was no love lost between SS officers: no room for natural emotions of any kind.

"Jawohl, Herr Oberst." The Captain clicked his heels to attention and threw out his arm in a Nazi salute. "Heil Hitler."

The Colonel responded, loosely. After a cold stare at Freddy the Captain marched out.

"You must forgive the Captain, Herr Professor. He is young and inexperienced in the ways of diplomacy." The Colonel was giving a good imitation of a hotel manager. Freddy expected him to go on "should you require anything, please do not hesitate to ring," but, of course, he didn't.

"You will now rest and will doubtless wish to wash and shave. Clean clothing is in the cabinet. You will join SS General Streyer for dinner in the Presidential Suite at nineteen-thirty hours. You will be collected. Lunch will be brought to you." He clicked his heels, considered saluting, remembered that you did not salute enemies of the Third Reich, about turned – which didn't quite work and caused him to totter sideways – and, without another glance, left.

Freddy heard the key turn in the lock. He guessed that there would be at least one guard outside the door.

He suddenly realized that he was very, very tired. Drained. For the moment he felt safe and, sighing with relief, sank down onto the bed.

But of course he wasn't safe, far from it. He was locked in a room, just an unusually comfortable cell really, in the heart of the Polish headquarters of Hitler's dreaded SS. About as **un**safe as anyone could be. Why did the mind, at times like these, dart from one sensation to its complete opposite? Confusion – and tiredness.

He lay back and his eyes started to close. This wouldn't do. He jerked upright. What time was it? He looked for his watch but his wrist was bare. Of course; they had taken it with everything else when they searched him at the villa. Now he looked around him. On a bedside table was a small clock. Ten in the morning. Was that all? He seemed to have been awake forever.

He crossed the room. The wardrobe had a suit hanging in it. He checked the label. His size and made by one of the finest tailors in Warsaw. Where was *he* now? The drawers had new shirts, ties, underwear, socks. A shoe-rack held a pair of new-ish brogue shoes. Who last wore those – and where was *he* now?

The bathroom was equipped with massive ornate furniture and gold taps. How had this building survived when the rest of Warsaw was reduced to rubble? There was piping hot water. All this in a city that was now dead. It didn't make sense.

He went over to the bed and was tempted to pick up the 'phone and ask for room service, or a call at 1 p.m. That would show them that there was still some spirit left in Poland. He couldn't resist picking up the handset but, of course, it was dead. He'd just lie down and rest. No need to doze off.

Two minutes later a heavy snore indicated that Freddy Crisciak, at the moment of the greatest crisis in his life was, indeed, fast asleep.

He was dragged back to wakefulness by a key being turned in the lock. There was laughter and banging. For a moment he was totally lost. Everything was in the wrong place: windows, door, the furniture. He lay there as two guards crashed in with a tray of food. One of them dropped it onto the table by the windows. The plate and cutlery clattered. The glass spilt its water...

Freddy closed his eyes remembering a morning at the villa. He and Peggy had been there a week and still his mother had insisted that they were on honeymoon; a life of total luxury, starting with breakfast in bed. A new maid had joined the household staff; she was on trial and very nervous, probably only fourteen or fifteen, the daughter of an estate worker. Inside the door stood the housekeeper, watching her, assessing her abilities. Such were the child's nerves that she dropped the tray heavily onto the table by the window making the plates and cutlery clatter, the glasses spill their orange juice. The housekeeper had come forward, distressed, but Peggy had sat up, smiling at the girl, "It's alright, Mrs Padeski, she is doing very well."

Freddy sat up now, automatically smiling – at an SS private soldier laughing at his colleague's carelessness. The laughter froze on the man's lips. He returned the smile with a snarl.

"Kommen sie Johann, schnell." The two of them left eyeing Freddy fearfully. He was obviously a maniac being prepared for the special skills of the basement "persuaders." The door was re-locked.

Freddy ate the food ravenously. It never occurred to him that it might be poisoned. But it wasn't. They were obviously not yet ready for the coup de grace.

He stripped, ran a bath and lay luxuriously in the hot water. It was the first hot bath he had had for – how long? Seven months; his last had been at the Research Centre, a lifetime ago. He shaved. There was even a toothbrush and a tin of dental powder. Then he dressed in the clothes provided for him and stood in front of the cheval mirror seeing himself, full length, for the first time since in his room on the Baltic. Despite everything he appeared to be fit and well; his old self again. At any moment he might expect the Chairman of the Polish State Scientific Association to knock discreetly on the door and invite him downstairs for cocktails, then to be wined and dined before assuming the role of principal speaker at the Annual Convention! Professor Frederick Crisciak was ready. His mind was up to its old tricks again. Ready for what?

He now had five or so hours to plan: to use his razor-sharp brain to work out tactics for the forthcoming encounter with SS General Friedrich Streyer. The aim was simple and clear; he *must* stay alive, not only for what he had stored in his memory – Project Omega – but also for his dear Peggy if, please God, she and his mother had survived the perilous Baltic sea crossing to Norway and, from there, the journey home to England and safety. And with her were his precious notebooks...

*   *   *

"But what does it all mean, Peg?" Pat was leafing through pages of one of the notebooks shaking her head in bewilderment. She and Peggy were sitting at the bay window in Alice Banbury's sitting room, the five notebooks open on the table in front of them. Peggy involuntarily stroked the surface of one of the pages.

"They mean Freddy to me, love. It's the only part of him I have." Her hands rested, pressing down hard on the pencilled hieroglyphics and symbols as if protecting them, gathering them into her care.

Pat saw that her mind was far away, locked in a trance. She too sat perfectly still, as if they were both in prayer, until the moment passed.

It happened suddenly. Peggy shook herself back to the present and feverishly started turning pages at random, quickly moving from book to book. Her mood now was a total contrast: urgent, almost frenetic. Pat put her hand on her arm to calm her.

"It's alright Peg. It's alright."

She felt this was totally inadequate but could think of nothing else to say. It was pointless, unfair even, to make trite comments such as "We'll get him back, just you see" when she couldn't see any hope of that ever happening. She felt that the path ahead was going to be even stonier than the one Peggy had already trodden, and how they were all going to deal with *that* as the drama developed she really had no idea.

"Did you do algebra at school, Peg?"

Peggy looked up. "Later on. But nothing like this. There's geometry too. It makes no sense at all – well, not to us – but to the right people it means everything. When Freddy brought me and his mother to live at the Research camp on the Baltic you could tell that everything the scientists were doing was so important and secret. No-one was allowed to say anything, but I heard enough to know that it's about beating Germany and that's what kept all of them working day and night. Of course at that time the war hadn't started but everyone seemed to think it soon would. That's why Freddy moved us from the villa to the camp."

For a moment or two they were quiet again as they thumbed through the books. The silence was punctuated by muttered comments as they explored the lines of pencilled notes.

"A lot of U235"

".05 MeV. What's an MeV?"

"Here Peg, what about this? $U^{238} + n - U^{239} - Ba^? + Kr^?$."

Pat handed the book to Peggy who checked the date.

"It's an early one." she added sadly, "I hope he solved the question-marks."

Briskly she packed the five books together wrapping them in the brown paper they'd travelled in from Poland. "The next time I look inside them." her voice grew strong "will be with Freddy."

"You must put them in the bank, Peg. For safe keeping."

"No." Peggy's tone was sharp, then she softened it. "Sorry Pat, but no. Freddy told me to keep them with me until he arrived and I shall. I've decided where they'll be hidden but it's best if only I know just in case," her voice trailed away, "in case someone tries to force it out of any of you."

Pat, too, was quiet now. Then she shivered.

"They're *that* important?"

"Yes love," whispered Peggy, "they're that important."

They went to their rooms for a rest before the show and then later met in the flat kitchen for a cup of tea to set them on their way to the theatre. It was a squash because Mountjoy's large wooden kennel covered much of the floor space. They'd all laughingly decided that, in the event of an air-raid, he'd have to squeeze up to make room for the three of them!

They wandered back into the sitting room with their tea.

"You really are an amazing lot." Peggy stood looking out over the roof-tops to where she could just see the highest point of the Pier Theatre's end pediment. "You're so kind. Everyone is in their own way. Dear Nell, of course, Belvedere – he's gentle behind that pomposity, but oh so sad. Even Tad." They both laughed. "I don't think he'd deliberately hurt a fly but he's the most unsubtle person I've ever met. Always putting his foot in it."

Pat came up alongside her.

"You must tell them, you know. They'd want to know – and help. Not all the detail, just what's important." Peggy sighed.

"I suppose I must. When I'm ready." Pat heard the determination in her voice and decided for the time being to leave it at that.

They crossed the High Street and strolled through the narrow passages between the houses to the pier.

"I just don't see why they should be burdened with my problems. Everyone has their own."

Pat wasn't having that. "Which pale into total insignificance beside yours, love. So let them help. We all want to."

Behind them at a discreet distance a tall man, his hat pulled down and coat collar turned up to hide his features, stealthily followed them.

*　　*　　*

They came for Freddy at seven thirty that evening in the Bristol Hotel in Warsaw. Two guards entered his room and roughly ordered him to follow them. He felt very confused. Here he was, a prisoner in Warsaw's Gestapo Headquarters about to be entertained by the most senior SS Officer in Poland, General Friedrich Streyer, in his private apartment, wearing clothes looted from the homes of his fellow countrymen who had either fled or been murdered on the orders of the thug who was about to be his host! He entered the Presidential Suite having no idea what to expect.

"Ah, my dear Professor. I have been looking forward to this meeting for so long."

The small man advanced, almost waddled, across the deep pile carpet with his hand outstretched. How often people had said that to him as his fame as a scientist had grown through the thirties but never, he felt, as insincerely as now.

This little man, ridiculously dressed in his black SS uniform with breeches and highly polished long black jackboots looked like a character from a Strauss operetta. He expected a tenor aria from Der Rosenkavalier to burst through his thin, mean lips at any moment!

There was something icy about his hand-shake as his staring eyes pierced right through Freddy. Although his eyesight was perfect he wore pince-nez spectacles having, very wisely as far as his career path was concerned, modelled himself on his master, Heinrich Himmler.

Released from his icy grip, Freddy was ushered to a chair in the Presidential Suite. The room was as sumptuously decorated as he remembered it. It was hard to believe in this desolate land, but it actually smelt of fresh paint! It was decorated in the style of a palace, the cream plaster-work richly moulded and ornate with the detail picked out plentifully in gold, the long windows framed with rich crimson curtaining. The heavy furniture matched the room colours and stood on a heavily designed Indian carpet. Freddy knew that there were bedrooms and bathrooms leading from the entrance hall; he'd used them in years gone by!

He sat in a deep armchair apparently more at ease than his host whose upbringing, until he joined the National Socialist movement in the early thirties, had been in surroundings which were the very antithesis of this: a slum dwelling lacking any form of indoor sanitation whatsoever. But Hitler had put that right and now General Friedrich Streyer was head of all SS troops, second only to the Governor-General, the ultimate Master of Poland.

The Führer, on appointing him to this coveted post, had told him that his orders were "to kill without pity or mercy all men, women and children of Polish race or language." This was music to the ears of Friedrich Streyer but, of course, there would be exceptions and, provided he gave his full co-operation, such a one was sitting opposite him now. And who would not fully co-operate, given the gruesome alternative?

With his brain functioning normally for the first time since he had been taken from his villa, Freddy had spent a useful afternoon planning his tactics. Outright refusal to co-operate would be the hero's way but achieve nothing. An unbelievably painful death would either mean that his secrets died with him thereby setting back Project Omega for years – long enough for Germany to vanquish all its enemies – or, before the last moments, he would give way and recite everything stored in his remarkable brain, in which case the Third Reich would be able to wipe out civilisation whenever they wished to do so within a year – two at the most.

There seemed to be no choice but he had spent much of the afternoon thinking calmly – an unusual luxury these days – and he saw a middle way. He would apparently co-operate until such time, if there could be one, when he was able to get information to England preferably, please God, in person. What he must do was to play for time.

"I must congratulate you, Herr General, on a quick victory. Our forces were overwhelmed before they could properly organise themselves." He choked on the words. This was going to be more difficult than he had imagined.

Streyer wasted no time. "The Führer is a master strategist. But you must realize, Herr Professor, that we and our good allies, the Russians, do not accept that we have occupied this land. We have, rather, liberated it. Annexed our former provinces." He chuckled. It was a chilling sound. "You have been working here, in *Germany* and living here, in *Germany* all your life." He was warming to his subject but Freddy couldn't resist interrupting.

"At the Treaty of Riga in 1920 Poland took back its lands…"

Streyer did not deign to hear. He ploughed on.

"And it is to Germany that you owe the priceless information you have concerning " he coughed hastily, struggled upright, and went to a bureau bringing back a file of papers. As he dropped back untidily into his chair he glanced, apparently nonchalantly at an inside page and recited slowly like a child "…nuclear physics."

He was angry now, not as might be thought, with Freddy, but with himself. He had spent time trying to understand the detailed background notes on this matter which was evidently of such overwhelming importance that Hitler, the great Führer himself, had broken with all precedence and penned a page of orders *in his own handwriting*. Streyer had ludicrously stood at attention as he read the page of scrawl!

He had been breathless and shaking but the euphoria had evaporated rapidly when he'd discovered that his failed academic education, interrupted so early in his life by the more stimulating opportunity to learn the act of indiscriminate murder and mayhem as a National Socialist street fighter, had made most of the background notes indecipherable.

Now he had revealed this inadequacy before the evening really started by forgetting the very name of this new science on which his Führer placed so much importance.

Streyer attempted – failed – to cover his confusion by pouring two glasses of Szampan and handing one to Freddy who remembered, like a knife in the ribs, when he had last drunk Russian champagne. It had been at the villa the night of his wedding feast…

He sipped the champagne; this was no time to dull his mind with alcohol. Streyer gulped his and poured another for himself.

"Yes," he slurred, "We are the liberators. In the east of what you call Poland are four million Russians – Ukrainians – and in the west a million Germans."

He emptied his glass and poured himself another. He didn't offer one to Freddy; the effort of displaying any form of manners was past him. Freddy nearly interpolated with, "and squashed in between these immigrants are nineteen million Poles," but he didn't. He *must* stick to his plan and say as little as possible.

This was made easier by the obvious intention of Streyer to do all the talking!

"You may, in your ignorance of these matters, Herr Professor, be interested to know that one of our illustrious Generals, during his rapid conquest in the west passed through his old family estates and occupied, as his headquarters, the very place where he was born!" He ended this on a note of triumph, slapping his knees with glee.

To Freddy his laugh sounded like a witch's cackle and his anger boiled over.

"Conquest, you say? Occupied? Not, I would say, the words of a liberator, Herr General."

Streyer's face darkened and he staggered uncertainly to his feet. Freddy wondered for a moment if he was going to be assaulted by this absurd little man. Then what? Freddy could lay him out with one blow but doubtless guards were on hand. All would certainly be lost.

The General unwittingly calmed the tension by marching unsteadily to the dinner table.

"We will eat." He waved his arm to a chair and sat in the other. Freddy felt that he shouldn't be surprised when his host tucked his table napkin into the top of his tunic.

Waiters – civilian, not military – appeared. Freddy remembered the bell-push under the table.

"I have chosen a meal to bring to you nostalgia, Herr Professor."
Streyer said this in a tone that suggested he now wished he hadn't
bothered. "Smoked eel as the hors d'oeuvres. Brought by lorry,
daily from the Baltic."

Freddy smiled, but only to himself. It wouldn't do for the
loathsome man to know that he had travelled with their
predecessors only seven months ago!

The meal was good. The eels were followed by beetroot soup, steak
tartare, as the Polish liked it, almost raw, potatoes, 'bigos', a sweet and
sour cabbage dish and, for dessert, a bowl of fresh fruit. All this was
washed down, liberally by Streyer, with Wódka czysta, a classical, fine
quality vodka. The talk during the meal was little and inconsequential
and Freddy wondered when they would be getting to the point of this
bizarre evening. It had better be soon or the Herr General would be
completely unintelligible.

He was motioned back to the armchair. It was strange to be a
guest *and* a prisoner. It was obviously equally confusing to Streyer.

"What do you know of the past seven-or-so months in Poland?
Since we liberated it?" Streyer lit an enormous cigar.

Freddy ignored the word 'liberated.'

"Nothing. I was alone in my villa. I knew nothing of the world
outside."

It was true. He had no wireless, naturally no newspapers, no
callers. The only awareness of other human life on the planet had
been the constant sound of aeroplanes and, occasionally, gunfire.

"It is as well," slurred Streyer. "You would not have been happy
had you known."

That was probably the understatement of the decade, but it
would be some time before the full level of the genocide of the
Polish nation was revealed.

"In a few days you will be taken to Berlin. There you will join
your German colleagues at the…" – he studied his notes –
"Kaiser Wilhelm Institute and continue your work into this…"
– again he checked the notes – "nuclear business." It was obvious
that he had no idea what he was talking about. As before, he
mispronounced the word 'nuclear' giving it a short 'u' as in 'uncle'.

Freddy knew the Kaiser Wilhelm Institute well. In the early
stages of Project Omega, before the restriction of shared

information ended collaboration with Germany, Freddy had been an honoured visitor. His was the brain they'd always wanted. Now, he noted dryly, it seemed they might get it! Freddy knew better; the cyanide ampoule would be broken first.

Again he decided to remain silent. To show his disdain for this stupid man he rose and went to the drinks trolley. Although he didn't really want it, he poured himself another vodka then, as an afterthought, one for Streyer. It would be better to silence him through drink and then this whole foul business could be over with.

Streyer took the glass with no acknowledgement. He emptied it in one long, loud gulp, some of the clear liquid escaping and running down his chin.

"Your house has been emptied of all your working documents. It is now destroyed. Razed to the ground." He searched amongst the papers, found one, read it and grinned, inanely. "You would not have known, of course, that two people were in the cellars. With a small child." He slammed the folder shut. "They have been eliminated."

Freddy felt sick. He couldn't breathe. It was as well that the shock had paralysed him otherwise he would have delighted in throttling the man there and then. Streyer slurred on.

"Your research papers are already in Berlin being analysed. Berlin requires your notebooks, Herr Professor." He smiled a deathly smile. "Where are they?" He asked the question like a child asking for a toy.

The truth of Freddy's answer was completely lost on the General. "I don't know."

Streyer eyed him. "Not in your house, not on your person." Then evily. "You *will* tell us." He leant forward. "You *will* tell us."

There was silence. In anger Streyer hurled his glass at Freddy. It missed and smashed against the wall. He spoke now in a fast gabble.

"What you know and have not recorded you will write down in your room. It will be two or three days before you leave. Then you and your notes will be put at the service of the Third Reich."

With great difficulty he rose to his feet. Swaying alarmingly he raised his right hand. It gyrated as if he were waving to Freddy.

"Heil Hitler." Streyer staggered to the dining table, just managed to press the bell-push, and without a backward glance, weaved out of the room into what Freddy knew to be the master bedroom. The door slammed. The convivial evening was evidently over.

Freddy was still sitting, in a state of shock, as the door opened and the two armed soldiers who had gracelessly brought him his lunch entered.

"Kommen sie hier, Herr Professor."

They ushered him out into the corridor to the lift which was waiting with the gate open. The little lift attendant, possibly the only Hotel Bristol employee left, was standing by the operating handle.

What happened next was such a blur that it took Freddy a while, when back in his room, to sort it all out. All four of them crammed themselves into the lift but before the gate could be shut the attendant went, quite simply, berserk. He started to pummel Freddy violently in the stomach and kidneys, flailing his small fists anywhere where he could find a target. Being small, much of his battery of punches were around and below the belt. The two guards hastily withdrew to the landing where they stood roaring with laughter.

The attendant gibbered away in a mixture of German and Polish.

"You are a traitor to the great German cause," he screamed as he punched, "an enemy of the Third Reich. We are all German. The Polish State has never existed..." and so he went on...

Freddy was, at first, helpless. He had been completely taken by surprise and was pressed to the rear of the lift, half falling backwards as if he was on the ropes in a boxing ring with this little flyweight undoubtedly winning on points. He could see the guards over the little man's head and, as the assault became more intimate, he found the strength to thrust the man back into the arms of the laughing soldiers.

He escaped from the lift as the guards flung the still gibbering attendant onto the floor inside it and one of them closed the gate on him.

"Well done" he shouted, "take yourself to the kitchens. You deserve some vodka."

The other guard laughed. "He seems well fortified with it already."

They took Freddy down the three flights of stairs to his room and propelled him inside. The door closed and the key was turned.

Sitting on the bed he tried to put the whole strange evening together. He now knew what was in store for him but it had provided no great surprise other than the news of the wanton killing of Jan, his faithful Estate Manager, his harmless wife and their little baby. They symbolised to him the nobleness of the Polish race and their death, the barbarism of their conquerors.

In a state of shock he started to prepare for bed. What a pointless charade the evening had been. He guessed that all the squalid little SS General had gained from it would be a king-size headache tomorrow morning and, maybe, a feather in his cap from his superiors in Berlin for delivering what he thought, by his semblance of hospitality, would be a willing accomplice to the German quest for the development of the ultimate weapon of destruction – the atomic bomb.

And then, to end the evening, Freddy had endured, in front of a highly appreciative audience, the indignity of a beating-up – albeit an ineffectual one – from a member of his own race calling him a traitor for not collaborating with the enemy!

In this mental state of shock he went through the automatic ritual of preparing for bed. It had certainly been a full day! He emptied his trouser pockets, as he had always done, but tonight, because of the strip search at the villa, all he would have in them would be his handkerchief. Out it came from the right-hand pocket but so did something else from the left-hand side. A scrap of paper fell to the floor. He frowned. It wasn't his. There were words on it, in Polish, hurriedly scrawled.

> *Ask the time. If the answer is the month,*
> *it is a friend. Do as he or she says.*
> *Margaret is well. Eat this now.*

He stared at the message. He read it ten, a dozen times. When the meaning of it had fully sunk in he fell back onto the bed, his eyes filled with tears and he broke down into uncontrollable sobbing. The emotion was just too great. For the first time in many months he felt relief and joy. He was not alone and Peggy was safe. He screwed up the paper, put it in his mouth and, with one gulp, it was gone.

In the room next door to Freddy's a man lifted a pair of headphones from his head. He talked to his colleague.

"Tell the Herr General's adjutant that the plan has worked. The Professor is crying. He is broken. He will co-operate."

*

In the cavernous kitchens of the Hotel Bristol the lift attendant raised his glass of vodka. To himself, in silence, he proposed a toast.

"To our dear Poland. We *shall* be free again."

*　　*　　*

The Crisciaks slept. Freddy in his bed in Nazi headquarters in Poland, Peggy in her bed in Alice Banbury's flat over the Post Office in Flaxton-on-Sea. But, paradoxically, it was she who had the more disturbed night.

In the early hours of the morning the inhabitants of this seaside town were suddenly startled awake by a series of violent explosions. A lone German Dornier bomber crew, probably lost and knowing the punishment for returning to base not having released their bombs or, worse, wasting them by jettisoning them into the sea, had dropped the full load of high-explosives on the nearby village of Orfield.

On this April night Hitler seemed to be closing in on the Crisciaks...

CHAPTER FIVE

__Mid April 1940.__ Fighting in Norway continues. In Poland all intelligentsia, clergy and nobility are to be exterminated.

The British Expeditionary Force, together with their allied armies, are drawn up to defend an invasion of Holland and Belgium.

For the people of Flaxton much of the following week was spent discussing in homes, shops, pubs and on the pavements the two 'sensations', as the Flaxton Chronicle described them: the stick of bombs dropping on nearby Orfield and what the editor, Vernon Rogers, called in his headline, 'The Station Murder'. It was a sign of the times that the bombs received far more column inches than the violent death of an elderly railwayman.

Everyone was irritable. In the seven months since Chamberlain's sombre voice had announced that the nation was at war much of the country had relaxed back into its peacetime ways of living. People's behaviour was the very antithesis of the Government's and deeply aggravated those in command. By exhortation, threat, fear and new emergency laws they entreated the population to take this conflict with Germany seriously. They were, it was stressed, now fighting on the 'Home Front'.

Sandbags appeared at the doors and windows of strategic buildings, air-raid shelters were built – some, as Alice Banbury described them with a shudder, looking like concrete public lavatories. Her customers nodded forlornly during their stamp-licking and one had the temerity to suggest that her simile didn't stop merely at their appearance judging by the smell emanating from them!

To add to the cheerless mood housewives were having to cope with the newly introduced food rationing which was none too extreme at this time but never-the-less demanded a forced change in the management of their homes. All in all it was an exercise in restraint and discipline which the people of Britain were going to have to get used to and, in fairness, most were doing so.

And then suddenly, with no warning whatsoever, a stick of bombs had fallen, out of a calm night sky, on the small hamlet of Orfield, just a few miles down the coast from Flaxton-on-Sea. The war had arrived in earnest – at last!

The whole area was frightened out of its life. The bombs had exploded away from buildings on farmland but this was no comfort to the farmer who, in the local pub the next day, swore that *four* of his cows had been killed – even if only *two* carcasses had been found!

"The other two disintegrated" he answered his nodding cronies in the bar, "but I'll want compensation from the Min. of Ag. for all four."

Such was the mood at this time. No-one seemed to realize that the war would create for everyone, in the coming months, maybe years, suffering, pain, misery and, for this farmer as a start, financial loss. The price of eventual victory. But Churchill's fine rhetoric hadn't yet got up steam; Chamberlain was still Prime Minister.

If the murder of the Ipswich train guard, Mr Alfred Spiggins, attracted scant attention in the Flaxton Chronicle it received only a little more from the overstretched police force. With the prospect of an imminent invasion anywhere along the East Anglian coast every available officer was deployed as part of the meagre defence force.

Routine enquiries were, of course, carried out. The station master – now, with so many men called to serve in the forces, doubling as booking clerk – said in his statement that he had seen a shadowy figure race past the ticket window just before the train left. The police, after much deliberation, concluded that this would have been the one-and-only passenger known to have travelled on the last service to Ipswich that night.

It was the signalman, coming off duty down the platform who had come upon poor Mr Spiggins. His alibi – for the diligent police, despite more important matters to attend to, required one of him – was that the guard must have been shot before the train left, otherwise he would have been on it, and up to the moment of departure he was chatting to the driver and then setting the signal to 'off' at which moment the train steamed out of the station.

After lengthy deliberations the police accepted this explanation but, for absolutely no reason whatsoever other than to achieve *something* from the time spent on the case, warned the poor man as to his future behaviour.

'It was probably an accident' wrote Vernon Rogers, the Chronicle's editor now doubling as crime reporter. 'soldiers and airmen aren't used to the guns they've been issued with.'

Ignoring this opinion from a much respected member of the community the Inquest returned a verdict of 'murder by person or persons unknown.' The only consolation for Mrs Spiggins was that the case would remain 'on file' and the suspect's description circulated to all police stations around the area.

Down at the Pier Theatre the troupe had a much more interesting topic to chat about rather than murder: Nell had taken on a new act! For some time she had been concerned about the 'balance' of the show; she wanted something to make the audience gasp – other than Tad's jokes – and now this funny chap had turned up at the stage door. He was tall, blonde and clean shaven and wore a very long, ill-fitting brown overcoat which flared so that it flapped around him like a bat when he moved. On his head was a wide-brimmed, brown floppy hat with a band of crimson material which hung down at one side onto his shoulder and he carried a long black ebony cane.

The first surprise for Nell and Vi when Don showed the man into the office was that he handed them a carefully written note.

> *Please you must excuse me I am Marvo.*
> *My voice went with the bombs in Hungary.*
> *In my country I am famous Illusionist. Top*
> *performer in theatres. I like work here where*
> *it is safe. I live in camp so am no trouble.*

"Well I never," said Nell. "An answer to a madam's prayer."

Vi touched Marvo's arm and he jumped as if he'd been stung. "She means maiden's," she whispered, but he seemed none the wiser.

Together with this note there was a letter from the Camp Commandant up at the golf course addressed to Nell and commending Marvo to her. "The more chaps I can get working the less strain it is on our beleaguered nation," he had pompously written, adding, bleakly "P.S. He's dumb."

They went onto the deserted stage where Marvo unpacked two large suitcases of props. He enthralled them with his magic as streamers, flags and brightly coloured silk scarves appeared from nowhere and objects of all shapes and sizes disappeared from view. All this accompanied by a series of grunts. Nell was entranced. She even handed over her precious fob watch – a wedding anniversary present from Masters – which he wrapped in a cloth and smashed into pieces with a small hammer. The pregnant silence was broken by him retrieving it from Vi's handbag!

They all wildly applauded and Nell, once she'd got her watch – and breath – back, engaged him on the spot. It helped that he asked for very little pay!

Rita and Rena 'adopted' him and, developing their own sign language, soon began to understand what he was trying to say before he wrote it down! Then they helped him to move into an old storeroom where they created a comfortable nest for him with the mysteries of his act stacked, hung and squeezed amongst discarded props, costumes, lights and sound equipment.

On the second day of Marvo's appearance the twins went to Nell and, in great excitement, suggested that, as well as Marvo's magic act which would be slotted into the first half of the show from that evening onwards, he could also do an 'illusion' act in the second half in which he would like them to take part. With pencil drawings and much arm waving he had explained to them how it worked and what was required. Nell jumped at the idea.

"The audience will be smellbound."

They left giggling at Nell's latest word confusion and started rehearsing with Marvo who was now included on the billboards as 'The Great Marvo – with Rita and Rena'.

The next morning Nell made her way to the scenery dock feeling already tired even though it wasn't yet midday. She knew that it was the years catching up with her but today she put the blame mainly on the hours she'd spent with the many and various authorities getting permission for Marvo to work for her.

"A refugee...?" they had said down their noses, "having Gainful Employment...?" (she felt the capital letters in their disgusted voices) "on the Stage?"

Being Nell she had her way and the necessary pile of papers was angrily stamped.

Now she was ready for another battle. Since the start of the season the scene dock door had sported a rough hand-written sign, 'Band Practice Room. Keep Out'. She didn't; she strode in. There was immediate confusion. Playing cards were hurriedly put away, a copy of 'Men Only' with its carefully airbrushed pictures of naked young ladies was hidden behind a back. The six men looked at Nell sheepishly.

"Reg, Bob, go and make yourselves useful somewhere. I wish to speak with the band."

Noting the threatening quivering of the tell-tale ostrich feather and the jutting of her several chins they scuttled out. Nell was not one to beat about the bush...

Before the season had started Nell, with arthritis now reaching her fingers, had decided to gamble on providing the summer show with a pit orchestra rather than rely solely on her on-stage piano. She didn't have to look far for players. The various bands in the town, Salvation Army, British Legion, Church Brigade and the Flaxton Town Band, had all suffered serious decline as the young members went off to war. The old ones were left to do what they could and now they leapt eagerly at the advertisement placed by Nell in the Flaxton Chronicle for string, brass and percussion players.

She mentioned a morning for auditions in the theatre and she and Vi were thrown into every sort of confusion when over twenty elderly men turned up, coughing and wheezing, carrying, tugging and pulling on small carts their various instruments in weirdly shaped cases.

Being a fine pianist herself Nell was well up to putting them through their paces but it was sad that, whilst all of them could have handled the relatively simple work, only four were needed.

In the end she selected those who were most versatile being able to play a selection of instruments and also convince – or persuade –

her that they were relatively fit; six nights plus two matinées a week could quickly take their toll. And so Alf Parson (trumpet), Claude Eckersley (trombone), Geoff Sanderson (piano) and Fred Spriggs (percussion) became the 'Pier Theatre Orchestra'.

Now, amongst the ordered chaos of the Scene Dock, she stood before them, a good foot shorter than the shortest. They saw the ostrich feather quivering and knew they were in for a scolding. As if drawn by magnets they all bent forward towards her.

"Look here, boys" – their average age was over seventy – "you've got to learn to keep a regular beat. You're cordistant"...

It was a short, sharp meeting notable for the fact that none of the musicians said a word throughout it! Nell left them in no doubt as to their shortcomings and suggested a little more practice and less 'partying', as she called it. Alf Parson (trumpet) was even advised that too much reading would affect his blowing! His grey face took on a tinge of reddish blush. He feared that she may have noticed the copy of 'Men Only' concealed behind his back – but she needn't have worried, Alf only bought it for the pictures; the only thing he could read was music...

*

That afternoon, the traditionally quiet time when performers relax before their evening exertions, a stranger made his way, unescorted, along the backstage corridor and knocked firmly on the door of the dressing room marked 'Pat and Peggy Baker'.

To them the knock meant that probably one of the troupe wanted to borrow something; all of them were constantly lending and borrowing make-up, safety pins, cotton and needles, shoe-laces, all the bric-à-brac of theatre life.

With a sigh Pat put the brush back into the nail varnish bottle and, blowing on the newly red-nailed fingers of one hand, opened the door – to a complete stranger. Her first reaction was to close it again, but the caller had foreseen this. He put the verbal equivalent of his foot in the door by saying in the perfect clipped English of a foreigner, "Please tell Peggy that I have news of Freddy."

Pat was speechless. Almost immediately the door was pulled out of her hand by Peggy. She stood stock still but also said nothing.

Both the girls had been completely thrown off balance. Pat could sense danger here and, pushing past the man, went to Nell's door, knocked and rushed in without waiting for an acknowledgement.

Nell was dozing. She jerked awake. "Pat, really dear, I do think ..." Pat's look stopped her.

"Please, Nell, there's a man trying to see Peggy."

Probably no other news – not even Germans landing on the beach – would make Nell move so fast. Pat found herself trailing behind this tiny woman who, brandishing her walking stick, shouted over her shoulder "Get the men."

Pat reversed, hearing the visitor say in his near perfect, slightly accented English, "Mrs Masters, I do assure you I mean no harm. I am a friend of Freddy Crisciak. I've come to give Peggy news of him."

Pat looked back at them. Here was a man who had infiltrated into the very heart of the theatre, knew all their names and, it seemed, the secret that they believed was only shared by the three of them! It was all too preposterous. She saw Peggy still motionless at the door and Nell, defiantly looking up at the man, ushering him into the dressing room.

Nell looked over her shoulder and said firmly to Pat "I want Don or one of the hands outside this door. Any disturbance and they come in."

The tone of her voice was clear to all of them: Nell would stand no nonsense. Pat ran off to find Don whilst Nell went in and closed the door.

The three of them, Nell, Peggy and the stranger, stood in the small cramped space and studied each other. The man was tall, slim and obviously athletic, but with a pallor that suggested an indoor rather than an outdoor life.

He smiled which, thought Nell, seemed to be an effort for his face to manage: it remained taut and no warmth reached his eyes.

"Do please sit. I will go over here."

Peggy sat on her chair, Nell on Pat's. The man went to the outside wall, and stood incongruously framed by the rails containing their hanging stage clothes.

"First let me introduce myself." He removed his trilby hat and stiffly bowed very slightly from the waist. "My name is Ludovic Henschel. I am from the refugee camp."

Pat came back in. She felt frightened and her voice was tremulous.

"Don is outside in the corridor with clear instructions. He says he doesn't know where this man's come from."

Nell nodded. "Well done, dear. Mr Henschel you must understand our precautions. It is not usually possible for strangers to enter the theatre. We all have keys to the back stage door."

Henschel waved his hand impatiently. He wanted to get all this stupid detail out of the way; there were much more important matters to discuss.

"The front doors were open, Mrs Masters", he lied easily, "I assumed anyone could enter."

Nell signalled to Pat. "Tell Don to get someone to lock the front doors. We could be invaded any minute."

She turned back to the man. "Now then, Mr Henschel…"

He smiled. "Please call me Ludo." He turned to Peggy and gently shook her hand, "Good afternoon Peggy. I've been so looking forward to meeting you."

Peggy instantly knew that she didn't like this man; there was something insincere, almost eerie about him. She pulled her hand away, perturbed. Everything was happening too quickly. She knew that she was starting to panic. She could feel it in her breathlessness.

"How do you know I'm Peggy? Who are you? What do you want?"

These questions were met by Henschel swinging around and closing the small head-high window on the back wall adding to their fear, as if the door had been bolted on them.

"I know you from your picture." His voice was quiet now. He took out his wallet and, from it, an old, much folded and creased photo which he handed to her.

Peggy gasped and tears prickled in her eyes. It was of her and Freddy taken probably about a year ago at the villa by his mother, Anya. She stroked it, ironing out the creases with her fingers; such memories. Nell gently took it from her and Pat looked over her shoulder at the blurred black-and-white image of two people, arms around each other, so obviously in love.

Henschel was getting impatient again, this time with their strange reaction to what was, to him, a rather poorly taken photograph but he managed to mask his irritation.

"It is good, is it not? You with Freddy, your dear husband – my dear friend."

Peggy felt that there was something wrong with his voice; not just its foreignness but a feeling of intimidation, almost as if he was threatening them. She roughly rubbed her eyes. She was getting cross now. This man seemed to be playing with them with no regard for the anguish he was causing her.

"But who are you? I don't understand."

Henschel slipped the photograph back into his wallet.

"Let's just say that I worked alongside Freddy at the Research Centre. I left before you arrived. I was not as brave as him. I got out of Poland before it was too late." He realised that he was on dangerous ground and needed to move on swiftly. "I can tell you no more than that, I'm afraid – except that we are in contact with him and we have been ordered to bring him out."

Now there was a long pause. None of the three seemed able to breathe.

Peggy whispered, "You mean – back here – to England?"

Henschel nodded. "I have to stress how secret all this is. One word outside this room and everything – and I mean everything could be jeopardised."

Peggy was weeping now.

Pat shook her head. "But I don't understand. It doesn't follow. You say you're a refugee in the camp, and yet you behave like a secret agent…"

Henschel broke in, stopping her. "It provides a very good cover. I'm afraid you'll just have to trust me for the time being. Let's get Freddy safely back here first."

Pat stirred from the door. "If it's going to help, Peg, I think we should tell him about – you know."

Again Henschel's face smiled, but not his eyes. "The notebooks?" he asked quietly.

Peggy jumped up, angry again now, her eyes blazing. The others thought she was going to strike him but he appeared not to notice.

"How do you know about that?"

Henschel waved her dismissively back to the chair and said airily, "Freddy told me everything before I left. He kicked himself for having put you at such risk – and that's why I'm here in the

99

refugee camp. I can say no more than that my job is to keep an eye on you – and I've certainly been doing that."

Pat came forward. "You mean you've been following her – us? That was a horrible thing to do. Spooky."

Nell shook her head, "What's all this about notebooks? Something new to me. Another piece of the rickshaw."

"I'm sorry, Mrs Masters, but really the fewer people who know about them the better – for everyone's sake. But you are all now too close to this, too – how do you say – embroiled, to be kept in ignorance. They are notebooks full of the scientific calculations created by Freddy's brilliant brain for a weapon that would end the war and, whoever has it to use, will win outright – game, set and match. But the books mean nothing without Freddy here to interpret them, so the orders from the very top are to get him here."

They were completely overawed. Their minds were in turmoil. The suggestion that there was a link between them and the country's leaders was too fantastic, totally unreal. There was another long silence.

Henschel waited impatiently tapping his foot on the floor. Being the man he was it hadn't occurred to him to break the news more gently. He couldn't understand their reaction and wasn't sensitive enough to note from their expressions the shock he had caused them. What was now occupying *his* mind was the fact that he really shouldn't be there anyway; Charles Turville was *not* going to be pleased but he had seen no alternative, events were moving too quickly. There was no time for sensitivity and, anyway, he couldn't see any need for it.

Pat was the first to break the silence.

"But why did your Freddy saddle you with the notebooks if they are so important – and dangerous?"

Peggy's voice was dull now, almost monotone.

"He thought he'd be following me as soon as the brave Polish army had repelled Hitler." She was bitter now. "He *had* to go and fight," she cried, "why are men so *stupid?*"

Pat went to comfort her and Nell, leaning forward and stroking her hand, looked up at Henschel.

"Why will you bring him to this little place? Someone so vitally impotent."

At any other time they would find this funny, but not now. Henschel had asked the same question a thousand times himself and he gave them the answer always thrown back at him.

"Because Peggy – and Freddy's notebooks – are here and he'll only come to where she is. And..." he added unnecessarily coldly, "I've been told not to move her for reasons quite beyond my comprehension." He realized he had gone too far and quickly added "It's also one of the shortest routes from the continent. Just within range of a small aeroplane."

Peggy stirred, "When will this be?" She said it quietly but couldn't hide the excitement in her voice.

Henschel moved towards the door.

"I can't tell you exactly when Freddy will arrive, but I promise you it will be soon. I'll be in regular touch." He turned and added harshly, "and for God's sake keep the notebooks safe. If they were to fall into enemy hands the war would be lost. Without any doubt."

Pat stood to one side of the door.

"Wouldn't it be better to let this – Ludo – have them? It seems someone will do almost anything to get them. It's not fair on Peg." Henschel was too good an operator to show any reaction to this unintentional but very useful initiative by Pat but it was to no avail, Peggy answered her with passion.

"No. No. Freddy entrusted them to me. No one will have them until I hand them to him – personally."

Now she broke down. She could control herself no more. The shock and suddenness of it all was too much to take. Pat knelt to comfort her.

"Of course, love. Of course, of course."

Henschel opened the door. He was confused by their reaction and had no idea how to handle it; crying and what he took to be hysteria were totally beyond his comprehension. Incongruously he bowed again, slightly, from the waist.

"You have friends who can help very close by. We shall meet again soon." It would have helped if the warmth of the message had been matched in the tone of his voice.

Nell went to the door. "Don, please show our guest off the premises." She loosely shook Henschel's hand. "Thank you for coming. You will realise that for us, all this is very difficult to understand. We are casting around in the park."

Don saw Henschel out through the stage door. "She means dark, you see. Casting around in the dark."

Henschel hardly heard him, his mind was elsewhere. He wasn't sure that anything had been achieved by the visit, certainly not his main aim of getting hold of the notebooks and, as he started back to the camp, he decided with uncharacteristic perception that it would be wise to keep Charles Turville in the dark regarding this meeting.

Back in the dressing room Nell was fanning herself with a flapping hand.

"I'm all of a da-do. What's it all mean, Peg love? If we can help, you know we will..."

Peggy wiped her eyes then leapt up and, grabbing a small bag from the floor started feverishly shovelling everything on her dressing-table into it.

"I'm sorry, Nell, I really am. It's better I go." Nell leant forward and touched her arm.

"Stop it, love."

Peggy went on at manic speed. Nell tugged at her.

"I mean it."

Her voice was stronger and firmer than either of them had experienced before and it had its effect: Peggy dropped the bag and collapsed onto her chair, her head in her hands. In despair Pat put her arm around her.

Nell stood; she suddenly appeared to be taller and years younger, almost agile again. Striding to the door, stickless, the ostrich feather straight as a ramrod, she turned and commanded them.

"You two and Vi are coming up to the house – *now*. I'll have no more bargy-argy. We'll have some lunch and then you can tell us all about it. Come along. Sout-tweet."

She opened the door and swept out. Pat and Peggy looked at each other. With Nell in this new decisive mood there was only one thing to do: they followed her.

*

Because Belvedere Galbraith – *tragedian* – was the more-or-less agreed representative of the troupe through his age and stage experience, Nell suggested that he should attend the meeting rather than her having to brief him later and Peggy had somewhat reluctantly agreed; she wanted to bare her soul to as few people as possible.

Nell, fully understanding this, took the precaution of instructing Belvedere to say not a word from start to finish, to which he had rather testily suggested that she would be better inviting Marvo who was dumb anyway. "As Matthew Arnold hath it, I shall be dumb, inscrutable and grand," he had assured her.

Now, he, Pat, Peggy and Vi were puffing up the steep steps to Clarence Road trying to keep up with Nell who, thinking of Peggy's plight, was leading them at an unusually brisk pace.

As she strode ahead of them she was fondly remembering Peggy's arrival on her doorstep. She had brought a letter from a London theatre manager addressed to her. It had obviously had an immediate effect because Nell had received her like a long-lost daughter and had mothered her ever since. "You poor thing" she had murmured as she read the letter. "Left on your own."

After turning over the page she added, "Yes, I remember, the Palace Theatre so well. Dear Beresford Clarke, such a fine manager."

She had rested the letter on her lap and looked at the two of them with far-away eyes. "He was so kind to Masters and me when we were going through difficult times."

Peggy, sitting forward, had said. "He sends his love to you. He felt I'd be better getting work outside London because of the danger."

Nell had shaken her head back into the present time away from painful thoughts of her dear Masters. "I remember you, dear. Such a pretty thing. Careless Rupture. Dear Ivor will have been delighted to have you in his little work."

It was the next day that she had come up with the brilliant idea of the two of them teaming together. Elsie and Doris Waters were at the height of their fame as a comedy double-act so why not emulate them? "Imitation is the highest flat of formery," Nell had declared.

So a new act was born: Pat and Peggy Baker 'Flaxton's Answer to Elsie and Doris Waters'.

Nell paused to get her breath back and, in doing so, shook herself into the present. With her arthritic joints aching she reached the top of the long flight of steps as the others caught up with her. "Damn old age" she muttered to no-one in particular – and moved on.

Clarence Road ran parallel to the shoreline, well above the High Street with splendid views of the sea and, in the foreground, the pier and its precious – particularly to them – theatre.

That afternoon, at number 23, all the curtains were flung open and the black-out frames down, so that the warm April sun shone in on the group gathered in Nell's front living room. She, Vi, Pat, Peggy, and Belvedere were settled on the three-piece suite. They sat spellbound as Peggy, nervously, recounted the story of her first meeting with Freddy, the whirlwind courtship, marriage and their all-too-brief seven months together on the Crisciak estate in Poland.

"Well I never, luv," Vi was confused. "So you're a Mrs Count or something?"

Pat took pride in her friend's eminence. "Countess Margaret Crisciak."

Vi stood and performed a little curtsey but Nell waved her back to her chair. She was not often impatient with Vi – or anyone for that matter.

"But it doesn't stop there does it, dear?" she said. "Those weren't tears of joy I've been seeing, were they? They were tears of sorrow. Great sorrow. A very different kittle of fesh."

Pat saw that Peggy was about to cry and sat on the side of her chair putting an arm around her shoulders.

In a small voice Peggy continued. "On the third of September Freddy put us on a fishing boat."

"Us?" Vi asked.

"His mother, Anya, and me." Peggy's voice was so quiet now that they had to sit forward to hear her. As she spoke she nervously revolved her engagement and wedding rings on her finger.

"It was a terrible crossing to Norway. A high wind, driving rain, enormous waves. There were about twenty of us huddled on the deck. We tried to crawl under the tarpaulins but the deck was slippery with bits of fish. It was horrible. We were allowed one suitcase each. Freddy had told us before, so that's all we had with us, but most of the others had to leave anything extra on the quayside. Those poor people had travelled – some had walked –

hundreds of miles pushing their few remaining possessions in prams and on carts and bicycles, and at the end of it all they had to throw most of them away. They were heartbroken, but then we were all in a state of complete shock.

"The captain of the boat told us that we may be fired on or even sunk by German warships or aeroplanes, but, thank God, a thick fog came down. He was amazing. Somehow he guided us to the harbour he'd been aiming at and we were safe. As soon as we landed all the rest went trudging off. No-one spoke to anyone else. As I said, we were all in shock. But Anya and I had other plans which Freddy had instilled into us."

Whenever Peggy mentioned Freddy there was a pause. It was hard for her to go on and they sat perfectly still in their hunched positions until she continued. Pat gave her friend's shoulders a little squeeze which brought her thoughts back to the present time. Then, in a whisper, she re-lived the journey.

"Anya and I went to the harbour master's office. I showed him my British passport which, as Freddy said it would, impressed him. The poor man was in a terrible state. The Norwegians knew that the Third Reich was getting closer and closer to them. He and the other inhabitants around the harbour saw in us and all the other boatloads of defeated refugees, themselves in a few months' time. They had little confidence in being able to keep the enemy at bay although, thank God, they still seem to be doing so."

Vi broke in. "Only just. The news this morning isn't good." As she said it she knew she shouldn't have.

Peggy broke down. In floods of tears she wailed, "Anya is still there. She wouldn't come."

Vi was embarrassed at having caused her extra distress and glanced at Nell expecting admonishment but there was none.

It was obviously time for a break. Pat stayed to comfort Peggy while Belvedere went out to the hall. He found himself blowing his nose. "Emotion is so near the surface of a great actor," he said to himself. "To be able to cry when required. Such skill." He wiped his eyes, took an extra large pinch of snuff, checked that he hadn't been seen doing so, and re-entered the room.

In the kitchen Nell and Vi made some strong coffee and Nell took a bottle of brandy from the cupboard.

"Put a dram in Peg's, love. She's in a state of shock." Vi put a trickle into Peggy's cup and then, on an impulse, did the same into the other three cups.

When they went back into the front room Pat and Peggy were standing at the window looking out onto the sunlit scene. It could have been any Spring day if it hadn't been for the anti-blast tape, stuck in diamonds on the panes of glass and the grey shapes of warships out at sea laying mines in the shipping lanes.

They sat down again. Peggy apologised for breaking down and they all made appropriate noises of understanding until her quiet voice stilled them.

"The harbour master was amazing. He made a 'phone call and took us to his house where they made us tea and put us in their beds. We slept deeply. I didn't think I would ever sleep again unless" she almost shouted "*until* I had Freddy once more beside me."

There was a long silence. They didn't move or speak. With a superhuman effort she controlled herself and went on.

"In the morning a car collected us. Can you imagine it, a *car*! All the way from Oslo. They took us there. It was difficult for Anya. They treated her as my servant! They were really only interested in me, being British, but I wouldn't let Anya out of my sight. Darling Anya, she became more and more uneasy.

"We were taken to the British Embassy. My passport gave me automatic protection, but they wanted to send Anya to a refugee camp. I was so determined, so difficult, that they let her stay with me. Then they said we'd be moving to Bergen to wait for a boat to take us to England. This was too much for Anya. We had a terrible row."

Peggy was silent again. After a moment she stood and, going to the window, looked out to the far horizon of sea and sky, talking very quietly.

"Anya said she had to go back to Poland. To Freddy." She was angry now, shouting as she turned on them. "Didn't she know that I had to be with him. Not her. *I'm his wife.*"

She paused as they sat in embarrassed stillness. Then she whispered

"She said that Freddy had to know that I was safe. And I knew why. I had – I mean I *have* – his notebooks, you see. One each for

106

the last five years of his work. They contain all the ground work on this secret project but only he can interpret them. He had told me to hide them and I have, but I know that there are many people who would – *will* – kill for them."

They were all silent, still hardly breathing. Belvedere stirred and said very quietly,

"Then you must give them to me, my dear, for safe-keeping."

Peggy turned back to the window. She hadn't heard him. She was wringing her hands, tightly, painfully and was so quiet now that they again had to strain forward to hear her.

"I promised Freddy, you see. Solemnly promised him that I would reach England and never let the notebooks out of my possession. He said he would join me once the battle was over. He was sure the army would win and Hitler would see the futility of invading his country. There's so much of Germany already in Poland, he said. There's no need for them to fight us yet again."

She swung round on them so suddenly that they all flinched backwards in their chairs. Tears were now streaming down her cheeks.

"My beloved Freddy. Such an innocent when he's away from his calculations." Vi passed her a handkerchief and she wiped her eyes.

"They laughed when I told them at the embassy." She was angry again now. "They said they'd never heard such ill-informed rubbish." The last three words were spat out as she punched her fist into the palm of her other hand.

"Freddy *has* to get back to me. Not just for my sake," her voice sank to a whisper, "for the sake of the world."

This was really too much for them but they understood; Peggy was obviously confused; it was hardly surprising after what she had been through. Belvedere felt he had to break in.

"How will he find you?"

She smiled weakly, "We agreed that he'll come to the London Theatre where we met. They know I'm here." She sat back in her chair.

There was another silence, eventually broken by Pat. "Go on, Peg, what happened next?"

Peggy struggled on, whispering so quietly that they had to strain to hear her. "Anya left. One night. From her room. Just left. She had slipped a note under my door. It was very loving. It ended, "I shall see you again on earth or in paradise. God bless you." – her voice drifted into silence. Vi wiped her eyes, Nell cleared her throat, no one moved.

"I was taken by car to Bergen. There were little fishing boats sailing endlessly backwards and forwards between Norway and the Shetland Isles. The Shetlanders were so incredibly brave. The boats would arrive loaded with guns for the Norwegians and then return crammed with refugees and resistance fighters. I had to wait a week to get a place on one..." she shuddered, "the sea was full of ships – British *and* German – wanting to sink each other and the skipper said we had to dodge all the mines that had just been laid! It was twenty-four hours of sheer terror before I landed at Scalloway in the Shetlands. From there it was a relatively safe sea trip to Aberdeen. I had some money left and caught a train to London and went to the only person I knew, the Palace Theatre manager." She got up again, restlessly, and went to the window. "I felt such a failure. I'd walked out on them full of happiness for my new life and, in no time here I was back again, a destitute refugee."

Pat wouldn't have this.

"It wasn't your fault, Peg. It's the war. There are probably thousands, tens of thousands like you."

Peggy, in her nightmare, was by now unaware of any of them. The telling of the story was proving to be a form of exorcism for her.

"Beresford was so kind. He took me back to his flat and he and his wife looked after me for a couple of days. I slept, I lay in hot luxurious baths and bought some clothes with money I still had in the bank but I was in a continuous dream – a terrible, terrible dream." There was silence; no-one moved. "I suppose I still am really..."

She dropped down into the chair again but sat well forward, almost whispering as if she felt she was being overheard.

"It was so odd. I told Beresford on the first evening that I had a weird feeling that I was being followed." They reacted, amazed. "I couldn't explain how I knew. I just knew." They were watching her intently.

"The next day Beresford walked behind me, at a distance, and he was sure I had someone tailing me. He said that it could happen to girls in London but he wasn't going to take any chances. Anyway, I couldn't stay doing nothing and there was no part for me in the few London shows that are now playing, so he packed me off to you, Nell. It's the best thing anybody has done for me in many a long month." She lay back in her chair, exhausted, and closed her eyes.

"You poor dear," said Nell. "You're safe with us *and* you're a good actress. We're thrilled to have you with us. Dear Beresford has done us all a great flavour."

Vi was about to correct her but thought better of it. They all nodded and smiled at this girl in the large armchair who looked so vulnerable and small, and who had been through so much.

Nell tugged at her fob watch.

"That's enough for now, my loves. It will do everyone good to have a nap this afternoon. Not you, of course, Belvedere. You're a man."

As the oldest person present he failed to see the significance of this remark but bowed never-the-less and, after raising his hand in farewell – he had seen dear Donald do it in Hamlet to such effect – went out into the hall.

Nell caught up with him, ushering him down the path to the road, giving him urgent whispered instructions as they went. He had to lean his tall frame over the little woman to hear what she was saying. A casual viewer at the window of a neighbouring house might have thought he was about to kiss her! Nell wouldn't have been too worried if he had done so. She certainly liked the old rascal and saw a strong, warm character under his theatrical façade. More important than that, in this time of crisis she knew that she could totally rely on him.

She waved him off more as a signal for him to get down to work than a fond farewell. But, in fact, she *was* fond of him and to his immense surprise and some embarrassment she gave him a tiny peck on the cheek.

After two gigantic pinches of snuff with their accompanying sneezes he made his way back to the theatre, realising that the duty he was to perform had more of a military than theatrical nature to it. He wasn't aware of it but by the time he reached the pier his actor's nonchalant saunter had turned into something approaching a slow march!

He was back twenty-and-more years but, thank God, the mud of Flanders was now the sunny pavement of Flaxton-on-Sea.

*

Charles Turville only just made the mid-day Norwich train. The meeting with the Poles in St John's Wood had gone on far longer than he'd intended and he'd had to heavily bribe the cab driver to get him to Liverpool Street Station in record time.

Now he sat looking out from a window in a First Class compartment in a state of such anger that he was oblivious to the smoky grime of London doing battle with the pale Spring sunshine as the train crawled through the depressing muddle of terraced houses that crowded against the line.

His anger was directed towards one man; Ludovic Henschel. It wasn't any surprise to him that he was angry; any thought of his colleague put him in that frame of mind but what was causing this particular fury was more to do with his own uncharacteristic weakness in not acting upon his gut feelings at the start by letting himself be persuaded by Sir Philip to put Henschel in charge of liaison with the Poles in London.

It had proved totally disastrous.

The call had come from Miss Gilbert on behalf of Sir Philip. "C wishes you to attend the next Polish Liaison meeting rather than your colleague," she had carefully enunciated down the 'phone. "He has been informed that they are a wee bit unhappy with his manner."

Turville might have guessed by the tone that it was a typically Lothian understatement; they were actually enraged. Within fifteen minutes of his arrival at the meeting it emerged that Henschel had, from the start, sought to dominate this group of proud, humbled statesmen and soldiers.

With all the artlessness he could muster – which in his case was well above the average – he had regaled them on the hopelessness of the Polish situation, the carelessness of their defences, the arrogance of their leaders and – a particularly insensitive remark considering his adopted nationality – their foolishness in relying on the British to come to their aid and repel the Germans.

Having got that off his chest at the start of each of the five meetings he'd attended over the last two weeks he had gone on to tell them what must be done and by when they must have done it. All this from a man who had led a conspicuously undistinguished life in his homeland to a group of their finest and most able citizens! Henschel's position as a British Secret Service agent had gone to his head in a monumental way!

It took Turville all his diplomatic skills to calm the group. The ten of them sat bolt upright, unmoving, expressionless around the table in the Polish Embassy, the civilians in their black suits with high-cut coats, wing-collared shirts and black ties contrasting with their military colleagues in dress uniform and medals. Turville was surprised and relieved that his Polish, far from deserting him at this tense time, actually blossomed and obviously delighted them.

Within half an hour the task was successfully completed. On the understanding that Henschel never again darkened their doors they relaxed into animated chatter and insisted on Turville joining them in the drinking of several toasts, raising brimming glasses of Zytnia, the finest of vodkas, from the Embassy's fast dwindling cellar.

But then the mood reverted into a sombre discussion regarding the enormity of the task that lay ahead. They reported to him that the partisans on the ground, the Armia Krajowa, who had been closely watching Freddy Crisciak since they were alerted to do so by London, had seen him disappear into Gestapo Headquarters in Warsaw and, with the utmost bravery, had infiltrated the building itself.

Now they had reported back that releasing him would be a near impossibility until he was taken from the building at which time, they had grimly added, he would probably already be dead: the torturers in the basement left no-one alive. The partisans were willing to risk a blood-bath but even then they doubted whether they would prise him alive from the SS.

Try as they might, those at the meeting could come up with no solution to the dilemma. For a start it wasn't easy to issue orders from the safety of London to people with infinitely more knowledge of the situation on the ground; only the people there could know what might or might not work.

But all this was hypothetical anyway because they didn't have any orders to issue! None of them could come up with a plan that would have the remotest chance of working. The Gestapo was undoubtedly the most evil gang of villains on earth but they were no fools; their security was watertight and their methods of dealing with those who stood in their way, absolute: elimination.

With these depressing thoughts Charles Turville now sat in the train gazing straight ahead of him. His empty stare was just above the head of the woman sitting opposite who, deeply worried, put her hand up to her hat. Had she in her haste, she feared, put it on back to front...

*

In Flaxton the men of the theatre company assembled at tea-time looking at each other with some surprise as they sauntered into the auditorium. The twins had been despatched by Belvedere to their various lodgings to "oblige them," as he put it, to attend an urgent meeting from which they could retire to the Pier Head Tavern "prior to performance." It was not made clear who would buy the round of drinks required by the landlord as a condition of them entering his premises but of one thing they were pretty certain: it would not be Belvedere!

No one was in a good mood as they arrived. Marvo swept in, his long coat flapping at his heels, and slumped down in a rear seat. Norman, George and Elaine appeared at the same time and saw Don coming down from the stage. This was evidently going to be a serious meeting, they thought; it took more than a pep-talk to get their highly respected stage manager into the audience area. It was true; Don never felt comfortable in front of the proscenium arch and his air of authority withered away as he descended into the stalls. He had been told to have the footlights fully 'up' and the auditorium in semi-darkness. "I need maximum effect, old boy," Belvedere had said, slapping him on the back. Bill, Reg and Bob followed Don by the same route, fed up that a game of whist had been left unresolved.

Then Belvedere made his entry. It was a strange sight. He almost seemed to march across the front of the main curtains to the centre of the stage. His right turn to face them was somewhat uncoordinated but not bad for a near septuagenarian.

The assembled, lolling group of artistes and stage hands were amazed at his opening, totally un-Belvedere-like remark.

"Stand at ease."

They were all sitting but arranged themselves rather more elegantly as they sensed something unusual was about to happen.

"Fellow troupers." the words – almost a command – shot out at them. "we are now on a military footing and as your leader..."

"Whatcha, tosh."

Tad appeared at the edge of the stage and dropped lightly down the steps. His clothes were more outrageous than ever. Most colours of the rainbow shone out from various parts of him, and he seemed to have managed to invent quite a few new ones.

"Can't stay long. Customers waiting. Train was late. Know what I mean?" He collapsed into a seat and looked around at his male companions. "What's up Belly, old boy? Wouldn't the girls play ball? You mustn't blame 'em. You posh ones are always the most dangerous."

He would have gone on but Belvedere, having had his much rehearsed entry ruined yet again by Tad, was standing no more of it. He took a large pinch of snuff, sneezed and then, adopting a theatrical stance, bellowed at them,

"Oh heart be at peace, because nor knave nor dolt can break what's not for their applause."

There was a stunned silence followed by Norman's Halifax twang.

"Can we be fairly quick please, Belvedere. I've got my lines to learn."

But Belvedere hadn't finished. "William Butler Yeats." He felt a little literary education could benefit them all.

"I've asked you men of the Theatre Company to this meeting because, unbeknownst to you, you are in the midst of..."

"I beg your pardon?"

A lilting Welsh soprano voice, delivered fortissimo, rang out from the stalls. In the silence that followed Belvedere shielded his eyes and gazed into the blackness.

"Dear lady," he purred. He had experienced Elaine in this operatic mood before. "I had summoned only the men, do you see? A thousand pardons."

An unidentified growl from the blackness further damaged the effect Belvedere was trying to create.

"Summoned?" said Reg, "He should be summoned."

Belvedere was saved finding a suitable reply by Elaine.

"George and I are a team. And he agrees with me. Whenever we are in the theatre we do things together."

"Aye Aye…" it was Tad's unmistakable voice, " as I suspected. And we thought the noise was you two rehearsing."

There was now chaos. Belvedere strained to see who was doing the shouting, and who was being shouted at. He could hear the tip-up seats banging and the sound of scuffling. The deteriorating situation was saved by Bill Colbourn taking matters into his own hands by jumping onto the stage and putting the auditorium lights to 'full'. Everyone froze. Tad, somewhat lost underneath Elaine and George, emerged and re-arranged his blazer and tie.

"Can you speed things up, Belly old boy. As I said, my customers are waiting."

Belvedere gave Tad a withering look. After another dose of snuff he took a deep breath.

"As I was saying, we are all embroiled in mighty Affairs Of State which could well rock the very fabric of our Society." When he wanted to Belvedere could hold an audience in the palm of his hand, and he didn't read Hansard from cover to cover – a regular birthday gift to himself – for nothing. He was at one with flamboyant oratory and now it had its effect; they all sat forward awaiting his message.

Belvedere was no fool. He may have sat with his eyes closed apparently asleep at Nell's whilst Peggy told her story, but in fact he had assimilated every word of it. Now, in his own style, he repeated it to them but not before he warned them.

"You are all under an oath of secrecy at its very highest level." His next statement may have been slightly over-dramatic but, given the nature of the operation into which they were all being inextricably drawn, it wasn't far off the mark. "Should you break your secrecy you may well be shot."

In other circumstances he would probably have been laughed off the stage and pelted with some over-ripe fruit, but his mood was infecting them and they stayed silent. The older ones would have heard such chilling statements before in other far away conflicts.

Belvedere then went on to give a clear, accurate resumé of Peggy's story. His voice was unusually quiet and totally lacking in bombast. This was a Belvedere Galbraith they had never met before and they were riveted by his narrative. Their concern for Peggy grew by the second and each, even Tad, remembered moments when they could have been kinder and more helpful to her.

Belvedere now reached the part relating to the five notebooks which Freddy had handed to Peggy without any real thought for the danger they would put her in. Now the possession of such treasures could be a death warrant and Belvedere could only hope that no one other than Freddy himself would find them of any value.

"We must relieve her of them and deposit them safely in a vault. There is no time to lose. This I intend to do before another day is over."

Then, as any good actor could, he completely changed his personality. The pose of statesman dissolved into a taller, more military figure. Could the Agincourt scene from 'Henry Five' be about to unleash itself upon them – yet again?

"I believe that we should organise ourselves into a disciplined fighting force." That did it! Now they stirred. They hadn't joined Nell's Theatre company to become a disciplined fighting force, thank you very much.

They all talked at once.

"I don't think Elaine would want me to…"

"with *my* chest…"

"I'm only just starting to get my lines right…"

"too old by half…"

"forget it, Belly old boy…"

Belvedere calmed them down. The volume of his voice easily drowned them all and he dropped it as they quietened.

"I don't mean we join up. We carry on exactly as we are but, in matters relating to the Peggy business we work as a group." He consulted some notes he had quickly prepared. "We'll devise a roster. Whoever is on duty will keep an eye on her wherever she is."

Everyone now wanted to say something regarding this plan. Don, well used to getting his voice heard above those of actors, stood up.

"That's all very well, Belvedere, but it's a bit personal isn't it? Peggy won't like it."

The others nodded and muttered their agreement, settling back again into the theatre seats, but Belvedere had been ready for this. If only they'd let him finish before butting in.

"We shall, of course." he boomed, "be discreet. When she's here we guard the stage door and keep an eye on her dressing-room door. When she's home we stand at the flat entrance and note who comes and goes. And we follow her at a fair distance when she goes out. Simple. We will operate 'Peggy Patrols'." Even Field Marshal Viscount Gort would have been impressed with the command in his voice!

Norman stood up and asked, almost apologetically.

"What do we do if we're suspicious or something?" He sat down very quickly. It was like school. He'd never liked standing up in class whether to ask or answer a question.

"You immediately contact me, of course."

Belvedere was just like his school teachers, Norman thought, so abrupt and cross. He wished he'd never asked.

George, with no such inhibitions regarding questioning the great man, quietly said, "And how will we know where you are, old chap?"

Tad popped up. "Belly will give you the number of the Pier Head Tavern. No problem. Know what I mean?" They all fell about laughing and the tension was relaxed.

Belvedere's voice at his grandest, rose above the noise. "This is no time for levity as I attempted to point out at the start of the meeting."

They hushed again into silence.

"Peggy's safety, the safety of all of us, depends on us taking this seriously. *And...*" his voice rose in volume. "that will depend on complete secrecy by all of us. Don't tell her or the other girls, it will only distress them."

There was a quick mutter amongst the stage group and then Don was on his feet.

"Bill, Reg, Bob and I are fully with you, Belvedere. Like you we were in the last lot and we know first hand what the Hun can do. We'd all be wise to take this very seriously." He sat down to nods and sounds of agreement.

"Thank you, Don – and the others, much appreciated. Are there any questions?"

Norman couldn't believe that he had put his hand up again.

"Yes Norman?" It was the weary voice of a tired schoolmaster.

"You didn't actually say how we could contact you." Norman was right, Belvedere hadn't, but that didn't excuse the bounder reminding him.

He said, testily, "I shall always tell the person on duty where I am. In the event of something happening you will all be summoned as quickly as possible." He went on without a pause to prevent further interruptions. "I will devise this week's roster in the Pier Head Tavern now to attempt to fit in with your arrangements." He looked at his watch as he tried to remember a military word to end the meeting. "It is now eighteen hundred hours. Dismiss."

They retired to the saloon bar where each bought their own drink and Belvedere gave them their orders. As a sign of true leadership he himself would undertake the first stint of 'Peggy Patrol' being discreetly on parade near the door of the Post Office flat at nine the next morning.

*

Charles Turville watched them all climb the steps to the stage and follow Belvedere through the centre join of the crimson curtains. Smiling and shaking his head in a fair degree of disbelief he made his way down the steep tiers of the dress circle and leant on the dusty brass rail. For a few moments he stood there looking down into the darkened auditorium trying to decide whether this initiative by the men of the Theatre Company helped or complicated the mission. It needed some thinking about but it would probably do no harm; the more people who kept an eye on the girl, the better.

As he made his way up the hill out of the town his mood slowly changed until, by the time he reached the Station Hotel, he was in a thoroughly bad frame of mind.

Later that evening he would be with Ludovic Henschel, briefing him on his meeting with 'C' and the Polish exiles in London. It would, he had no doubt, prove to be a vindictive session.

It was probably just as well that he was yet to hear of his subordinate's afternoon visit to Peggy's dressing-room.

CHAPTER SIX

Mid April 1940. In Poland the programme of evictions, death marches and mass shootings continues at great pace. Field Marshal Walter von Reichenau dares to speak against the SS 'bestialities' in the occupied land.

The Royal Navy destroys a German naval force at Narvik in Norway and lands British and French troops.

It was now nine-fifteen on this damp mid April evening. Tad Stevens, dressed in a loud check sports jacket, cream flannel trousers, brown and white brogue shoes, a wide gaudy bow tie and trilby hat set at a jaunty angle on his bald head, was nearing the end of his second spot in tonight's show.

"Just been out for a quick one at the Dog and Duck.
Do you know how much a pint of beer is now? *(licks fingers)*
Threepence.
And I reckon there's a farthing of froth on the top, know what I mean? *(licks fingers)*

This chap came into the pub with a lump of tarmac under his arm.
'What would you like?' said the barman.
'A pint of beer and one for the road,' the chap replied. Get it? *(licks fingers)*

The landlady handed me a pint.
'Looks like rain,' she said.
'I don't know about rain' I told her, 'but it certainly doesn't look like beer.'"

Each joke was rewarded with loud laughter, cat-calls and whistles. This reaction was as much – more – a release of tension amongst the audience in these dark times rather than a true appreciation of the joke's worth.

No-one knew if Tad was aware of this but, even if he was, it never dampened his supreme confidence or enthusiasm. As he had often said, "a laugh's a laugh in'it. Know what I mean?"

Tad always referred to this spot near the end of the show as 'The Star Turn' much to the infuriation of the rest of the cast – which was the main reason why he did it! He even said it as if each word began with a capital letter! The other artistes may have been infuriated with good reason but Tad's boast was probably true as far as their average audience was concerned.

Discounting the evening's batch of refugees from the camp on the golf course who understood little but enjoyed the relaxed atmosphere of the place, most of the people occupying the rickety red plush seats were from the service camps in the area. Unlike the townsfolk they much preferred quick-fire, risqué humour to sentimental songs and high-brow recitations.

Nell and Pat were already standing in the wings waiting for the finale, watching Tad with more than a little despair.

"My mother-in-law's in hospital.
Good thing really. I couldn't cope with Hitler *and* my mother-in-law.
(pause) I'd choose Hitler any day... *(licks fingers)*
The doctors are so baffled they've put a suggestion box at the end of her bed.
One of them told her: 'You're suffering from Alice.'
That even confused my mother-in-law.
'What d'yer mean?' she asked. 'What's that?'
'We don't know,' said the doc, 'but Christopher Robin went down with it. Know what I mean?'" *(licks fingers)*

Nell smiled at Pat.
"A time of the signs, dear."
She yawned and did a bit of long royal blue dress adjusting and checked the position of her many necklaces, brooches and bracelets. For the finale the felt hat with its ostrich feather was relegated to the hook behind her office door. She glanced at her fob watch. Finished

by nine-thirty. Home, Horlicks and bed. She'd be taking a bow in the finale which, once Tad deigned to finish, would follow closely behind him. Pity about the Marvo Act. It had all gone wrong. A special rehearsal for *him* tomorrow. She yawned again.

"We'll all need our sleep tonight, Pat. Those bombs made me slump out of my gin."

Vi, who had joined them, whispered to Pat, "she means jump out of her skin, love." She didn't like the cast to feel that Nell was becoming confused.

Tad was warming to his work. The reaction of his audience was heady stuff to him.

"I was on the bus yesterday.
'A three-ha'penny to Mapleness,' I said to the conductor.
'It's twopence now,' he said.
'What do I get for the extra ha'penny?' I said.
'You get to stay on the bus.'
I could have punched his ticket machine. Know what I mean?
(licks fingers)
I fell over twenty feet last night – trying to get to my seat in the cinema."

"I'm worried about Peggy" Nell whispered to Pat.

"She's worried about Peggy." Vi's whisper was slightly louder. She wanted to make sure that Nell's worries were clearly understood by Pat.

Nell whispered on "It's all too much for her." Pat nodded.

There was no time for a reply because all three of them saw Peggy approaching from the rear back-stage doors.

They had a joke running around the troupe that not even the ARP Wardens could black-out Peggy because of her beautiful engagement ring. Freddy had bought it for her in London a year ago last February at the same time as her wedding ring.

The diamond cluster – a large central one with five smaller ones around it – seemed to act like a torch beam even in the darkest conditions. Now, like Tinkerbell in Peter Pan it heralded her arrival.

"Hello love," said Nell. "Soon be over."

"Soon be over," echoed Vi.
But not if Tad had his way...

"It's good to see our usual truck load of refugees here
this evening. Hi gang. Some of my best customers."

There was mild applause. The refugees shuffled uncomfortably;
these proud folk didn't like being dismissed as refugees.

"Any Poles in the audience tonight?"

Tad leant forward, hand shielding eyes, peering over the footlights.
An elderly, tall, emaciated man automatically stood up. In Poland at
this time he would have been shot for not doing so. There was
embarrassed applause as the spotlight, wielded by Fred Prentice,
settled on him.

"It's good to have you with us," shouted Tad. "Look at
the height of him."

There was more uncertain laughter.

"Be careful mate. Another foot higher and they'll be stringing
telephone wires from you. (finger lick)
D'you get it? Our very own telegraph pole."

Half the audience groaned, the other half laughed. The servicemen
liked a good joke. The elderly man looked around him, shaking with
fear. Stringing up? Gallows?
Peggy let out a gasp of anger and stumbled, assisted by Pat, to a
hamper where she sat down, weeping. Tad waved dismissively at the
old man.

"Sit down friend. You're blocking the view of paying
customers."

Nell's sighs were joined now by a chorus of "tuts" and "oh dears"
from the rest of the cast who were assembling in their seaside
costumes for the finale. How was it that such crass humour could
arouse this audience to such heights when 'quality', as Elaine and
George, *The Welsh Nightingales*', were quick to point out,
seemed to pass over their heads?

"You've been a wonderful audience, both of you.
I'd like to end with a ditty which many of you will know.
I dedicate it to those wonderful lads, the Royal Observer
Corps. Geoff, a chord of mild and bitter please..."

Tad had at last realized that if he wanted to get to the Anchor Inn
for a few after-hours drinks with bar-maid Pru before they slipped
off to bed he'd better bring his act to a grand conclusion. He pulled
the microphone on its stand to the edge of the footlights and
embarked on a doubtfully worded version of "Bless 'em All"
which the military members of the audience augmented with even
more doubtful words. Nell, unable to decipher any of it, was
none-the-less sure that everyone was thoroughly enjoying themselves.

Belvedere, George and Norman decided that tomorrow must be
the day of reckoning as far as their fellow artiste, Tad Stevens, was
concerned. The orchestra struck up the finale and the men pranced
– as best they could – onto the stage.

"Pom, Pom, Pom,
P-P-P-Pom, Pom, Pom..."

The girls, as if they hadn't a care in the world, joined them.

"Oh, I do like to be beside the seaside,
I do like to be beside the sea..."

Another Pier Show was nearing its end...

*

The thirty or so refugees shuffled out of the theatre and along the
damp, darkened pier to the two waiting army lorries. The drivers,
seeing them coming, put out their cigarettes, wedged them behind
their ears, put on their berets and started the engines. The short
run back to the camp on the golf course would be the last duty
of their idle day.

They and their mates were confused and somewhat embarrassed
to find themselves running a bus service for foreigners instead of
becoming heroes in the front line. That's what, they boasted to
each other and anyone else who would listen, they had joined the

army for. They didn't know how lucky they were – or perhaps, deep down, they really did...

The refugees clambered up the steps on the lowered tail-boards and slumped onto the metal benches running down each side of the trucks. They shook the rain off their hats and overcoats. It was strange – eerie – that no-one talked.

All of them were still in a state of shock. Uprooted from their homes and daily lives, and with many separated from their loved ones, their existence would have been unbearable if it wasn't for the knowledge that the alternative to it would have been instant, or worse, lingering death.

Not even *they* could know the true horror that had awaited them if they hadn't at a moment's notice dropped everything and fled their homes.

Now that the excitement of the show was over, these sad people were sinking back into the permanent state of depression into which their hopeless situation had thrown them – except for one of them. He was the elderly Pole who unwittingly had become Tad's stooge in the theatre. He was still seething and deeply humiliated by the experience. Tad had picked the wrong one here! This school headmaster, for that's what he had been, was a member of the refugee camp committee and his influence could seriously damage a certain person's black-market business dealings amongst the camp inhabitants. He was angry, too, with himself for forgetting, as he stood up in the theatre, where he was. The image of the military courts set up to try and, of course, convict his compatriots had, for a moment, been too strong. He had experienced blind, naked fear. Tad would pay for that.

*

Peggy was very quiet after the show. She changed in silence and Pat, sensitive as ever, knew better than to try lightening the atmosphere with the inconsequential patter they usually delighted in once they got back to their dressing room. She understood why Peggy was so angry with Tad. For the second consecutive evening she had seen her weeping through the finale whilst apparently singing, smiling and dancing with the rest of them.

As she took her make-up off in front of the dressing-table mirror, dressed in her petticoat with her hair held up out of the way in a head scarf, Pat had time to consider the collapse of Peggy's composure which, until last night, she had managed to maintain since she first had come to Flaxton three months ago.

How could Tad – even Tad – be so insensitive? He actually visited the camp selling his tawdry black-market wares, and surely must be more aware than any of them regarding the terrible suffering those poor people had been subjected to and the despair they must now be in. And shouldn't he know of Peggy's plight? Belvedere had said up at Nell's house that he would pass on the gist of her story to the troupe so that they'd understand her problems.

Pat stepped into her frock, Peggy did the same and, almost as if it were part of their well-rehearsed act, they zipped each other up. Pat paused as she was putting on her hat and coat.

"Tad's a fool, love. We all know that. But I'm sure he didn't mean to hurt you."

Peggy, lacing up her shoes, spoke sharply

"I know Pat, I know. I understand. But it's not easy." She immediately regretted her tone. "I'm sorry, love." She kissed her on the cheek. "Off you go now. Grab one of the boys for escort. I'll be along in a jiff. Something I've got to do first."

She propelled Pat out of the dressing room as Vi and Nell were coming out of Vi's office. Nell was shaking her head.

"Takings are down again." Vi bent down so that the key tied round her neck reached the lock.

"I don't think Mr Chamberlain had us in mind, dear, when he declared war on that Hitler."

Tad put his head out of the boys' dressing room door.

"Walk you home, girls?" he winked at them cheerfully.

"Tad Stevens," Pat rounded on him, "After what you did tonight to that poor old Polish gentleman in the audience you can walk off the end of the pier for all we care. And good riddance."

She pulled herself up to her full height, gave a tiny disgusted shake of her shoulders and sailed past him, pushing him back through the door as she did so.

"So say all of us," added Vi with a loud sniff and, giving him an equally sharp push, she marched after Pat.

"Unconstipational" was Nell's contribution which no-one could interpret but they all felt that the point had by now been well and truly made so without another word, they left through the rear stage door into the pitch-dark night.

"Was it something I said?" shouted Tad in mock innocence as he retreated into the men's dressing room but he got no answer from the three other occupants. No-one was talking to him.

Belvedere, George and Norman left next. They needed to get to the bar at The Pier Head Tavern – a non-Tad pub – in time for some very much needed alcoholic refreshment. It had been a gruelling evening making all of them on edge because of a very thin 'house', a rowdy group of soldiers who had been loud in their lack of enthusiasm for the 'class' acts and, to cap it all, Tad's disgraceful humiliation of that poor old Polish gentleman. Drinking – and a suitable anti-Tad action plan – was on the agenda. Nothing, Belvedere had warned them, was to be said about Peggy. You could trust no-one these days.

George and Norman were all too aware of the established procedure when the three of them entered the saloon bar. Belvedere removed his heavy black overcoat with its astrakhan collar, which he wore in all weathers, and doffed his floppy wide-brimmed hat to the ladies present. The rain dropped off it onto the floor.

"Dear ladies," he murmured and they tittered, flattered, in return.

He placed the hat and coat with loving care on a nearby hook sporting a label which said, grandly, "Belvedere Galbraith Esq." He then took up a commanding position in a large Windsor carving chair behind the table by the fire. A 'reserved' sign was placed on it each evening by the landlord in return for occasional free tickets to the show.

George and Norman were in charge of buying the drinks and bringing them to the table. They all shared the cost with scrupulous precision but Belvedere had never understood the strange self-service procedure common in British pubs, having been used, in the good old days, to waiters fussing around him.

Now he sat back, his hands smoothing the brown knitted cardigan which he had been reduced to wearing. A large gold chain spanned his ample stomach, threaded incongruously through a button-hole but the evidence of better days still manifested itself in the nonchalantly knotted crimson silk cravat which certainly caught the eye but tended to accentuate rather than hide his many chins.

"Make it a large one, dear boy," he bellowed in his fine baritone voice to George at the bar.

Everyone paused and looked at him with respect. The three of them were 'stage stars' and you didn't share the same pub with many of *them* in Flaxton. Aside from Belvedere's commanding presence was the remarkable wobbling of his many chins when he loudly proclaimed. It was a moment not to be missed.

George and Norman carried across the drinks. The evening's 'slate' had been opened behind the bar and was, as a matter of honour, settled in full each Friday pay day. With Belvedere's large scotch, diluted with soda to make it last longer, would be George's pint of mild and bitter and Norman's Guinness. Norman's pint would last all evening, George's about ten minutes.

Their dress, once the mackintoshes were removed, was a great disappointment to the regulars in the bar. George wore a rather threadbare three-piece dark blue suit and looked for all the world like a bank clerk. Norman, on the other hand, much preferred the schoolmaster look in old fawn corduroys and a Fair Isle jumper which had certainly seen better days.

They now sat at their reserved table and all three of them, in unison, raised their glasses to their mouths. It was surprising to the onlookers that the return of them to the table top was also in unison because considerably differing amounts of fluid had been transferred. Belvedere reduced his whisky and soda by half, Norman sipped the cream off his Guinness and George poured in a third of his pint which seemed to be taken in one gulp. This done, the business of the evening could be started.

"It was inexcusable behaviour, and Elaine agrees with me." George wiped some beer froth from his upper lip with the back of his hand. He invariably included his partner in his pronouncements and she did likewise. Welsh Nightingales must stick together.

"Up North they'd pelt him." Norman's Halifax brogue matched his bluntness. "I've seen all kinds of fruit, old shoes, even a ferret hurtle through the air onto the stage." He added as an afterthought, "not always at me though."

George was concerned – for the ferret, not Norman. "I didn't know ferrets could fly."

"Nor did this one," Norman was mournful, "but it soon learnt how to. It landed with a thoomp and scuttled off back stage shaking its…"

George broke in, "Fist?"

"No," even more mournfully, "its head."

*

Tad was the last of the artistes to leave the theatre. All except the emergency lights were now extinguished and he felt his way carefully towards the rear stage door and opened it onto the dark night.

As he stepped outside, a fist propelled with considerable force, landed with perfect accuracy onto his right eye and, with a frightened yelp, he collapsed back into the building. The pain was immense, as if a thousand sharp pins had been driven into his eyeball.

Crawling to his feet he staggered back into the dressing room. The sight in his mirror was horrendous. Where there once had been a perfectly serviceable right eye there was now a most unpleasant black, blue and purple swelling. He sat at his dressing table in shock.

It was much later that he remembered the last image he had seen before the fireworks display invaded his brain. Advancing towards the now fully closed, swollen eye had been a bright pin-prick of light surrounded by a cluster of five smaller ones. Tinkerbell had struck…

*

Back in the Pier Head Tavern, blissfully unaware of the splendid fate which had befallen Tad, Belvedere had been sitting through all the chatter about ferrets no more amazed now than he usually was when George and Norman got going. He knew it was he who would have to provide the serious, meaningful content of this important meeting.

"When I was at The Theatre at Stratford" – 'the theatre' was said very grandly. He got no further.

George sank the rest of his beer. "Did they ever find the ferret?" he asked Norman.

"I don't know." Norman was even more mournful now. He took another sip of his Guinness. "The management released me after that night's performance. They said they couldn't risk more damage to the back-drop – and anyway rodents weren't allowed backstage."

There was a silence.

"When I was at The Theatre at Stratford..."

George leapt up. "Time for another round." He collected his and Belvedere's empty glasses and went towards the bar. Norman rubbed some Guinness blobs into his Fair Isle jumper.

"I had an Auntie who lived in Stratford. When I stayed with her she used to take me for walks on Hackney Marsh. I'd never seen men and women doing – that – before." He shuddered, "It put me right off it..." the pub was silent, Norman took another sip. "...for life."

The sigh from Belvedere was more of a rumble.

"Not Stratford in London, you northern know-nothing. Stratford-upon-Avon. Home of the Bard. The shrine of the English theatre." The inhabitants of the bar shuffled uncomfortably. They felt they'd all been admonished.

"I'll put them on the slate, Mr Noble." The landlord wiped the bar nervously with his cloth. "Could you ask Mr Galbraith to lower his voice ever so slightly please? No-one dare drink and that's not good for my takings. I'm sure he'll understand."

George nodded unconvincingly and picked up the whisky and beer. As he moved away from the bar the landlord had one last contribution to make.

"Oh, by the way, a ferret isn't a rodent. It's a species of polecat. I know, my Dad keeps 'em." He smiled, hoping that he'd eased the tension.

George set down the drinks at the table. Belvedere took a large swig of his whisky and soda.

"I'll have no more interruptions." People dared to start chattering again – but quietly.

"We're here to discuss how we deal with that infuriating bounder Tad. When I was playing in Richard Three at Stratford." he glared at the two of them, daring them to interrupt him and they quickly buried their faces in their tankards. "…dear Donald was incensed to notice out of the corner of his eye…"

"Donald who?" Norman would never learn.

In a voice which silenced not only the saloon but also the adjacent public bar Belvedere bellowed, "Wolfit."

"A little quieter gentlemen, if you will." That was the best the barman dare do.

Belvedere now punched each word separately at them in a stage whisper. The rest of the customers drew a little nearer and a number crowded in from the public bar.

"Donald, dear Donald noticed out of the corner of his eye that a young fellow – one of the Lords or other Attendants – had started to acknowledge the tumultuous applause a split second before he, our revered leader, did." He leant forward to make even more point and the end of his cravat dipped, apparently in reverence, into his whisky. "Began his bow, do you see? Before Donald." He sat back exhausted.

George and Norman were silent as were the audience scattered around the bar. They drank, wiped their mouths and looked at each other. Norman, as always it seemed, dared to speak – but not much.

"So?" he said.

"So," said Belvedere taking another fair swig from his whisky, "here's the point."

"Thank the Lord for that," whispered the barman. Belvedere slammed his hand on the table. Everyone jumped. The audience retreated a step.

"Donald cut him dead. Cut him dead. Just like that. For all of the next week when they passed in the passage or wherever Donald looked right through him." He strove to make the point even clearer. "As if he wasn't there. He pretended not to notice him. Invisible. Do you see?"

No-one could have taken more trouble to get his point across but sadly the meaning of it was lost on George and Norman. George gulped his mild and bitter to help him concentrate.

"How did the poor lad take it?" There was another bang on the table.

"Poor lad? Poor lad? He was a bounder. An upstart. Amazingly he didn't seem to notice at the time. Carried on quite normally. I would have been mortified but this lad just went on being a Lord – or Attendant – or whatever. What is even more remarkable" the audience was close in again now, "is that he went on to become a leading actor himself. I played with him once. Abraham to his Romeo." He finished his whisky and added quietly in the silence, "somewhere."

Neither of them felt it wise to remark on the paucity of Abraham's part in the play; they realised it would be cruel. George, with tact which only a Welshman could muster at a time like this, changed direction.

"What's that got to do with Tad, then?" Belvedere had been miles away thinking of those better times. He stirred.

"Cut him dead, of course. Take no notice of him."

Norman finished his Guinness. "We already do, when we can. Cut him dead." He stood up. "*He* doesn't seem to notice either."

They stood up and put on their coats.

Belvedere felt that the meeting hadn't gone as well as the afternoon one but he had one more trick up his sleeve. With a final tip of his glass to see if the tiniest drop of whisky could be coaxed from it he said, "Then we'll go on doing it."

With a flourish of his hat to everyone in the bar and the ever-patient landlord, he swept towards the door only to be knocked backwards into the room by a dishevelled, dripping and extremely agitated Tad holding a handkerchief to an already swollen, black, blue and purple right eye. He yelped as he saw the three of them.

"Had a problem, Tad?" Norman was, as ever, observant.

Tad, with another yelp, turned and ran off into the blackness.

"Well done, Norman. So much for cutting him dead. A really good start." George was not impressed.

Belvedere merely sighed. You can't *make* someone into a real actor.

They set off towards their respective lodgings discussing the good fortune that had caused Tad some much deserved, if only temporary, pain.

The three gunners who had made up the evening detachment on the Bofors gun at the far end of the pier, and had a clear view of the stage door, were in the public bar. They had finished the last of their evening intake of four or five pints and had watched events with relish.

"That were quite a lass that landed him that one, weren't she?" They nodded appreciatively.

"Reminds me of my missus" said the second one. "I miss her beltings."

"I like a strong lass," agreed the third. "You know where you are with a strong lass."

The landlord looked at the clock behind the bar. If only his three special customers had left two minutes earlier he could have called for one last order. Dare he risk it? He saw one of the town councillors sitting with his wife in the corner. No, he daren't.

"Time, ladies and gentlemen, please," he shouted ringing the bell. This hadn't been a good evening as far as the takings were concerned. He would have to pluck up courage and get those three to keep themselves to themselves. Times were hard enough as it was without a nightly bombardment from Belvedere Galbraith.

*

At eleven-fifteen that night Charles Turville and Ludovic Henschel faced each other across the desk in the Commandant's office at the refugee camp. The thunder of wind and rain on the wooden roof and walls of the creaking, rickety structure heightened the obvious tension in the room. They were probably the only inhabitants of the damp, soulless camp to be pleased with the weather; it would drown whatever sounds they made.

They had greeted each other with the briefest of perfunctory nods and Henschel knew that all was not well from the curtness of the coded message ordering him to attend at this late hour. The lateness was of no concern; it was the lack of time to prepare his planned onslaught on Turville regarding the lack of co-operation by the Poles in London that annoyed him but, more by luck than judgement, he decided to hold it back until he'd heard what the meeting was to be about.

Turville's voice was only just audible above the cacophony of the tempest lashing the building but this was deliberate. He had carefully planned what he would say, changing it a dozen times during the train journey from a blistering tirade against his foolish subordinate to a bald statement laying out, clearly and unequivocally, the reversed roles they would play in the assignment from this moment onwards. He saw no value in censoring Henschel for his past behaviour now; that could wait until he wrote his final assessment for the man's confidential file.

"I have been with the Poles today. As a result of my meeting I shall, in future, be handling all negotiations with them. You will look after this end."

The predictable explosion from Henschel matched the worst the weather could throw against the building. There was nothing new in what he said and his disdain for the Poles was even more evident than at their last meeting.

Turville sat looking through his file of notes whilst Henschel raved which, he appreciated, only added to the man's fury but he couldn't think of anything else to do; he certainly didn't want to look at him and anyway, he reasoned, Henschel might just as well get all the bile out of his system at one go.

As with all storms it slowly abated until Henschel fired his last salvo.

"I resign," he barked, standing up and putting on his raincoat and hat.

Turville had been ready for this.

"Very well," he said quietly, "but you must understand that due to the importance of this assignment you will be held incommunicado until it is over, one way or another."

To Turville's surprise Henschel, with no further argument, now reversed his actions. Without a word he took off his hat, then his raincoat and sat down. He was even more amazed at the man's next question.

"What are my orders?" It was asked bleakly in a voice Turville had never experienced in the man before.

He gave Henschel his briefing clearly and concisely. He was to shadow Peggy, never harrass her, but protect her from any form of danger so that she – and the notebooks – were available to be reunited with the Professor when – if – he could be evacuated from Poland.

Henschel opened his mouth, and closed it again. He had been about to tell Turville of his fruitless visit to the dressing-room but, wisely for once, realized that it might not be the best moment to do so. Unable to leave well alone he instead embarked on his well-trodden path of disagreement with the philosophy behind the proposed tactics.

"The girl is of no importance. It is the notebooks we must have. The package can then be reunited with them and get on with his duty to the free world."

Turville fixed Henschel with a cold stare.

"And the girl?" He said it quietly, his voice hardly audible against the noise of the vicious weather. Henschel gave a dismissive gesture.

"She doesn't matter. No part of the equation."

Turville sighed. This had all been made clear time and time again.

"The package will not co-operate regarding either travel or work without the girl. You already know this, my friend."

Henschel leapt up, leaning forward with his hands on the table.

"You British. So sentimental. If you had lived in *our* world you would think differently. The package should be *made* to work."

For a moment Turville said nothing but his eyes didn't waver from Henschel's as the Pole sank back into his chair. Then he spoke in a voice little above a whisper.

"You are one of very few people to label me a sentimentalist. I am flattered, yet I think there are many – alive and dead – who would disagree with you."

The menace in his voice added weight to the statement. There was a silence between them as the building fought against the weather.

"The girl *is* important – vital – to this operation. The package is no value to *anyone* if he does not wish to co-operate. No one, not even the SS, has yet found a way to operate a brain without its owner's consent. You have already been told that he will only co-operate when he is reunited with the girl. Neither must be allowed to be under any pressure. Those are our orders. I am responsible for the package reaching us safe and well, *you* are responsible for seeing that the girl is here to receive him – *and* the notebooks. Comment?"

134

The last word was said abruptly and coldly. Turville did not expect to have to repeat himself. He fixed Henschel with a bleak stare and received an equally penetrating one in return.

They held the tableau for almost a minute before Turville embarked on another tack which had been gnawing at the back of his mind for some time. It was the death of the wretched train guard. It seemed obvious to him that he was the intended victim; he must have been pushing past the man almost at the moment he was shot.

One possible suspect needed to be, as the police put it, 'eliminated from his inquiries' and that man was sitting opposite him now. He wouldn't put it past Henschel's embittered impetuosity to take a pot-shot at him and, if he had, the matter would need to be dealt with swiftly – and terminally. In a strange way he rather hoped it *was* him and then the far more dangerous and worrying alternative explanation would not apply.

He broke the silence.

"Why do you think the train guard had to die?" Turville asked this almost conversationally and was surprised at the quickness – and unexpected wit of the answer.

"I really have no idea. Were you attempting to travel without a ticket?"

Turville couldn't help himself; he roared with laughter.

"I wish I had thought of that when the matter was discussed in London. It seems the bullet was from an army service revolver which *could* mean carelessness. Too few servicemen are familiar with the weapons they are now required to carry, and many feel there's little point in doing so unless they're loaded." He leant forward and spoke quietly. "But why such an accident should happen late at night on an apparently deserted railway station platform is hard to imagine."

Whilst saying this he had been staring into Henschel's eyes almost boring through them into his brain to detect any signal, however tiny it might be, that would suggest that the man was lying, concealing the truth. He saw nothing, only a semblance of boredom that time should be wasted on such an unimportant matter. So, thought Turville, the unpalatable alternative would need to be considered.

"We are ordered to take extreme care. It would not be surprising to find that others have traced the girl and are in competition with us to secure the package *and* the notebooks."

Henschel appeared puzzled. "You mean the bullet was meant for you?"

Turville shrugged. "Maybe. Maybe not. Whichever, it means extreme caution."

They lit cigarettes and sat silently for a short while. Henschel was considering the possibility of another group in the area, obviously Britain's enemies, planning to abduct and spirit away Peggy – or the Professor if he were got here. That made his part of the assignment far more interesting. Turville had the same thoughts but, rather than interesting, he saw a battle at the Flaxton end of the operation with Henschel in charge fraught with danger for this woman, Peggy.

The wind outside was so strong that it seeped into the wooden hut dispersing the cigarette smoke. At last Turville stirred.

"The rest of the actors are now tailing the girl to protect her. Get to know what they look like but *don't* interfere. A bit of extra protection will do no harm."

Henschel again exploded. "It makes my job impossible. They *must* be removed. I insist."

Turville smiled. "Perhaps you'd like them all shot? With a service revolver?"

Henschel had no answer.

Turville's smile vanished. "They stay. You can protect them as well as the girl."

He stood. The meeting was over. Henschel followed him out feeling that little, other than a flea in his ear, had been achieved. Without a word they split and went their respective ways.

Henschel went to his hut and climbed up onto his bunk. The others around him knew better than to acknowledge him; each had been curtly dismissed when they first tried. They sympathetically put his harshness down to hidden grief; they all had that in abundance and were aware that it affected people in different ways. He lay back and lit a cigarette. He was glad that he hadn't mentioned to Turville the meeting with Peggy. Now was not yet the time to incur the undoubted wrath that would have resulted from such an admission. He smiled wryly to himself. That would be part of the greater plan and *that* required a visit away from Flaxton.

He took one final deep draw on his cigarette, stubbed it out on the metal bed frame and, as those around him settled down to sleep, dropped silently to the floor, pulled on his heavy coat and hat and let himself out into the foul night.

*

Tad was alone in the snug bar of The Anchor with Pru, the barmaid. She was gently dabbing a damp cloth on his blackened eye. Leaning across the bar counter to do this Tad noted that her top blouse buttons were undone – it had been a busy, hot night pulling the pints – and even with only one eye in working order he was still able to appreciate the magnificent chasm which was on display before him. The lacy brassière that was designed to push its contents 'upwards and outwards', as the label had assured him it would do, – it was one of a gross he had bought at a cut-down price – was certainly doing its work; doing overtime in fact. Tad looked forward to its removal later.

His groans and grunts were caused by a mixture of what one damaged eye was feeling and the other was seeing.

"There they were," he explained to Pru, "three of them. Ruffians. Of course I took them on. You'd think we'd all be fighting on the same side, wouldn't you?"

The landlord, washing glasses in the public bar, was overhearing all this and almost dropped a tankard as he heard Tad admonishing others for their lack of national spirit in these hard times. He knew very well the shady black-market dealings that this crafty character got up to although he was not averse to making use of Tad's services to help augment his dwindling stock of spirits, liqueurs and cigarettes. Where the crafty beggar got them from heaven alone knew but the margins were good; it was the only reason why he tolerated Tad and his loud boasting ways.

He admitted that the man was good on stage – the best – but in his snug bar he was a pain in the neck. If it hadn't been for the regular supply of contraband he'd have warned Pru to steer well clear of him, not that she'd listen; she liked the cheery cheekiness of him and, the landlord feared as he breathed air on a glass and re-wiped it, more besides.

"So I laid them all out. In a row. Like a packet of Woodbines. Out cold they were, my love. Cold as a dead baboon's bottom."

Pru giggled.

"Language in there if you don't mind," shouted the landlord.

Pru giggled again and the chasm wobbled and heaved.

So did Tad. "I think I'll need helping home, love." He made his voice small and pained. "Dizzy you see. That last one got me just before he fell. It's terrible to be wounded so early in the war."

This was, at last, more than the landlord could stand. He sighed, "Take him away, Pru, for heaven's sake. If Mr Chamberlain hears of his injury he'll probably surrender!"

They left. The night, for them, was still young...

There was more nursing going on in another part of Flaxton in the flat above the Post Office where Pat and Peggy lodged with Alice Banbury, the Postmistress.

"You poor love. Straight into a lamp post." Alice was bathing Peggy's hand. "Our first war wound. Hitler's got a lot to answer for. What a horrible bruise." She dipped the cloth in a bowl of warm water and gently pressed it over Peggy's knuckles. "They're deadly in the dark. They should put lamps on them so that we can see them."

Pat smiled and brought over a tray holding three cups of steaming Horlicks. She considered explaining the point regarding the black-out and lamps on lamp posts but thought better of it. She looked at Peggy's swollen left hand which, around the knuckles, was turning a bruising shade of blue.

"Lucky it didn't damage your engagement ring, love, bashing it into the post so hard. Still, better your hand than your head."

Peggy said nothing.

It was just after eleven. The three of them were sitting in Alice's cramped kitchen plus Mountjoy the black labrador and Harriet the cat. The animals were keen to help by licking Peggy's fist better.

Alice was already in her nightie and dressing-gown. It was good to be free of frock, tight shoes and corset, and hours standing behind the counter made her body ache.

She stood up, exhausted, her eyes red-rimmed with tiredness and went out to lock the front door. Suddenly Peggy jumped out of her chair and startled Pat by grabbing her with her good hand and pulling her to the fireplace. They stood facing each other. The cue for action was the adoption of their stage, cast London, voices...

PEGGY	"I had a terrible night. My Charlie's snoring.
PAT	What did you do?
PEGGY	Moved into the spare room, of course.
PAT	You would.
PEGGY	The lodger was very good about it. Moved over a bit *(pause)* Still took most of the blanket...
PAT	They do. How was Charlie this morning?
PEGGY	He said he felt a little hoarse.
PAT	No wonder the milk cart was late reaching our end of the street...
PEGGY	Talking of milk, how are you getting on with food rationing?
PAT	Getting thinner. Jack doesn't worry though. He just drinks more beer. I don't know why they bother with barrels. It'd be easier to fill him up at the brewery.
PEGGY	It's clothes rationing that affects me.
PAT	So I see...
PEGGY	What d'you mean? This is one of my best frocks.
PAT	*(appalled)* You mean you've got another like it?
PEGGY	I went to buy some bloomers yesterday but I only had enough coupons for one.
PAT	How much did it cost?
TOGETHER	Half a nicker..."

Pat and Peggy fell into each other's arms giggling like schoolgirls. Alice, standing in the doorway, was amazed at the resilience of the young and, laughing with them, chivvied them out of the room turning off the gas fire and the light as she did so.

"Let's hope we have a better night tonight. No more bombs."

The animals followed them out. Mountjoy, despite his grand wooden kennel in the corner of the kitchen, would often spend the night 'visiting' their rooms. The three of them never knew who would be honoured with an extra deeply breathing presence until they reached their bedrooms. Tonight he chose Alice which meant that Harriet would probably wander between Peggy's and Pat's rooms.

*

The theatre creaked. The tide rolled under the decking with a regular swish and crash followed by the tumble of the pebbles as they were pulled back into the North Sea. Each surge caused the framework to shudder and the building above it did the same, in sympathy. The smell of sweat and tobacco still hung in the air, a legacy of tonight's noisy audience and, adding to the bending and stretching of the structure, the furniture and stage equipment bedded down for the night with clicks and clatters.

But there was another sound now. Very faint, irregular, man-made. It was the frenzied dit-dot-dit of Morse code. There was no doubt about it. Somewhere in the theatre someone was sending a message by wireless transmitter in Morse. It stopped briefly, resumed and stopped again.

In this building that jutted out over the sea, pointing like an arrow at the rapidly expanding territory of the Third Reich, a secret conversation was taking place.

Dit-dot-dit...

Late on this April night Flaxton-on-Sea's Pier Theatre was staging another performance; a solo turn with an audience far across the North sea – in occupied Europe.

CHAPTER SEVEN

Mid April 1940. Rudolf Franz Hoess is appointed Super-intendent of the newly completed Vermichtungslager – extermination camp – at Auschwitz. He would boast after the war that he had massacred two-and-a-half million people there.

There is concern in Britain that butter, sugar, bacon, ham and meat are now rationed.

"So, the Herr Professor cries." The Gestapo Captain sneered. "It would be better to put your energies into your work. There is much for you to write. General Streyer commands it."

He pulled himself to attention as he uttered his master's name. "You would do well to obey."

That had been early this morning. Freddy had slept badly. The euphoria at finding, through the lift attendant's note, that there were friends on hand and that all might not be lost had soon passed. He had cried in relief – which surprised him. He put it down to a release of tension and the evening with the SS General had certainly been tense.

Short snatches of shallow sleep had been punctuated by long periods of uneasy wakefulness. He turned from side to side, got up and paced the floor and slowly his mind settled towards its usual sharpness. Towards – but not yet there. Different new disciplines were being called for: theoretical science needed to give way to practical solutions to the danger he was in.

He was surprised to be awakened by the key being turned in the lock and the door opening. It always seemed the case that after a bad night, deep sleep came with the dawn. He sat up, bleary-eyed, as a military orderly brought in a tray of breakfast. Not knowing who Freddy was he turned towards the bed, sprang to attention and threw his right arm up in a Nazi salute. Freddy nodded. A vicious yell from the corridor made them both jump and the soldier scuttled out, petrified. At any other time Freddy would have found the episode amusing but humour was the last thing on his mind as he forced himself out of his deep sleep.

As if to make the point, Captain Fengel, who had been his junior escort on the journey from the villa, marched into the room. His was the vicious yell, and his dislike for any courtesy towards a Pole, which was hinted at yesterday, was very evident this morning. His sneering remarks regarding his crying showed clearly how he intended to approach this unwanted duty as Freddy's gaoler and, flinging open the curtains as if he was providing room service, he marched to the door.

"You will get up now and work. You have little time Herr Professor." And then, evily, "Very little time."

He clicked his heels then, remembering where he was, tried to un-click them – a move which no-one in the German army had yet mastered – and, in fury, stalked out. The key turned in the lock.

Fear was mixed with confusion. Freddy was living two lives at the same time; a guest occupying one of the best bedrooms in the finest – and now only remaining – hotel in Warsaw with full room service, and a prisoner for a frighteningly uncertain length of time in Gestapo headquarters. No wonder his mind, for all its legendary brilliance, was seriously confused.

He went through the mechanical process of rising, washing, shaving and dressing, as if he was about to start any other normal academic day. Then he sat at the window to eat a perfectly satisfactory breakfast which included a pot of delicious strong, black, Polish coffee kept warm on a spirit heater.

Fattening the lamb for the slaughter? Freddy couldn't help his mind thinking such thoughts, but there was something else troubling it, detached from the overall drama of his situation. He knew the feeling of old. It was an 'electric' feeling, a tingling excitement. He experienced it – or, at least, he certainly used to – when a scientific formula or equation was about to make sense and then would suddenly slot into place either from his ever-present note-book jottings or from an overheard remark.

Freddy thought back, carefully checking every detail of the last few hours with as much precision as he would a scientific equation and then, with an involuntary gasp, he solved the riddle.

It was the Captain's first sneering remark that morning – "So the Herr Professor cries." How did the man know? Freddy knew that the only time he'd wept in that room was in relief, last night, on reading that note – *and he had been alone.*

That was it! They were listening to him – then – and now.

Somewhere there must be a hidden microphone.

The realisation that he was being spied upon, that he had no more privacy than a goldfish in a glass bowl, terrified him. He was shaking, panting with short, shallow breaths, paralysed not only with fear but a reluctance to move – and be *heard* doing so.

The moment of panic passed and with his brain functioning again came a burst of inspiration: he could turn their sordid invasion of his privacy to *his* advantage! He set out to find the instrument without letting the eavesdropper know. Any disturbance of its camouflage would give the game away. He padded quietly around the room. Surely there couldn't be many places where a large bulbous microphone could be hidden plus its connecting wire, could there?

Bulbous – bulb? Wire? It was probably the connection of words that made him look up at the heavily ornate chandelier in the centre of the room. He switched it on. One of the six lamps wasn't working and under normal circumstances that wouldn't surprise him in these terrible days. He quietly fetched a chair and, standing on it, could just reach the glass bowl from which was coming no light. Sure enough, rising from it he could see an extra wire leading to the centre chain and up through the ceiling-rose.

Now that he knew, the panic briefly returned but then he quietly put the chair back in its place and sat at the window table.

"Now to work," he said out loud. "There is much to do. My German colleagues at the Kaiser Wilhelm Institute will need all the detail I can give them. If we Poles cannot split the atom, why not them? So be it."

It was a crass speech and he felt very foolish making it but, not being an actor, it was the best he could do. He mumbled as he started to scribble meaningless formulae and equations onto the sheets of paper helpfully provided by his hosts.

*

In the room next door the eavesdropper smiled. The words the prisoner had spoken were written neatly on his pad which he handed to his colleague to take, at speed, to Hauptmann Fengel. He adjusted his headphones and settled down to intense listening. He heard humming interspersed with murmured letters and numbers. The Herr Professor was obviously playing into the ever beckoning arms of the Gestapo...

*   *   *

The morning after his meeting at the theatre Belvedere took up position at nine o'clock at a discreet distance from the front door of Flaxton's Post Office flat and, to avoid looking conspicuous, – as if he ever could – was pretending to look in other shop windows in the High Street. He discovered that if he stood at a particular angle he could see a reflection of the door in the plate glass.

Finding himself gazing into the window of the Flaxton Chronicle Office his attention was diverted by a display of a page from one of last week's papers giving a write-up on the Show.

"Droll?" he muttered, "Bygone age?" louder, "Corpulent?"

"Don't worry love." Spinning round he saw Peggy standing alongside him. "They think you're great. Look how they cheer."

Belvedere considered this. "As I leave the stage, I think." He allowed himself a wry smile.

She squeezed his arm. "Come up for a coffee. It's a cold morning."

In no time he found himself sitting in a chair which was rather too small for him – most chairs were – in Alice Banbury's front living room above the Post Office.

The room was delightful; it had a friendly, cosy 'parlour' feeling reflecting the comfortable life-style of its owner. Chintz covers in a summer flower pattern covered the chairs and sofa; there were vases full of fresh Spring flowers, photographs of relatives of every age and a glass-fronted cabinet full of porcelain ornaments and glassware, all set neatly and tidily on a rich Axminster carpet.

But Belvedere, for a number of reasons, was aware of none of this comfort around him – in fact he felt distinctly *un*comfortable, partly due to the tightness of the chair, partly to his evident lack of ability in the art of surveillance but mainly because of the frenetic attentions of the black Labrador, Mountjoy, who assumed that this large stranger was either here as a playmate or, even better, a play-thing.

Belvedere wasn't used to dogs and his embarrassment was exacerbated by having this very personal attention witnessed by Peggy who was sitting opposite him. It annoyed him that she either didn't seem to notice or care that he was being physically – even sexually – assaulted! He tried all the friendly rebuttals he could think of but they just spurred Mountjoy on to greater effort.

"I do impress upon you, Peggy, the need to free yourself of these dangerous tomes."

He seemed incapable of using ordinary English but exception proved the rule with his next exclamation: "Ow!"

Mountjoy had gone too far – far too far – and Belvedere cuffed him away. This, to the dog, was a signal that games were about to start in earnest. He pulled back on his haunches and let out a playful snarl. Belvedere, trying not to rub himself and thereby show the assaulted area, said between his teeth.

"I would be grateful if the hound might be removed to another room."

Peggy was amazed. It hadn't struck her that anyone would want to see Mountjoy banished but if it would relax poor old Belvedere then, so be it. She took the reluctant dog by the collar and plonked him into the hall giving him a playful farewell pat. Belvedere was supremely grateful to see her close the door.

"About the notebooks. You see I can't, I really can't. I gave Freddy a solemn promise that the notebooks would stay with me until he was here to receive them and I will not – ever – break that promise."

Belvedere feared that she was going to cry. He wouldn't know what to do if she did. He hoped he had put a clean handkerchief in his pocket; it might help but he wouldn't, shouldn't, touch her, that would be most improper and far too embarrassing.

"Peggy, your husband obviously didn't realize how dangerous it would be for you to have his notebooks. It would seem that they hold secrets that the wrong sort of people would," he wanted to say 'kill for' but it might set her off. He settled for "go to some lengths to steal from you."

Peggy wiped her eyes. She transmitted her anguish in each word. "They're all I have of him, you see. If I lose them, I'll lose him. To me it's as simple as that."

They were quiet for a few moments, unlike the dog who, sensing a friend in danger, pounded on the door. Belvedere shuddered, imagining himself, rather than the stout oak, as the subject of the frenzied scratching of the animal's claws.

"Shush, pet." Peggy was still looking at a now deeply embarrassed Belvedere as she crooned the injunction, and it took him a moment to realize it was directed at the dog, not him. Amazingly it stopped scratching instantly.

"Why not deposit them in a bank vault? Remember Prospero in dear William Shakespeare's 'Tempest'. 'Deeper than did ever plummet sound, I'll drown my book'. Ah, dear Johnny – Gielgud, you know – played it so movingly."

Peggy was totally perplexed. "Lovely," she said hoping it might help him.

She did wish that he'd go now. She knew that he meant well but he was a bit peculiar and she couldn't work out why he was concerning himself in her dilemma. She rather wished she hadn't recounted her story yesterday. She should have kept it all to herself. Freddy would probably be furious.

"I don't trust bank vaults, Belvedere. Did you read in the Chronicle of that raid in Ipswich? They got away with everything. People are waving guns around these days like, like..." she couldn't think like what, but she hoped she'd made her point.

Belvedere got up with some difficulty from the chair. He wasn't used to such prevarication when he issued instructions to people.

"Peggy, I have to tell you, nay, *order* you to give me those books. I will ensure their safety against all manner of folk, so help me God." He felt that an oath from the Coronation Service of only two years ago might help to sway things his way.

Peggy also rose.

"I know you mean well, Belvedere, but I would rather you stopped bullying me." She stamped her foot. "Until I hand those notebooks to Freddy..." her voice became shrill, "and I will, they stay in my possession and no one..." shriller still, "no one will take them from me."

Now she started to cry quietly. Her eyes were full of tears. Mountjoy, hearing her distress, resumed his battle with the door.

Belvedere was mortified. He hadn't intended to upset Peggy but rather to help her.

In great embarrassment he mumbled as he made for the shaking door, "My dear, I am really so very sorry. Unforgivable. Only trying to assist. Meant no harm."

He felt her hand on his and turned as she collapsed into his arms, shaking with giant sobs. He found himself gently stroking her hair and holding her tightly. He was amazed at how easy it was and what deep contentment it gave him. He realised that he had never experienced anything like it, either as the giver or receiver of such love and his own eyes filled with tears.

"It's alright, my love. It's alright. We'll protect you and, please God, we'll have you re-united with your Freddy."

They stayed close together for a while and, as if sensing Peggy's grief, the dog was silent now. Eventually she eased herself from his arms, wiped her eyes and opened the door. The dog was sitting obediently outside in the hallway.

"Thank you, dear Belvedere. I feel safe knowing that you care. You – all of you – are so kind."

Belvedere made his way to the Pier Head Tavern. He needed a very stiff whisky. The mission had been a total failure – or had it? Two doubles later it occurred to him that, maybe, it had actually been a success. Peggy at least knew she was surrounded by friends.

He realized that he'd handed her his handkerchief to wipe her eyes and that she still had it. Such a thing had never happened to Belvedere Galbraith before. Never.

*

That evening at the de-briefing George, who had come on 'Peggy Patrol' at midday, solemnly reported to Belvedere that Belvedere Galbraith had been seen leaving her flat at twelve fifteen. He told Belvedere, with a totally straight face, that the reason for Belvedere Galbraith's visit was not known. Half an hour later, he reported, Peggy left the flat with a large black dog. He had followed them for some distance to a patch of green grass at the edge of town where, before their return, the dog "performed mightily". George took his surveillance duties very seriously. He added that the dog seemed "very frisky". Belvedere didn't need to be told *that*!

*

In the afternoon the stage was fully lit as if for the show. Nell had called a full dress rehearsal of the Illusion act after the chaos of the previous evening's performance.

"Marvo, you'll have to make a better signal than that. I'm all at an angle now like last night. I'll tipple off in a minute." Rena, lying on a plank apparently floating unsupported on the stage was seriously head down and likely to slide off at any moment.

"Or grunt louder." Rita, normally calm and sympathetic to Marvo's inability to speak, was at the end of her patience. He, judging by the whiteness of his tightly clenched fists was in a similar frame of mind.

It really shouldn't have been a difficult trick but if, as happened last night, it went wrong it looked stupid and the audience, not known these days for their tolerance, turned what should be a hushed appreciation of illusion into a fairground spectacle.

The stage set looked absolutely right; an air of mystery suspending rational belief. The back and sides were covered in hanging, sparkling gold and silver tinsel which glittered and flashed in Bill Colbourn's low, subtle lighting. Pinks, blues, reds and greens – every colour of filter he could find – covered the batten of lamps he was using, and the three of them, Marvo, Rita and Rena, moved from colour to colour.

An antiquated machine (when it worked) puffed out imaginary smoke which ranged in intensity between thick fog almost completely masking the action and thin wisps that suggested that a fire was about to engulf them all. If the machine wouldn't work at all they hoped for a sea mist to permeate the theatre and do the job for them!

Marvo, resplendent in gaily coloured kaftan, fez and rope sandals sulked about the stage waving his magic wand, grunting and adjusting his 'magic' box which, when pointed at the supine Rena, would magically lift her, unaided, seven or so feet into the air from the trestles on which she lay along the back stage flat.

Rena didn't wear her glasses for the act; she'd rather not see how high she was being lifted!

When it worked, accompanied by a slightly over-zealous roll on the drums from Fred Spriggs followed by a crashing of cymbals and a more-or-less together triumphant chord in C major from the rest of the 'orchestra', it worked well and the audience was gratifyingly amazed. No one could see how the illusion was done.

Last night had been a disaster. As Rena had teetered and wobbled on her plank, the soldiers in the audience had delighted at the prospect of a catastrophe and a jettisoned Rena displaying even more than her scanty costume already revealed.

They had yelled "tip the lady out of bed", "two goes for a tanner", and one, immediately ejected by a burly corporal, attempted to leap onto the stage via Claude Eckersley's lap knocking his trombone out of his hand. Claude, going through considerable mental concentration for the forthcoming triumphant C major chord blew his false teeth out of his mouth and under the piano. This turned out to be a blessing because the recovery of these two revolting, but precious, objects diverted attention away from the stage where Marvo, grunting and waving his wand in the manner of the celebrated orchestral conductor Sir Thomas Beecham, was trying to level Rena.

The note of high – but unintentional – farce wasn't helped by the beating the apparently mad Illusionist was giving the curtains each end of the supine Rena as if he were trying to force dust out of a carpet. This, for reasons which the audience would never know, severely exacerbated the problem. Rena suddenly dropped with a bump onto the trestles and let out a small scream and, as Rita rushed forward, the soldiers got the view they had all been waiting and hoping for.

Nell, backstage and in a fair state of alarm shouted at Don to "till the crabs" which even *he* couldn't interpret. So he closed the curtains and Bill Colbourn pushed his dimmers down to nought. Later Vi, with her uncanny ability to 'read' Nell's malapropisms, explained to them that 'till the crabs' would have been a mixture of 'kill the lights' and 'pull the tabs': theatre parlance for switch off the lights and close the curtains!

The evening had been saved by Tad going front-of-curtain and brilliantly extemporising a stand-up routine which had the audience in stitches.

He recounted a joke involving an army padré who, giving a talk to recruits on the dangers of making love, advises them that if they must indulge in it, to save the lady distress, they should never prolong it for more than five minutes. One recruit leans over to his neighbour and says, 'How does he make it last five minutes?'

The yells of delight from the other side of the curtain relaxed Nell who was by now on stage berating a grunting Marvo whilst Vi calmed Rita and Rena. It was just as well that none of them knew the cause of the laughter. Nell just thought that Tad was doing a grand job.

"A real trooper," she whispered to Vi.

*

As a result of the fiasco a grim Nell called an extra rehearsal the following afternoon. She and Vi met Pat and Peggy at the bottom of the steps by the Post Office and they all slipped into the seats at the back of the auditorium. The ostrich feather pointed itself accusingly straight at Marvo!

Pat whispered to Peggy "You've got *me* going now, Peg. That weird feeling of being followed."

Marvo, in a seethingly bad mood, banged down his 'magic box' which was, in fact, an old tea chest painted in all the colours of the rainbow, equipped by Bill Colbourn with flashing coloured lights powered by cycle-lamp batteries. He pointed the 'magic ray' tube (rolled-up card stuck on with glue) at Rena. Despite knowing what it really was, Rena still recoiled when the infernal machine was aimed at her.

Rita advanced angrily on Marvo. "It's no use getting cross Marv. It was a near disaster last night and you know it. Poor Rena could have broken her neck landing on her head like that. It's lucky she has the gift of foresight and managed to turn it into a cartwheel – although, she added doubtfully, our costumes aren't designed for cartwheels…"

"I think the tabs were closed before that," Rena anxiously whispered as there was another jolt.

Nell sprang up with unusual agility and strode down the aisle, her ostrich feather looking angry. She couldn't put up with this any longer.

"Marvo, for heaven's sake grunt more clearly. They can't understand you. You're un-un-uninterlectual to them."

She mounted the rehearsal steps and marched across the stage. Rita, Rena and Marvo, who hadn't known she was in the theatre, stood frozen in the position they were in when they had first heard her voice.

Nell went to the rear scenery flat which, unknown to the audience, had an alcove in it in which lay Rena on her plank. This was, in fact, a stretcher 'borrowed', unbeknownst to Nell, from the local WVS emergency store. The handles at the two ends of it poked through the side tinsel curtains of the alcove in which were hidden, on one side Reg and on the other, his mate Bob on small ladders. On a clear cue from Marvo that they were supposed to hear, they would raise Rena off the trestles, lifting the stretcher handles high up to their shoulders and hold her there until another clear cue told them to lower her. Because they were behind the rear flat they couldn't see anything. If only one of them heard the cue he lifted and the other, sensing the movement of the handles, tried to follow suit, but it would be later and slower – or faster – and the result was a switchback ride for Rena.

Now Nell faced the tinsel behind which she knew was Reg – or Bob. She yelled, unnecessarily, "Can you hear me, Reg?"

As fate would have it she'd chosen the wrong side for Reg who now answered away to her right. "Hello, Nell". It seemed the only thing to say.

Nell moved across past Rena who was now lying back with her eyes closed. She shouted to the place from which Reg's voice had emerged.

"Bob?"

"Yes, Nell", came from the left-hand end where she had first stood.

Vi, in the back of the auditorium, clicked her teeth. It would be better to let the five of them sort all this out for themselves. She made her way to the front and went up the steps onto the stage where Nell was making frantic, but pointless, signs to Marvo who was sulking and picking at a sleeve of his kaftan.

She whispered to her, "Best leave them to it, love. They'll sort it out." Then she turned to Rita. "You take charge. Stand near Rena and tell the boys when to lift. Much the best."

151

Vi took Nell gently by the arm and lead her backstage. "Shall we go to the office and do some paper work?"

There was a slight movement, which no-one saw, in the darkness of the dress circle as a figure moved back to the dusty staircase. It avoided the cobwebs as it descended to the foyer and past the "no entry" sign. In mackintosh and trilby Ludovic Henschel slipped silently out of the theatre and back down the pier, now more certain than ever that he had been charged with protecting a group of lunatics.

*

At the other end of the High Street from the pier Councillor Edward Bradley, Chairman of Flaxton-on-Sea Town Council, was having trouble with a dog somewhat smaller than the Labrador, Mountjoy. He was standing on the pavement at the gate of a neat, well maintained cottage separated from the road by a small, pretty, wild garden. He'd made the mistake of opening the gate and standing on the path which the dog very much saw as its territory. Now this small, more-or-less white Yorkshire terrier was snapping at his heels unaware and uncaring that this human, dressed as a postman, was such an august member of the community.

'Postman Ted', as the opposition parties on the council – and the Flaxton Chronicle – delighted in calling him, found the day job very demeaning, and had plans to forego the postal heritage handed on to him by his father, and his father before him, and become a Member of Parliament and then, he would say to those who couldn't avoid listening to him, "Probably Prime Minister."

The aspiring future leader of the nation was already in his late forties so he would need to make his dizzy way upwards soon, but to mix with the right sort of people who would secure his elevation he needed a commodity which, to a lowly postman, *should* be in short supply: money.

Councillor Edward led a life which caused much speculation amongst the electorate of the town and, his bête noir, the Flaxton Chronicle. No one really knew where his funds came from to buy him membership of the Golf Club, a smart seventeen horse-power Sunbeam Talbot, a new chintz three-piece suite bought in

Ipswich and delivered on a lorry that was required by the Councillor to drive twice up and down the High Street before delivering it to his house (the Chronicle was offered a photo opportunity but declined) and, most recently, a large eighteen inch blade Webb *motor* mower.

This last symbol of wealth, far beyond the pay of a humble postman, could be seen *daily* being driven up and down the tiny front lawn of their house in Approach Road by Councillor Edward usually dressed in one of his many smart suits. If his wife Phyllis hadn't, yet again, threatened to walk out on him, (Ted would first and foremost see this as damaging his political ambitions rather than losing his wife) he would wear his chain of office whilst pretending to cut the now almost totally bald patch of grass! He wore it whenever he could and was extremely miffed that the GPO, in its wisdom, forbade him to wear it with his postman's uniform.

Now he was having his ankles snapped at by this aggravating dog. As if that wasn't humiliating enough, the dog belonged to his deputy Chairman, Councillor Winifred Ledbury, who was now calling it to desist in a voice vibrating with authority.

"Josey, Josey, Josey," she called, "Put the Chairman down this instant."

Councillor Winifred was used to being obeyed holding, as she did, commanding positions in most of the town's voluntary organisations and coming, as she also did, from locally landed gentry. No one disobeyed Councillor Winifred for long and Josey reluctantly obeyed her command now.

"You're late again this morning, Bradley."

Councillor Edward, who did *not* approve of his vice-chairman referring to him by his surname replied, haughtily, "Civic duties and the war madam. They must come before conveying His Majesty's post."

He patted his gas-mask and slightly turned to proudly display his steel helmet, strapped onto his back-pack. He had ordered the council signwriter to stencil the word CHAIRMAN in white paint on the front of it. Mrs Ledbury was, of course, not impressed. She noted with satisfaction that, during this pomposity, Josey had squatted and urinated on his right boot.

"Will you kindly remove your dog, Councillor. There is a matter I must discuss with you urgently before tonight's meeting." Councillor Winifred, noting that the chairman was unaware of his wet boot, smiled and felt it would be a nice surprise for him when he went to take it off back at home.

Picking up Josey she patted her clever dog. "I suppose you'd better come into the porch."

She led the way down the straight path to the little lean-to that protected her front door. Each side was glass paned, criss-crossed with white sticky tape to prevent flying glass splinters caused by bomb blasts.

Beneath the side glass walls of the porch were narrow planks of wood serving as seats or shelves for garden implements. Mrs Ledbury ushered the chairman/postman to one side and sat on the other, their knees almost touching. It was as if they were in a very narrow train compartment and, whilst she knew that they looked ridiculous, she considered it a better alternative to inviting this insufferable man into her home.

"I'll come straight to the point."

Pigs might fly, she thought. He'd already wasted more than five minutes of her time – and time to her was very precious.

"The Theatre Company. I have decided that their lease of the Pier Theatre should not be renewed."

Mrs Ledbury stiffened. "Have you indeed. Democracy was never a strong point with you, was it Bradley?" As was his custom he ignored this admonishment and sailed on.

"I have been monitoring their performances from the start of the season. Very poor quality. There's that disgusting comedian and a fat pompous oaf…" Mrs Ledbury murmured, "it takes one to know one." but he didn't hear and ploughed on "…spouting Shakespeare, a grunting madman who prances around in a night-shirt, two nearly naked young girls…"

Mrs Ledbury interrupted, "You're obviously very well informed. I hope your numerous visits were not charged to your excessive expenses bill."

The chairman squirmed just a little. "Of course they were. This is council business."

Mrs Ledbury watched with satisfaction a spider which had descended from its web onto his shoulder.

"Is it indeed," she said. "You will know that my work brings me into contact with a very wide cross-section of the electorate. Whilst I hear the odd complaint it would seem to me that, by and large, the town is proud of its Theatre Company. The troops, who should be our greatest concern, thoroughly enjoy their evenings on the pier and the poor refugees see it as a welcome interlude in their sad, dreary lives. It costs us nothing – in fact it provides the town with much needed revenue. In the vote I and my party will oppose any suggestion of closure."

The spider was now exploring the chairman's GPO shirt collar.

Councillor Bradley would have none of this defence of what he saw as a 'frivolous anomaly in these dark times' – a Churchillian phrase he had prepared for the evening meeting.

"You know very well Mrs Ledbury, that I and my party have a majority. That is why you were chucked out as chairman. We will vote for non-renewance..." Mrs Ledbury winced at this invented English, "...of the lease when it comes up for..." he tried to think of another word but couldn't.

Mrs Ledbury helped him. "Renewance?"

"Precisely. At the end of the month."

She stood. He stood. They were only about a foot apart which suddenly made Mrs Ledbury feel unwell so she retreated and stood in her doorway. She noted that the spider had disappeared.

"You'll have a fight on your hands."

The chairman smiled indulgently as if he was dealing with a child.

"I see no reason why there should be a fight. I hope, you and your little party will support us in the motion. Much better that such an important decision is seen as being unanimous."

The chairman made his way back down the path towards the High Street.

"And my post, Bradley?" He was brought back with a cruel bump to the reality of being a postman and grumpily handed her a bundle of important looking letters.

"I shall see you this evening, Mrs Ledbury." He strode away with all the dignity he could muster. Why was it that this infernal woman always made him feel uncomfortable? And why did his right boot squelch? And why did his vest tickle so maddeningly?

Mrs Ledbury closed the front door. She was sorry for the Pier Company – and for the spider.

*   *   *

"But, my dear Jozef, do you really feel it will work?"

In the Polish Embassy underground air-raid shelter in London Charles Turville sat at the head of a long table with, ranged down either side, the small group of Polish exiles who were, at this time, the only free representatives of the defunct Polish State. At the far end sat another Pole who stood out from the rest not just because of his rough shabby clothing – a stark contrast to the formal black suits and braided uniform of the others – but more for his rough peasant features: a deeply lined, dark, strong face dominated by a livid scar above his right eye.

The group had moved to the shelter as soon as Turville had arrived. This was to be a meeting of the utmost secrecy, and in their virtually sealed concrete bunker they knew that their deliberations would be secure from any prying eyes or ears.

Turville, as he did when concentrating his thoughts, methodically began to fill his pipe and the visitor, Josef, taking the hint, brought out a tin of powerfully smelling tobacco and rolled himself an enormous cigarette. The small group, fearing imminent asphyxiation, swung their eyes from one to the other as if at a tennis match.

With thick smoke already swirling around the naked light bulb hanging above them they waited until Jozef had taken an enormous draw on his cigarette. His reply to Turville's question began with a deep throated chuckle, almost a gargle.

"It *has* worked, my friend. For *me* it worked. From prison." He pulled his shoulders back and crashed a fist onto his wide chest. "And they never found me. It is *I* who found *them*."

Again a deep chuckle. "And then I am free."

Turville knew the story; the details were carefully tabulated in his brain. Jozef Raczeck. A life sentence for murder. Committed to Warsaw's impregnable city prison. One night he escaped from his cell. The bars had been sawn through, the small window dismantled. Outside, a sheer drop, forty feet to the ground across which was a constant patrol of guards. He disappeared and

156

wasn't seen again until, with irrefutable evidence proving his innocence, he gave himself up. Despite intensive interrogation he refused to provide a single clue as to how he had escaped.

All this had happened in 1938 and, with his pardon and rehabilitation, he again disappeared, this time into the ranks of the Armia Krajowa who were hastily organising themselves into a disciplined underground resistance movement in readiness for the inevitable conflict with Germany.

And now he was here in this cramped, smoke-filled room which, bearing a close similarity to his erstwhile cell, made him feel quite at home. But not the others. Even Turville was experiencing the effects of the airlessness and moved the proceedings on with some haste. Rough drawings were passed around, questions asked, doubts and fears expressed and through it all Jozef sat puffing at his cigarette and reassuring everyone that what he had successfully done once he could do again. He had the team, he had his contact in Gestapo Headquarters – a fellow resistance fighter – and he knew he could spirit the man known as 'the package' out of the building under the eyes of the guards – and out of Warsaw.

"It is agreed then." This should have been a question, but Turville had no intention of allowing a committee to debate the issue; this, he knew, would lead to no decision being made. His ploy worked; they all nodded and adjourned upstairs for a considerable dose of fresh air – and vodka.

Jozef, who had been plucked from the heart of Nazi-occupied Poland in a small Westland Lysander aircraft at dead of night, would now be delivered back on the end of a parachute, his first duty to train his team to such perfection that nothing could, or would, go wrong in the mission to free Freddy Crisciak from the clutches of the Gestapo.

*   *   *

Back in Flaxton, Norman Jackson – *Over the Garden Wall* – was pleased with himself – on two counts. First he reckoned he was doing a jolly good job tailing Peggy; she and Pat were some thirty yards ahead totally unaware of his presence and, as usual, chattering away oblivious of everything around them.

157

It was half-past five and the girls were on their way to the theatre to rehearse a new sketch. The second reason for Norman's pleasure was his faultless run-through of his act: he knew he was word perfect. The townspeople were growing used to seeing this fair-haired man wandering around muttering to himself and those who hadn't witnessed his stage performances were saddened that such a young, good-looking chap should have been inflicted this way.

The two girls had now turned in through the pier's wrought-iron gates, past the notice that said 'Access only to the Theatre' and were on the narrow walkway between the side of the theatre and the balustrade.

Norman was relieved as they disappeared from view behind the building. He knew that they'd now be entering through the rear stage door and would, of course, be safe once they were inside. He quickened his pace eager for the solitude of the men's dressing room and another run through his lines.

Head down against the strong east wind he pushed out along the pier and into the walkway alongside the theatre – and then suddenly took off into space. He felt himself being propelled at great speed in a vice-like grip, his arms locked to his sides and then being bodily lifted with enormous strength.

The surprise was so total that he put up no resistance whatsoever and being completely off-balance found himself literally sailing through the air, over the balustrade, and down.

Two thoughts struck him during his brief descent to the water: first it was lucky it was a full tide and second, it was less lucky that having been brought up in landlocked Halifax, he'd never learnt how to swim! Then, with a mighty thump or, as he later described it, thoomp, he was in the tumbling waves.

CHAPTER EIGHT

Tuesday, 16th April 1940. *Estimated figures suggest that the Germans lost 50,000 men, 700 planes and nearly a thousand tanks and armoured cars in their invasion of Poland.*

In Britain barrage balloons have become a regular sight over and around towns. One old lady remarks "If those Germans think they can frighten me by sitting up in those balloons all the time, they're very much mistaken!"

In the theatre, up above the pounding waves, Pat and Peggy were on stage rehearsing a new 'charlady' routine. Their prop was a cardboard model of a high explosive bomb! It sat, some three feet high, at a slight angle to the ground with its nose apparently embedded in the centre of the stage. In case there should be any doubt in the minds of the audience as to what this masterpiece was, its creators, Reg Prentice and Bob Bennett, had stencilled BOMBE along the side of it and a large swastika on its tail fins! Pat and Peggy, in cheap outdoor coats, head scarves and carrying shopping baskets, stood each side of it...

PAT	"Before the war the park keeper would never put up with a thing like this in his flowerbed.
PEGGY	Before the war we *had* a park keeper.
PAT	True. I heard Alvar Lidell this morning on the news saying that Mr Churchill wants us to send all our old metal for munitions.
PEGGY	*(kicks bomb)* Kind of Adolf to join in. Perhaps he'll send us his saucepans.
PAT	*(kicks bomb)* My cousin Fred's in bomb disposal.
PEGGY	I thought he was a bomb aimer in the RAF.
PAT	He is. He disposes of them over Germany. Do you think we should tell someone it's here?

PEGGY	Better not. They might think *we* put it in the flower bed.
PAT	But what if it goes off.
PEGGY	Then everyone will know it's here.
PAT	I suppose so. Here, my Alf's joined the Fire Service.
PEGGY	Why? Were they falling apart?"

Rita and Rena, forever sewing up tears in tights, leotards or other over-stretched garments, were sitting in the audience having a good laugh at the new routine. Apart from helping Pat and Peggy it eased their own tension. Would Marvo get it right tonight? If not, all three of them might be out of a job.

Alone in her dressing room Elaine was practising her scales and snatches of the medley of songs she and George would be performing that evening. They'd decide after each show which six – two spots of three each – from their repertoire of twenty or so they would do the next day, so that the orchestra had time to rehearse and she'd have time to din the order into George's brain! After a number of disasters when he'd launched into a selection from, maybe, 'Lilac Time', whilst she and the four doughty players had started into something completely different (at which point he inadvertently would let out a rude swear word), she put the title and order of the chosen songs on a blackboard in the wings which worked provided no one stood in front of it – which they invariably did.

Tonight they had decided, for their second spot, to sing some current favourites – 'Yours,' 'I'll be seeing you' and 'A nightingale sang in Berkeley Square.' She sat at her dressing table, starting to work on her hair and humming snatches from the melodies, feeling very contented.

In the nearby dressing room her partner, George Noble, was *not* humming snatches from their song selection, he was in a far less amiable frame of mind.

"It was a disgraceful joke." He was brushing his tail coat with such force that the elderly material was in danger of disintegrating. "I went to buy a war bond on the way here," (he and Elaine lived frugally and believed in saving *and* helping the war effort), "and Mrs Proctor who was buying some stamps in the Post Office gave me – *me* – a piece of her mind. She'd brought her niece to the show last night and tried to cover the child's ears when Tad told that terrible joke about – you know – five minutes." He was now punishing his dress trousers with the clothes brush. "But she was too late. The child heard everything."

Belvedere put down his nose hair scissors. "Mrs Proctor introduced me to her niece the other day. She's about twenty-five."

He was getting rather tired of George's frenzied wielding of the brush and, rising magisterially, rested a firm hand on the waving arm. His mighty voice reverberated around the room.

"In peace there's nothing so becomes a man as modest stillness and humility. Shakespeare, Henry Five." He sat back and picked up his scissors for the other nostril. He felt he had done his bit.

There was silence, but only for a moment before George resumed the attack on his clothes – and the absent Tad.

"Well, we're not at peace, we're at war – and Elaine agrees with me." He seemed to feel the point had finally been made.

Belvedere sighed, "I..." the sound was so silly that he stopped nose hair snipping for a moment. "I suppose *I* shall have to speak to Tad *again*." It was a heavily modulated speech. "I shall warn him of the powers of the Lord Chamberlain. I shall..."

His next very loud vibrant exhortation was interrupted by the entry of the culprit himself.

"You're early, Tad," George studied his watch. "Or is my watch wrong?" He panicked and started to tear off his clothes.

"Relax, George," Belvedere sighed deeply, "still an hour and a half to curtain-up."

Tad picked up Norman's enormous padded brassiere which had fallen from its hook in the confusion and hurled it at George who deftly caught it and re-hung it amongst Norman's stage clothes.

"Chucked out."

He sat unTadlike, shoulders down, dejected, at his dressing table. The unfamiliar sight was embellished by the splendidly shut black eye.

"Chucked out. By the guards on the gate." He crashed his fist on the table top sending pots and brushes flying. "And *I* supply them with their comforts. Life wouldn't be the same for them – or the town girls – if it wasn't for me." Another crash. "And they pointed their rifles at me and told me the camp is out of bounds to me – *ME*. Orders of the Commandant." A louder crash still. There was nothing left on his dressing table and one of his precious six bulbs went out. "And I get him his piles ointment," they winced, "They're right out of stock in the chemists, but I..."

"Tad Stevens, shut up and come with me." Belvedere rose. Tad was in such a state of shock that he did as he was told and allowed himself to be led to the door.

Belvedere turned. "It is a far, far better thing that I do... Dickens. A Tale of Two Cities."

He propelled Tad into the corridor and followed him out. The door closed.

It was undoubtedly one of the best exits Belvedere had ever played and it had the desired effect on George who sat in silence looking at the closed door. Something was missing. It was eerie. He closed his eyes, screwing them up tightly which he thought might help.

Then he got it; it was the quietness. This room was not known for quietness. No Belvedere humphing, puffing and snuff-snorting, no Tad endlessly prattling and no Norman line muttering. He could account for the first two but where was Norman? He was usually here in plenty of time. Perhaps at last he'd been arrested for suspicious behaviour; murmuring with intent... George chuckled at his witty thought and went back to his violent clothes brushing.

In her office Nell was sitting in her deep armchair with her eyes closed thinking back to yesterday and Peggy's story of her flight from Poland. She realized that she was very tired and could so easily sleep. This uncharacteristic thought disturbed her and she stood up as quickly as she could, automatically moving to the photograph of her beloved Masters on the wall by her desk.

"My darling," she whispered. "It's time to move on. Never, ever, have I felt too tired for the evening's performance. It really is all too much without you. The war. Poor Peg. No holidaymakers. No income. Living on our savings, my love. It won't do. It just won't do."

Not for the first time since her terrible grief after his death Nell's kisses on the photograph were mingled with her tears. She made her way blindly to the chair, dropped into it, and sobbed herself into a doze. The ostrich feather on her hat dutifully drooped in sympathy.

But sleep didn't bring an end to her thoughts. A dream carried her into retirement to her sister's home in Scotland. Back to her roots, to where she was born...

She was awakened violently by the tinny clanging of the telephone bell. At first she couldn't place the sound. Why wasn't her sister answering it? Then her surroundings fell into shape. Her sister's pretty cottage in the Scottish Highlands became her office in Flaxton's Pier Theatre. Later, thinking back on this moment that was to become pivotal in her life, she would recognise that the realization of fact over dream had created a feeling of deep disappointment.

"Flaxton four five seven." Her voice, uncharacteristically low and flat, deceived the caller for a moment.

"Nell Masters?" The query, friendly but booming, invaded her ear. "Nell, my dear. This is Winifred Ledbury here..."

The telephone call from the Vice-Chairman of Flaxton-on-Sea Town Council knocked out of her whatever stuffing Nell had left at this low ebb in her life. She replaced the hand-set and wearily called in Vi. It was easily done. One bang on the partition wall and she was in before Nell was sitting back at her desk.

Vi was excited. "Some really good news, Nell love. Word's got around via the Chronicle about Tad's – ahem – brave deed, laying out those three as yet – ahem – unknown assailants. People are coming to cheer him on tonight. Evidently the shopkeepers have heard no other chit-chat all day. And the refugee camp is laying on another truck. The rumour's spread there through – ahem – someone who came to the gate that the three are probably German spies. We know what the refugees think of them."

Vi's throat clearings were intended to indicate a message to Nell regarding the authenticity of these statements many of which she was sure were dubious bearing in mind that Tad was involved. But at this time it was all wasted effort.

"We're closing." Nell's voice was dull, her face cupped in her hands. "Shut down. Finished. The Council are going to vote tonight not to renew our lease."

It took Vi, in her high spirits, a moment to take this in.

"Closing? They can't. Why? We always pay the rent on time. We owe them nothing." Vi's pride at her book-keeping took precedence over everything else. "Who says?"

Nell, lifted her face, rubbed her eyes vigorously and put on her glasses letting out a strange hissing sound through her teeth. Vi knew the signs well: her Nell was ready for a fight.

She looked up at Vi and said briskly, "Councillor Ledbury. She's just telephoned me. She's in a state about it herself but she can't see what she can do. Hers is the minority party now. She'll verbally clout them, but the votes will mean the Council's motion, proposed by their idiot Chairman Edward Bradley, is adopted."

She looked at her calendar. The picture with it was of a pretty Highland scene and it caused a tiny frisson of excitement to shudder through her which she would remember later.

"We'll soon be going into May. We have until the end of that month. Then we're out."

There was a knock on the door.

"Half an hour, Nell." Don was alerting the troupe ready for curtain-up.

"Say nothing for the time being, Vi, except that I want a meeting of all the staff – troupe and back-stage – tomorrow morning at…," she thought, "nine sharp. I want to get to them before they hear it from elsewhere."

She went to the door and stood, bolt upright. This was the old Nell, a fighter who had taken up, and accepted the challenge handed to her by her dear husband, Masters. The bull-dog spirit.

Her sharp glinting eyes were fixed on Vi. "If we have to go…," she declaimed, "We'll go with a bung."

On that belligerent note she swept out.

*

It was a very young policeman on patrol along the promenade who put in hand the rescuing of Norman. His attention was drawn (as his written report phrased it) to a group of young ladies waving and shouting words of endearment (it looked good in print) apparently at the wooden supports of the pier.

Upon closer inspection (his Sergeant would be pleased with this) he ascertained that their behaviour was directed towards a person (he couldn't resist adding 'or persons' even though he could plainly see it was a single body) waving at them.

Upon even closer inspection he identified the waver to be a male in his thirties (or twenties or forties; he wasn't very good yet with ages) and immediately alerted the coastguards, local Defence Volunteers, Fire Brigade, Ambulance Service, Military Garrison Command and finally his Police Station.

First on the scene was the WVS tea wagon! It was a pity that he hadn't alerted his Police Station before all the others; it would have saved them all from turning up, but he'd never used a Police telephone box before and he wasn't sure how they worked.

No-one in the theatre was aware of the drama being enacted beneath them. Those in charge of the operation assumed the theatre would be empty until the show started.

The pier was surrounded by armed troops and the police cordoned off the area as most of Flaxton descended upon the scene. The Fire Brigade lowered a ladder from the promenade to the beach (alongside the steps but in the drama of it all they hadn't noticed them), stretchers were deployed, a Bomb Disposal Unit, thoughtfully alerted by the Garrison Orderly Officer, plotted a mine-free path to the nearest support not under water and they all prepared for action. Safety catches were released and rifles cocked. If this was a spy or a shot-down Luftwaffe pilot his war was well-and-truly over.

At this moment a small coast-guard motor boat phut-phutted into view and plucked Norman from his perch. It then disappeared at speed towards the lifeboat slipway at the southern end of the town.

The population cheered, covering the curses of the military and civilian emergency services who retired to the WVS tea wagon for a free cuppa and a thick dripping sandwich.

It had certainly been a dramatic episode and, they assured each other, all the time spent in training had been well and truly vindicated.

*

Norman, having been home to change – and resisting his landlady's efforts to send him to bed with a glass of hot milk – had arrived at the theatre during the first half of the show and received a severe wigging from Nell, but as soon as she heard his story she gave him a kiss on the cheek, a nip of her precious whisky as an 'up-me-pick' and summoned Belvedere to look after him. She felt that Norman was appearing to be in somewhat of a daze...

The show was now well into its second half. It was ironic that the very night when, if they had known the shattering news about the impending closure, they would have been at their lowest, the troupe was actually in the highest spirits. There was nothing more stimulating to actors than a good sized 'house' showing their appreciation in the right places. Tonight the auditorium was over three-quarters full and, of particular satisfaction to Nell, a fair majority of them were townspeople.

She, having recovered from her despondency, was at her sharpest. All her cunning learned from years 'winning' her audiences was in full play. She changed the order of the acts, putting Tad on directly after the opening ensemble. The rest of the troupe were somewhat miffed by this but quickly realized Nell's astuteness because Tad was, for whatever doubtful reasons, the hero of the hour.

Rising, as ever, to the occasion he was on his finest form and best behaviour. He'd even written a monologue especially for the occasion. In four verses he had the audience in the palm of his hand. Coming down to the footlights he waited for silence and then embarked on the terrible doggerel in a voice quivering with mock emotion...

> "Hitler needs to watch himself
> The stupid little clown.
> He sends his spies to Flaxton
> To destroy our lovely town.
> But he doesn't know that Flaxton folk
> Are tough, resourceful, bold.
> And if we see his Nazi thugs
> We'll knock 'em out. Stone cold."

Belvedere fretted in the wings. How could he follow this rubbish with his renderings of the Bard? And why did they enjoy it so much? By the end of the fourth verse, all finishing with the same last line, the audience was ecstatic; some actually stood to applaud Tad. If he had been anyone else he would have been quite overwhelmed, but not he. With a deprecating wave he launched into his patter.

In the wings the rest of the troupe – even their resident tragedian – applauded him on. They now saw how astute Nell had been. Even Peggy, who painfully knew where the black eye had come from, had a wry smile. You had to give it to Tad, she mused, if he fell into a pig sty he'd come out smelling of roses!

After that start the show really couldn't fail. George remembered to sing the right songs and the *Welsh Nightingales* brought many a tear to many an eye as, when invited, the audience joined in the choruses. Even the soldiery, for once correctly sensing the mood, refrained from substituting rude words to the songs!

Belvedere, with a point to make, performed mightily. He had decided that his – others referred to it as Shakespeare's – Agincourt speech from 'Henry Five', as classical actors liked to call it, would be most appropriate and, dressed in full stage armour over his kingly robes (all hired hastily from the Amateur Dramatic Society) he bellowed it at the marvelling audience. Larry, Donald and Johnny would, he was sure, have been proud of him.

And Marvo got it right. His grunts, helped by Rita's unseen prompting to Reg and Bob, caused Rena to rise magically – and horizontally – towards the roof. The smoke worked, the lighting worked; it was illusion at its very best.

Then Pat and Peggy delighted the audience with their repartee. The curtains opened on the dummy bomb set in the centre of the darkened stage lit directly from above by a solitary blue light. In the smoky atmosphere the beam was clearly visible, widening down to the sinister prop which looked so eerie and menacing that the audience gasped. On cue Pat and Peggy strolled on from either side in old mackintoshes and headscarves and launched into their patter.

Norman was next. When the curtains opened the only prop was his garden wall. He more or less hobbled on – looking terrible, not only because of his recent ordeal but also due to the stage costume he was wearing. For his *"Over the Garden Wall"* act he was the worst possible female neighbour anybody could be unfortunate enough to have. His frock stretched tautly over the enormous padded brassière, his stockings were doubly wrinkled, his wig of unruly auburn hair was covered by a headscarf. Throughout the act he occasionally brought out a filthy hanky and loudly blew his nose. He had, of course, been muttering his lines, very fast, in the wings. Now, once the initial laughter had died down, he leant his massive bosom on the wall, and was off in his slow, north country voice...

"She's a funny woman next door. Have you met her?
She's so big. Muscles here, here – and even here...
Well, she says they're muscles. I have me doubts...
Muscles are meant to *help* you walk; not flap along behind you.
I said, 'You ought to get a bike.' She said, 'I'm on one.'
You'd never know...
Hello luv. Just putting out the washing? They're big.
Reminds me, did you see that barrage balloon yesterday?
Enough material on that to go round you twice...
And you, luv. And you."

Norman went on in an inwardly serene state through his act and the audience loved it. He was word perfect. Now, for the first time, he knew that his father in Halifax would be proud of him; he'd done something without – indeed against – parental push and he'd made it work. Perhaps he needed a soaking every day!

The orchestra saw him off with a suitably rousing ditty and the audience rose to him. With one last hitch of his bosom, he left the stage waving his hanky at them all. Many of them had neighbours just like Norman's awful woman, others, not realizing it, *were* that awful woman and, as happens in life, the latter group laughed the loudest!

The show neared its end with another spot from Tad whilst the rest of the troupe gathered in the wings for the finale.

Nell watched it all in a strangely detached frame of mind. From the start the show had become a background echo to her.

Something, from the time of that telephone call, had readjusted itself in her brain. Where there had been turmoil, now there was peace. She now knew precisely the route she had to take and this evening had, in an obtuse sort of way, reassured her that this present way of life should end. She would, of course, see that Peggy was alright but her guiding hand was not needed anymore as far as these talented people were concerned; they were now ready to fly the nest. Everything she could teach them regarding the theatre had been taught and absorbed in their totally differing ways and they all knew their individual strengths at winning and holding an audience.

Nell was deeply satisfied. She saw, again, in her mind the calendar picture of the Scottish Highlands, *her* Highlands, and linked it to the dream she'd had that afternoon of her sister's cottage in its quiet, peaceful village. She needed to be there, Masters would want it. She would be able to emerge from his shadow and *share* the last part of her life with him. And now *she would do it...*

She clicked her mind back to the present. Everyone was now packing onto the stage for the finale. She would just have time to adjust her splendid evening frock, tidy her hair and squirt on a bit more scent. She strode purposefully back to her office. Nell Masters wouldn't go without a fight; the troupe deserved all her efforts. The next six weeks would be a busy and exciting climax to her theatrical life as she launched her talented troupe into the outside world.

Even *she* couldn't envisage how shortened, as well as busy and exciting, that climax would be...

With the show over for another night Peggy sat in her dressing room in her petticoat feeling absolutely exhausted. The strain of the stage act on top of her desperate fear for Freddy's life and the responsibility of the note-books was, she felt, asking too much of her.

She looked at herself in the mirror as she rubbed on cleansing cream and saw an older, sadder face emerging from the stage make-up and it made her angry. She hadn't started out ahead of the rest of the world in strength and stamina, bravery and cunning; she was just an ordinary girl who had decided to try her luck on the stage. After her parents' death no further dramas had rocked her life until that wonderful moment when she had met her beloved Freddy. And then life only got better and better until, she sighed, until…

This was stupid. She shook herself out of her confusing moods which lurched unpredictably from good to bad and back again. It was unusual to have the dressing room to herself and she was pleased with the rare chance of being alone for a while. They were all so kind, so very kind. Since the gathering at Nell's house and her account of the escape from Poland, the whole Theatre Company had hardly left her alone for a moment. She still couldn't decide if she'd done the right thing in telling her story but it certainly had reduced the pressure considerably. She hoped Freddy would have – would – approve. She *must* stop talking of him in the past tense…

It was rather sweet, but also a darned nuisance, that the men seemed to follow her everywhere! First one, then another, then another. There was a time when she would have found this very flattering but there were limits. She'd have a word tomorrow with Belvedere who seemed to be in charge.

It was odd. She was wiping her face on her make-up towel and something, just something, was wrong but she couldn't work out what it was. She felt her routine was disturbed and it annoyed her.

The thought was broken by Pat charging into the room. She was still in her finale sailor's costume and started tearing it off as she chattered excitedly.

"We've been listening to Bill's wireless set. I like that Sandy McPherson on his theatre organ. Really soothing. Oh Peg really, you are messy."

She hung up her skirt and blouse with the blue square collar.

"He's just played a selection from 'Lilac Time'. We were all singing along trying to follow Elaine and George – oh, what is my handbag doing over there? Did you need something? I'm sure I'd fastened my case. Peg, what are you looking for?"

All this was said at great speed and now, in her underwear with her hands on her hips, she was standing in the centre of the room.

Peggy, totally bemused, was looking for her frock which she knew she had hung on its hanger on its usual hook. Now she saw it lying in a crumpled heap on the floor. Those girls, Rita and Rena! Pat and Peggy didn't mind their intrusion into their dressing room – all the girls used each other's clothes and make-up as one big communal happy family – but it would be kind to rummage tidily for what they needed to borrow rather than leave the room like this.

Never mind, all theatre people were forever in a frenzied rush and Pat and Peggy knew that they tended to do exactly the same. None-the-less, they'd give those two young rascals a piece of their collective minds tomorrow…

The troupe left the theatre in a rowdy, elated mood. Sometimes, just sometimes this extraordinary profession paid back all the toil and heartache it injected into so much of an actor's life. These were heady moments. Tonight, as Rena had said excitedly, feverishly polishing her glasses, "it has fizzed for everyone."

The cheerful atmosphere carried them to their immediate destinations. Belvedere, George and Norman were set for their reserved table at the Pier Head Tavern, Tad would sample more of Pru's delights in The Anchor snug and then her bed and Rita and Rena were off to the Cottage Café where two lucky and, hopefully, well brought-up airmen were waiting. Marvo went goodness knows where and Elaine and George hurried home to boiled eggs and an early night.

Nell and Vi wended their way up the steep steps to 34 Clarence Road, the two of them chattering rather breathlessly about Pat and Peggy.

'Quite their old selves', mused Nell. Could it be that Peggy's mind was, just for the moment, free of the fear for Freddy's safety? And Nell herself was calm; happy for the two of them, and all the cast. Just for a moment she felt totally detached from all the dramas that were so much a part of running a theatre company in these impossible times.

Whilst Vi made the two of them Horlicks in the kitchen Nell went into the front room, put off the lights and pulled back the blackout curtains. She looked out and sighed.

"I can't get used to not seeing any lights. And no stars." She shivered and her voice was a whisper. "If I can see a star I know that Masters is watching over me."

Wearily Pat and Peggy climbed the stairs to the flat above the Post Office. Alice was dozing at her window in the first floor sitting room, a comfortable person in her comfortable home. Harriet, her tabby cat, was lying asleep on her lap and Mountjoy, the black labrador, was at her feet alternately snoring, sighing and doing an occasional bit of noisy washing. Now he joyfully bounded up as the two of them came in to say goodnight. The cat arched its back but took little notice of the upheaval.

After a quick word about the show – Alice always wanted to know because she liked and admired the spirit and determination of her friend Nell and was possessively proud of the two girls' performances – they all went off to bed.

They'd only just reached their rooms when Pat and Alice were frozen by a frightened scream from Peggy. They rushed to her bedroom and found her standing with her hands clasped to her head.

The room was devastated. The furniture had been pulled from the walls, the contents of drawers, wardrobe, suitcases, boxes – everything that might hold anything – were strewn around the floor. Mattress and pillows were slashed and the stuffing, like snow-drifts, was mixed with the jumble of broken and torn objects.

Nothing had been left untouched by the frenzied searching of an unknown intruder.

CHAPTER NINE

Mid April 1940. The Germans are experiencing stiff resistance in Norway. A German Offensive in the West is expected soon.

In England most children evacuees have returned to London from the country.

That mild April night, before the developing drama enveloped them all, was a peaceful one for the artistes of the Pier Theatre Company except, of course, for Pat and Peggy. Poor Peggy, already suffering more than most, hardly slept at all. Pat was all for bringing in the police straight away but her friend was adamant: the door to her room would be locked until they both had more strength to face the chaos tomorrow and tonight she'd sleep on the spare bed in Pat's room. As it turned out it wasn't surprising that neither of them really slept at all.

Rita and Rena, in their twin-bedded room in Nell's house slept very peacefully. The act with Marvo had gone well, the two airmen had taken them to the cinema – each, of course, paying for their own ticket – to see George Formby in 'Let George do it', then tea and buns in the café before kisses pecked on blushing cheeks outside the house and firm separation caused by the front door being opened at exactly the right moment by Vi.

At the Anchor pub the evening ended with the Landlord performing the time-honoured ritual of flicking the lights and calling 'time'. Tad had experienced more gentle ministrations from Pru on his still multi-coloured eye – and thereby more glimpses of the magnificent chasm – and whilst she cleared up he'd had time to negotiate a shady deal or two before the two of them went back to Pru's lodgings, where he combined a lustful night with making plans for the re-establishment of trading with the refugee camp. Tad liked to keep his mind occupied even when his body was on auto-pilot.

In normal circumstances Norman would go to his lodgings after his session in the Pier Head and creep into the house. His landlady, Miss Reed, was a small dynamo. She was a spinster and treated him like the son she'd never had, cooking, washing, ironing, darning and dosing him with castor oil whenever she felt he looked a bit bilious – which was often.

Norman couldn't be happier. After all, he was not forty yet and still felt very insecure – particularly away from Halifax. She worried when he was out late and being led astray by the awful, loud elderly gentleman and his Welsh friend. That meant she worried most nights. The only thing that really aggravated her was the sound of him mumbling his stage lines, on and on, from the moment he came in with a cheery north country "Hello, Miss Reed. It's only me," until, at last, he fell into a deep sleep.

She would lie in her bed, pressing her head into the pillow, stuffing her ears with cotton wool, humming tunelessly to herself, even wrapping a scarf round her eyes and ears but, in the distance, the mumbling would always be there. She often scolded him, but he didn't know he did it. Not to worry, she loved him as much as any mother would, so that was alright.

But tonight things hadn't been alright, not alright at all. Norman was in a very confused state after the show. The elation at his splendid performance on stage had been injected with a dose of ice-cold fear as the reality of his near-death plunge, propelled by someone who obviously wanted to murder him, seeped into his nervous system.

He had just been mastering this lethal mix of emotions and was leaving the theatre with Belvedere and George for a restorative session in the Pier Head Tavern when the Press, in the shape of Vernon Rogers, editor (and every-kind-of-reporter) of the Flaxton Chronicle waylaid him.

He was already flustered by a row in the dressing-room caused, of course, by Tad who, with his usual intention of teasing people into a state of fury, had suggested that anyone who had seen Norman's act in the previous week should be suspected of his attempted murder! Now this news-hound was barking at his heels looking for the lead story in the next day's edition.

Belvedere had taken control.

"Ill news hath wings and with the wind doth blow" he had bellowed at the editor, shouting over his shoulder, "Michael Drayton, The Barron's Wars."

"I wish I'd had wings" muttered Norman.

Whilst stopping to jot all this down in the howling wind and rain that swirled around them, Vernon Rogers looked up and saw a woman advance on Norman who allowed himself to be led away from the group into the darkness. Miss Reed had come to claim her own. Castor oil awaited!

But Vernon Rogers had not reached the dizzy heights of editor for nothing. He caught up with Belvedere and George and led them into the saloon bar where he bought a round of three double whiskies and it was in that smoky, airless atmosphere during the next half hour that the seeds of a highly dramatic 'front page spread' were sown.

Belvedere, much later that night, managed as usual to infuriate his landlady. Mrs Florence Chumley had great affection for him and he always treated her like a Duchess with old world charm. Whereas Mr Chumley referred to her invariably as "Floss" or "Ducks", our tragedian made much of the title "Dear Lady".

Mrs Chumley preferred to have Belvedere rather than Mr Chumley around her except when he returned from 'The Pier Head' at around eleven-thirty. It was then that he gargled mightily in the bathroom, just one thin wall away from her bed headboard, and other mighty noises followed as he went to his room humming an operatic aria. The sound was of the Flying Scotsman railway train passing through a station. Now fully awake she'd have to try all over again to shut out her husband's snoring and get to sleep.

As usual there wasn't much to say about George and Elaine's night. Until he got back from The Pier Head Tavern Elaine listened to the radio, darned socks and sewing-machined together odds and ends of material into sparkling frocks, her tiny feet twinkling away on the pedals. As she prepared a light meal she sang. Practice, as the *Welsh Nightingales* were forever infuriatingly exhorting their fellow artistes, makes perfect.

The only charge that could be laid against the two of them was that they were sensible and worthy. They were in bed before midnight and, unless Hitler intervened, they'd sleep deeply until the clockwork alarm went off at 7 a.m.

Marvo, it was assumed, slept peacefully in the refugee camp, but no one would know if he did or didn't. He lived in his own very private world. Nell had been exasperated with him for refusing to tell her, via his notepad, anything about his past life; he obviously didn't want to be reminded of it. It was as much a mystery as the conjuring tricks in his stage act.

The British Secret Service, charged with protecting this disparate group of players, was apparently off duty that night. Charles Turville slept soundly in his Albany Chambers in London, but of Ludovic Henschel there was no sign. His bunk in the camp was empty.

But someone went to bed long after Flaxton had settled down for the night. From the darkness of the Theatre, inaudible to passers-by, came the dit-dot-dit of Morse code.

*　　*　　*

In Warsaw's Bristol Hotel Freddy slept fitfully. It was the uncertainty of what lay ahead that sapped all this energy and confused his brain. The Gestapo were no fools. The longer he was kept this way the more vulnerable he would become; they were experts at this new form of psychological torture and knew better than most that the way into Freddy's brain was to disorientate him and then re-programme him to do their bidding. Cunning, not force.

And it was working; he was getting more fearful by the minute. Today he'd been left alone to his meaningless equations but he knew that the scribbled pages wouldn't take much effort from a physicist to be seen for what they were. Then what?

And then there were the notebooks. Everything was in them. They mustn't find them. Never. Freddy tossed and turned, knowing that all the time every sound was being monitored. What if he talked in his sleep? Did he? Only Peg would know that. And now off his brain went down the most terrible of all memory lanes; his darling Peggy. Peggy! He wanted to call out her name; just to say it out loud would be some form of closeness, but of course he couldn't. The eavesdropper must be fed nothing other than his deliberate deceptions. Peggy – and his mother? Where were they? Were they safe? Were they even alive? Restlessly he turned over again.

Twice he'd asked the civilian orderly, when he'd brought in his lunch and supper, "what time is it?" He had held his breath, desperate to hear the month given as the answer, the code which would mean this was the friend that would, by a miracle, engineer his escape. But each time the orderly had looked at the clock on his bedside table and peevishly repeated the time to him, and his spirits had sunk to new depths.

The sheer terror and uncertainty of it all exhausted him and mercifully he fell into a troubled sleep.

Next door the eavesdropper noted in his log that the prisoner Crisciak was restless. This was good. Lack of deep sleep would quicken the process.

*   *   *

Back in Flaxton another player in the developing drama was passing a poor night. For Councillor Edward Bradley things had not gone according to plan and he was not pleased. He kicked himself for having blurted out to that blasted Winifred Ledbury his decision to chuck out the Theatre Company.

He blamed it all on the dog. When he had got home his wife Phyllis had complained about his smelly feet. As she often did so he took no notice until, later, he changed from his coarse postman's outfit into his natty 'Chairman of the Council' suiting.

It was better not to describe the condition of his right boot, sock and foot. The first two he handed by thumb and forefinger to his protesting wife. He would have had her wash his foot as well but, in truth, there were occasions when she actually frightened him by her vehemence and this was just such a time. So he took himself to the bathroom, ricked his back lifting the offending, offended and offensive foot into the washbasin and did what he could to remove the, by now, putrefying dog's urine from between his toes. After all that the discovery of an enormous and now very dead spider in his underpants was but a trifling inconvenience.

But none of this, cataclysmic though it was, was the cause of Councillor Edward's poor night. Mrs Ledbury had been busy since his visit to her. She had rallied her own party forces but, more astutely, had informed three of the ruling party councillors, all of whom had a great admiration for Nell and the therapeutic work the troupe was doing, of their Leader's plans. It helped that none of them liked Councillor Edward but, in all fairness, few people did. The result was a tied vote and a motion to send a delegation to the theatre where, unencumbered by a noisy audience, they could ascertain the quality and probity of the show and report back to the members of the Council at its next meeting in a week's time. This was carried by a large majority and a very bad tempered Chairman stumped out of the meeting showing, even for him, a remarkable quantity of ill grace.

*

The next morning Nell made her way down the hill to the theatre, unusually early, for the nine o'clock meeting. She called at the Post Office on the way to say good morning to her dear friend Alice Banbury, buy her local paper, and hear the latest news.

How the Post Mistress knew so much overnight detail so early in the morning after only a quick scan of the Chronicle was a mystery but she was never wrong.

First they talked about Norman's drama which covered the front page. The work Belvedere and George had done in the saloon bar the previous evening had created a story of such valour and heroism that Vernon Rogers's prose resembled a citation for the George Cross!

Alice Banbury had no difficulty in reading between the lines but on this occasion she got it wrong.

"I reckon the wind blew him over", she said to Nell, "There's nothing of him" and then, with pursed lips, added after a pause "when he's dressed like a man." Alice did not approve of men pretending to be women – particularly ugly women – whether on stage or, for that matter, anywhere.

Nell didn't hear her. She was reading an item on page two which caused her considerable satisfaction. It was a report on the previous evening's Council vote regarding the future of the Pier Theatre Company. Nell was naturally delighted, but it wouldn't change her decision to retire and return to Scotland although it would, she felt, be much better if she could go on her own terms rather than be pushed.

All this occupied her mind as, having exchanged the usual cheery waves with the gun crew at the pier end, she made her way by the stage door into her office.

Vi was already there. She had left the house even earlier than Nell to meet Don at the theatre and to get things ready for the meeting. Nell had decided that she wanted everyone on stage rather than, when she was dealing with show matters, having them looking up at her from the stalls. This was to be – had to be – a very different sort of meeting. Vi and Don arranged chairs in a wide semi-circle facing up-stage. Nell, with Vi beside her, would sit in the centre of the rear wall. She had planned to have the tabs closed but decided when she reached the theatre that it would be too claustrophobic so they were open. Bill had put the necessary lights on, Reg had put the necessary kettle on and Nell was in her office receiving news from Vi of two early morning telephone calls that had seriously confused her.

"No sooner had I put the telephone down than there it was, ringing again. That's more calls before nine o'clock than we usually get in a day! What makes them think we're here before nine when we work through the evening?"

Vi was at full steam ahead now. "I told them we weren't usually here and all they could say was, 'well you are now'."

Nell would actually like to have known what the calls were about. She tried to soothe Vi.

"Well you were, love, weren't you? They will have known that you were here because you were talking to them." She paused. "Do you see?"

Vi was still very worked up. "Well, I know I was but I was trying to tell them I might not have been, and usually wouldn't have been."

Nell couldn't help looking at that photograph of the Highlands. Perhaps all this was getting a bit too much for Vi as well. She decided on a new tack.

"Who was calling us, Vi dear?"

Vi consulted the back of an envelope which contained scribbles of bits of the two conversations. It was all she could lay her hands on when the telephone bell had made her jump out of her skin.

"They got me very confused."

So it would seem – but Nell was glad she had kept that observation to herself.

"They were shouting at me. I called one of them a bully. I said, whose side are you on, anyway? That set him back, I can tell you. He didn't like that."

Nell fixed Vi with a look normally reserved for Tad. This was all getting too much – and it was nearly nine o'clock.

"Set *who* back, dear?"

It was said quietly, but Vi knew the signs and pulled herself together.

"Didn't I say, Nell?" More patience was required.

"No, Vi. Not yet. But you're going to now, aren't you dear?"

"ENSA." Then she added, to provide more weight to this brief statement, "Entertainment National Service Association."

"Yes dear," sighed Nell, "I do know what it stands for. What about them?"

Vi was surprised that Nell didn't understand. Perhaps she hadn't told her yet.

"They're coming. Here." Vi was frantically trying to decipher her scribbles. "They can only manage this Thursday, the second of May, at 10 a.m. They say." she read in a prissy voice, "they wish to evaluate our show. They wish to see a cross-section of our acts. Two only, because their time is limited."

Nell looked at the calendar under the Highland picture.

"Cheeky devils. Masters would soon sort them out. Thursday, you say. The day after tomorrow. The troupe won't like it. Mind you, I doubt if they'd be sent to France; it would be a series of draughty halls and sheds around Britain. They're better off here..."

Vi looked up from her envelope, "In *this* draughty hall." She regretted it as she said it but Nell laughed and went on.

"There are plenty of troops – and the refugees – to entertain here. They're doing their bit."

Vi went to the door. "I'd better go and see that everyone's assembled."

Nell shouted after her, "The other telephone call, dear. Who was that?"

Vi was confused again. She consulted the envelope.

"Ah, yes, of course. Mr Griggs from the Council. They want to see the troupe at work. Two of them are coming on…" she turned the envelope this way and that "Thursday, midday." She left for the stage.

Nell sat back and closed her eyes. There it was again. The soft green hills. Heather. Sheep. The lowing of cattle. Masters leaning on a gate with her. Afternoon teatime, homemade cakes and her sister pouring tea from her bone china pot into the delicate bone china cups. She opened her eyes, checked her fob watch – nine sharp – and stood up.

"Thursday morning," she informed the photograph of her dear husband, "both sets of requisitors. Oh Masters, come and sort this out, my dear old boy. And on top of everything else."

She took a deep, wheezy, breath and made her way to the stage.

*

George and Norman were on 'Peggy Patrol' that morning. Belvedere had decided that from now on they would work in pairs. Norman had insisted that he should go straight back 'on duty' so as to keep his nerve. He was slightly flummoxed – though flattered – at the pats and thumps on his back from passers-by accompanied by "Well done," "That's the spirit," "Damn good show," and so on. He knew that his stage performance last night had been good, but wasn't all this going a trifle far?

Now the two of them trailed along behind Pat and Peggy as they walked from the Post Office flat to the theatre. Peggy, they noted, seemed very distressed. Whilst the two girls went into the ironmongers the men paused several shops away and pretended to look into the window. It took them a few moments to realize that they were staring at a display of lingerie! Greatly embarrassed they turned away and studied the empty sky until the girls reappeared. They would report to Belvedere that all was well.

As they walked on to the theatre the two girls were discussing the ransacking of Peggy's room. A large fat policeman had 'attended the scene' and, after puffing and blowing up the two steep flights of stairs from the street front door, had surveyed the mess with what he hoped looked like a professional eye – he was rarely let out of the station – and declared that it looked just like his daughter's bedroom.

His chuckle was cut off in mid-flight by the look the girls gave him. He checked the window and expertly noted that no panes of glass were broken nor locks forced.

On being assured by Peggy that nothing had been stolen he gave her a long stare, and remarked that the entire police force was, at this time, working out ways to stop Hitler invading the town.

He put away his rarely-used notebook which he had got out with much ceremony and trudged carefully back down to street level. Noting that the front door had not been forced he suggested that it was probably 'an inside job'.

Pat, now heavily exasperated, suggested he question the dog and the cat, a joke totally lost on the constable who, having told them to change the lock, left shaking his large head. It didn't strike him that someone expert in such matters may have entered without a key.

The girls reported all this to Alice Banbury in the Post Office. Mountjoy peered at them with his head on one side, a sign that he was giving his full attention, and seemed to suggest that, much as he would like to be in two places at the same time, his place was behind the counter with his mistress to repel armed robbers. On their way along the High Street they commissioned Mr Best, the ironmonger, to fit new locks to the front door that morning.

Before they reached the theatre entrance there was a question Pat just *had* to ask Peggy. She knew that it was none of her business but she had to know.

"What about the notebooks, Peg?"

Peggy patted her arm. "They weren't there, love, thank the Lord. They're quite safe."

It was agreed that nothing would be said to anyone at this stage. Let Nell get her important meeting out of the way first.

Going in through the foyer Pat suddenly stopped. Peggy, just behind, bumped into her.

"Pat dear, could you make some signal or other when you stop?" Pat took no notice. She turned, whispering. "Our dressing room yesterday evening," her voice was urgent. "Things in different places. I think someone had been in there, searching. Like your bedroom."

Peggy's face crumpled and the tears flowed.

"Oh Pat, love, what am I to do?"

George and Norman followed the girls in through the theatre entrance and made their way, via the stage, to their dressing-room not knowing that they too, had been followed. A few moments later Ludovic Henschel entered the foyer and drifted silently past the 'No Entry' sign and up the dusty, dark stairs to the dress circle.

For some time now the cast had been arriving at the theatre in every sort of mood. Bob Bennett had been sent by Don to unlock the main doors in the foyer because the gun crew, evidently having come to some secret non-aggression pact with Hitler, had disarmed the air and sea defence of Flaxton from the enemy occupied east by dismantling the Bofors gun!

It lay in dozens of parts all over the outward end of the pier totally blocking the theatre's rear stage door. The sergeant in charge stood there scratching his head wondering how on earth they'd manage to reassemble it and how many parts would be left over when they had!

He was grateful to Reg Prentice, who had been in the Royal Artillery in the last war and knew all about guns, for promising that as soon as Nell released him he'd nip out and help them to put it together again; he'd soon get to grips with a Bofors rapid-firing dual-purpose forty millimetre job. Until then the troop of gunners would thoroughly enjoy themselves in the warm sunshine covering everything in oil and rubbing it off with rags made from every type of old garment – some unmentionable – kindly given to them by the WVS from their store of donated, but too unpleasant to re-allocate, clothes.

Due to the early hour, Belvedere was in a bad enough mood even before he found his way past the theatre to the rear stage door blocked by a roughly worded 'Use Front Door' sign resting haphazardly on an old chair. How would Larry – or Johnny – or dear Donald react to such a brusque, untidy message directed at *them*? He strode back to the front entrance, banged in through the doors, clumped through the auditorium and crashed onto a chair.

"I am not in the habit of being summoned to the theatre at this unearthly hour in the morning. I remember dear Donald saying…"

"What's up cocks?" Tad had bustled in wearing his very loud sports jacket and yellow flannel trousers and carrying his ever-present suitcase. His black eye was now covered, to give more effect, with an eye patch.

"Can't stay long. I've got silk undies and stockings to flog at the camp." He licked his fingers. "Know what I mean?"

He flopped down next to Belvedere, who lowered the Times newspaper he was about to read and moved up a space thereby creating an empty chair between himself and Tad who, without thinking, moved up into the empty chair. Belvedere, as he usually did with anything relating to Tad, despaired.

Rita and Rena, already in place, sat meekly in identical frocks and cardigans mending their leotards and sequinned tights which were finding the strain of Marvo's illusions almost too much for their delicate stitching. Rita looked up.

"I thought you weren't allowed inside the camp, Tad. That's what Vi told us."

Rena also looked up. "She did."

The two girls liked to be in agreement.

"Sorted it." Tad opened his case to do a little stock-taking. "Now I'm a hero having rid the British Empire of three spies, they can't do enough for me. I was there at eight this morning. Welcomed with open arms." He was counting pairs of frilly white knickers. "Took a lot of orders too. I'll have to find another supplier for these little jobs. *My* supplier's been called up. Bloomin' cheek." He licked his fingers. "Know what I mean? Pair each, girls? Free fitting. Special price to you. Two and a tanner." He held up two pairs for their inspection.

"They were two and threepence last week," said Rita doubtfully.

"Ah," quick as a flash. "That was last week."

The girls, in perfect unison, looked at each, blushed and shook their heads. Two shillings and sixpence was a large slice of their weekly wage packet.

"Dear Lord preserve us." Belvedere had heard about all he could take.

George and Elaine swept into the auditorium. They moved rather as if they were taking part in a ballroom dancing contest, George swirling Elaine before and around him.

Belvedere again lowered his newspaper and acknowledged George.

"Ah, the great Caruso." He stood to help Elaine to a chair.

Tad nudged him, "And his Girl Friday."

They all groaned.

"What's the matter? Robinson Crusoe and..."

Further embarrassment was prevented by the sight of Norman coming onto the stage from the rear in his usual day clothes, but also wearing, outside his sweater, his enormous padded bra.

"I can't stay long." His northern accent was, as ever, mournful. "I'm having trouble with my boosoms. They're lop-sided." He sat punching the left bra cup which did it no good at all.

Elaine winced at the blows. "Take that off, Norman pet." Her Welsh was husky this morning. "You're making us girls feel inadequate and George agrees with me."

Norman advanced on Belvedere who, looking up, saw this grotesque apparition bending towards him. He pulled back as far as the chair would allow him. Norman nodded violently, gave a huge wink and a thumbs up. Then he went and sat down, removing the bra. Elaine, watching this strange behaviour, assumed that it was probably a Halifax custom and hoped she would never be on the receiving end of it.

Pat and Peggy now arrived from back-stage and it was immediately clear to everyone, except Tad of course, that Peggy had been crying and seemed very unhappy.

Pat led her to a chair. "Hello everyone. Sorry we're a bit late."

They all made suitable noises and gestures except Tad who, having counted – and probably allocated – the knickers, was now doing the same with tiny bottles of scent. Belvedere could stand it no more.

"Tad Stevens, for heaven's sake. Stop treating these hallowed boards like a Turkish bazaar. Put those nasty little things away."

Tad went on counting them. "These, Belly old fruit,..." Belvedere just refrained from blacking the other eye, "are phials of priceless perfume. I should know. I spent all yesterday afternoon transferring it from a beer bottle into these..." He held up a phial, "with an eye-drop squeezer." He licked his fingers. "Know what I mean?"

Norman *had* to ask. "Beer bottle?"

Tad snapped his suitcase shut. "All I had available." He saw their doubting faces. "I washed it first."

In unison they shook their heads in disbelief.

Tad couldn't understand it. Were they thick or something? "The WVS keep on being given nearly empty scent bottles – for the war effort. Seems daft to me. Mavis Runcorn, who owes me a favour, lets me drain them. Easy." He licked his fingers.

With one voice all of them, less Belvedere and Peggy, chanted, "Know what I mean?" and fell about laughing.

Marvo now sidled silently onto the stage. For some reason he'd dressed in his full stage outfit of turquoise kaftan, fez and open-toed sandals.

"Talking of Turkish bazaars…"

Tad winked at Marvo who gave him a withering look and then, grunting at Rita, sat between her and Rena scribbling notes in their own form of shorthand which he thrust into their hands.

Vi appeared, obviously very flustered.

"The telephone shouldn't ring before nine," she announced to a bemused audience. "Everyone here?"

Norman, with his brassiere now resting, enormously, on his knee, replied for them all.

"Whoever isn't, say so now."

It was said in such a deadpan way that no one knew if he was meaning to be funny or not. Nor did he. To be on the safe side no one laughed.

There it is again, thought Norman. One minute your jokes are funny and the next minute they're not. What *was* the secret?

Vi sat down facing them all. She'd now augmented the old envelope with a notepad and pencil. They all sat sipping their mugs of hot tea wondering what this unusual meeting could be all about.

Nell made her way purposefully to the seat beside Vi.

"All present and correct, Nell."

Vi reported the obvious and made a scribbled note. Belvedere lowered his newspaper and folded it. "I wouldn't call Tad correct in any respect."

They all laughed. They needed to. They could all feel a tremendous tension and everyone, excluding Tad, was uneasy. Something important was about to happen.

Marvo stood. This, in itself was startling. Not so much that he stood, but rather that this shadowy figure who, unless he was on stage acting, never claimed the limelight wished, apparently, to do just that. Dressed in his finery he waved his arms about, grunted, gyrated around the group, stamped his sandaled feet and dropped exhausted onto his chair. It was extraordinary how the twins managed to interpret these wild movements into words.

Rita, with help from his shorthand notes, translated. "Marvo wishes you to know that he would like the stage cleared quickly so that he can rehearse a new illusion for tonight's show."

Rena, polishing her spectacles, took over. "He wishes Rita and me to go and change, and isn't it time we had stronger costumes?" She looked at Nell. "He's right on that one, Nell. You should see the gusset of my leotard…"

Elaine patted her knee. "I think most of the cast have, dear."

Tad chipped in, "And George agrees with her."

As he always managed to do, Tad caused pandemonium. The cacophony of admonishments ended with a solo from George saying "Anyway gussets are all the same," for which he received a slap from Elaine.

Nell banged her walking stick on the floor.

"Right dears, stop bickering. If Masters was here you'd all be watching your P's and carrots…"

Vi chipped in. "Qs. They certainly would."

Nell didn't really hear her. "He wouldn't stand prefabrication from anyone." Nell was obviously in sparkling form. "And as for you, Marvo, I would prefer you to prefect your *present* illusion before you try another one on us. Stronger costumes indeed. You must realize that they're designed to give here and, um, there."

Rena whispered to Elaine. "They certainly do that, every show." Nell, luckily didn't hear her. She was in a real paddy, almost shouting now.

"Reinforced gullets. Made to stand up to anything."

There was a stunned silence. No one dared speak. They didn't know what she meant by that last remark, and Vi felt it would be better that way. She patted Nell gently on the knee. She was cross that they had upset her.

"Now look what you've done. Upset Nell. And she has important things to tell you."

Marvo subsided, grunting.

Nell shook herself a little, adjusted her hat so that the ostrich feather didn't droop in front of her eyes, smoothed her frock over her knees, took a deep breath and smiled at them.

"You are a wonderful troupe. I love you all," she looked at Tad, "yes, *all*, very much. But in these troubled times we are, like everyone else, facing uncertainty. You will have seen how our audiences are getting thinner..."

Tad sat up. "That's rationing for you. Ow!" The exclamation of anguish was caused by both his brown and white brogue shoes being stamped on heavily at the same time, the left one by Belvedere and the right one by George. Nell took no notice. Her mind was on the job in hand. She was tense.

"And there are those who evidently feel that it's inappropriate for there to be gaiety like ours when our troops in France are fighting for their lives. And then there are others who obviously feel exactly the opposite and want us to take our gaiety *to* the troops." Nell was warming to her message now. She banged her stick on the stage.

"Contraception." They all sat forward. Was Nell about to issue a new edict? She felt their confusion.

"It's a contraception in terms. Opposite views."

Vi felt she must help, "Diction, dear."

Nell swung round to her. "Vi Ulthwaite, *no-one* speaks with better diction on stage than I do. I've won every electrocution prize that's worth having."

Vi sat there, head down. She didn't know what to do. Perhaps have a little cry.

Help came from an unexpected quarter: Tad.

"Nell," his voice was so commanding that everyone sat up and forward in surprise.

"You are being most unkind to Vi. She is the best friend, even including us, that you've ever had and she was only trying to help. By mistake you said contraception instead of contradiction. We were all confused until she explained."

188

The troupe shifted on their chairs and looked away. Perhaps a lick of the fingers and "know what I mean?" might have helped but there was none.

"I'm very sorry, Vi. I misunderstood you. But you can be a little muddling at times. I'm sure you understand, dear."

Nell patted Vi's knee, Vi patted Nell's knee. Norman noticed there seemed to be a lot of knee patting this morning. Definitely *not* a Halifax custom...

Nell easily resumed command.

"The reason I've called this meeting is to give you two bits of important news. First, we are to be visited by ENSA who – what did they say, Vi?"

Vi looked at her scribbles on the envelope and read in her put-on prissy voice, "wish to assess us to see if we are good enough to entertain the troops..."

There was general pandemonium.

Belvedere – "I who have worked with the greatest names..."

Rita – "bloomin' cheek..."

Norman – "They love my boosoms..."

George – "We lift their spirits, and Elaine agrees with me..."

Elaine – "Always after my autograph – and George's of course..."

Pat – "You should see their faces when we..."

Rena – "My friend Arnold likes us..."

It was a simultaneous explosion of anger.

Marvo continued to sit, stony faced. Peggy said nothing. Tad's contribution was rather different to the rest.

"I couldn't go near the front line because of my brittle bones. Know what I mean?"

Belvedere punched his shoulder. "Everyone of which I'd now like to break."

Vi stamped her foot, hard, on the floor. She shouted.

"Stop it, everyone. You're upsetting Nell."

They quickly quietened down and Nell smiled.

"But what *spirit*. An understandable refraction. But I had to fill out their beastly form, and they're sending people to elevate us this Thursday at – when is it, Vi?"

Vi consulted the scribbles on her envelope again. "Ten o'clock, Nell."

There was dark murmuring from the troupe.

Belvedere, thunderstruck, found his voice. "We're in the pub by then, Nell."

Tad chipped in, "Pru would never allow it."

George added, "We need to get to bed early. And Elaine agrees with me..." Elaine nodded, blushing.

Tad elbowed Norman. "Aye Aye. Know what I mean."

Vi shouted, "A.M. In the morning."

That silenced them – but only for a moment.

"They're coming at 10 a.m. *in the morning*?" It was Tad's turn to be thunder-struck. "No audience? I can't perform without an audience. I *must* have an audience."

"Ah," said Belvedere with the utmost malice, "But think, Tad, my revolting colleague, what a service you'd be giving to mankind if you *always* performed without an audience."

Tad, sensing an unexpected compliment in this remark, smiled.

"Would I? Thanks, Belly old chap." There was an explosion of laughter and the tension was broken.

"Can I get this straight please, Nell." Elaine held up a hand to quench the noise. "We are required, by law I take it, to put on our complete show, costumes and all, before two complete strangers who will assess us," her voice rose, "to see if we – WE – are of a high enough standard to perform before a bunch of soldiers."

Her Welsh lilt ended with a crashing crescendo somewhere near a top A flat. Nell remained totally calm.

"Not quite, dear. Only two acts." They were very slightly relieved, but it was short-lived. "They say they don't have time to stay for more."

There was another silence. No one wanted to ask the obvious question but rather than sit like dummies they found things to do. Loose buttons, hanging threads, nose blowing, glasses wiping, hair slide adjustments or just, as Belvedere did now, an examination of his suède shoes. He pushed his legs out in front of him, turning the feet up and slowly revolving them, in perfect unison, from left to right, back again, and so on.

At such moments Tad was at his best, "Think of the baby goats they killed to make *them*," he said, pointing at the Belvedere suèdes.

Belvedere involuntarily pulled his feet back swiftly and hid them under his chair, then, realizing he'd displayed weakness, pulled them out again.

"Poor little things," Rena was upset.

Feeling that it was time to get back to important matters Belvedere used his seniority, "Well, Nell, which two acts?"

Nell had no idea and decided to play for time but she was saved from saying anything for the moment by the arrival on stage of Don, Reg Prentice and Bob Bennett. They were all covered in varying amounts of oil, having had a splendid time trying to put the Bofors gun together with the troop of soldiers. Reg evidently scored for the Theatre by finding a place for the last piece. It was now complete – but not yet tried in action. That would be the acid test.

As often happens when a cheerful group suddenly invades a sombre gathering, there was embarrassment all round. Don quickly took the other two backstage to make amends by boiling up another kettle of water. The idea of a fresh brew cheered up everybody but the interlude had served another useful purpose: it had given Nell the opportunity to change tack.

"There's another important matter to be considered first." She had all their attention and was now way beyond finesse. "The Town Council want to chuck us out. They don't wish to renew our lease. They obviously feel that their own Pier Theatre Show is expandable."

George's question broke the silence. "Can they really do that, Nell?"

Belvedere stood and paced the floor in front of them, his voice at its magnificent best.

"In wartime the authorities can do virtually anything, however monstrously unfair and downright stupid it is. We must go as a group and invade the offices of our crass Town Council, find that idiot chairman with that idiot name – um…" He pointed at Tad like a schoolmaster to a small boy, "What's he called?"

Tad smiled a wicked smile, "Belvedere?"

"Yes – no, you fool, *his* name."

Vi tried again to stop the slide into chaos, "Bradley. And anyway we can't. The lease is due for renewal at the end of May, just a few weeks away, and each side can give a month's notice. That's what they've done. Legal and above board."

In the ensuing silence Marvo stood up and walked out, his sandals flip-flopping and his kaftan billowing out behind him.

"However," Nell pulled her shoulders back and sat bolt upright. "They have offered us a chance to change their minds. They will also assess us. They are sending representatives to see the show, though why they haven't come anyway since the season opened is anybody's guest."

Elaine, still smarting from the presumptions of ENSA, waded in again. Her voice was quiet, "And will we know, Nell, which evening they will grace us with their presence?"

They could feel that the Welsh volcano was about to erupt again and sat forward as if to get a better view. Vi decided to, as it were, stand in front of Nell and take the onslaught.

"Not an evening, dear. Another private viewing." She consulted her envelope. "Thursday at noon. Just after ENSA."

"Do I take it," smoke was rising from the crater, "that we are to parade ourselves ... " her voice rose through an octave, "*audition*, as it were, before two lots of ignorant, arrogant and self opinionated little Hitlers who will march in, one lot at ten and the other at noon, ON THE SAME MORNING?"

The note 'A flat' was reached and raised by a semitone to 'A natural', "THE DAY AFTER TOMORROW?"

Nell quietly surveyed Elaine. She liked a girl with spirit.

"That's it, luvvie. In a nutcake."

Once again there was uproar. "I for one – never have I – how dare they? – who do they think? – monstrous – refuse to – wouldn't demean" – and so on.

Nell clapped her hands and Vi added volume by doing the same. They quietened down.

"And we'll do it," the ostrich feather straightened to attention, "there is nothing to fear, we know we're good and we'll give them our best."

Tad could be very logical when he bothered. "So ENSA see we're good, disband us and send us to the front line and the Council decide we're good after all and say we can stay, only we can't because we're dodging bullets and bayonets."

This understandably caused a long, awkward silence. For once no-one wanted to rebuke Tad because he was dead right.

"Nell?" Rena was busily wiping her glasses, which they all knew was a sign that, unusually, she was going to say something before Rita did.

Nell smiled at her. "If you must dear, but try not to be long."

"Why don't we do our acts really badly for ENSA so that they leave us alone, and really well for the Council so that they let us stay?"

After a brief silence there was a little indulgent laughter, and they prepared to return to the problem but Tad slapped his knees causing Belvedere, who was rubbing an itching eye, to nearly poke it out.

"Fool," he bellowed, but Tad took no notice.

"She's right. The little darling is dead right." Rena blushed attractively. Tad suddenly wondered why and how she had escaped his notice – and attention; such matters must be dealt with later. But first things first.

"Excellent. Belly can do his usual act and the Nightingales can squawk some of their songs at ENSA. That should send them running. And I, with a bit of support from Rita and Rena doing some gymnastics in their scanties, can woo the Council. Done." He slapped Belvedere's and George's knees each side of him. "Know what I mean?"

There was, of course, a return to wild confusion. It was surprising that these intelligent people didn't realize that Tad was forever teasing them; provoking them into angry reactions that he gleefully witnessed.

Nell, however, was rarely taken in – and certainly not now. She banged her stick.

"Thank you Tad for your, as usual, perspective comments." Whilst the others were still huffing and puffing she was actually smiling! "Rena has come up with an excellent idea. Well done, luvvie. However, we shall not be following Tad's advice with regard to the selection of acts." She looked at Tad. "You and Belvedere will provide rubbish for ENSA."

They all found this highly amusing – except, of course, Tad and Belvedere who were loud with their protests but Nell held up her hand.

"Because, dears, you have the years of stage experience which enables you to *act* as well as perform. All of you perform well, or you wouldn't be in the troupe, but you two can, if called upon *act* a role. Here it will be the role of a poor performer. For the sake of the whole Company I ask you to do so."

There was a respectful shuffling of feet. Nell certainly knew how to handle her troupe. They were overawed by her call to arms, not least Tad and Belvedere. They simpered a bit, wriggled and made some deprecating noises. Tad had never been so complimented before and was uncharacteristically silent but Belvedere, being no stranger to compliments, or rather what he was sure were compliments, easily created a suitable script for the occasion.

"Nell," he said, trying to emulate dear Larry in 'Henry Five' at Stratford when he had knelt before Katherine and wooed her, "Dear Nell" – he was now going a bit far – "we humbly kneel before you and will willingly do your bidding."

Tad found his voice, "Will we, old fruit? All right with me Belly, if you know what I mean."

Nell swept on. "I don't want Pat and Peggy emboiled in all this." They both started to protest. Nell, with a tiny movement of her hand, silenced them.

"So I'll ask our songbirds and Norman and his wall to win over the Council. Now that's all for the time being. You know what you need to do. Quite enough chatter-chitter. And there's a show to put on tonight. Rita, Rena, go and find that Marvo. I've got a bone to pluck with him. And tell him that if he must wear an afghan in his act, at least have it at a decent length. His uncles look ridiculous." Vi whispered, "ankles."

Nell rose, they all rose. They realized it was still only a quarter to ten in the morning and they'd have an awful lot of nothing to do for a very long time; usually their day had only just begun.

"Afghan?" Norman was confused.

Tad sighed, "Kaftan, old fruit. Obvious. Know what I mean?"

For Nell and Vi it was going to be a very busy day. They went into Vi's office. Nell was in top gear now.

"Brief Don for me, will you love? Prepare him for Thursday. We'll all be busy so I want Reg or Bob in best tuck and bibber to meet our honoured guests and get them seated. Row F, 15 and 16. Good view and safely far back. Belvedere tends to spit rather a lot these days, bless him. I'm telling Rita and Rena to take Pat and Peggy into town for that morning. It'll be best for Peg to get away from it all. Give them some pocket money, love. To buy coffee or whatever. I'm off next door to sort a few things out."

Nell went into her office and sank into the big armchair. She must pick the right moment to tell Vi, in strictest confidence, of her plans. Retirement at the end of the lease. She looked up at the calendar with its beguiling picture. Six weeks. Friday, the thirty-first of May. The final night – unless Hitler decided to retire them all before that...

She yawned. It had been another bad night's sleep. Despite the multitude of problems she was facing she dropped into a doze.

The lone audience for this involuntary stage performance by the theatre company left the dusty dress circle. His opinion of the troupe hadn't changed; he was just amazed that such an ill-disciplined bunch of amateurs could have in their midst someone who, in a roundabout way, held the fate of the world in her hands. Ludovic Henschel passed silently through the foyer and out into the sunlight.

*　　*　　*

In Warsaw Freddy had his usual bad night's sleep. The log in the room next door showed several entries of murmurings and mutterings and the sound of violent turning over and banging of pillows. The Herr Professor was clearly not enjoying a restful stay in the Hotel Bristol.

The door was thrown open. Another morning – but something was wrong. Freddy, in a befuddled state, felt it immediately. That cold, icy fear was back. He held his breath. Captain Fengel seemed pleased to wake him which in itself was sinister. He bent down over the bed to within a few inches of Freddy's face.

"The General will see you – downstairs," he made the word sound evil "in thirty minutes. You will prepare yourself *now*."

The last word was barked, and Freddy smelt the foul breath. He just stared, that was all he could do. The door was closed and locked.

For a moment he lay, paralysed, in the security of the warm blankets fighting the need to throw them back and lose their protection, then, in dread, he got out of bed trembling, ice cold yet perspiring.

He was in deep shock by being awoken to fear and still only half conscious he opened the curtains. No light. It was still pitch dark outside. He looked at the clock. Four-thirty in the morning. *Four thirty?* The Gestapo knew their business. A lamb to the slaughter.

And that's what undoubtedly it would be. But how slow the slaughter? And how cruel? Books talked of bravery; of fine, last words, a challenge thrown mockingly at the torturers; of brave, firm steps to the gallows, head held high. Pride. Inner strength. Calmness. Freddy had none of these and the realization made him want to weep for the thousandth time since this nightmare began. But no tears would come.

Feeling desperately sick he washed, shaved and dressed automatically. Would he ever go through the familiar ritual again? Should he tell them everything he knew? Why? He would be annihilated anyway. Where were these friends? Had they been discovered? Destroyed? Like his mother? Or dear God, like Peggy?

He could answer none of these questions, gain no comfort.

Two guards came to collect him. They said nothing as he was taken to the lift. He saw that it was a new lift attendant and his heart sank, if it could drop any further. There was no acknowledgement from the man who was apparently oblivious to the prisoner's presence.

Very slowly, as if the lift itself wanted to add to the torture, they descended to the basement: the basement of Gestapo Headquarters in Poland. Freddy Crisciak was led along a corridor flanked by cell-like doors...

*　　*　　*

Later that afternoon Charles Turville and Ludovic Henschel sat facing each other across the desk in the Commandant's office at the camp on the golf course. The Commandant was not pleased. As an elderly Colonel who had fought through the last war, retired, and been recalled to the Colours to undertake this thankless task, he didn't like to receive orders from civilians or be made to vacate his office and clear people from the surrounding area.

He had no idea what was going on but the telephone call he had been ordered to make by the Polish refugee who had barged into his office a couple of weeks ago had connected him to a General at the War Office who told him brusquely to obey the man and remember he was still bound by the Official Secrets Act.

The General in London had been angry; the Colonel thought it was directed at him but, in fact, it was at the Pole who seemed to be acting in a very high-handed manner. He had slammed the 'phone down, pleased to get back to his cup of tea and The Times crossword.

Turville stretched his long legs under the Colonel's desk. Both men were smoking, unaware and uncaring of the Commandant's dislike of the habit. The lingering smell of ash and the smoke haze would add to his fury at the inexcusable violation of his authority.

"If they close the theatre we can spirit her away."

It was this kind of loose, not-thought-through thinking that particularly annoyed Turville. He had decided not to rise to it; it was a waste of time.

"They musn't close," he said firmly. "Certainly not until the mission is successfully completed." He waved away a planned interruption from Henschel.

"The situation is ideal as it is. The girl feels secure, the East coast is the nearest point between us and occupied Europe to bring the package to, and he will continue his work on Project Omega *here in Britain* if he knows that she has not been threatened in any way. To achieve these three basic aims the theatre company *will* continue to present their show as it is now – *with our help.*" The last three words were spoken by Turville with great emphasis.

He saw this threat of the closure of the Pier Theatre as an added aggravation to the smooth running of the assignment, no more than that. One order delivered from London would put the Flaxton Council firmly in its place but he'd rather it didn't come to that; it would obviously cause a raised eyebrow or two and that was the last thing he wanted just now.

All this was trivial compared to the lifeline that had been thrown to him that morning at the Polish Embassy by Jozef Raczeck which, at a stroke, had turned improbability into a degree of possibility as far as evacuating Freddy Crisciak to England was concerned.

He would find it difficult to explain to his Chief, Sir Philip, but he had decided, for a reason that he couldn't quite fathom, to say nothing to Ludovic Henschel about it. He acknowledged that it was odd, even bizarre, not to share every scrap of information with a colleague on an assignment but he convinced himself that it was to avoid fruitless discussion on what was now an agreed course of action. Deep down he knew it was something more than that.

He banished the matter from his mind.

"We will lead on to the Norman Jackson incident." He said this slowly and quietly, staring with cold eyes at Henschel. "If I were to believe that you were the unknown assailant I would have you sharpening pencils, desk-bound tomorrow. You do understand, don't you?"

For once it was Turville who was surprised by his colleague's reaction to a threat. Henschel laughed.

"Let me assure you my friend..." he used one of Turville's terms of endearment with equal sarcasm, "...that had it been me he would have been dead before he hit the water. What you and I need to give our minds to urgently is who *did* try to kill this stupid insignificant little man – and why?"

Turville had to admit to himself that the full significance of Henschel's remark had not struck him fully until now. He had been so certain that it was his subordinate who had, in his usual impetuous way, carried out the attack that he hadn't considered any alternative. But if it wasn't Henschel, then who?

"So you feel this is proof that someone else *is* on our patch?"

They sat silently for a while. The only sound in the room was the wind making the wooden building creak.

Turville stood up preparing to leave. "I want you to comb the town. You're good at that." he hoped a little flattery might get greater co-operation, "Find out what you can. We've got to eliminate any rival for the package's co-operation before he does serious damage. We'll meet again tomorrow."

Turville moved to the door but Henschel hadn't finished yet.

"Those damned actors will have to be warned off. It's impossible for me to trail the girl when I've got one of them between her and me. The distance is too great."

Turville turned. "Disturbing them will achieve nothing. Come on, man, they're helping to do the job for you. Trail them and you're trailing her. They'll soon show you if she falls into any danger. The less fuss the better."

Henschel shook his head in anger but said no more. They left, one back to his hut, the other towards the railway station.

The Commandant, seeing them leaving, emerged from the Guardroom.

"How good of you to allow me the use of my office again," he said as he passed them but the sarcasm was totally lost on the two men.

"We shall require it again tomorrow at the same time," was all he got by way of a reply.

Henschel stood and watched the departing figure of Turville, tall, alert, supremely confident, his precise military step in perfect timing with the click of his immaculately furled umbrella as it struck the ground. He smiled a twisted smile.

"You fool" he said quietly to himself.

*   *   *

Freddy was pushed roughly into the cell by the Gestapo guards. He was expecting the worst but even *he* was surprised by the sheaf of papers hurled from the centre of the room at his head. They scattered, gently brushing his face, as they fluttered to the floor.

A bright light directed at him restricted any vision behind it. He was forced onto a chair, his hands pulled behind it and manacled tightly so that he couldn't move. The screeching voice from behind the light was undoubtedly that of SS General Friedrich Streyer.

"You insult the Third Reich? You insult the Führer? You abuse my hospitality and try to fool me? You scribble worthless rubbish and think I will be fooled by you? Have you no fear? Do you not know? We are wiping out your race. Poland is ceasing to exist. Extermination. A total cleansing of your wretched nation." This manic performance ended in a high-pitched screech. "Where are the notebooks?"

The effect on Freddy was extraordinary. The fear went. He was totally calm. It suddenly all became completely clear to him. He had a secret weapon that no force or persuasion could ever breech: his mind. If they wanted its contents they would have to play it *his* way – otherwise the ampoule of cyanide awaited...

"It will help considerably if you will stop screeching like a wounded baboon." As he said it, in such contrasting quietness to Streyer's ranting, he wondered if he hadn't gone a little too far.

The force of the fist on his head was numbing. The second hit seemed less so, the third and fourth merely continued the pain. His two guards were warming to the task.

"Stop"

Even Freddy himself was surprised at the power of his own voice – and it had the desired effect. Amazingly the guards obeyed him. Maybe they thought the command came from the General.

With massive effort he controlled his voice back into a seemingly calm state. "You may not be aware, Herr General, that every blow on the head destroys, for ever, millions of brain cells. You have so far killed four times those millions in *my* brain."

General Streyer broke his own rules. He came into vision on Freddy's side of the light and thrust his face inches from his.

"That is only the start..."

Freddy's voice was loud and sharp, "Silence."

Streyer obeyed! A fist hit the side of Freddy's head and again he summoned every last reserve of strength so that, to them, he apparently hadn't felt the blow.

His voice was still totally calm, "Another few million cells. What are your orders, Herr General?"

All this was going seriously wrong for Streyer. He was being made a fool of in front of his own guards. His voice was evil.

"It is now that you will feel the exquisite pain delivered with such skill by my operators. You will be taken away and stripped. A mirror will be provided for you to view, for the last time, your body as it now is. And then my surgeons will start to operate. Bone by bone. There will be no anaesthetic..."

Freddy's voice was still completely calm. The ampoule was touched by his tongue.

"And in this way you expect to provide for your Führer my full co-operation for the task that lies ahead, as we use my *fully functioning* brain to solve the immense intricacies facing the German Third Reich in creating the weapon that will bring victory over the world? You are a fool Streyer..."

The General stopped with his hand another blow that was about to descend on Freddy's head and it was at this moment that Freddy knew he had won. Now the advantage must be pushed home.

"Will you personally deliver my dissected carcass to your – *our* – Führer, or will you wisely commit suicide and send some other poor unfortunate as your messenger?"

Streyer retreated behind his light and for a moment there was silence. Freddy, realising how total it was, assumed that these rooms were sound-proofed and suppressed a shiver. *Nothing – nothing* must show. This was literally, he was sure, the moment between his life and his death.

"When this is over," Streyer's voice was icily quiet, "I shall ask for you to be delivered to me. For slow extermination."

The guards were harshly told to return him to his room. They were surprised and disappointed having hoped for so much more. Roughly they undid his manacles.

The lift, laden with the three passengers, slowly ascended. Already confused, frightened and in considerable pain from the blows to his head, Freddy was suddenly aware of his hand being squeezed and, looking down, saw that it was being held by the lift attendant. It was an urgent pull, like a child seeking attention. He gasped and the guards chuckled totally unaware of the significance of the sound.

With his heart racing and fighting for breath, he asked, almost sobbed, "What is the time, please?"

With another squeeze the attendant mumbled, looking through the gate at the passing lift-shaft wall, "It is May."

CHAPTER TEN

Wednesday, 1 May 1940. Hans Frank, Nazi Governor General of Poland, states that all Poles capable of leadership in Poland have been eliminated.

In Britain families are advised to have one suitcase per person packed with essential clothing and other items for use in the event of sudden evacuation caused by an invasion.

The beginning of May; the longer, warmer days now providing the first hints of the coming summer which, traditionally, was a time of rising spirits. But not this year. There was no escaping the fact that, at last, the mood of the 'ordinary' people of Britain was starting to change.

The eight months of apparent inactivity, the 'phoney war' as it was called, which had not, as had been expected, produced any attacks by sea or air on the mainland had lulled the population into a belief that everyday life could continue its peacetime tempo. But now, almost imperceptibly, it was being injected with a realisation that hostilities had not been avoided, only postponed.

The wireless and newspapers were mainly responsible for this. The news from Europe was grim, and whilst the degree of barbarism perpetrated by the Third Reich on its northern neighbours was still unknown, the aims of its mighty war machine as far as the West was concerned were becoming all too evident. Vast concentrations of their land and air forces were being massed on the Dutch, Belgian and French borders, and the reports from news correspondents in the front line with the British Expeditionary Force were grim. It was this news that was discussed, dissected and often inaccurately assessed by the British population as it steeled itself for what undoubtedly lay ahead.

The people of Flaxton were no exception. In the butchers' and grocers', whilst the assistants juggled inexpertly with ration books and scissors, tongues wagged as they did in every shop and pub in the town. They spoke in varying degrees of fear and bravado, and it was these two extremes that often led to the fiercest arguments – and even fights.

Nerves were on edge and here, so close to the threatened continent, they had good cause to be: the east and south coasts would bear the initial onslaught of an attack on mainland Britain.

For Nell Masters that May morning, wrestling with the accounts of the Pier Theatre Company, financial survival was an even more immediate problem than thoughts of invasion. It was now two weeks after the troupe meeting and Vi had placed the previous week's accounts in front of her as she did every Wednesday. They were neatly drawn up in large letters and figures with her special broad-nibbed pen which made it easy for Nell to see.

She glanced at them and shuddered but at the same time gained a crumb of comfort from realising that the financial state of her Company hardly mattered anymore. Their fate would be decided one way or the other by ENSA or the Council tomorrow.

"If things go on like this, Vi love, you'll be able to use indelible ink soon. There'll be nothing to write."

Vi sighed. "Invisible, dear."

Nell sat back, her ostrich feather and chins quivered in unison.

"Exactly. Try to keep up, love. Jokes are hard enough to make as it is these days without you getting them wrong."

Vi decided to say nothing in answer to this unfair attack on her; Nell was under great strain and should be forgiven for any little flare-ups which erupted from time to time. Vi saw it as her clear duty to protect her friend in every way that she could and it was deeply upsetting when she, even if wrongly accused, was the cause of an eruption. Standing unseen behind her friend she wiped an eye with her hanky. Nell felt the moment and put her hand on her arm.

"I'm sorry, love. That was unkind of me. You are my Rock of Ages."

Vi would have preferred 'Gibraltar' but wisely decided to leave it. Nell went on.

"It's the troupe, you see. If I decide to close, whether because of the Council or lack of income, or..." she hesitated and continued lamely, "or whatever, what will become of them? I'll have let them down. Masters would not expect that of me."

She suddenly sprang to her feet and banged her desk with her walking stick sending the accounts book crashing to the floor, her chins wobbling more frenziedly than ever.

"Damn this war. Damn Hitler," she shouted, the swear word as startling to Vi as the vehemence. "He should be oiled in boil."

Vi would have been surprised to know that Nell's anger was as much directed at herself for even contemplating retirement and thereby abandoning her troupe, as it was to Hitler.

As Vi set about restoring some sort of order to Nell's office – and Nell herself – three members of the troupe were only a few yards away from them, leaning on the balustrade at the end of the pier, enjoying the warm afternoon sunshine. Elaine, Rita and Rena were in light summer frocks unwittingly showing the gun crew the backs of six very shapely legs, the seams of their stockings – supplied, of course, by Tad at a 'special' price – perfectly straight.

The crew were polishing the gun yet again, there being so far no other use for it, and with their eyes firmly on the girls the same small portion was being polished, and polished, and polished, their mouths open and their thoughts on matters far removed from buffing a piece of army ordinance.

Wednesdays, like Saturdays, were hard work for the theatre troupe. They were matinée days and for some reason the afternoon show was far harder to perform than the evening one; the afternoon didn't lend itself to strenuous stage activity but conversely the audiences seemed to love it. Usually there'd be sixty or seventy at a matinée, nearly all of whom were thoroughly bored other ranks given time off – town leave – by frustrated officers who had run out of duties for them to undertake.

For them, what better way to spend the long afternoons than sitting in the darkness of the Pier Theatre or the town cinema cuddling someone whose name you kept on forgetting or had never known? But delightful though this activity was, most of them found this idle life frustrating and wondered when the real war would start. Worse still, being stuck here with no battles to fight did nothing to enhance their prowess with the girls!

The cinema manager, who had suffered the mud of Flanders, watched these youngsters pour into the darkness of his auditorium, only children really, the boys keener on the dark cavern awaiting them than the girls they were pulling behind them, and he shuddered. How were they to know, he ruminated, that the starting pistol, and many other more lethal weapons, would be going off very soon – probably in their innocent faces.

Unaware of the gun crew, Elaine, Rita and Rena were looking along the beach southwards with the town on their right and a very calm North Sea to their left.

Like most of the Suffolk shoreline it was a fairly steeply shelving pebble beach now covered, not as in the past, with happy families sitting on towels in bathing suits, but with giant concrete anti-tank obstacles, miles of barbed wire spiralling like coiled springs in every direction and, most sinister of all, signs every twenty yards or so displaying the skull and crossbones and the three frightening words – MINES. KEEP OUT.

There was a lethal welcome awaiting the expected visitors from the sea. Winston Churchill, who already seemed to be the voice of the Government, had said that not an inch of British land would be surrendered without a fight to the death.

On this beautiful afternoon it all seemed to the girls to be so incongruous, as if a weird fairground had been erected on the beach. All it needed now were the crowds and according to rumours circulating in the town, they, in German uniforms, could arrive any day! Talk of imminent invasion was in the air, but still it was hard to imagine.

Elaine gave a little shudder.

"I hate all this," she talked quietly, as if the enemy was close enough to hear her.

Rita touched her arm, she felt it trembling, "Perhaps it will all be over soon. They'll find a way of stopping it."

Rena took off and wiped her spectacles, a sure sign that she was starting to panic. "They said it would be over by Christmas."

Elaine turned between them and leant back on the balustrade causing the gun crew to lose one pair of straight seams.

"Hitler wants to rule the world. He won't stop until he does. George says so, and I agree with him." She said it in such a way that brooked no argument.

Rita felt that it was as well that the British Government and High Command were not aware of George's military assessment! She was watching activity at the south end of the beach involving a crane which was lifting a giant gun barrel onto an equally large turret.

"That's the gun Tad was talking about."

Elaine turned to look. "Yes. He said they were putting two big naval guns, like they have on battleships, on the beach. He said they would – what was it? – draw the enemy's fire, and George agrees with him."

Rita sighed, "Charming. We can always rely on Tad to keep us cheerful."

As if on cue the sun disappeared behind some light cloud. It wasn't cold, but they shivered. This was not the world they wanted to grow up in.

"Come on, let's go in." Elaine lead the way to the stage door as if the familiar interior of the Pier Theatre would wipe away this disturbing scene. The gun crew closed their mouths and stopped polishing. It was time for a NAAFI break.

*

There was tension in the Commandant's office at the refugee camp. Again, to his extreme annoyance, its rightful occupant had been pushed out and had driven off in a huff in his little Tilly van. He had ended the last war in a staff car and the thought of this come-down didn't put him in any better mood as he bullied the little van towards Ipswich where he intended to give his so-called superiors a piece of his mind regarding the invasion of his office. On his return later he rather wished that he hadn't; they had suggested that he might prefer to command a Local Defence Volunteer Force – civilians with pitchforks...

Charles Turville glared at Ludovic Henschel across the Commandant's desk, "You went to the girl? Identified yourself? You must be mad. Everything could be jeopardised." Turville's voice was cold.

Henschel shrugged, "I had no option. You could do nothing. This end must be prepared for the package. That is now *at your insistence* my job. When he arrives it is imperative that he is quickly reunited with the notebooks."

Turville got up and looked through the window at the long line of drab wooden huts, the scene incongruously softened by multiple rows of washing hung on lines like coloured flags. But he didn't see them, nor the people moving between the huts, always slowly, the horror of the last few weeks having sapped their energy. They shuffled, like old men in carpet slippers. There was nowhere to go, no rush.

The silence in the room was ominous. Turville, still looking out of the window, spoke first.

"Ah yes. The notebooks. What news have we of them?"

Henschel smiled, "You are inconsistent, my friend. You berate me for visiting the girl and then want to know what came of the visit."

Turville's voice was colder still as he repeated the question, "What news have we of the note-books?" Henschel sat back and put his hands together behind his head and frowned.

"The girl will not, *voluntarily*, be parted from them. My fear is that she will suffer an accident in which case they may never be found. And, we are assured, without them, not even the brain of the package will be sufficient to achieve success in time..."

Turville finished the sentence for him, "in time to save the world." He turned and resumed his seat, frowning. "That will not do. Time is fast running out."

Henschel was quick with a riposte, "When will the package be sprung?"

Turville replied calmly, "Very soon. We have disturbing news regarding Demon's tactics. Unless we move quickly the package could well be broken into."

Henschel jerked forward and fixed Turville with his cold, dispassionate eyes. "That must not happen. Do they understand you?"

Turville was surprised that the man was so agitated; he had shown remarkably little concern regarding the whole project until now.

"Believe me, my friend..." his stare was equally cold, "...that will *not* happen."

Turville had a habit, infuriating to Henschel, of tidying himself, adjusting his cuff-links, minutely tweaking his tie and smoothing down the lapels of his suit, which meant to those who knew him that it was time to change the subject. He leant back and lit a cigarette, his mood now almost cheerful.

"Now to this Pier Theatre Company. What is the latest news?"

It was Henschel's turn to move to the window. He didn't want eye-to-eye contact at this moment.

"They are such imbeciles." He crashed his fists onto the sill. "I repeat what I said earlier. We must discount them from this operation. Take the girl, extract the notebooks from her by whatever means necessary and lock her up until the package comes to claim her..." he added balefully, "if it ever does."

He knew the wrath that would descend on him but frankly he didn't care anymore. Turville hadn't witnessed the inane behaviour of this bunch of idiots on stage who fought amongst themselves, told crass jokes, made stupid plans and were led by an old, muddled woman who couldn't even speak intelligently.

But as his mind dwelt on this he knew that, yet again, he'd played the wrong card at the wrong time. To succeed – and it was no exaggeration to say that his future depended on success – he had to stay on this assignment. And Turville had the power to decide one way or the other.

But there was no wrath; just silence and then a quiet, encouraging question, "What, to use your word, *stupid* plans did they make?"

Henschel felt it safe to resume his seat and gratefully took the proffered cigarette.

"They will act badly for ENSA and well for the Council." Turville looked up, surprised.

"Is that it? Just that?"

Henschel, more confident now, copied his master and leant back, drawing deeply on his cigarette.

"I said they were idiots."

Turville jerked upright and stubbed out his cigarette. All this had gone on quite long enough.

"On the contrary, the simple plans are often the best. We'll help them. I will see to ENSA. They can have the lot when we've finished with them, but not until then. You will sort out the Town Council. Remember, the English worship democracy and any overt attempt to interfere with it will undoubtedly break this assignment wide open. So be subtle."

As he said the last three words his heart sank. Henschel – subtle? But before he could impress the order on this most unsubtle of men the absurd happened.

With a loud crack the glass shattered in the window facing the perimeter of the camp. All their combat training slipped automatically into gear. In an instant the two Secret Service agents were huddled together under the commandant's desk. After the customary ten seconds to allow for possible detonation the two of them peered out. On the desktop, rolling between inkwell, blotter and two cups and saucers – was a golf ball!

It was that ludicrous scene that was afterwards so often described in great and embellished detail by the delighted Colonel's clerk who had peered round the door to check on the noise of breaking glass.

*   *   *

In his office in the Hotel Bristol in Warsaw SS General Friedrich Streyer put the field telephone down with obvious satisfaction.

It was an incongruous scene. This dumpy little man in his immaculate black uniform, black jackboots, black belt and pistol holster sat at an enormous desk in this enormous room. It had once been the Grand Salon on the second floor of the hotel, a sumptuous feast of ornamentation which, before the bombing of the city, had been walled in mirrors. On occupying it in late 1939 Streyer had the vanity to have the hotel renovated to its former glory by Polish craftsmen – instead of paying them they were put to death on the completion of their work.

The Salon, which was entered through twelve foot high double doors as a mark of its opulence, had been – and still was despite the lack of its vast mirrors – a wonderful room. Streyer was satisfied that the sheer scale of it befitted the Head of the SS in Poland, enhanced as it was by the ultimate accolade of a large, personally signed framed picture of Adolf Hitler on the wall behind his desk.

The desk was, in fact, a beautiful Louis Quinze table, rich in gold leaf ornamentation, which was matched by chairs and sofas around the room.

The military telephone, the only permanent item on the desk, looked out of place but was essential; the Polish civilian telephone network lay, a mass of jumbled wires, in the rubble of the city and across the scarred landscape.

In all his evil works Streyer was a perfectionist. His movements were slow, precise and tidy, his brain evil and his face expressionless with small, staring eyes behind his 'Heinrich Himmler' spectacles. Now, with the telephone handset back in its cradle, he examined his small podgy hands, the fingernails perfectly trimmed. Such care by someone who spent much of his time ordering the removal of these items, without anaesthetic, from his less fortunate guests housed in the converted store-rooms in the basement of this very building, summed up the man perfectly.

The Herr General was pleased. His adjutant had brought him good news in the form of a decoded Enigma message from the SS in Norway. The person he had been seeking had been found and was even now being transported south. He rubbed his hands together. Nobody made a fool of Friedrich Streyer for long.

But he found the news from Berlin less good. He had received a signal to the effect that the Führer who, with his brilliant brain, busied himself with every detail of the war, was understandably too preoccupied at that moment to deal with this scientific business. He wished the work of the captive, Professor Count Freddy Crisciak, to continue in Warsaw until the time when the volunteer nuclear physicists from other annexed German States were identified and able, together with their German colleagues, to receive the invaluable contents of this man's remarkable brain. This could not be for at least another two weeks.

The coded signal which, unlike the earlier handwritten message, Streyer feared was not personally compiled by the Führer himself, ended with the phrase, "Guard and protect him well."

Streyer read a veiled threat in these final words. He was too vain to realize, of course, that had it not been for Freddy's halting of the beating in the cell yesterday, he would have had to spend much anxious time trying to compose a coded reply to the Führer, explaining why the Herr Professor was now a pile of pulp! To the Führer even SS Generals were easily expendable...

Streyer pressed a small bell-push. His adjutant came in silently and stood at attention at the desk.

"What is the surveillance report on prisoner Crisciak?" The adjutant consulted a sheaf of papers in an eagle-embossed folder.

"He is writing again, Herr General. He is heard muttering figures and letters." The adjutant was obviously under some strain. He hesitated and Streyer was too good an operator to miss the signal.

"And?" he said dangerously quietly. The adjutant stumbled over his words.

"He spent some time after breakfast bathing a bad bruise..." there was a pause, "on his head."

Streyer stood, not suddenly in panic, but slowly, in anger. His voice was now very quiet, almost a whisper, "Caused by?"

The adjutant was as loyal to his fellow officers as he dared to be.

"The prisoner insulted Hauptmann Fengel. He was punished as any prisoner would be, Herr General. Hauptmann Fengel ordered the guards to hit him..." and then he added like a child, "but he's alright now."

Streyer moved to one of the high windows which ran the length of the room above the entrance to the hotel. He didn't see the piles of distorted rubble and gutted buildings that were Warsaw in 1940; he saw instead, in his mind, a gallows and a man hanging from it.

"Send Hauptmann Fengel, disarmed and under escort, to me." He pounded the glass pane with his fist.

"Now."

*

Up on the fifth floor of the hotel Freddy was lying back on his bed with his hands behind his head muttering every now and then arbitrary numbers and letters. His head hurt and the bruise was quickly coming out. He'd bathed it in cold water, and now had a soaked handkerchief resting on it. Where were these friends? He could do with them *now*. Judging from the latest assault it seemed that time was running out.

It had been a short, sharp, vicious attack. Unprovoked. By the shouted remarks between the obscenities hurled at him by the Captain, it seemed that it had all sprung from a report from the guards regarding Freddy's treatment of the General down in the cells yesterday.

The three of them had burst into the room and, with no warning, the guards had started to hit him around the head. The soldier manning the listening post next door didn't know what was happening and inadvertently saved Freddy from worse injury by calling for help which came in the shape of the Colonel who restored order with one loud command. Since then, he'd been left on his own and the headache had got worse.

Now, suddenly it all changed. Two men in white coats entered the room and the guards – new guards – stood each side of the door. Freddy was in such a confused state that blind fear gripped him even when they introduced themselves as doctors. This could mean anything; medical care – or something much more sinister.

Amazingly it seemed to be the former. Gently they examined his head, ointment was applied, temperature taken, pulse taken and heart checked. *And they apologised!* It was a mistake. Orders were misunderstood. The error, they assured him, would not reoccur. He was given tablets and, in a daze, he took them. They left and not for the first time, or probably the last in this infernal room, Freddy was thoroughly confused. It then struck him that the tablets could be poison but, if so, why go through the charade beforehand? Just force them down his throat and make him swallow. Or why not just shoot him? He lay down more confused than ever and closed his aching eyes.

The pills did their work and he slept lightly for a while but when they wore off he awoke to considerable pain. He decided to mutter a few numbers and words to keep the eavesdropper happy but as he started the key rattled in the lock and the accustomed fear gripped him. One of the doctors had returned for a further check-up but, much more interestingly, so did a trolley pushed by an orderly with covered dishes of hot food – and a bottle of vodka!

The orderly said, "The Herr General wishes you to enjoy your dinner." Then, unbelievable, he saluted and left.

This had been another extraordinary day. The reviled prisoner and the pampered guest. Was this part of the psychological treatment for which the SS was renowned? Freddy Crisciak didn't believe it was; far too unsubtle. With aching head and a brain filled with unanswered and, it seemed, unanswerable questions he attacked the food…

*   *   *

The first day of May ended for the Theatre Company in Flaxton with quite a few headaches as well. A second pounding through the evening performance was gruelling for all of them. Such a small cast demanded an almost non-stop appearance by all of the troupe on stage in one guise or another throughout the two hours of performance and that, coupled with the fetid atmosphere and the loudness of both the audience and the 'orchestra' meant that, on matinée days, there was many a sore head by bed-time.

Marvo had been out-of-sorts again giving a crotchety perfor-mance in the afternoon, and one only slightly less irritable in the evening. Luckily throughout all this, Rena on her stretcher, mainly thanks to Rita, Reg and Bob, stayed more or less horizontal!

The song-birds had often sung better and the comedy acts had been known to be funnier but, showing the infuriating perverseness that makes the theatre so stimulating, the takings were excellent. Good attendances for both performances.

Before they left the theatre Nell impressed on Belvedere and Tad the need for an early night because of the visit of ENSA the next day. Belvedere was insulted, reminding Nell of his professional standing in the theatre.

"Did dear Larry, or Johnny or Donald carouse until the early hours when there was an early 'call' on the morrow?"

Nell had no idea whether they did or not, and was not in the least interested to know one way or the other.

"Don't burn your end with both candles", she told them, and left it at that.

They winced at the mere thought of such a thing. Belvedere followed George and Norman out of the theatre and found that, through habit, he was already in the Pier Head Tavern and sitting in 'his' chair before he realized it and so he thought he'd stay for just one scotch.

Tad, seeking other distractions, was convinced that a night with Pru would set him up well for a memorable performance, whether good or bad, the next day and decided to try to double his efforts with her. As it turned out she had other ideas and a hard dig in the ribs when she'd had enough told him so.

On the way home from the theatre Nell and Vi came upon Alice Banbury on the pavement outside the door that led to her flat over the Post Office. She had just let out Harriet, the cat, for her 'nightly necessities' as Alice described the feline call of nature and had already walked Mountjoy to his favourite spot for the same purpose.

The three women chatted about the mysterious break-in and Alice showed Nell the new locks – two of them now for added security. Harriet finished and, with much rubbing of body and tail around their legs, announced that she was ready to resume her arduous duties – sleeping, washing, eating and a lot more sleeping – upstairs in the warm.

"Pat and Peggy went straight to bed. Peggy seemed exhausted." Alice was sure that Nell would want to know. She had been very firm about a sensible routine for 'the girls' when she entrusted them to her.

Nell and Vi made their way up the steps to Clarence Road. Neither talked; they were too tired. The sky was clear and they were able to see their way easily by the light of a fullish moon. As they reached the house Nell looked up at the stars and saw the one she always felt was her dear Masters looking down on her. She knew nothing about astronomy and didn't care which star it was, but she knew it was Masters.

"Good night, my love," she whispered, and blew him a kiss.

In the kitchen Rita and Rena were drinking mugs of hot milk. Nell sighed. It was just like the family she'd never had.

*

In his bed Belvedere put down his scrapbook. In it he had pasted the history of his stage life. Photographs, cuttings from newspapers, letters from fans and, in pride of place, kind notes from his gods – dear Larry, Johnny, Donald, Sybil, Gertrude and so many more. Many had actually spelt his name correctly.

Whenever in the depths of despair, and the awful truth of how far he had sunk choked him making him wish for a merciful end to it, he would take up this book and gain strength from what had, and might have, been.

He sighed, but rather than a smooth sound he found that it was broken by emotion. He wiped his damp eyes and put out the light. His alarm was wound and set for eight o'clock. At nine he would be on duty at a discreet distance from the door of the Post Office flat. His turn for 'Peggy Patrol' tomorrow.

The night – the last peaceful night for the people of Flaxton-on-Sea for many years to come – would pass quietly. The sea was calm and a light warm breeze freshened the air.

*   *   *

In the cockpit of his Dornier 17 bomber Leutnant Hans Rechtner checked his altitude and position. He noted that his plane was twenty-eight thousand feet above the vast North Sea and that the east coast of England was ten miles, two hundred and eighty-eight degrees to the west.

A casual observer would have assumed that either the pilot was under the illusion that he was performing at an Air Show, or that he was drunk! But Leutnant Rechtner was neither performing nor drunk; very far from it. He had taken off at 6.30 a.m. from his base near Bremen with a full crew and three bombs to test a number of new flight systems devised by the army of scientists and inventors employed by the Third Reich.

He had a programme of manoeuvres to carry out which would put the loaded bomber through every contortion it might have to make to avoid enemy fighters and anti-aircraft gunfire and Rechtner was required to return with a completed log. Now the mission was over and his orders were to jettison the heavy bomb load and return to base.

Then his day could really start – and it would be a memorable one. The second of May 1940 was Hans Rechtner's twenty-first birthday and his comrades had an evening of riotous celebrations lined up for him. Until then he'd be off duty; a reward for volunteering for this routine and rather boring mission.

And Rechtner *was* bored. Flying the equivalent of a test-bed was not his idea of war or his planned route to glory. There could be no Iron Cross, First, Second or Third Class, at the end of *this* flight.

He prepared to drop down to ten-or-so thousand feet to release the bombs and then his bomb-aimer could judge how closely they could be clustered in the sea; another test for accuracy. He put the control column forward and started the descent in as steep a dive as the Dornier 17 was designed to take. Three splashes in the sea would be the boring end to a boring mission.

But why? Could he not celebrate this milestone in his life in a more glorious way? As the plane dived steeply a tingle of excitement passed through him. He already knew the feeling well; it came with the start of a bombing run, or a report through the intercom of enemy fighters, or the fear as flak burst around him. They all brought with them that electric charge to the nerve endings.

He made his decision in a instant. Still diving he pointed the bomber westwards towards the English coast and ordered his crew to stand-by at action stations. This would be one birthday Hans Rechtner – and the damned English – would never forget!

*   *   *

Flaxton was waking up to a new day. Another fine one. No clouds, a blue sky and, for this part of the country, an unusually warm westerly breeze blowing off-shore. To most people the nights were still as they always had been; calm sleep and innocuous dreams. It was the days, the waking hours, that were now so different, and each morning renewed the painful knowledge of the frightening times that lay ahead.

They were now constantly reminded that it was these seaside towns on the south and east coasts that would be the first to be made aware that the phoney war was coming to an end and real hostilities were imminent. They knew that the military war machine was literally taking them over. The evidence was all around them.

Flaxton was part of the first line of defence, a line that extended far inland from the fortified beaches and, as such, street and road signs had disappeared and the town and countryside around it were pock-marked with pill-boxes, their gun embrasures pointing towards the sea and north and south along the coastline. Barrage Balloons were sited haphazardly in the fields, air-raid shelters had sprung up in the streets and gardens, sandbagged ARP posts led off the pavements, emergency water tanks had been set up and filled to the brim at strategic points and guns – naval, anti-tank, anti-aircraft, anti-personnel – were sited within and outside the town. Flaxton was now ready for war, not if, but when it came.

Its inhabitants had slipped into the war mode with resigned efficiency. They had fortified their homes by protecting their windows, strengthening ceilings and, in many cases, sealing a room against gas attack. Provisions had been stored, candles stockpiled, lawns dug up (not Councillor Bradley's yet; the Webb lawnmower was still very active), vegetables planted and everyone carried their gas mask in its cardboard case wherever they went. The police and wardens had their steel helmets strapped to their backs, and the fire brigade and ambulance service were on constant alert.

The roads were busier than a year ago; even though nine out of ten families didn't own cars, military vehicles were everywhere and the streets were full of khaki and airforce blue uniforms.

So Flaxton was ready for Jerry – or so it thought…

*   *   *

The Dornier 17 bomber dropped to two thousand feet some five miles from the coast. The crew of five were tense now; excited. This is what they had joined the Luftwaffe for and to them Leutnant Rechtner was already a hero.

In only a few moments they would reach the coast and involuntarily they held their breath as the pilot dropped to a thousand feet. Very low. The land rushed at them. They skimmed over a small cluster of houses and a tower or two but none was worthy of three of the Third Reich's five hundred pound bombs.

Rechtner pulled the control column to port and the aircraft banked steeply towards the south. He corrected the plane's trim and altitude so that it was flying low along the shingle shoreline towards a sizeable town dead ahead and, having carefully checked that there were no barrage balloons on his flight path, he pushed the throttle forward to attain maximum speed: two hundred and twenty miles an hour.

There was no retaliation; no guns fired, no enemy fighters intercepted them. It was 8 a.m. Hans Rechtner, on his twenty-first birthday, had the skies over Flaxton-on-Sea to himself. The bomb-aimer in the nose of the plane rested his finger gently on the release button…

*

On the ground the throbbing of the two mighty Daimler-Benz engines of the Dornier grew louder and louder until they became

217

a deafening shriek. The terrible sound bounced off the ground making it vibrate, shaking all the buildings and the objects inside them.

In terror the citizens of Flaxton froze, immobile, staring at each other, their ears pounding with the noise and then, in the last moments, the explosions.

The earthquake struck once – twice – three times in quick succession. Fifteen hundred pounds of TNT.

As the ground rocked people fell, not crumpling, but rigidly, like poles being snapped and in an instant the air was filled with flying debris of every kind. Daylight disappeared as a pall of smoke blotted out the sky.

The noise was still shattering even though the aircraft had disappeared to the south, the shriek of the engines being replaced by other terrifying sounds. Debris was landing heavily in the street and through the roofs of buildings, screams of pain and fear came from all directions as people staggered around, some unscathed, but many clutching wounds and dripping blood. With it all was the never-ending crash of breaking glass.

It seemed an eternity but, in fact, it had all happened in seconds. The clanging bells of the fire engines and ambulances grew louder as they sped in from the town stations inland, and the military machines joined them from the surrounding camps.

The sight that greeted then as they turned into the High Street was apparently one of complete devastation. Buildings had collapsed into the road, some were on fire, bricks and masonry were everywhere and a dazed population was staggering around clutching at each other for support. There was no panic. The screaming had died away now and in its place was a deathly hush.

As the fire engines, ambulances and other emergency vehicles picked their way through the rubble the extent of the damage became more clear. Most buildings on the High Street and in the surrounding roads had superficial damage – roofs and windows mainly – but only a handful had been destroyed, amongst them the cinema, thankfully empty, which had taken the first direct hit and was now a blazing mound of rubble. At the far end of the street the Methodist Chapel had suffered a similar fate from the third bomb and taken the Minister's house and another two with it.

It was the second bomb's direct hit which was drawing most people to it. The Post Office had been destroyed. There was no fire; just a high mound of rubble and twisted masonry and digging frantically into it a beautifully sleek black Labrador dog.

Mountjoy was searching for his mistress.

*

The crew manning the Bofors gun on the end of the pier had no hope of at last firing their highly polished weapon at the Dornier: it came and went far too quickly and anyhow the gun's arc of fire was seawards and not inland; they would have taken the roof off the theatre if they had tried a shot at the speeding plane.

The soldiers sat around the gun as immobilised as the rest of the population, but with a grandstand view of the low-flying bomber and the three bombs that lazily fell from it, first horizontally and then, nose heavy, dropping down behind the buildings to be replaced by enormous sheets of flame and billows of smoke and that ear-splitting noise.

But theirs was not the only anti-aircraft gun in Flaxton. At the furthest end of the narrow spit of shingle which ran for half a mile along the shoreline south of the town was a Martello Tower. Built in 1815 it was designed as a defence against earlier feared invasions and had four large 24 lb cannons mounted on it. Now, alongside them, sat another sleek, highly polished Bofors gun and, as luck would have it – about the only bit of luck in and around Flaxton that morning – the crew were at action stations carrying out their morning drill.

The detachment commander, a sergeant with a row of First World War medals on his chest that suggested he was long past the 'caught napping' stage had shouted, "This is for real, boys", as soon as he had heard the tell-tale throb of German aero-engines and to see the Dornier coming straight at them had been too good to be true.

Other guns were now firing from inland, but they had a low, sideways-on, fast moving target and no real hope of hitting the plane. The Martello crew only had to fix the plane in their sights and watch it grow bigger and bigger.

With more experience they would have scored a number of hits with the rapid-firing gun in the seconds it took to fly over them –

but they did score once – and once was enough. The forty millimetre shell went straight through the under-belly of the fuselage just behind the wing roots and, exploding, severed all the control lines to the tail unit.

*

On its bombing run along the High Street the big plane, nicknamed the 'Flying Pencil' because of its long, sleek shape, bucked and rocked as the shock waves from the explosions hit it. The crew, hanging on for dear life, were deafened in their intercoms by the ecstatic and almost maniacal yelling coming from their pilot.

And then the Bofors shell hit, killing one of them outright.

Rechtner tried in vain to keep control of the aircraft. He was a good pilot and instantly calmed as the plane ceased to react to the controls. The rudder bar did nothing, the control column was sluggish and, with both engines still screaming at maximum power, the plane slipped, almost gracefully, towards the sea. They were too low for the crew to bale out – and there was no time anyway.

The impact came in the shipping lanes approaching Felixstowe harbour.

What made Leutnant Rechtner decide to descend to five hundred feet to drop his bombs will never be known. It was a foolish height for a heavy bomber and the hours of discussion in pubs, clubs, homes and more official quarters which followed the horrific event came to the conclusion that it was the act of an over-excited, impetuous young dare-devil.

The bodies of the five crew members were recovered by an Air-Sea Rescue Launch and brought ashore and, in accordance with the tradition of the time, they were afforded a full military funeral.

Leutnant Rechtner was eight and a quarter hours into his twenty-second year. It was ironic that he and his crew would be buried some time before his Flaxton-on-Sea victims.

CHAPTER ELEVEN

__Thursday, 2 May 1940.__ Himmler complains of the amount of work suppressing an obstructive population (Poland), carrying out executions and evicting crying and hysterical women.

In Britain the blackout at night leads to people being told to 'wear something white'. Men leave their shirt- tails hanging out and owners of white Pekinese dogs are urged to carry them!

As with everyone else in Flaxton that May morning the three explosions froze Nell, Vi, Rita and Rena. For seconds they stood motionless in the house and then ran to be together, meeting in the hall.

Looking back they saw how ludicrous it was. Nell had been in her nightie and dressing-gown in the kitchen, Vi was fully dressed letting out the cat into the back garden, Rita came rushing downstairs in her underwear and Rena, a towel wrapped almost around her, hurled herself out of the bathroom and down the stairs.

The sound of all the windows at the front of the house shattering accompanied their arrival together. By sheer luck no-one had been in a front room because, although the sticky tape had more-or-less held the glass together and prevented flying fragments, the blast had still blown the panes across the room.

Their ears rang with the residual noise. They, like everyone in Britain at this time, were totally unaware of what to do. It would only be a short while before most of the population would, in this situation, take immediate cover in whatever area of the house they had designated as the 'strong room', gas masks would be at the ready and they'd be waiting for the next bombs. Now, being amongst the first few to experience war from the air, the four of them did what every other inhabitant of Flaxton was doing; having thrown overcoats over their various items of clothing they went out into the road to see what was going on!

Looking down on the High Street from above they should have had a grandstand view but in fact there was nothing to see but a wall of thick black smoke, punctured by flames, which was drifting away from them in the westerly breeze out to sea. It was a young lad on a bicycle careering along the road who brought them the news.

"The cinema's gone," he yelled excitedly. This was indeed desperate news for the town's young folk. He passed, then swung his body around almost losing his balance and shouted an afterthought, "And the Post Office."

It took a second or two to sink in and then, with a terrified glance at each other they were off, running towards the steps leading down to the High Street. Their thoughts were confused as they raced along, Rita and Rena out in front, Vi helping Nell who was showing a remarkable turn of speed.

She was muttering, "Pat? Peggy? Alice? Surely not. Please God no..."

A certain amount of order was now being exercised at the three scenes of devastation. The Emergency Services were in charge and the towns-people, who had immediately thrown themselves at the piles of smoking rubble, were now behind rope barriers. An army of dedicated workers, police, firemen, ambulance men, doctors, nurses and ARP wardens, were tackling the grim task for which they had undergone months of training.

Ladders and hoses were everywhere and the emergency vehicles were crowded around the perimeter of each demolished building. The air was filled with the noise of pumps feeding water to the hoses and their loud clattering further invaded ears still ringing from the immense noise and blast of the explosions. Strangely, no-one was talking; there was some whispering but the workers attacking the rubble communicated only by rehearsed sign language. The need to listen was paramount: for cries, groans or moans and for creaking or rumbling which could mean a further collapse and the probability of more injury.

At the site of the demolished Post Office, the dog continued frantically digging. Mountjoy would know the scent of the victims better than anyone...

Rita and Rena reached the High Street first. There was no hesitation. They ducked under the ropes strung around the ruins of the Post Office and started to climb clumsily up the pile of bricks and lengths of broken timber. There was no discussion between the two of them and the thought of any danger never entered their heads. It was simple: they had to find Pat and Peggy. And they were somewhere in that pile of rubble...

Nell and Vi arrived and pushed through the crowd who, recognising them, gave way and helped them through. They saw a fireman talking to the twins and then handing them to a policeman who gently brought them down.

"We have a list of three occupants," he said to Nell. He hadn't yet mastered the art of tactfulness adding, "Not much hope for them. It was a mighty blast."

The tears were rolling down all four faces now. He glanced and did a double-take.

"Sorry, I'm new here. Did you know them?"

Nell mustered all her strength and in a clear, low voice said simply,

"We loved them."

She looked at the pile of rubble. Half-way up, at a crazy angle, the dog's kennel stuck out from the wreckage. Nell remembered Alice telling her that it would make a good air-raid shelter – but even through her tears she could see that it was empty...

Two women who knew them slightly came up and led them off to a WVS mobile canteen, its side opened up and a counter of buns, sandwiches and a large, steaming tea urn attracting a crowd around it. Ladies in the familiar dark green WVS uniform were taking trays of tin mugs filled with hot sweet tea to the ropes for the emergency workers. Recognising the four of them, dining chairs were brought out of a house and they were led to them.

As she sat down Rena's coat fell open, exposing a bare leg. None of them, less Vi who was fully dressed, had given a thought to the lack of clothes under their overcoats. Nell put her hand on Rita's arm, her voice quiet and amazingly calm.

"Take Rena to the house, love. Get yourselves properly dressed. You'll do yourselves no good catching a cold here."

After only a slight protest the two of them trudged back to the steps and, without daring to glance at the heap of rubble, climbed up to Clarence Road.

And still Mountjoy, the black Labrador, sniffed, dug and searched the ruins for his mistress...

"They're letting the dog stay."

One of the ARP Wardens, covered in dust and grime, streaked with sweat, was blowing on a mug of tea at the van counter. "He'll know the scent. Do more than the rest of us put together."

Other voices around Nell and Vi wafted in and out of their numb minds as they sat, tightly holding hands.

"The cinema manager says no-one was in the building..."

"Four are missing at the Church, including the Minister..."

"A body's been blown onto the roof of the library..."

"Over twenty seriously injured. The wards are full..."

"Geoff says the plane came down in the sea..."

"Why us? What've we done to annoy Jerry?"

"The dog's found something."

It was the worst news Nell and Vi could hear, and yet it was what they were most fearing. They couldn't hold back. They joined the crowd at the rope and saw a group of the emergency workers squatting down around a hole that had been cleared in the rubble. The steel helmeted heads of two of them, one with WARDEN and the other, POLICE painted on them, were just visible over the edge of the hole. A stretcher was handed up and any quiet murmurings that there were in the crowd stopped.

Everyone held their breath. A blanket completely covered the body being borne, with difficulty, down the slope as the stretcher was passed from worker to worker. Nell and Vi admitted afterwards to the same confused thoughts. They didn't want the body to be Pat, or Peggy, or Alice Banbury, but it had to be one of them.

A worker slipped and the stretcher nearly spilt its load. The crowd gasped.

Nell had the stupid thought of Rena, on stage, having to do a somersault as Marvo got it wrong again.

The tilting of the stretcher caused a hand to drop down from under the blanket and a worker hurriedly put it back but not before a wedding ring had glinted in the sunshine. Two of the three had been married, Peggy and Alice, but this was the thin, veined hand of an elderly person.

Alice Banbury was leaving her Post Office for the last time. Mountjoy, now held on a piece of string, followed her.

The men doffed their hats. Women wept, but in a controlled, British way. It was still all too hard to take in.

The ambulance, with its precious load, left slowly, its bell silent. Vi, holding Nell's hand, felt that it was the saddest sight of all.

She stood up. "Come on love. Let's go home for a moment. You need to dress. Then we'll come back."

Nell allowed herself to be shepherded by Vi towards the steps. All the troupe was there, scattered in the crowd. They didn't know what to do. They didn't trust themselves to mix and share their grief. Some of them experimented with something they hadn't done in many a long day; they quietly prayed.

Nell and Vi, slowly climbing the steps, missed the next episode in this terrible day. Why it should happen simultaneously no-one would ever know but, as if on cue, Tad emerged from one side of the rubble and Marvo from the other. They clambered up the bricks and masonry, met at a point and, without acknowledging each other, started to throw large and small chunks into what was once the back yard. The police and wardens shouted at them but they chose not to hear, the time for finesse was over; the Flaxton Theatre Company would now take charge of its own.

Belvedere, George and Norman advanced on the pile. A little man wearing a steel helmet with the word 'CHAIRMAN' on it tried to intervene and was sent flying by one of Belvedere's strong arms. The helmet fell off and was ground underfoot. The rescue workers were now experiencing something not in their training manual but they saw the sense of the initiative by the troupe: it was time that was important now – but it would almost certainly be too late anyway. More men and some of the women joined in. Human chains were formed and the pyramid of rubble started to shift back into the rear yard.

And now everyone was talking, almost shouting, willing on the voluntary team. No one paid any attention to the tall, thin stranger digging as feverishly as the rest of them. Ludovic Henschel needed those notebooks...

Councillor Bradley picked himself up, dusted off his steel helmet and noted, in dumb fury, that the word CHAIRMAN had been

scratched so badly that the only discernible letters were CHA-R—.
He wouldn't wear it again until the council signwriter had redone it
with tougher paint. He started to issue orders to all-and-sundry, but
all-and-sundry took not a blind bit of notice…

Nell and Vi reached their house to find that there, too, there had
been feverish activity. Don, Bill, Reg and Bob had been straight
round after the bombs had dropped. Now every front window
that had been shattered in the blast was boarded up and the front
door was lockable again.

When the twins had come back to dress they had tearfully told
the four of them about the Post Office and, quickly finishing
their carpentry, had rushed down to the High Street to see what
they could do. Now they were digging with everyone else.

Nell dressed in a daze. It seemed a lifetime since she had last
stood in the house preparing breakfast for the four of them and
then, like everyone, she had heard the deep throb of those
engines getting louder and louder. She shuddered and sat down at
the kitchen table. Vi was firm: they would all have a cup of tea
and some precious bacon on bread before they went back. They
must keep up their strength. She didn't add the obvious: it was
going to be a gruelling time ahead.

They were startled by a knock on the front door. Vi found on the
step the agitated form of the Chairman of Flaxton Town Council
holding in his hand a steel helmet bearing the word CHAR. Vi
did not like, never had liked, and never would like Councillor
Edward Bradley and in that she was at one with most of the
discerning inhabitants of Flaxton. Now she showed it.

"Yes?"

"I will speak with Mrs Masters, if you please," said the pompous
little man.

"Will you indeed," retorted Vi. "Just put the post through the
letter-box. You should be able to manage that."

She started to shut the door, but Councillor Edward forgetting
for a moment the mishap to his steel helmet thrusts it in Vi's face.

"I am not here in the capacity of postman, madam. This is
Council business," he snarled.

Vi turned and shouted through the hall. "Nell, a char wishes to
speak with you."

226

Curious, Nell poked her head around the kitchen door, saw who it was, and came down the hall followed by Rita and Rena. "I see you have a new job well suited to your talents, Councillor. What can I do for you?"

Councillor Bradley ignored the jibe, which was easy for him because he didn't understand it, took a deep breath and launched into his speech.

"As Chairman of the Town Council I have to tell you, Mrs Masters, that if you fail to comply with the instructions issued to you regarding the staging of a performance of your little show today before my chosen representatives I shall assume that you accept the Council's decision to make your lease non-renewable."

For a moment the four of them stood mute with disbelief that even this wretched little man could deliver such a message when he knew that as many of his electorate as could be accommodated on the bombed site of the town's Post Office were searching for the bodies of two of Nell Masters' troupe!

Suddenly the tableau was broken by a fist hitting Councillor Edward Bradley smack on the nose, making him reel backwards with blood pouring all over his smart shirt, tie and suit. Dazed, he turned and staggered to the pavement and was off, running blindly along Clarence Road, eyes watering, seeing nothing in front of him and holding his hand over a severely blackening eye.

Rena picked up the CHAR steel helmet from where it had fallen on the doorstep and Rita led Vi, who was clutching her right hand in pain, back into the kitchen. She had obviously learnt from Peggy how to deal with the lack of sensitivity in men!

Now it was Nell's turn to minister to one of her troupes' bruised fists...

*

Flaxton Cottage Hospital was on a war footing. The moment the bombs had dropped the Matron had put into effect the Emergency Plan so often rehearsed and now about to be tested. She smoothly went about her duties preparing, with her staff, the wards for an influx of casualties and all those off-duty immediately made their way to the hospital including both the resident and town doctors who would, in relays, tend to the arriving wounded.

The Plan was working splendidly. The seriously injured were patched up and sent on to Ipswich and those with lesser wounds, many from flying glass, were dealt with in Flaxton's own Operating Theatre and then put into a male or female ward. Not all the injuries were caused by flying debris; some people passing by on the High Street pavements when the bombs fell were thrown considerable distances by the blast and there were broken bones and deep bruising among the casualties.

Every admission was documented. Most of those who couldn't give details had wallets or handbags which identified them, and the few who had no means of identification and were unable to speak had a red disc attached to their treatment sheets at the foot of their beds; they would be named soon enough once the townspeople took stock or when they themselves regained their full faculties...

*

Back at the bombed site of the Post Office, despite the feverish activity by the army of volunteers, Pat and Peggy's bodies had not been found. Why, when they slept on the top floor *above* Alice Banbury's bedroom, was the search yielding nothing? Those trained for such emergencies blamed the vagaries of bomb blasts. They might be anywhere.

Nell, the twins and a bruised fisted Vi made their way with heavy hearts back down the steps to the High Street. They digested through dulled senses the manic clearing activity going on. Of course there was no longer any hope. People came forward and gently led them back to the WVS mobile canteen and the four chairs where four exhausted workers sprang up and guided them to the seats. They sat, wearily, with wan smiles of thanks to these kind, compassionate people and mugs of sweet tea were put into their hands. They didn't want it but it would have been churlish to refuse.

Again they heard in a blur snatches of conversations.

"Obviously forced right through to the cellar..."

"Could take all night..."

"It was a direct hit. Straight through the roof. A big bomb..."

"The bastards..."

"Sssh, ladies present…"

"They were such nice kids…"

"Are you going to see your two at the hospital?"

This was all too much. Nell longed for her office and its deep chair. More than anything she longed for her dearest Masters. He would have taken charge, given her comfort, known what to do. She had told Don to put up CLOSED signs at the theatre. There would be no performance tonight – or probably ever again.

Her arm was being gently touched.

"Are you going to see your two at the hospital?" She had just heard that. There it was again.

"Excuse me." It was a gentle and concerned voice. A man was squatting now in front of her holding her hand.

"You *are* Nell Masters, aren't you?" She nodded dumbly.

"I'm Doctor Cartwright. I've just finished my shift at the hospital. Stopped for a cup of tea. Your two young ladies. I've seen them on stage doing their charladies act. They're in shock. Bomb blast. No identification. Only had nighties and overcoats on. I bet they'd love to see you."

*

Councillor Edward Bradley was at the Police Station. The entire Police Force was in the High Street except for an elderly constable who leaned wearily on the counter.

"That's a nasty bump you have there, Councillor. Jerry is no respecter of status, is he? You need the hospital, not us."

Constable Budd, recalled from retirement to bolster Flaxton's first line of defence, had seen it all before – and much more. He had served in the army through the last war and had, until he reached the statutory age, policed this area of Suffolk ever since.

"I wish to report an assault on my person." Councillor Bradley was at his most pompous.

"Right-ho, Ted."

The Councillor bridled at this lack of respect but knew that this was all he would get from a man who had known one or two of the darker secrets of his life over the years. "An assault, you say?"

Slowly PC Budd took a large ledger from a drawer, slowly he opened it at the next clear page and slowly he picked up a pen which he slowly dipped into an inkwell. Constable Budd wished to illustrate to the Council Chairman that the Flaxton Police never panic even in the face of such a heinous – alleged – crime.

"Assault, eh? I shall see that Herr Hitler is interviewed about this immediately."

Sarcasm was lost on Councillor Bradley. He explained that this had nothing to do with Hitler, suggested that Constable Budd should pull himself together and outlined the details of the incident which had occurred on the doorstep of number 34, Clarence Road.

By way of a return match Constable Budd explained how trivial this all was compared to the carnage in the High Street, suggested that the Councillor should forget all about it and outlined the text of an apology that he should make to Nell Masters for his crass lack of sensitivity. He did his duty, however, and logged the complaint which would, unless it was withdrawn, have to be proceeded with.

Councillor Bradley, satisfied that the law would prevail, made his way back to the High Street, two tufts of cotton wool sticking from his nostrils. He hoped that people would think that he, too, had suffered war wounds.

When the Councillor left the Police Station, Constable Budd picked up the telephone which miraculously was still working, the Exchange being in a building detached from the Post Office, and asked for a number.

"Hello. Vernon? Ronald Budd here..."

*

Councillor Bradley was standing, looking important, at the bombed site that had been, only a few hours before, the Methodist Church. He had decided to give the Post Office ruins a wide berth in case those wretched stage people set on him again; he knew they were all there looking for the two girls who did that stupid charlady act. His nose and eye hurt appallingly and, to add insult to injury, no-one took any notice of any orders he barked at them. He thought this was because his voice sounded different now that his nose was blocked up – and also because he had now lost his status symbol: his steel helmet. He almost jumped out of his skin when a hand

230

clamped onto his shoulder, twisting him around to face one of the town's opinion leaders whom he disliked more than most, Vernon Rogers, the Editor of the Flaxton Chronicle.

"Well now, Ted…"

And then the newspaper man went on to explain in a mock fatherly tone how he was going to cover the story of how the Chairman of the Town Council reacted when his town was devastated by enemy action and so many townspeople had been killed or injured; how he had left the scene to invade the grief of a woman – a pillar of the church and town – who was the surrogate mother of the two young ladies feared dead in the ruins of the Post Office and then how he had gone on to threaten her on her own doorstep. Surely a resignation issue?

"Of course," he concluded, "all this nasty business could be avoided if…"

Councillor Bradley, more gloomy than ever, made his way back through the town to the Police Station where Constable Budd was expecting him. The charge was dropped and the stern policeman reminded the Councillor of the seriousness of wasting police time.

*

"I got up early, you see." Peggy, in a quiet, wavering voice was giving her four visitors details of her and Pat's incredible escape from certain death.

"Mountjoy had spent the night in my bedroom." Ears in other beds around her pricked up.

"He'd been washing himself, slurping, and I couldn't stand it any longer so I slipped a coat over my nightie and took him out." Other patients in the ward were confused and pitied the poor girl. Men; they were all the same…

Nell was far from confused. She was sitting on the chair between their two beds. The red 'unidentified' discs had been removed and replaced with the girls' names. She held one of Peggy's hands and one of Pat's who was lying back with her eyes closed.

Pat's heart still thumped, her body shook and she had that cold, unpleasant feeling of fear inside her but the sedatives were helping and the bruises would heal. Peggy was in a better state and reckoned that Pat had probably shielded her from some of the blast.

Vi sat the other side of Peggy's bed and the twins were on the edge of it. Such was the scale of the incident that Matron had waived all her strict rules and, provided everyone was quiet and not disturbing other patients, they could stay and comfort them.

"We walked down to Mountjoy's special patch of grass and then he obviously saw something that needed investigating." Peggy's speech was fast and urgent, broken by tiny sobs.

"He tugged at the lead and it came away from his collar. I can't have clipped it on properly. And he was off like a dart. He just disappeared. I called and called and tried to follow him but he'd just gone."

She took a sip of water. Nell stroked her hand.

"I went back and got Pat. She slipped a coat on. It was only about seven and very few people were about. Mrs Banbury wasn't up yet."

They hadn't told the girls about Alice. They'd just said that she was poorly. There'd be time later when it would be right to break the news to them.

Peggy rushed on.

"We went off in search of the rascal. Someone said he'd been seen haring up the High Street towards the Martello Tower. We searched and searched and people kept telling us that he'd been seen somewhere else. And then, in despair, we started back to the Post Office to break the news to Mrs Banbury, and we were just opposite the Methodist Church when this terrible aeroplane ..."

She broke off, sobbing and shuddering and Vi leant forward and squeezed her hand with her unbandaged one.

"Mountjoy got back alright. He's being looked after..."

Nell stopped her with a sharp look but luckily Peggy was too distressed to take in the strangeness of the remark. They settled her down and quietly left them.

Belvedere, hidden in the shadows outside the hospital, watched the four of them leave. He had suffered as much distress through the morning as everyone else but he found his mind darting from concern for Pat and Peggy to fear for the loss of the notebooks which, if Peggy was telling the truth, would have been close to her in the flat. He was ashamed that he was giving any thought to such relatively unimportant matters when the lives of those two lovely spirited girls were in doubt, but he consoled himself that it was probably what Peggy would have wanted.

Now, with the amazing news that they were alive, he needed a quick, urgent word with her. He strode into the ward to which he was directed and saw the two of them lying peacefully, seemingly asleep. Sitting on the chair next to Peggy he quietly whispered her name. She opened her eyes and, to his chagrin, started crying. He leant close to her and, for some reason, gently kissed her on the forehead. She smiled and gripped his hand.

A quarter-of-an-hour later he was walking as briskly as his portly frame would allow away from the hospital and back towards the devastated town centre. He had a clear plan and he knew just what he had to do. His first stop was at a shop in the High Street but when he reached it he found men boarding up the shattered windows and a roughly drawn sign assuring him that it would be 'BUSINESS AS USUAL TOMORROW'. Belvedere, noting the 'bulldog spirit', nodded in satisfaction. He would be there the next morning as it opened.

There was also business as usual in the little flat behind the High Street shared by Elaine and George. Despite the day's drama, Elaine insisted that the never-wavering routine of their lives should not be disrupted. The familiar domestic harmony so appreciated by George was evident in the clean, tidy sitting-room, the furniture polished to perfection, the pretty flower-pattered curtains gently fluttering in the breeze wafting through the open windows, and the reassuring sounds of the BBC – news to listen to, music to sing along to – through the big bakelite wireless set.

Now, sharp at five o'clock, Elaine brought in the tray of boiled eggs, bread with a hint of margarine, and a big pot of tea. As if on cue, George settled at the little dining table in the window, now cleared of its ever-present dressmaking paraphernalia.

It seemed all wrong to him that everything was so quickly back to normal but the Emergency Co-ordinator who had arrived from nowhere and assumed command of the rescue operation had sent all but his trained teams away from the scene and, with Pat and Peggy safe, Nell had sent the troupe home 'to reciprocate'.

Elaine had just settled opposite George, serviettes had been tucked under chins and spoons were poised to crack eggs, when the door bell rang. It was no ordinary ring but went on and on as if it was stuck. George, ever the pessimist, groaned and rushed into the hallway expecting to find a posse of police or firemen announcing another full-scale drama. Instead he found the large and imposing figure of Belvedere completely filling the door frame.

"Dear boy," boomed the familiar voice. "So here is your little house. 'I crown thee king of intimate delights, fire-side enjoyments, home-born happiness' – dear lady."

He was by now in the sitting-room having squeezed past George in the narrow hallway whilst declaiming and was bowing deeply to Elaine.

"William Cowper."

Elaine, who could never get used to Belvedere, nodded, the top of the egg in her spoon transfixed inches from her mouth. Suddenly the room seemed very full and thoroughly disorganised.

"Good evening Mr Cowper," she said apparently in all innocence, "you look just like Belvedere Galbraith," and she smiled sweetly at him. Belvedere, thoroughly confused, produced his snuff-box.

"I need, dear lady, to speak with George – alone."

Elaine lowered the spoon, "You may choose the hall, my kitchen or the lavatory, Belvedere. That is all the space that is on offer – and," she added loudly, "no snuff in my home thank you very much."

It has to be said of Belvedere that whenever his total lack of grace and manners was pointed out to him he deflated like a punctured balloon and was immediately overcome with remorse.

He stood now like a very large naughty schoolboy, "Of course, of course, of course."

He bowed again, causing Elaine to wince as various parts of him brushed against her prized knick-knacks carefully placed around the room. Then he turned, causing more wincing, to George.

"England hath need of thee," he bellowed as he led his host into the hall adding over his shoulder to Elaine should she be in any doubt, "William Wordsworth."

Elaine shook her head and smiled. For all his bombast she liked Belvedere and felt safe with him in the troupe. She was sure that beneath it all he had a kind heart and a wise head on his shoulders. She jabbed a soldier of bread into the yolk of her egg and wondered what his surprise visit to their flat was all about, and as she chewed on the, by now, cold mouthful she heard loud whisperings followed by the front door slamming shut.

George re-entered the room, plonked himself down opposite her and tucked into his egg.

"He hath urgent need of me," he said, "Belvedere Galbraith, nineteen-forty." They both laughed but George would say no more.

"Better you don't know, luvvie," he said in his light Welsh tenor voice feeling it unwise to tell her that he had been instructed to parade at the Pier Tavern at twenty-one hundred hours for a quick snifter before night exercises.

They finished the meal in a mixture of gossip from Elaine filling in lurid details of the day's drama, and grunts of acknowledgement from George as he painstakingly worked out, using mental arithmetic, that twenty-one hundred hours was 9 p.m. What on earth had Belvedere got in mind – other than a longer than usual evening in the pub?

*

George entered the saloon bar at the Pier Head Tavern sharp on 9 p.m. He knew better than to be late on parade! He saw that Norman was already there with Belvedere and had been sent to the bar to get the round of drinks. George joined him.

"I've been here ages." Norman's mournful north-country voice matched his mood. "I worked out that twenty-one hundred hours was eight o'clock. I don't know how to do the sum."

They carried the drinks back to the table where two startling things caused George to spill the froth from his beer – a very rare occurrence. First it was the bunch of flowers resting on the table in front of Belvedere and second, it was the big man's whispered pronouncement that they only had time for this one round. Belvedere whispering was startling enough; to restrict his inflow of alcohol was unheard of.

An hour later, after three more quick rounds, Belvedere led them out of the pub and more or less marched ahead of them holding the bunch of flowers vertically in his right hand like a sword. They tried to keep in step but Norman kept on tripping over his own feet and decided a slow trot would work better. It was as well that most of the population were indoors licking their real and imaginary wounds caused by the days' events and that very few lace curtains remained in the High Street to be twitched...

It was dark now, intensified by low cloud and a heavy drizzle of rain. The pyramid of rubble that, only a dozen or so hours before, had been the smart town Post Office with a cosy flat full of happy occupants above it presented a gaunt, dead image through the wet gloom.

Belvedere gave them no time to brood. With a sweep of the flowers he sent his troops through the rope barrier and aloft over the broken bricks and masonry, handing the bouquet to George as he passed. He had briefed them on their mission and, with cut and bruised hands and twisted ankles, they inched their way upwards towards their goal.

"And what do you think you three are up to?"

The voice, coming from close behind his ear, made Belvedere jump out of his skin. He turned to see a steel helmet with ARP stamped on it and beneath it, eyeing him balefully, the face of Reg Prentice.

"Bel," he jerked back, "What the blazes are you up to?"

Belvedere, never one to lose an opportunity when it was presented to him, clapped Reg on the back.

"There you are then, old love. Remember the Bard? 'Our bridal flowers serve for a burial corse, and all things change them to the contrary'."

He turned and yelled up into the darkness, "Plant them at the top, men. On the kennel."

He turned and fixed Reg with a stern expression. "Romeo and Juliet," he said with finality.

"The kennel?" Reg had to ask, it was his duty. He'd been sent on patrol to ensure that the good people of Flaxton didn't forget themselves for a moment and resort to a little looting and now here, of all people, was Belvedere Galbraith shouting upwards at nothing other than a pile of bricks in the pitch dark.

"Flowers, you see." The usual boom was quite sepulchral, "For Alice." His voice dropped to a whisper, "We felt it our duty."

He removed his hat and bowed his head looking meaningfully at Reg who, whilst wishing to share the moment, didn't know whether it was correct to remove his helmet or salute. Being on duty he felt the latter course would be correct and so they stood at attention until a small avalanche of bricks and stones announced the re-emergence of George and Norman, their clothes, hands, faces and hair covered in brick and concrete dust. The two of them looked as scared by the whole episode as they undoubtedly were. Before they could say anything Belvedere put his arm around Reg's shoulder and led him down the pavement.

"You know how we all feel, old laddie. Less said the better, don't you think? Careless talk…" his voice trailed off. He couldn't remember how the new catch-phrase ended.

"Costs lives," murmured Reg. "Say no more, Bel, your secret's safe with me." With that he set off down the High Street.

Belvedere gathered his troops and led them back to the Pier Head Tavern where, after a wash and brush-up in the Gents, they carried on where they had left off, but not before an oblong package, carefully wrapped in brown paper and tied with string, had been transferred from Norman's coat pocket into Belvedere's safe keeping.

"Fastened in the roof of the kennel, Bel. As you said."

George gulped deeply, Norman sipped and Belvedere smiled.

"Another round, if you please, landlord," he bellowed in the general direction of the bar.

* * *

In the Hotel Bristol in Warsaw there seemed to be something of a stalemate between the SS and the enemy of the Third Reich, prisoner Crisciak. Neither quite knew how to handle the other. Freddy felt more secure with the knowledge that friends were somewhere on hand to extricate him from these evil clutches, though how he couldn't imagine. He also felt that he'd won the battle over whether General Streyer should keep him – or, to be more precise, his brain – in one piece or annihilate him. Streyer would, of course, have much preferred to do the latter but knew that he couldn't. There was even the terrible prospect of the prisoner being received in Berlin by the Führer himself!

What really worried the General was how he would be portrayed by this damned Professor if the wretched man was honoured by an audience with Hitler. It was a ludicrous situation for him to be in.

But Streyer was not a Gestapo General by chance; intrigue and cruelty had been necessary – and pleasurable – throughout the course of his meteoric advancement through the ranks of the Waffen-SS and he had devised a way to solve the present quandary. A person had been plucked from hiding in Norway and brought 'under the protection' of SS General Friedrich Streyer into Poland. That person was now imprisoned in a former Austrian Cavalry barracks near Cracow whilst the construction of a special camp nearby was being completed.

Streyer now summoned Freddy to his office. The guards marched him in – in fact *they* marched, he sauntered. It was a room he knew well; he'd been entertained in the Grand Salon on many occasions. Now he stood before the General's ornate desk and, there being no chair, had no option but to stare down at this repulsive little man.

"I have some news for you, my dear Professor. I now intend that, voluntarily, you will start work – *accurate* work – on the project which the Führer has decreed you shall be engaged on as a service to the Third Reich. You will not make any mistakes, you will be diligent and you will work day and night until such time as it is decreed that you shall be taken to Berlin. You will also inform us of the location of your wretched note-books."

He banged the table viciously.

Freddy wondered what on earth this terrible man was talking about. They knew they couldn't use force for fear of damaging his brain, so how else could they persuade him to co-operate?

The General's voice was oilier than ever.

"Your mother is Anya? Countess Anya Crisciak – is she not?" Freddy stiffened and cold fear gripped him. He couldn't breathe. He stared without any expression at Streyer. The General returned his stare with an icy smile through his rimless spectacles.

"Your mother is now under our protection. She will shortly be transferred to a new camp which we are building near Cracow."

His hand slid underneath a folder on his desk and he brought out a black-and-white photograph which he pushed across the desk towards Freddy.

One look was enough to see that it was his mother but the finery and noble bearing were gone. Her hair was shorn; her look, defeated. Worse than all this was the shapeless dress she was wearing. It had broad vertical stripes like a pair of men's pyjamas. General Streyer smiled, an evil, deathly smile.

"She is held in a small town you Poles call Oswiencim."

His piercing stare totally immobilised Freddy and his voice was now no more than a whisper.

"We call it Auschwitz."

CHAPTER TWELVE

Friday, 10th May 1940. *The German offensive in the West begins with the invasion of the Low Countries. In ten days they surround the capital of Holland, The Hague.*

In Britain Winston Churchill becomes Prime Minister. Children and some mothers are evacuated from the east and south coasts.

In the week following the bombing of Flaxton there was considerable talk ranging from idle chatter to serious debate, a lot of action and, for some, time for contemplation.

The talk ranged through how and why such a terrible incident should happen to a harmless, small seaside resort and what should be done to prevent it happening in the future. Many, particularly women, saw it as they would an unprovoked attack on a defenceless child; they wanted the culprits punished.

It was an insight into the mental state of Britain at this time, after over eight months of non-aggression, that few immediately saw the bombing as an act of war! Wanton, meaningless, unprovoked, unfair, unkind, mean, vicious, these words, and so many more like them were used constantly, but veterans from the last conflict merely nodded and said yes, that's what war was all about.

As so often happens when people are flailing around in the dark for someone to blame the final destination for all the abuse and recrimination was, inevitably, those who govern. The central Government, already in a state of collapse as the Prime Minister, Neville Chamberlain fought for his political life after the military fiasco in Norway, bore the brunt of the local vitriol.

Flaxton was a bit of a celebrity having beaten all other towns to win the unwanted distinction of being the first to suffer a severe bombing raid. The nightmare was compounded by the descent onto the already shell-shocked Community of a host of Government Ministers, the Member of Parliament, military bigwigs, petty officials and, worst of all, reporters from national newspapers and the BBC. They all arrived in smart cars guzzling large quantities of petrol which was now as precious to the nation as gold dust.

None of them stayed long. They came expecting stiff upper lips and flag waving as the British were believed to indulge in when up against it or when faced by their leaders, but they went away with multiple fleas in their ears. Flaxton-on-Sea was *not amused*...

Before they hurriedly left they were asked why it was possible for an enemy aircraft to fly over any part of Britain without prior warning to its inhabitants, why the barrage balloons whose only value was to snare low-flying aircraft weren't sited at each end of the town from which an enemy aircraft would – and did – make its bombing run and what was going to be done to compensate the bereaved and injured, many of whom would now have no income?

And many asked the simple question, "What is being done *now* to prevent it happening again?"

Some even dared to veer away from the local issue and ask what was happening to our – in many cases *their* – boys in France?

The Flaxton Chronicle, double its usual size, asked all these questions on their behalf and, in stark headlines, formed the conclusion that none of this galaxy of civil and military super-stars could answer directly any of them! Those more experienced in the art of gerrymandering, in other words the politicians, managed to swing their statements into gung-ho rhetoric of the 'we can take it' kind. It was they who received the biggest fleas in their ears at the hands of Vernon Rogers – who now added the title of 'Chief War Reporter' to all his other functions.

The only saving grace of this reportage and the often bitter verbal exchanges that took place face to face was that word got around in the high places. The posh official cars, some polished black, others khaki with flags fluttering and stars on their bumpers, stopped purring down the now cleared High Street towards the Council offices. Flaxton was left, as it wanted, to lick its own wounds...

It was now that the town's population turned to – and on – its local bureaucracy, the Town Council. Something very strange was going on here. It was generally accepted that their leader, Edward Bradley – Ted the postman – was less than loved by many of the electorate but he *was*, and had been, fairly elected to that Office and, until the last month or two, had done the job officiously but well. Now he seemed to be behaving very strangely as if, to put it charitably – and only his nearest cronies would be bothered to do that – he was under great stress. Perhaps the state of the world was getting too much for him. Probably not. Few reckoned Councillor Bradley saw far beyond his postman's boots...

Despite Vernon Rogers keeping to his word and *not* printing the story in the Chronicle, news got around regarding the Councillor's extraordinary behaviour on the day of the bombing – indeed many had witnessed much of it. There were angry demands for his resignation. The Chronicle was under an obligation to print letters denouncing his callous behaviour and the shops and pubs were full of acrimony towards him.

The solution to this discontent was a political masterstroke engineered by the ever-calm leader of the minority party, Councillor Winifred Ledbury. She persuaded the members that for the duration of the war they should, indeed must, abandon party politics and form a 'Town Council of National Unity'. A straw poll in the Chronicle gave the plan almost unanimous support so, constitutionally or unconstitutionally – no-one cared which – they did just that. Councillor Bradley remained Chairman but lost nearly all his power because Councillor Winifred, his deputy, had the support of most of the members.

It was encouraging to the new Council and most of the electorate of the town that the politicians in Whitehall, many of whom had been along to plague them during the previous week, soon followed their example and formed a National Government. In their case they got rid of the leader, Neville Chamberlain and appointed as Prime Minister, Winston Churchill.

So, through idle talk and serious debate the cruel act of a twenty-one-year-old German airman resulted in a unified Flaxton being at least slightly more ready than most other towns and cities in Britain for the onslaught that was undoubtedly to come.

And with all the talk came action. It was probably the shock that caused people, with no previous experience of the act of war, to treat the bombing as they would a gas explosion or similar civil incident. Everyone was out clearing up. Most of the shops in the High Street, which were the lower portions of substantial three and four storey houses, had suffered some form of structural damage. Many roofs were holed by flying debris and, of course, most of the windows in the vicinity of the three blasts had been shattered. Whereas in the years ahead there would be temporary patching and boarding-up after air-raids, now an army of building contractors moved in and the East Anglian glass companies did a roaring trade. Flaxton was to be restored, not to its former glory because the sites of the Post Office, Methodist Church and Cinema would remain empty weed-covered holes, but certainly to a semblance of the smart, neat town it had been only a week before.

A sign that the authorities *had* learned a lesson or two from the raid was apparent to everyone: barrage balloons were now sited along the coast to the north and south of the town. Gently ducking and weaving in the breeze, the cables connecting them to their winches would prevent any more low-level bombing runs down the High Street.

The people themselves were now much more alert, as the country had been in the first few days of the war. Everyone was carrying their gasmasks again, the air-raid shelters had been cleaned out – many in people's gardens had become garden sheds for every type of rubbish – and fighting the ARP wardens and the strict blackout rules had ceased to be an honourable pastime; now everyone was willing to 'knock up' those they found infringing the rules.

*   *   *

In Poland Freddy Crisciak had passed a most unpleasant week since he had been forced to look at the photograph of his poor mother in SS General Streyer's office. This once proud, noble, happy woman was now shown as a defeated, cowed and frightened creature. It was as if both her blood and her spirit had been drained from her. Over what period of time this metamorphosis had been achieved by this evil regime Freddy could only guess. Months? Weeks? He would have been even more distraught, if that were possible, to know that it had been concentrated into a matter of a few days.

He had been pushed into the lift. The same attendant who had given him the coded answer to his question was there but gave no sign other than the minutest shake of his head. He seemed deeply worried and Freddy soon saw why.

"Down."

It was a curt order from one of the guards. Down? Oh dear Lord. The cells and...

He was thrown into a small windowless cell about eight feet by six feet. There was a wooden shelf some three feet wide raised a foot from the floor with a rough, stained, blanket on it and a small table on which was a pad of paper and a pencil. Against it was a chair and in the corner a bucket for sanitation. That was it: nothing more. The door slammed shut.

There was no sound and the fetid air hung around him like a mist. It was cold and damp but that wasn't the only cause for the shivers that wracked his body. His brain, the brain that was supposed to be crystal clear and full of the formulae that it had deduced along the road towards nuclear fission, was jammed with fear and dread from the situation he was now in. It must be so with all hostages, he thought. No-one knows that I am here. I can rot; die a slow lingering death.

Then his brain, yet again, had started to click into gear. Friends were still on hand and the lift attendant would report where he was. He looked at the solid door and the plastered walls and ceiling from which hung a solitary low wattage bulb. Impregnable. A rat in a trap. The word 'rat' reminded him of the swine Streyer's delight in calling his mother an alley rat. He would surely die for that if not for the long list of heinous crimes he'd already committed. Freddy would see that he died for that insult.

Empty threats. Pointless. He had already decided what he would do if this happened, and had spent some time guessing what he was sure the Berlin Research Institute would already know. He knew that they were quite some way along the scientific path regarding the background structure of Project Omega but he was pretty certain they didn't know where to go next. He – and only he – did. So he picked up the pencil and started regurgitating the background. There was weeks of work here and, to those not knowing the detail, his scribbles were undoubtedly authentic. It would have to do for the time being and, above all, it would bring him – and the friends outside – some time.

244

For a week Freddy wrote, recreating the old formulae and equations in the finest detail. Unknown to him it was passed to a Nazi physicist working in Warsaw assigned to some project to do with the new concentration camps being built in Poland. The man put aside his research on the effects of Zyklon-B gas to give a cursory look at Freddy's work. He could see that it was certainly not rubbish, there was high grade physics being put together here.

On having this reported to him Streyer was satisfied that he had, at last, tamed this Polish animal who had dared to defy him. He allowed himself one of his wintry smiles and poured himself a large portion of the finest Szampan.

Freddy was undoubtedly suffering as Streyer had intended that he should. He had no change of clothing, a bowl of cold water and a brick of soap were passed through the door each morning, his overflowing latrine was emptied every two days and the light bulb was never extinguished. Watery, luke-warm potato soup in tin bowls and lumps of stale black bread were thrown in to him sometimes once, sometimes twice a day.

At night he lay on the wooden shelf facing the damp, plastered wall and, amazingly, drifted into a light sleep. Despite the soundproofing he would hear in the deep silence of the night cries and sobs, shouts for lost loved ones, and sometimes brief screams that would suddenly cut off into echo.

Psychologically he was a wreck – as Streyer had intended he should be – but despite his dire condition he still clung to the vain hope that he could save his mother and that his beloved Peggy was still alive. With his tongue resting on the ampoule of cyanide he worked on...

*   *   *

For the Flaxton Pier Theatre Company it had been a busy week getting things back to as normal a state as possible. Pat and Peggy made rapid recoveries and were discharged, still badly bruised, into Nell's tender care and, at their own insistence, immediately returned to the stage determined to 'show that Hitler what we're made of'.

They were amazed to discover that a tidy little sum of money to replace essential items destroyed or damaged in the bombing awaited them. All those who lost possessions were eligible for a share of money donated by the townspeople doubled, pound for pound, by the Town Council under the direction of Councillor Winifred Ledbury.

The Chairman, Councillor Edward applied for aid on the grounds of 'the trauma of High Office during the outrage'. The phrase, and the capital letters were his from his neatly completed application.

Whilst no money was forthcoming, Councillor Winifred was very sympathetic and the Council voted their colleague a long, extended, (they used both words to make the point) leave of absence and his wife duly despatched him to a dragon of an aunt in Pontefract.

He left, surprisingly willingly, on the understanding that his aunt's whereabouts were not revealed to anyone, whoever it might be. His wife joined with the people of Flaxton in expressions of relief and applauded the appointment of Councillor Winifred to the 'High Office' to which Councillor Edward had referred. And a further benefit emerged: in the hands of a replacement postman letters started to be delivered on time!

It was after the late unlamented Edward Bradley had left that a story circulated in the town regarding two mysterious visitors who had visited the Councillor shortly before the bombing. His harassed secretary had been sworn to secrecy by him after what she described as 'two burly London men in dark suits' had barged into his office and, after some very heated words during which she heard, doubtless with her ear pressed to the door, 'overdue', 'pay now' and 'times up' they had left without so much as a goodbye and thank you. Now that he was gone she felt she could unburden herself to her best friend but, of course, in such a close-knit community it only took a day to be all around the town!

One thing was certain, when he left his trappings of wealth that he had constantly flaunted in front of everyone – his 17 horse-power Sunbeam Talbot, the Webb motor mower and his smart clothes disappeared from view. Much to the relief of the members he also resigned from the golf club. The least lurid explanation for all this – that a mysterious and doubtless illegal form of funding had dried up – was probably nearest the truth.

In her newly elevated role Councillor Winifred threw herself into a frenzy of activity. She approached Nell with a request that, for a very handsome fee, the Pier Theatre should be lent each afternoon to the cinema owner for the screening of films. Nell was delighted. In one stroke it eased the Company's financial position and rescued the troupe from the exhaustion and frustration of the two weekly matinée performances.

Don, Reg, Bob and Bill Colbourn entered into the new arrangement with enormous enthusiasm – not least because each received an extra dollop of much needed cash in their wage packets.

A large roll-up screen was borrowed from the Army Kinema Corporation and fixed to the proscenium arch and Don took the opportunity of the long ladder to replace the R on the word PIER. 'Nell's Rs' joke was removed from the witticisms of the military members of the audience at a stroke! A portable projector was housed upstairs in the Dress Circle which, they reckoned, would just about take the weight of it and its rather portly projectionist.

Nell was not only pleased to help the cinema manager who had been devastated by the loss of his precious building which had been run by three generations of his family but also delighted to have the Pier Theatre so busy.

"We're multi-medical," she proudly proclaimed to Pat and Peggy. They thought she meant the two of them having been in hospital but Vi explained to them later that Nell had meant 'multi-media'. They were none the wiser and nor was Vi or anyone else who heard the phrase. Nell was way ahead of her time, but Masters had often used the word 'media' to describe the theatre and cinema and what Masters said...

Nell was in her office during one of these afternoons working at some script alterations Tad and Norman wanted to make to their acts when Vi put her head around the door and said that Councillor Winifred was outside and would like a word with her. The mumblings she'd heard as she sat at her desk were, when the door opened, transferred into the mellifluous voices of Clark Gable and Joan Crawford becoming well acquainted in some film or other. She'd nip out and see the end of it once the work was done.

"Show the dear in," she smiled at Vi. It was so good, thought Vi, to see Nell her old self again.

Councillor Winifred appeared with Josey under her arm. They were given the large armchair and the dog settled comfortably on her lap hoping this would be a long stay. She felt comfortable and safe here.

"Nell dear, I'm much exercised by this ridiculous audition business," the Councillor never wasted time in idle chit-chat; she believed in getting straight to the point.

"It's yet another Postman Ted nonsense I'm having to sort out. Heavens knows what devious little scheme he had in mind in trying to get you out of here but take it from me that it won't happen. You're all doing a wonderful job and long may it last. I hope this nasty conflict will be cleared up soon and then we can all settle back into our peaceful, uneventful lives."

All this was said in the tone of a directive. Nell smiled. Were Hitler to be on the receiving end of Winifred Ledbury in full flow there's little doubt, she thought, that he would quickly agree to her demands, apologise, withdraw behind Germany's boundaries and promise not to do anything so foolish again!

Nell tried to keep up with all this but the blessed relief in Councillor Winifred's statement was almost too much for her.

"You mean no audition?"

"Certainly not. An insult. Keep up the good work. The lease is renewed."

She jumped up from the chair rudely awakening Josey who found herself being neatly tucked under the arm of authority. They shook hands warmly and Councillor Winifred was off to sort out another of Postman Ted's nonsenses.

Nell sat down again for a moment. Such relief. One hurdle removed. Just the wretched ENSA to go, then a few months of good work until blessed retirement and – she looked yet again at the calendar picture – to her sister's in the Highlands. She strode, hardly needing her stick, into the corridor. After giving Vi the good news and telling her to pass it around the troupe she was off into the auditorium.

With only one projector available there were frequent breaks in the films whilst the projectionist changed the reels and during this time the lights stayed out so as not to spoil the mood of the film. The soldiers and airmen loved these moments whistling and cat-calling up to the poor man at the front of the dress circle who, with a cycle lamp attached to a piece of his wife's elastic around his head, sweated to lace the film through the intricate sprockets.

It was during one of these breaks that Nell appeared at the edge of the stage by the steps. There was an immediate, respectful, silence. Everyone these days seemed to be expecting momentous announcements, and this could well be such a moment. She felt she should say something.

"Multi-medical. That's what we are."

Why she said it she had no idea but an approving murmur went round the audience and two sailors, home on leave, rushed forward to help her down the steps. She settled into one of the more comfortable rear seats with no-one around her and immersed herself in the steamy world of Clark and Joan. In no time she was asleep, gently snoring.

*   *   *

In the Hotel Bristol in Warsaw Freddy had no idea that ten days had passed since he had been incarcerated in the underground cell. With no window, clock or watch he was completely disorientated. His only reference to time was the arrival of the bowl of watery potato soup but this appeared to be a haphazard event. Sometimes there would be long gaps so that his stomach filled with acid pains and he was doubled up on the bench bed, other times it seemed to arrive within an hour of the last lot but he ate it for fear that it might be the last food he'd ever get.

He was by now emaciated and very weak, his eyesight often blurred, and when he closed his eyelids there were sharp flashes which made him wince. But what really concerned him was that his brain was now playing strange tricks. He was amazed at what he had written or left out in the calculations on the pages and often he would drift into a sort of 'awake dream' pacing around the floor murmuring and muttering.

His filthy clothes were hanging loosely on a filthy body. He had no razor and a scraggly beard was starting to fill a face further darkened by sunken, dead eyes. Luckily he had no mirror but his condition was graphically brought home to him by the nose-holding of his guards when they brought him his disgusting food, almost throwing it at him with the words, "Here pig," or "rat."

There was no spoon anymore, no bowl of water and soap for washing, no toilet paper. Professor Freddy Crisciak was being reduced to the status of an animal and, although he was unaware of it, he was beginning to behave like one. He slurped the soup which tasted more foul each time it was thrust at him and shuffled around the floor trying to pick the lice and bugs from his clothes and body.

And still the guards collected his work each day. The deterioration from clear neatness and lucid thought to the haphazard jottings on filthy, streaked paper was a clear indication of his rapid collapse into this pitiful state. With increasing frequency he considered the ampoule lodged in his teeth but the thought he clung to of Peggy being still alive and in England made him hold back the final crunch on the glass phial. Of his mother he held out no hope; he could see in her eyes in that terrible photograph the knowledge that death for her was very near.

The final ingredient to his torment was the lost awareness of time. He believed that he had been in this hell-hole for weeks, not just a few days. The guards couldn't understand why the SS General bothered to keep the pig alive. Could there not be some sport in the torture room? It would come, they comforted themselves, soon enough...

*

Two floors above the cells, in the splendid opulence of the Grand Salon, SS General Streyer was very angry, so angry that he hurled the field telephone at one of the large picture windows and shattered both!

The non-stop ringing of the bell in his adjutant's office suggested to the frightened officer that all was far from well and in trepidation he made his way to the high double doors, took a deep breath and entered.

He found the General standing behind his desk, his palm pressing down on the bell-push and his other hand smashing his baton on the table top with all the force his little body could muster, doing the superb surface irreparable damage. As the adjutant fearfully approached him the baton broke causing even wilder fury; it had been presented to him by Heinrich Himmler himself on Streyer's elevation to General Officer rank. The Reichsführer SS was not in the habit of performing the same ceremony twice.

"Berlin." Streyer said the word with every ounce of venom he could muster.

Then he screamed, "They are sending an inspection team to examine the prisoner Crisciak and ensure that he is being well looked after." He pounded the desk with his fists. "On the orders of the Reichsführer SS himself." The sentence ended in a shriek.

Now he started to pace, almost run, around the room stamping his highly polished jackboots on the thick-pile carpet. The fact that there was no sound from the stamping made him, if it were possible, even more apoplectic than ever!

"The Reichsführer SS trusts that the Herr Professor is in good spirits and ready for his work to the glory of the Third Reich *and...*" he stared at the picture on the wall over his desk and his voice was hollow and broken, "...our Führer."

The adjutant was surprised to see the General apparently shrink before his eyes. He was small enough already, but now it was as if a black balloon had sprung a leak and was slowly deflating.

"Your orders, Herr General?" He asked the question quietly. The situation spelt doom for him as well as his master if the matter could not be put right. Adjutants fell with their Generals.

Streyer walked slowly back to his desk and sat down. He drummed his well manicured fingers on the damaged top of the table.

"Take him to his room. Give him all he needs. Get the doctors to restore him to full health – *on pain of death.*" The SS had simple ways to have their will done.

"What is the date?" For a moment the adjutant had to think. "The date, fool?"

"The tenth, Herr General. Friday the tenth."

Streyer stared at the far wall. He spoke quietly, "We have four days." The stare he gave the adjutant was very explicit. "You will see that they are well pleased and that the Herr Professor speaks well of us, otherwise..." He flicked his hand in dismissal.

The adjutant left knowing exactly who would be the lamb to be sacrificed.

*　　*　　*

Throughout the week Norman and George had become more and more worried about Belvedere. He just wasn't himself. The clientele of the Pier Head Tavern had to strain their ears to hear his 'bon mots' – and there weren't many of *them* anymore. Worse still, during the week after the bombing he'd 'dried' twice during his act; an unheard-of occurrence. Luckily Don, doubling as prompter, had quickly set him going again and no one in the audience really noticed but Belvedere was mortified. *So* unprofessional, *so* unlike him. His only comfort had been that he knew why it was happening.

For the past five days he had been working into the early hours of the morning and through much of each day up until the theatre call of seven o'clock. The task he had set himself was awesome and entailed not just hour after hour at the little table in his bedroom but also frequent visits to the reference section in the town library.

But now, with the week behind him, the work was done and he was celebrating, back to his old fortissimo self, in the Tavern. His Saturday performance had gone splendidly and he was at his most expansive. Others might have celebrated by buying a round of drinks but Belvedere restricted himself to the 'dagger' speech from Macbeth. The audience was suitably impressed but the landlord wasn't; his customers felt that it would be impolite to drink during the virtuoso performance and that didn't help his takings one little bit.

*

"I will not have Pat and Peggy's undermentionables handed around the troupe."

Nell was in a considerable state. Vi, Belvedere, Norman, Elaine and George were with her on stage preparing to rehearse some new routines for their acts.

"Banded, dear." Vi needed to explain it to the others.

Nell banged her stick. "Nor the band." They were confused as much by Nell's invented words as by the reference to the girls' 'undermentionables'.

Belvedere, as always, stepped into the breach.

"I well remember dear Gertrude – Lawrence, you know, once confiding in me..."

Vi saw Nell becoming troubled. "I'm sure, Belvedere, I'm sure."

Norman polished his glasses furiously. "I had a cousin, she was older than me – is – and she once showed me her..."

Now it was Elaine's turn to step into the breach. "Cousins can be like that, Norm. Don't let it worry you."

He replaced his spectacles in relief. It was good to get these things off your chest.

Nell sniffed. It didn't solve the business of Tad and his fellow troupers' underwear. She banged her cane.

"Too much chatter-chitter. There's work to be done."

To the casual eye the action on stage now became a sort of ballet. Each artiste went to their position where they would be performing their act and started to mime their way through the changed routines. Nell sat on Don's chair watching them with affection. Vi, as a good lieutenant would, stood to one side just behind her peering through the ostrich feather. For the moment undermentionables were forgotten...

Don, Fred and Bob were busying themselves with new scenery and Bill Colbourn was adjusting his lighting and blowing intermittently on his woolly gloves to stop them singeing. They wished the cast would clear off and let them get on with their jobs, believing, as all backstage crews did, that except during performances the stage was their domain, not to be invaded by actors.

Nell's concern for the girls' underclothing went back to late last week. They had mentioned to her that when the time came for them to leave the hospital they would have nothing to wear other than the nighties and overcoats they had on when the bombs fell so, before they were discharged Nell, with Vi's help, had swung into action.

She had gone to the outfitters in the High Street, climbed the stairs to the ladies lingerie department and bought some 'sensibles', as she called the undergarments, and Elaine and Vi had donated a couple of frocks until the girls could choose their own. She had then taken the frocks and the 'sensibles' to the hospital.

The girls had never worn such boring and uncomfortable underwear before and, across the gap between their beds, agreed that their use would be very brief.

What had outraged Nell was to hear that Tad had been to the hospital and toured the wards selling quantities of lace knickers to the bedridden injured who found that they hadn't the strength to withstand his sales patter and what had annoyed her even more was that he had made Pat and Peggy pay for theirs which she felt was not in the spirit of the Theatre Company. She was even angrier that he had dared to engage the females in her troupe in such intimate matters at all.

To the girls' dismay she had grabbed the garments from their bedside lockers still, of course, unworn, and taken them back to the theatre where she had thrust them into Tad's protesting hands. He had voiced his surprise and dismay to any and everyone who would listen at this, to him, inexplicable behaviour. Hence Nell's outburst on stage.

On being discharged from hospital the plan was that, in the short term, Pat and Peggy would move into the one remaining spare room at 34 Clarence Road. Nell was gleefully telling everyone in town that she now had "a theatrical bawdy house"! Luckily most knew her little speech problem and those that didn't were soon put right. Mr Beavis provided his taxi free of charge and on this bright Friday morning, in ill-fitting frocks and itchy 'sensibles' they were deposited, with Vi, on the doorstep of number 34.

Nell was on the pavement to greet them. Their first surprise was to see a steel helmet with the word CHAR on it stuck on a bamboo cane in the front garden, but beyond it was an even more bizarre sight. All the windows on the front of the house were still boarded up but it's what was on the boards that really caught their eye.

Don had rushed to the scenery store and grabbed what he could after the bombs had dropped. Now the front of the house was a kind of museum for many of the past productions in the Pier Theatre. Downstairs front left sported scenery flats showing a scene from 'The Mikado', bottom right, staying in the Orient, 'Chu Chin Chow', Nell's bedroom, middle left was Nöel Coward's 'Hayfever', middle centre (the bathroom) was 'Dick Whittington', Peggy's bedroom, middle right was 'The Ghost Train', and the attic windows sported 'No No Nanette', 'Private Lives' and 'The Dancing Years'! The girls thought this was marvellous but Nell and Vi were somewhat embarrassed as was Councillor Winifred who felt that the sooner the window frames were restored to glass the better; it was all a bit gaudy for Flaxton.

Pat and Peggy were relieved to be moving in with Nell. To Peggy, showing outward gaiety whilst inwardly grieving was no new experience and she was therefore coping quite well with the death of Alice Banbury, but for Pat, who had known her for longer, it was a nightmare that just wouldn't go away. Alice had been a mother to them and her sudden death had left an unfillable void in their lives. The only consolation they had was that the doctor assured them that she had died in her sleep and would have known and felt nothing.

When they had settled into their room they joined the others in the kitchen where Vi had news that, if it were possible, added to their depression. Before she had left the theatre to collect the girls from the hospital she had received a telephone call from the ENSA office to say that the postponed visit would take place the following Tuesday morning if this was alright with them.

Vi had found herself saying in a little voice, "Yes" and, as easily as that, the fate of the Flaxton-on-Sea Pier Theatre Company was set for sealing three days hence.

It was remarkable how quickly everything returned to near normal – until the funerals. In all, five people had been killed: the Methodist Minister and his wife, a young woman thrown onto the roof of an adjoining building by the blast and her baby found in its cot in the ruins of the house alongside the church, and Alice Banbury. All the funerals took place on the same day and, as a mark of respect, all places of entertainment were closed. The Anglican Church at the north end of the town was the scene for both the Methodist and Anglican burials, the Rector having made his church available to the Methodists for as long as they wished.

All the troupe attended Alice's funeral not only to support Pat and Peggy but also Nell who had been her close friend. So many relations arrived from other parts of the country that Nell opened the theatre and the wake was held on the stage. Alice would have been amazed and, in her humble way, very moved.

So Flaxton-on-Sea ended a week it would always remember but would rather forget. In its near thousand years history it had experienced the ravages of pirates, plague, pestilence and Popes, smugglers, privateers and, interspersed with them all, the sudden fury of the North Sea. Now the act of one reckless young man ranked alongside each and every one of them. The *real* war had visited this tiny patch of the British mainland.

*　　*　　*

In Warsaw it was early morning. Friday, May the tenth. But no-one in the cells of Gestapo Headquarters would be aware of that. The pain in Freddy's stomach was unbearable and, to try to alleviate it, he lay on the low shelf with his knees drawn up tightly to his waist. Each spasm caused him to gasp and hold his breath. He clenched his fists so tightly that the long filthy nails dug deeply into his palms. More blood.

His face was contorted in a wild grimace, eyes tightly shut. They were poisoning him, slowly, to cause the maximum suffering. It must end soon. Despite everything it couldn't go on like this. Peggy would understand. His mother would understand. Not that either of them would ever know. Mixed with his cries of pain were the sobs and tears of defeat.

He was now juddering uncontrollably, his whole body shaking. The distant voice took time to register in his numbed brain.

"Up". More shaking. "Now".

Rough hands were pulling him. Another voice, even further away. "Be gentle. He is ill."

Painfully he turned on the shelf. Through his watery eyes he saw two guards and behind them, in the doorway, the horrific spectre of two men in long white coats. What form of death they had planned for him was beyond imagination. The decision had been made for him. His tongue sought the glass of the ampoule.

Then it was blackness.

CHAPTER THIRTEEN

__Saturday 11th May 1940.__ The German offensive in the West gathers momentum. They break through the Belgian lines at Maastricht.

In Britain the evacuation of children to the country is reintroduced with added urgency. One child writes home, "Dear Mum, I am learning to be a poacher!"

"C will see you now." Miss Gilbert captured the few stray hairs that had escaped from her tight, severe bun, forced them back into place, moved behind her immaculately tidy desk, smoothed her frock beneath her and sat down. A little rearranging of her pencils and pens and the task was done.

Charles Turville had seen it all before, in fact every time over the past ten years or so when he had been summoned to Sir Philip Southern's office. Miss Gilbert never wavered from her precise routine and it was a foolish man – as he had once found out – who interrupted her until she was settled back at her command post.

She whispered up at him as he opened the door, "he's a wee bit unhappy."

Frowning, Turville made his way towards the large settees, glancing at Sir Philip who was, as usual, busily scratching away with his large fountain pen filling pages of foolscap with his statutory green ink. Unhappy? What had caused that? His mind raced back through the most recent twists and turns of the assignment and, other than Ludovic Henschel, everything seemed to be running smoothly.

"Over here laddie, if you would." Sir Philip's gentle voice belied the severity of the summons. His fountain pen was pointing at an upright chair opposite him at his desk which looked only slightly more comfortable than the one Turville had just escaped from in Miss Gilbert's office. He diverted to it and, try as he might, couldn't sit on it in any other position than that of a naughty boy summoned by the Head Master. It struck him that that was probably exactly what Sir Philip intended. But why?

The pen was rested and the cap firmly screwed on to prevent the ink drying on the nib. The ritual was completed by Sir Philip carefully blotting his page with an ornate curved blotter and then, at last, he looked at Turville who was relieved to note a tinge of sadness rather than anger in the older man's eyes.

"We'll be needing your man Henschel back with the Poles."

Turville couldn't believe his ears. As if having Henschel described as 'his man' by Sir Philip who had forced him to take him wasn't enough, he was now arbitrarily demanding his reinstatement as the liaison with the Polish exiles who had refused to work with him! This wasn't like Sir Philip at all. He had never before interfered with, even questioned, his judgement once he'd assigned a mission to him – and he was damned if he'd let him now.

He found himself saying, "Out of the question C. The Poles won't have him and, since *you* forced him on me, I'll decide how I use him."

Never before had he spoken to Sir Philip so forcibly but, he reasoned, never before had there been need to. He was shocked at his own vehemence and the sudden fury that had sparked such a reaction from him and fully expected a justified angry response from Sir Philip but it wasn't forthcoming. Instead the big man levered his enormous frame from his chair and, ushering Turville to follow, lumbered over to the settee and armchairs, dropping himself like a full sack of coal into one of them.

Turville, now thoroughly confused, settled himself on the settee. This wasn't the C he'd grown to know and respect over the years. There was too much out of character. First there was the foisting of Henschel onto him. Before, he'd always been allowed to accept or reject his subordinates, it was an acknowledged fact that it was the only safe way to operate; each knowing and respecting the judgement of the other; their lives – literally – depending on it. And then there had been the order – that's what really riled him – the *order* to reverse roles: he to liaise with the Poles, Henschel to protect the girl. And now, again with no discussion, he was to reverse the roles to their original state!

He was glad to have the traditional pipe-filling-and-lighting time to consider all this because, he was sure, something lay behind this completely uncharacteristically erratic behaviour and, for everybody's safety, he needed to know what it was. Uncharacteristic behaviour? It struck him as he drew the first, always tastiest, mixture of nicotine and smoke into his lungs that he, too, was guilty in this respect. He had never been in the habit of sudden rage and intemperate outbursts and now he seemed to be behaving this way almost daily. It only took him a moment to find the two word explanation: Ludovic Henschel!

"Do you trust me?"

The soft lilt of Scotland seemed to add to the triteness of the question but, coming from Sir Philip, Turville knew that it was far from being that. It would be a precursor to something of the utmost importance.

"I wouldn't be here if I didn't, C. You know that. I apologise for my outburst just now but you must understand that I am somewhat confused. Orders, counter-orders. And all where, before, there had been no orders. In the past you trusted me to exercise my own judgement and, to this day, I believe – as I hope you do – that the trust has been justified."

Sir Philip merely nodded. It was obvious that he was deeply wrapped up in his own thoughts. There was a long pause and then, with some difficulty, he sat forward, put his pipe into an ashtray and rubbed his hands together as if they were cold. Then he was very still as he fixed his eyes on Turville.

"When I was handed this assignment by Winston, he used his very considerable store of grand rhetoric to impress upon me that this was by far the most important, vital, war-winning – oh, I don't know, use any superlative you can think of – assignment that any man had been, or would be given, in the history of mankind. He couldn't be content at telling me once; he repeated it with an abundance of grandiloquence that frankly left me breathless. In my own humble way I passed the gist of what he said on to you. Such is the unique importance of this assignment that it is inevitable that it will cause suffering and what will appear to be irrational behaviour. I am guilty of it, you are guilty of it, but within the scale of this assignment neither matters a jot *provided* we understand that such irrationality will occur, and it *must* be accepted without seeking or demanding explanation."

Sir Philip sat back, picked up his pipe and re-lit it. He had spoken quietly but with such intensity that Turville had remained totally motionless.

"You do understand, laddie, don't you?" This, though delivered more lightly than before, was clearly an order rather than a question.

Turville would like to have left it at that but it just wasn't possible.

"All that being so, C, we still have a major problem. I must stress that the Poles won't, under any circumstances, accept Henschel as their liaison. The present arrangement is, as I've reported daily, working very well and the evacuation of the package is in hand. I must impress upon you that it would be madness, and seriously counter-productive, to revert to the previous arrangement."

Sir Philip heaved himself upright and walked slowly back to his desk.

"I will speak with them. If, please God, all goes according to plan there should be little need for further close liaison anyway."

He sat down heavily at his desk. "I can say no more at this stage. One day I shall see that you understand my dilemma. Good luck."

Turville had been dismissed and as far as he could see nothing had been achieved. The rock on which, in the past, he had totally relied to guide him through every one of his assignments now seemed to be crumbling before his eyes. And this deeply troubled him...

*　　*　　*

"Is the pig dead?"

"He smells as if he's been dead for days." There was crude laughter.

Freddy came slowly out of the blackness. He was in the lift, supported under each arm by the guards who were totally confused at this unusual treatment of one of the many Gestapo victims that passed through the cellars of the Hotel Bristol every week. Their normal task was to throw the tortured bodies into a room near the rear exit – once the staff entrance – for removal and burning. This one, though, was still clothed, albeit in filthy rags, and they had been ordered to support the foul pig and take

260

him back to the luxury of the fifth floor! They'd all need de-lousing after this...

The lift attendant, his erstwhile ally, had the effrontery to join in. A Pole mocking another Pole.

"The pig comes round," he sniggered as he slapped Freddy's face. "You foul these brave soldiers – *and* my lift. You will do well to lie in a hot steaming bath – for hours, pig."

He ended the sentence with his eyes so close to Freddy's that the imperceptible movement of an eyelid was clear even in his fuddled state. Freddy felt his hand in the attendant's grasp and, as before when the code-word was passed to him, it was squeezed but he was now so confused with the sequence of events coupled with the pain in his stomach that he dropped back into unconsciousness.

He wasn't aware of the lift reaching the fifth floor and it being met by the two Wehrmacht doctors. They took him to his room and injected him with a painkilling drug, checked that his body systems were functioning adequately and then left him lying, still in his filthy state, on the bed.

Throughout the day the doctors returned. Nourishment was fed into him and slowly, as the evening approached, his periods of consciousness became more frequent. With a return of his mental faculties came more confusion. Why was he back here in the comfort of this luxurious room receiving the care of two doctors and several visits from a previously unknown officer who announced himself as General Streyer's adjutant?

"You must..." this officer assured him, "ask for anything that you require." The adjutant went on, with a touch of pleading in his voice, to suggest that when he felt strong enough the Herr Professor might care to take a long, hot bath. Fresh clothes – all necessary items, he stressed, were available in the drawers and wardrobe.

Freddy slept deeply, the drugs easing his pain and the liquid nourishment slowly rebuilding his strength. On one of the visits the doctors opened his windows to allow the smell of his unwashed clothes and body to disperse. The soft Spring air was the first to be breathed by him for well over a week but he was oblivious to it. Freddy slept on.

*   *   *

Freddy wasn't the only Crisciak to be thoroughly confused and not a little frightened at the strange direction the day was taking. Peggy was sitting at breakfast when Vi brought the post into the kitchen. There wasn't much – there never was; just a postcard or two and some official letters for Nell which Vi would deal with, but in amongst them was an envelope addressed to Peggy. It wasn't only the fact that it had no stamp on it and had therefore evidently been delivered by hand that caught Vi's attention, she was also surprised at the two words that were written on it in sloping, foreign-looking handwriting, 'Peggy Crisciak'. No-one locally used – even knew – her real surname; everyone called her Peggy Baker.

"Personal, for you dear," was the way that Vi made the strangeness of the envelope apparent to Peggy but at that moment her attention was wrenched away from the mystery by the arrival of Rita and Rena spilling in from their bedroom ready for a substantial breakfast. She was amazed at how they managed to eat so much yet stay so slim!

The frying of two large breakfasts diverted Vi's attention from Peggy and her unusual envelope and it was only out of the corner of her eye that she saw her leave the kitchen with the letter unopened.

*

Peggy climbed the stairs to her bedroom, shaking and near to tears. Surely it couldn't be from Freddy. It didn't look like his handwriting, but who else would call her Crisciak and write in such a Polish script? Was he free? Was he here? Had he been so close? She tore open the envelope and a moment later was on her bed sobbing uncontrollably. What a fool. How unutterably stupid. To even think...

The note was short:

> There are problems regarding F.
> Come to the camp this morning.
> Ask for me. Tell no-one.
> Ludo H.

The let-down was tremendous. To think for even a brief second that Freddy would announce his arrival to her, his wife, by way of a

262

letter in the letter-box was too ludicrous to even contemplate but such was the trauma in her mind at this time that it grabbed at the irrational before the rational. If this went on much longer, she felt, she would go mad.

The walk to the refugee camp calmed her. It took her a mile inland, out through the thinning sprawl of bungalows, paddocks and orchards to the heathland. For the hundredth time she wondered if she should have brought Pat with her, or at least told her where she was going but the message from this strange Ludo man had been quite clear, 'Tell no one. There are problems regarding F'. Dear Lord of course there were but what on earth could *she* do?

So deep were her thoughts that she wasn't aware of her surroundings as she walked but a passing army lorry and a cacophony of accompanying wolf-whistles jolted her back. She looked over the flat countryside, the rich arable land of East Anglia now pock-marked with defences of all kinds and, for a painful instant, it carried her back to those few happy months on the estate in Poland. Tears filled her eyes blurring the peaceful scene around her. Why couldn't she forget that one brief amazing episode in her life for a day, an hour, even a minute? Always, always it came back not to thrill, but to haunt her.

She found herself at the main gate of the camp. Two sentries stood idly each side of it more or less in the 'at ease' position with rifles loosely held at a slant, butts resting on the ground. As they saw her approaching they imperceptibly pulled themselves straight, giving their appearance at least a degree of military bearing. Both of them looked thoroughly fed-up; they hadn't seen their newly conscripted military careers as guards for a bunch of foreigners.

Wiping her eyes and in considerable trepidation Peggy approached the sentries.

"What can we do for you, love?"

This subtle refinement of the customary "Halt. Who goes there?" calmed her but before she could identify herself Henschel came out of the building by the gate signed 'Camp Office'. He appeared to shoo away a protesting officer who, even to Peggy, seemed to be of senior rank with red tabs on the lapels of his uniform. As

Henschel sauntered towards her the officer angrily threw himself into a small army van and, shooting gravel in all directions from his spinning wheels, drove at speed out of the gate. The sentries presented arms fairly smartly and Peggy, for reasons she would never know, waved him goodbye!

Henschel said nothing to her, there was no handshake, just a nod of the head suggesting "follow me". This riled her right from the start. The pecking-order was being clearly defined by this strange man who, although apparently only another unfortunate resident in this sad place, had sufficient authority to send a senior British army officer skidding away from his own command. This, she instinctively felt, was not the friendly man who had come to her dressing-room.

Henschel led her past tidy flower beds filled with Spring colours and the strange symbols of any military camp, war or no war, white painted half oil drums with posts sticking out of them, topped with signs – cookhouse, canteen, church, social hall, male lines, female lines, family lines and many more. Low post and chain fences each side of the gravel paths, again well white-washed, gave a clear impression of well-ordered discipline. All this had a strange effect on Peggy. She felt confined, a prisoner of this foreigner who strode so arrogantly ahead of her.

He led her into the Commandant's office and indicated to her to sit at the table then, ensuring that the door was shut, lowered himself into the seat opposite her. For a full minute he silently stared at her, sitting well forward, his face close to hers. She sat there, staring at him, not moving a muscle and hardly breathing. She knew that she was afraid; something very bad had obviously happened since their last meeting.

To her immense relief, after what seemed a lifetime, Henschel sat back and attempted a rather unsuccessful smile. His foreign, clipped English heightened the coldness of his speech.

"You know I am in contact with those who can rescue your husband." He didn't wait for – or want – a reply. It was as well. Peggy could find no voice to answer him, she just nodded.

"I have to tell you that they report to me that he is in very grave danger."

She was ice-cold now, her throat constricted as if a lump was blocking it.

"Such is his knowledge valued by Germany that he is guarded day and night." The next sentence was as toneless as the preceding ones.

"It may be that we have to terminate the mission."

Now she broke. Hurling her chair backwards she leapt up, leaned over the desk and shouted at him.

"How dare you? Who do you think you are to dismiss my husband like that? To sentence him to death. He is nothing to you but he is everything to me."

She punched the table with her fist. It hurt but she wasn't aware of it. She realized that the words were inadequate but there were no others she could find to express how she felt at that moment.

Henschel was completely unmoved. His intense eyes never wavered from drilling into hers as he slowly lit a cigarette.

"Sit down please. And if you love him you will not raise your voice. These are dangerous moments. Be aware that many people are risking their lives, risking unspeakable forms of death in Poland to bring Freddy out of the country. There are those who need him here, alive, as much as you do."

Peggy doubted that but was chastened by his remarks. She retrieved her chair and sat down.

"I am sorry. You must understand that I care for nothing other than having my husband safely with me."

Again his tone didn't change; "Then you should. You should care that his escape to the free world will help to ensure that it stays free. Your husband has the ability, with his knowledge and mental capacity, to help defeat Germany. That is far more important than personal sentiment."

What could she say to this man to whom love meant so little? She was silent, speechless and, as if it might dispel this terrible nightmare, she closed her eyes.

"There are things you must know, Peggy, but must not repeat to a living soul." He was softer now. "Freddy's mother, Anya, has been arrested by the Gestapo. We do not know where she is. She, and those hiding her in Norway, were betrayed."

She opened her eyes but her vision was blurred by tears. He went on apparently not noticing her distress – and if he had it would have made no difference.

"Freddy is in Gestapo Headquarters in Warsaw. Our report is that he is very sick. His room is guarded. You will understand the magnitude of the problem."

She remained silent, drained of anything to say. Whilst there may have been some reason to tell her all this she couldn't fathom what it was. He must know how powerless she was and the news only heightened her grief.

"We need the notebooks. Now."

His voice was quiet. There was no discussion here; it was an order. Now she understood; this was why she had been summoned here. Wisely she said nothing.

"Ideally they and Freddy must be reunited, but if it cannot so be then we will have to make do with just the books. Our people will have to attempt to decipher them."

The callousness of all this did an extraordinary thing to Peggy's mind: it cleared it. Crystal clear. No emotion offered, none absorbed to clog the thought processes. To Henschel's immense surprise, instead of a resumption of the expected hysteria from this distraught female pining for her lost husband, she returned his cold stare and said quietly and simply, "No Freddy, no notebooks."

It was his turn to be speechless but not for more than a moment. His voice rose as he lost the control he had fought so hard to maintain.

"We are not talking here about one man's life and some scraps of paper. You must realize that we are talking about the survival of the free world." She felt that he would dearly like to hit her.

Again quietly she replied, "I am talking about one man's life and some scraps of paper."

Henschel went to the window. His voice was deathly – deadly – as he gazed unseeing out into the camp.

"We will have them you know." Peggy's gaining of the high ground made her careless.

"The books are in safe keeping. Others will see that they remain so." She saw Henschel's eyes flicker in her direction. In hindsight she would never be sure why she said it; it was probably partly to shift the danger from her to no-one else in particular and to bring this dreadful meeting to an end.

She had no idea what Henschel might do next and it struck her that she had not told anybody where she was going when she left Nell's house. And then she remembered her ransacked room and the disturbed dressing room. Again she was on her feet, fists pounding the desk.

"You searched my room. You *dared* to search my room; *and* the dressing room." Her voice was high pitched now, her face white with anger.

His answer totally deflated her. "Someone had got there first," he sounded almost disinterested and later she realized she should have questioned this strange statement. Henschel swung round. His smile was icy, his voice now brisk.

"Right. Thank you for coming to see me. Let us hope my fears are groundless and that your husband will be with us soon. This can only be so if you maintain total secrecy regarding this meeting. Failure to do so will jeopardise whatever chances we have of bringing him out of Poland." He thrust out his hand. "Goodbye".

Peggy found herself being escorted at a fast pace back to the road. She wondered whether she could bring herself to say anything courteous in farewell but she needn't have bothered, by the time she passed out through the gates Henschel had disappeared.

"Had a good time?" One of the sentries winked at her. "Yes, thank you," she said tartly as she started the walk back towards the town knowing that the two soldiers would be eyeing her appreciatively. It took her a few moments to realize what was meant by the question.

She blushed furiously – and walked on.

*   *   *

Charles Turville strode out of the SIS building in London in a confused frame of mind. On leaving Sir Philip's office he had been startled to be offered a cup of tea by Miss Gilbert and ushered to one of the uncomfortable chairs to read a 'Most Secret' directive which, with a rare, warm smile, she handed to him.

What on earth was happening? Why had he not been given the file by Sir Philip? Normally he would have sat and read it and then, over a pipe, they would have had a friendly discussion regarding its contents followed, maybe, by a glass of sweet sherry. Then he remembered that he had just been cautioned by an unusually discomforted Sir Philip that nothing regarding this assignment *was* normal.

He would have been further confused to know what the faithful Gilly knew: Sir Philip had confessed to her his extreme embarrassment at the uncharacteristic way he was going to have to handle his protégé in the meeting that had just taken place and wanted to keep it as brief as possible. She, he purred at her, could help by giving him the new directive to read.

Turville sipped the tea and read of the next phase of the assignment which required him or, it strongly suggested, his subordinate, to travel to Stockholm, await the hoped-for arrival of the package from the clutches of the Gestapo and escort him to England. He noted that Sir Philip had allowed for any outcome of their meeting by, whilst stating a preference for Henschel, offering an option of either of them for the forthcoming operation. Turville could at last smile. He knew who it would be.

Miss Gilbert saw his smile and was greatly relieved. She would report the change in his mood to Sir Philip and it would relax him. She so hated to see him perturbed; it quite blighted her day.

She saw Charles Turville on his way noting again the blueness of his eyes, selected one of the precious horde of Edinburgh shortbreads from her desk drawer and, placing it in a prominent position on the tea tray, bore it in some triumph up to Sir Philip Southern's immense desk.

In fact Miss Gilbert had read Charles Turville's mood wrongly. The smile had merely marked his satisfaction at having the option of making his own choice for the leadership of the next highly dangerous part of the assignment, that was all.

His mood was certainly better than it had been earlier but had he known what Henschel had been up to in Flaxton in his latest abortive attempt to wrest the notebooks from Peggy he would undoubtedly have flown into yet another untypical rage brought on by the impetuous behaviour of his subordinate. He knew it was dangerous to leave the man to his own devices but there was no option. He assured himself that Henschel could do no real harm whilst he was away but in his heart of hearts he knew he didn't really believe that to be so.

*　　*　　*

In his evil-smelling room in the Hotel Bristol, Freddy regained full consciousness slowly and it was late afternoon before he emerged from the effects of his week's incarceration in the cell and the sedatives that had been injected into him during the day.

He found it difficult to separate the brief moments of wakefulness from the disturbing dreams, all now forgotten, which had plagued him since he had been roughly dropped on the bed by the guards that morning. The mental torture of the past few weeks had taken its toll and he would have been amazed to know that most of it had been unintentional and had been the result of the two extremes: the brutality that the Gestapo in Poland wanted to inflict on him and the care the Third Reich demanded he receive until such time as his usefulness was over.

But there was no middle way; the SS knew of no such route. As far as the torture of their enemies was concerned there was not even an 'all or nothing' state; it would always be 'all'. Now, to their fury and confusion, they were required to restore this prisoner, this Polish rat, to full health ready to receive an audience of eminent members of the Kommandatur from Berlin who would be representing the Führer *himself*!

Freddy knew none of this, of course, and understandably feared for the next phase of this roller-coaster death ride. Something was troubling him almost as much as his uncertain future and, with his main faculties restored, it revealed itself to him. It was the smell in the room. In the confines of the airless cell he had grown used to it and couldn't understand the reaction of the guards; he had assumed it was merely a crude form of abuse. Now, more-or-less mentally restored, with a gentle breeze blowing in through the open windows, it was all too apparent. He – and his clothes – were disgusting. He remembered two people, the doctor and the lift attendant, telling him through his fog of pain to take a hot bath. Why not – if the facility was still functioning?

He got up from the bed – and immediately fell onto it again. Dizzy. He must move slowly and carefully. He did so, shedding his filthy rags as he crossed the floor. Something strange again. What was it? The windows, open. He went to them. A low decorative railing was set into the sill but apart from that nothing to stop him falling out. A sheer drop down five storeys to the street below. There was no view as such; the Luftwaffe bombers had obliterated it. Where there had been expensive flats on the opposite side of the street were now mile upon mile, pile upon pile, of charred ruins.

Stupidly he muttered these phrases, mile upon mile, pile upon pile, as he went into the luxurious bathroom. Sure enough there was piping hot water – the Gestapo had what it demanded – and in no time he was lying in it up to his bearded chin. Very little of Freddy Crisciak was visible above the steaming surface.

Eventually he got round to washing. It took two bathfulls of water to restore him to Eminent Professor of Physics state although his hair, now clean, was still far too long for his taste. Now it would be the battle of the beard.

He was about to wipe the washbasin mirror with his towel when he was transfixed by the steam gathered on it. He looked, and looked again. A jumble of words had remained clear within the steamy background. As a child he remembered rubbing his finger on the bathroom mirror to make a silly message which the natural grease on his skin would prevent the steam covering. When the next person ran a hot bath there would be the message for them to read. Now the previous occupant of *this* room, probably a Polish cleaner – or the lift attendant – had performed the same trick on him.

In Polish the words revealed the escape plan to get Freddy Crisciak out of Gestapo Headquarters and out of enemy occupied Poland.

It is May.   Tonight.   Window open.   Wipe off.

He stood staring at the message. He didn't move, couldn't breathe, he just stared. Slowly he wiped off the steam with his towel and then, with his fingers, rubbed grease all over the mirror so that the message was permanently obliterated.

He allowed himself a smile, the first for weeks.

He knew Peggy wouldn't like the beard so with a dangerously light heart – he shaved it off!

CHAPTER FOURTEEN

Saturday 11 May 1940. *The German offensive penetrates deeper into Western Europe. Holland has laid down its arms. The Belgians are in swift retreat.*

In Britain 'Stop Me and Buy One' ice-cream sellers on their tricycles have been forbidden to sound their bicycle bells for fear it will be seen as an invasion signal.

The questions facing Freddy as he stood looking out of the window in the dusk over the ruins of Warsaw seemed endless. The microphone was a worry. He didn't know if he was still being listened to but he assumed that he was. He would need to warn any rescuer of the need for complete silence. But that seemed to be the least of his worries. How on earth could anyone reach him? He leant forward over the window sill and looked down the sheer wall of the hotel to the entrance five storeys below on the Aleja Jerozolinskie and saw the tops of the sentry boxes each side of the bomb-damaged canopy and black-uniformed SS sentries standing stiffly at ease.

Feeling dizzy he eased back and glanced to the left and right but there was no ledge along which a skilled climber could walk or even crawl. He wondered how professional these rescuers were, and if it would all end in a blood-bath. It surprised him that he hardly cared anymore. All this had gone on long enough. He wanted it to end one way or another.

After the bath he'd dressed in the new underclothes provided for him but had got no further realizing that he had no idea what to put on next! He recognised, yet again, the giant leap he had been forced to make from the security of his chosen profession where he was considered to be a leading authority into that of a scheming prisoner and would-be escapee. He really had no idea what to do. Would his gaolers come to his room again that evening, perhaps to bring him supper?

The clock told him that it was after seven; the doctors might feel that some solid food should be taken. It alerted him to the likelihood of a visit from someone before they left him alone for the night because for some inexplicable reason, having tried to destroy him, they were obviously now concerned for his health! He lay on the bed as he was and forced his brain into calmness by making it concentrate on the subject it knew best: nuclear physics.

He had devised this form of hypnosis on his first night in the cell and had found that it relaxed his body as well as his brain, taking away the lump in his throat and the violent beating of his heart.

And with it came sleep.

Freddy awoke, as he always did these days, in panic. It was dark and he was icy cold. For a second, still in a half dream, he imagined himself naked in a darkened morgue and, letting out a sob, sat up suddenly.

With relief he realised that it was the coolness of the evening penetrating his thin underwear that had made his body shiver and awakened him.

He calmed himself and involuntarily went to close the windows. Then he paused. Would they open again? This brief respite of having access to fresh air had reminded him how much he had been missing it but it had a far deeper psychological effect on him: with the windows open he no longer felt so hopelessly incarcerated; he could 'feel' the world outside.

He compromised by pushing the frames together and pulling across the heavy curtains blotting out the black evening.

Try as he might he couldn't begin to work out how his friends would get him out of this seemingly impregnable room. If he was to be sprung from the room it would, he reckoned, be during the night and there was still almost three hours left to midnight.

He decided to get into bed and pretend to be asleep when any visitors came in to check up on him. For a while he lay there but then another thought struck him. If the doctors called they may decide to give him a sleeping tablet and that would be disastrous. Up he got again.

This was ludicrous. Was he totally incapable of any rational planning? Had his mind been so damaged that he couldn't think logically any more?

It was alright. Why should he have any idea of what to do and how to do it? He'd try something else.

He slipped on shirt and trousers, socks and shoes, found the notepad the guards had brought back from the cell with him and, sitting at the table by the window, started to create another string of meaningless calculations. There would be no point in drugging him into an unconscious state if he was evidently already working again for the Third Reich...

*

Friedrich Streyer admired himself in the cheval mirror that stood in his office three floors below the toiling Professor. He was very pleased with himself. His black uniform was a perfect fit on his short tubby body, his black belt, pistol holster and jackboots gleamed, and the silver insignia of SS General stood out on his lapels and shoulders. He smoothed the material and, not for the first time, marvelled at his rise from obscurity to this high rank.

At his desk stood his valet and adjutant. The former handed him his service cap, again, awash with badges and braid, and his silver topped General's baton, invisibly repaired by a Polish master craftsman who, as payment, had been shot.

The adjutant, who had only recently returned to favour by reporting the quick recovery of the prisoner Crisciak, passed him his despatch case. With a final admiring look in the mirror Streyer led the procession down to the main entrance and out to the large Mercedes staff car. The adjutant checked that the General's cases were already safely packed in the boot. This was to be an overnight stay which would require at least two changes of uniform and, of course there were gifts for his host.

The Swastika flag was uncovered on the front wing of the car and with a frantic exchange of Nazi salutes and cries of "Heil Hitler" the car purred away towards the office of the Governor General. There Streyer would brief his host on the latest state of the extermination programme and the building of the Auschwitz camp and then tomorrow, prize of all prizes, he would go on to a meeting – an audience – with no less a person than the Reichsführer SS himself, Heinrich Himmler.

*

Freddy heard the noise of the General's departure through the curtains and it jolted him back to reality from his world of nuclear physics. The sound of the car was a welcome link with the outside world, desolate though it now was, that had been denied him when the windows were sealed.

The more he thought about the escape the more terrified he became. No plan, he was sure, could succeed. Who in their right mind would contemplate snatching a prisoner of the SS from their own headquarters in the heart of an occupied, destroyed and heavily policed city, a prisoner who was valued sufficiently for the Führer himself to take an interest in and, quite possibly, wish to meet!

And then there were the insurmountable obstacles to consider: a guarded room with a window opening out to – nothing; a hearing device to monitor sound in the room; a ruined city with little or no 'cover' and a devastated country to cross, and then another, and then another. Impossible. Add to this the risks any would-be rescuers would be taking: certain death to any who were captured, the worst death that could be devised.

Such was the condition of his tired and confused brain in this state of free-fall that he seriously considered if it would not be better to reject the rescuers and take his chances in Berlin. If, as seemed likely, Germany won the war quickly and decisively Peggy could probably join him and life could resume more or less as normal.

Freddy was saved from further dangerous and defeatist speculation by the door handle rattling. After the now accustomed moment of terror on hearing the key turn he was pleased to see the doctors coming in because their arrival cleared away two of his many concerns regarding the coming night's activity; first it gave him confidence to have predicted the movements of his gaolers but, more important than that, it would mean no interruptions until they returned the next morning. If everything went to plan he'd love to be a fly on the wall when *that* happened!

The doctors fussed around him as the guards looked on in amazement and disgust. They couldn't understand the behaviour of their masters at all. They knew how *they* would treat this Polish pig and one day they intended to put their thoughts into practice.

He was easily able to reject any further medical treatment. It was clear to the doctors that, remarkably, he was fit again and at last tamed into working hard on the strange hieroglyphics the Herr General required him to write down. They were very pleased with themselves and would report to the General's adjutant that their treatment, based on their very considerable medical knowledge, had worked.

Freddy asked them to ensure that he was not disturbed that night as he had much catching up to do with his valuable work for the Third Reich, and would they also instruct the guards accordingly.

"I shall work through the night and this will involve much pacing up and down."

He was pleased with that. He was getting quite carried away with this business of subterfuge, so much so that as they left he couldn't resist a final barb, "and please inform the person listening in to my every move of my intentions. But then he's probably picked them up already."

They all left in some disarray. He feared that he may have been just a bit too clever for his own good.

The strain of it all was now really beginning to take effect. He felt immensely tired and weak but through determination had hidden it sufficiently to mislead the doctors who, had they really known his condition, would have sedated him and sent him straight to his bed.

Their 'considerable medical knowledge' had missed the obvious symptoms of complete exhaustion; his heart was pounding, his hands were uncontrollably shaking and he felt stifled. Needing air he went to the window, drew the curtains back and opened the two door-like frames as far as they would go.

The rain was falling lightly on the dead city and the chill night air made him shiver but helped his heart to calm. He looked down on the Aleja Jerozolinskie. Nothing was moving. The sentries were obviously sheltering in their boxes.

Still fully dressed he lay on his bed and, using his nuclear physics method of calming his brain, fell into a disturbed sleep.

He was jerked awake by the paralysing sensation of a hand pressed over his mouth. The room was pitch dark and he could make out nothing, no object, no person. It was as if he had been gagged but he knew by the tiny muscle movements that it was a human hand on him encased in some type of glove. As his eyes grew accustomed to the very slight light coming through the window he saw that the hand was part of a figure dressed entirely in black. It motioned him upright and instructed him to be completely silent.

As if in a dream he allowed the man to help him into a black overall, rather like a boiler suit, and put a black Balaclava helmet over his head. Black socks over his shoes and black gloves made him as invisible in the dark as his visitor. In complete silence he was motioned to the window. Would he be given wings with which to fly? Stupid thought. He now saw a rope inside the room to which was attached a harness which the man now strapped around his waist and under his thighs. It was like – and actually was – the lower part of a parachute. The visitor checked the buckles and then led him to the opening. He fearfully closed his eyes guessing what would happen next.

He was gently eased out of the window, the rope tightening as his weight was transferred to it and then, amazingly, he was hanging a foot or so away from the wall – and rising very slowly. He gyrated on the rope as the fibres took the strain and up he went, past the curtained windows of the Herr General's splendid suite of rooms on the sixth floor and past a top floor of small windows which will once have been the hotel staff quarters, but now were probably barrack rooms. His heart, if it was beating at all, seemed to stand still as he rose silently within a foot of the sleeping soldiers, but all was well, their curtains were also drawn and they slept on.

He was now level with the parapet and found himself staring into the eyes of a man only inches away from him. The man's feet were against the top of the wall and his whole body was projecting outwards and upwards like the jib of a crane, the rope supporting Freddy fed over one of his shoulders keeping him away from the wall. The 'jib' was, in turn, held in that position by a rope around his chest fastened to another man on the roof. A fourth man was helping to lift Freddy's weight by pulling on the lifting rope. All of the team were dressed as he was, in black from head to foot.

Freddy had only a moment to credit the ingenious geometry of all this before he was being rushed through the gully of the pitched roof to the side of the hotel. Doubtless the man who entered his room was being lifted in the same way. They all paused, breathing deeply. There was no acknowledgement between any of them. No word was spoken. They had rehearsed this whole exercise many times until each knew precisely what their next move would be.

They waited for what seemed to Freddy to be an interminable time but was, in fact, little more than a minute and then the other three joined them and the entire procedure was repeated in reverse. The jib man was eased out over the edge with the largest black shadow wrapping the man's supporting rope around himself and lying back against the sloping roof with his feet against the parapet wall. The lowering rope was passed over the jib's shoulder and re-attached to Freddy who, with his eyes tightly shut again, was launched out into the night. Then, faster this time – much faster – he was dropping.

He dared to open his eyes. It was extraordinary. He could tell that he was in a lift shaft. He passed holes in the walls where the gates had been, but there were no floors beyond them, just space. These were obviously the ruins of the gutted building adjoining the hotel. Freddy realised that he was descending as if he was in the lift that had once been operating in this shaft!

Suddenly he was grasped by two sets of hands, the harness was undone and two black-clad bodies took each of his elbows and literally carried him at a canter along a path in the rubble to the road running behind the hotel.

Then he was dropped, like a sack of coal, down a black hole into even blacker darkness.

He was safely caught by hands that had obviously practised receiving a body thrown from above. These must be strong men; he was no light weight – although certainly lighter than when he first became a guest of the Gestapo – and, at six foot, he was a large object to be carting around.

The first thing that struck him was the smell. There was no need to try and guess where he was. In less than ten minutes he had exchanged the comforts of a fine suite in the Hotel Bristol – for the sewers of Warsaw!

He wanted to cry with relief. For the first time for so very long he was amongst friends. At the very worst he would die with them

rather than in the presence – and to the delight – of the most evil
men on earth, Hitler's SS.

*

In the deserted kitchens in the basement of the hotel the little
Polish lift attendant afforded himself a tiny smile. His cold cell-
like bedroom, which had once been a pantry, had a small grime
covered window slit set high in the wall but at pavement height
on the road running behind the building. The room was in the far
corner of the kitchens and, by standing on tiptoe on the ledge
which was his bed, the attendant had a fine view of a sewer
manhole cover at the near edge of the road. In the darkness of
the night it is doubtful if a casual viewer would have seen
anything but this man knew what he was looking for. He saw the
dark shapes moving at great speed, the cover lift and their bodies
dropping into the hole. First three and then, a moment later,
another four. The cover was replaced. All within a minute.

He climbed off the bed and collected his few belongings. Within
the hour he would follow their same route; the Hotel Bristol would
be no place to be tomorrow morning!

All his careful planning had paid off. He had offered to help clean
the 'Polish Pig's' room which gave him access to the bathroom, the
writing on the mirror had worked, the constant reference to his
smell had ensured that he had a bath and also that the windows
would be unbolted. Now his work was done and with considerable
relief he would return to his comrades in the Armia Krajowa.

*

The tunnel was large, about five feet in circumference, brick lined
and surprisingly clean. Whilst the sanitation system in Warsaw had
been destroyed, as had the city itself, the sewer network remained
intact. A small stream of water ran at their feet but virtually no
effluent;

They were only there for a few moments. The four who had lifted
Freddy up, over and down the building had now joined them. They
had abseiled down the ruins of the lift shaft and now, preceded by
their coils of rope, they dropped down the inspection shaft into the
sewer tunnel. The lid was replaced and the seven of them squatted

278

for a moment to catch their breaths. Still no word between any of them was spoken.

Two small lights came on. They all blinked; none of them had seen light for quite some time. The lamps were fitted to bands around the heads of two of the team, others were brought out and everyone except Freddy slipped them on. They showed the tunnel leading off into distant blackness and, at their feet, a canvas stretcher which was now being assembled. Everything was being done in total silence, with precision and at great speed, obviously practiced time and time again.

As they worked they tore off their balaclavas to get more air and Freddy saw that their heads were soaked in sweat. He did the same and was ashamed that his face was cold and dry. The leader nodded at him and he smiled stupidly back. He saw that the man had a vicious red scar above his right eye.

Now he was motioned to lie on the stretcher and two straps were fastened to hold him in place, his arms tight in beside him.

The next hour and a half was extraordinary. He was conveyed, as if on an underground train, at a fast trot, through the city's sewer network. Every ten minutes or so the two stretcher bearers were replaced by two other members of the team. They knew exactly which turns to take and, Freddy guessed, had practised the whole run until they had mastered the route and were at their peak of fitness. How they managed it, bent down to fit in the tunnels that sometimes were only about four feet high, and breathing a limited supply of air that was, at best, stale and foul, he would never know. What story had these amazing men been told that made this effort and danger worthwhile?

It wasn't long before Freddy closed his eyes; the closeness of the tunnel roof made the speed seem faster than it was and the flashing images of the bricks, so near his face, had become very painful.

Heaven knows what would happen next but for the moment the future was out of his hands. He afforded himself a grim smile. In the most unusual way imaginable he was leaving Warsaw but one day, he vowed to himself, he would return.

Eventually after what seemed like hours, they stopped. They were beside another vertical shaft leading up to a manhole cover.

With more signals for silence Freddy was released from the stretcher. If he had been feeling weak and nauseous *before* he had been lifted from his room the feeling now was infinitely worse but he felt ashamed to admit it in front of this group of men who were now bent double trying to get some air, however foul it was, back into their lungs. They were exhausted and, he was sure, would dearly have loved to retch and cough to ease the pain and yet, remarkably, they suffered in total silence.

The man who was obviously the leader checked his watch and signalled 'three' with his fingers to his colleagues who nodded and settled down. It was strange that no one acknowledged Freddy; they obviously felt that it was safer that way. As far as they were concerned they were delivering an anonymous package to its destination. He would have been amused to know that the SIS had labelled him exactly that: a package in transit between Poland and Britain.

It struck him that he had absolutely no idea of the time. He hadn't seen the clock by his bed in the moments between being woken with a hand over his mouth and hauled out of the window. Since then his roller-coaster ride through the sewers had left him totally confused. He edged up against the leader and pointed to his watch. The man pulled back his glove: two-thirty. So what was to happen in three minutes time?

Nothing! Time dragged by and the six men slept. Freddy tried to do the same but to no avail; the total uncertainty of every aspect of the escape prevented him, tired as he was, from relaxing. Where was he? Who were these people? Were they now safe or in more danger than ever? What would happen next? When? He was as near to floating around in a vacuum as any living person could be.

The time dragged on and on. Freddy reckoned that the three fingers must have meant hours, not minutes. At last the leader stirred. How he knew when to wake was a mystery to Freddy, but carefully he leant amongst his colleagues and, with a hand over their mouths, woke them. He reached Freddy, but seeing him already awake he moved on without a flicker of expression in his eyes.

Another look at his watch and the leader stood and motioned to him. They gathered round him and he was lifted onto the vertical ladder running up the side of the shaft leading to a manhole cover. He felt the cold metal through his gloves and realized that his whole body was numb through lack of exercise and movement.

A noise from above him invaded the silence and grew louder until it deafened him. He recognised it as a vehicle engine struggling against dirty fuel and clogged pipes. It drew closer until it seemed to be only inches above him and he guessed that it was actually over the cover.

The noise stopped and simultaneously there was a crash of metal on metal and a foul stench as the hands of two of his rescuers reached past him, lifting the heavy lid. Before he could clearly register any of this he was literally ejected upwards past a barrier of legs in filthy overalls and onwards through a hole in the bottom of the floor of a lorry and up into its evil smelling chamber. The manhole cover was replaced and he was alone. With a splutter and a jolt the lorry moved forward.

The men in the sewer moved off towards their planned exit point in the rubble of a nearby building where they would wait through the day for darkness before scattering into the night. Josef Raczeck, the scar on his cheek more livid then ever, and his team had done their work.

Any passer-by in that street of shell-damaged, run-down, houses on the outskirts of the city would have seen, if they had bothered to look, a dustcart stop for a few moments, the dustmen empty a couple of bins and then clamber into the cab and onto the running-board of their vehicle and move away. It was as normal as that!

The cart had a low domed body on each side of which were six sliding lids into which rubbish was tipped. There were three compartments but today the middle one was not being used. It was reserved for Professor Freddy Crisciak!

The vehicle stopped a few times for topping up with rubbish from the poor suburban houses and then, with only two dustmen remaining, it lumbered on to its depot. The dawn collection had been completed.

Freddy felt the vehicle jolt to a halt. The engine coughed into silence and he heard the cab doors open and footsteps retreat into the distance. A door slammed and then there was silence. He lay on the floor of the compartment in the stench of the rubbish around him – and he hadn't the faintest idea what he should do.

He was about to clamber down through the hole in the floor – which he knew would be stupid but he could think of no alternative – when he heard the sound of an approaching vehicle but, unlike the dustcart, this engine was well tuned, running on the very best fuel. He froze.

The vehicle stopped within a few feet of him, steps approached the outside of the compartment and a very soft voice said in educated German,

"Will you please drop out from under the vehicle, Herr Professor, and join us."

After all that there was betrayal.

Within the group of brave partisans who had done so much, risked so much to free him, must have been a traitor who, probably in return for his life, had handed the world's leading nuclear scientist back to the Third Reich. And now there would be no escape.

Freddy lowered himself through the floor and surrendered himself to the fully-armed crew of a Luftwaffe Personnel Carrier.

*

General Friedrich Streyer had enjoyed his evening and night at the official residence of the Governor General of Poland, Herr Dokter Hans Feltshaffen. In precedence he deferred to the Governor General as his superior, but each trod warily with the other. Feltshaffen knew that the SS deferred to no one. There had been a grand dinner attended by thirty or so of the most senior officers of the Third Reich, accompanied by their ladies (a few of whom were actually known to their escorts) sitting around a large table laden with some of the finest Polish silver. Fine wines and vast quantities of select foods had been flown in from Germany. The toast was 'The annihilation of the Polish People'. The Soviet guests present heartily endorsed this sentiment.

That night as his valet tried to undress his severely drunken master his adjutant craved permission to enter his bedroom to – smugly – tell him the good news that the prisoner Crisciak had made a remarkable recovery and was working in his room. The doctors – as smugly – had informed the adjutant that they had ordered complete rest with no interruptions until a late breakfast tomorrow.

Now, very early the next morning, and with a painful hangover, SS General Streyer, in a perfectly pressed new uniform, was being driven very slowly in his grand Mercedes staff car at the start of his journey to meet his idol, Heinrich Himmler.

*

Freddy approached the open-topped Personnel Carrier warily. Had he thought, he might have put his hands above his head but he'd never surrendered before and the idea didn't strike him. When he'd been arrested all that time ago in the hall of his villa it had appeared to be a fairly civilised affair.

These Luftwaffe airmen seemed far more war-like. They were wearing what Freddy took to be flying suits and each held a pistol at the ready. The Personnel carrier and the dustcart were parked close together in a gap between two buildings in a yard filled with foul household rubbish of every kind. Freddy saw two men in overalls standing at the entrance to the yard. Behind their backs they carried machine guns.

"Welcome, Herr Professor, to the Armia Krajowa. The Polish partisan army." The whispered voice of the most senior airman made him start, not so much because of the words themselves, but rather the warm, friendly tone of voice and the outstretched hand. Suddenly it struck him that no one was pointing their gun at *him*!

"My name is Leo. We four were all members of the Polish Air Force and today we fly with you to freedom. It will be dangerous, and if we are caught we will be summarily shot, or worse, for disguising ourselves as Luftwaffe personnel. This we do not mind. It is a risk we are proud to take for our country. If you dress as we are the same will probably happen to you. Do you share the risk with us?"

In a past life, only a few months ago, Freddy would not only have been amazed by the question, he would have refused with a dry laugh. Now he just nodded. He didn't trust his voice; to break down in tears before these brave men would have been unthinkable and leave them wondering if risking their lives for him was worthwhile.

He stripped off his black outfit and the shirt and trousers underneath it and they were unceremoniously flung into the rubbish in the dustcart and the lid closed. Next he was handed a set of thick underwear which covered him from shoulders to ankles and then helped into a flying suit, long fleece-lined boots and a forage cap. A belt containing a pistol in a holster was passed to him which he fastened around his waist and then a pack containing a flying helmet, rather like a swimming cap, an oxygen mask which would clip onto it, and a pair of thick gloves.

Lastly they gave him a small tatty wallet and told him to study its contents carefully and commit them to memory. Now dressed identically to the others he was ushered into a back seat of the personnel carrier, the canvas roof was pulled over it and they set off.

Freddy opened the wallet. The first thing he saw was a photograph of a man in full flying gear on an identity card. For a fleeting second he thought it was himself and, dressed as he was, he realised that it would pass quick scrutiny. He looked at the details. He was evidently Sergeant Ernst Bender of II J.G.77 (whatever that meant), aged thirty-five, married with two children, and his home was in Dortmund. He hoped that he wouldn't be asked too much about his home town; he'd only passed through it once! Now he was evidently stationed at the Luftwaffe airfield at Pruszkow. He knew that was twenty kilometres or so south-west of Warsaw and assumed they were on their way there now.

The wallet held other bits and pieces of paper amongst which was a photograph of a cheerfully smiling woman with her arms around two toddlers. On the back of it was a loving message. How did the Resistance think of all these details? What inventiveness. It was the person next to him, whom he'd been told to call Johann, who put him right. He took the picture from him and chuckled.

"Poor Sergeant Bender. He'll never see *them* again." Freddy, appalled, realized that he was, literally, in a dead man's shoes...

The Personnel Carrier drove slowly over and, where possible, around the potholes. They were now in a line of crawling military vehicles passing through similarly desolate landscape to that which Freddy had seen on his enforced journey to Warsaw six or so weeks before.

The sides of the road were lined with the burnt-out remains of a beaten army and a fleeing population. Military vehicles were mixed up with carts, prams, dead animals, piles of household belongings and amongst it all, the dead; the military and civilians of every age gunned down from the air by endless waves of fighter planes. One of the pilots may have been Sergeant Bender, thought Freddy, and seeing all this pointless carnage his sympathy for the man receded. He closed his eyes and memorised the details of his assumed identity.

His companion, Johann, had been given the task of briefing him. The vehicle carrying the genuine five-man Luftwaffe crew had been hijacked on leaving their billet at dawn that day. They had already been identified as the crew assigned to fly a Junkers JU 52 transport plane to Oslo that morning.

"How did you know?" asked Freddy.

"We have people everywhere" was Johann's enigmatic reply. Freddy now understood. The German occupied Western half of Poland was still teeming with good, brave Polish fighting men with no longer an army or airforce to fight in. They spoke German fluently, indeed many had grandparents and even parents who were born when their homes were in German territory and, in their youth, German had been their first language, so impersonating the hated Hun was no problem whatsoever. And here were four of them, all crack fliers of the now defunct Polish Airforce!

"What of the original German crew?" Freddy asked, really knowing the answer he would get. A single word reply.

"Liquidated." Their uniforms had been taken and photographs changed on their identity documents. To all but those who had known the doomed original crew – and they were far away in Germany – the passengers now in the vehicle were the same five that had left the billet at dawn.

"What about at the airfield? They'll know we're not the original crew." He wondered why he went on asking questions; they'd obviously thought of everything.

"Let me tell you what you will find when we get there, my friend."

Johann, speaking quietly but intensely, painted a picture of escalating chaos at the Luftwaffe's hastily constructed airfield at Pruszkow. What had been open grazing land before the war was now a giant building site, as Engineer battalions armed with every kind of earth-moving equipment battled against the clock to complete a mighty Luftwaffe bomber base which would, in time, make a major contribution to the intended war against the Soviet Union.

Whilst bulldozers and mechanical diggers were on the move day and night to complete the task by the date set personally by the Führer, by far the largest quantity of earth was being moved by a seemingly inexhaustible supply of expendable energy: Polish slave labour.

This scenario played conveniently into the hands of the Armia Krajowa. The chaos engulfing the whole area and the frequent acts of sabotage they inflicted on the occupying forces meant that there was no established order which would be alerted by any unusual activity. The Luftwaffe aircrews were all strangers to each other, coming and going as the war ebbed and flowed around them. They would land their bombers and fighters, eat and sleep whilst they were refuelled and re-armed, and then take off again on another mission. It was a recipe inviting mischief, and mischief, on a grand scale, was what the well-trained Armia Krajowa had in mind.

"Unless something totally unforeseen happens we will have no problems."

As Johann spoke these words of confidence something unforeseen *did* indeed happen. With a growing volume of motor-horn bleeping, four German military police motor-cyclists surrounded their vehicle. The partisans, less Freddy who didn't think to do so, released the flaps on their pistol holsters and massaged the butts of their weapons. They'd die, but they'd die fighting. Freddy felt the ampoule of potassium cyanide with his tongue.

The military police signalled their vehicle to the side of the road. Guns were carefully taken from their holsters and safety-catches released.

But now the police moved forward to the next vehicle in front and went through the same procedure.

As they stared in disbelief there was a growl of a well-tuned car engine and a large staff car, carrying the Swastika flag on a front wing and the insignia of a general on its front bumper, swept past them. With one accord his colleagues threw up enthusiastic Nazi salutes but Freddy felt too silly to do any such thing and huddled down in the back.

Yet again he was in a cold panic, heart thumping, breathless. For a fleeting second he had seen a face at the rear window of the car. There could be no doubt who it was. Could it be that SS General Streyer was coming to the airfield to see him off? Not for the first time since this whole appalling business started he didn't know whether to laugh, cry – or be sick. Maybe it would be all three at the same time!

Ahead of them at the airfield main gate the Guard Sergeant felt rather as Freddy was feeling at that moment. Confusion was occurring all around him and had done so every hour of every day he was on duty since he had landed this loathsome job. Everyone used the gate, airmen, soldiers, construction traffic and the lorries carrying the slave labourers to and from their squalid prison camp.

He had no hope whatsoever of controlling the mass of entries and exits that clogged the gate in a non-stop stream and all his pitifully small guard detachment could do was give a cursory glance at the vehicles, their occupants and their ID cards. Now the Sergeant had just been informed that a Very Important Person would be arriving at the camp in fifteen minutes. His identity was kept secret for security reasons but he was entitled to a full Guard of Honour which suggested someone of top military rank.

"Why, oh why," the Sergeant said to his Corporal, as he chivvied his already overstretched guard into some semblance of ceremonial order, "why can't we be given more notice?"

He commandeered the one mirror and muttered to himself angrily. Generals didn't just appear out of the blue. The Camp Commandant, to whose office this VIP was to be escorted, must have known hours, even days, ago that he was to have such an important visitor. Now his little troop of men had to throw themselves into their Dress uniforms with all the trimmings and prepare to parade in three perfectly formed ranks and, on his order, Present Arms with their carbines. In return the VIP would either dismount and inspect them or drive straight past. The Sergeant fervently hoped it would be the latter.

The sound of vehicle horns approaching alerted him to parade his Guard and they quickly fell in, just inside the gate beside the road. The Sergeant took up his position and shouted his orders as the four motor-cyclists rode past in perfect formation. The large staff car followed closely behind and the podgy face of the little General appeared at the open rear side window. He waved his baton at the guard and sank back. A camp motorcyclist joined the other four to lead the General on to the Commandant's office. The Sergeant sighed with relief and sent his troops to change back into their working uniforms.

Throughout all this charade, vehicles and people had been streaming into and out of the camp unchecked including a Personnel Carrier, one of many, bringing a fresh crew in for its designated flying sortie. With splendid irony General Streyer had removed another dangerous hurdle on Freddy Crisciak's path towards freedom!

Freddy couldn't understand why the driver of the Carrier had moved out and immediately behind the Mercedes as soon as it had passed. Were these freedom-fighters merely dare-devils who took delight in taking the greatest possible risks? He fervently hoped not! But now inside the airbase he understood their tactics; being so close to the General they had sailed through the gates unchecked. If it could, his admiration for their astuteness increased even further.

The driver of the Personnel Carrier flung it around the confusing, cluttered perimeter of the airfield as if he made the journey on a daily basis rather than for this first and only time in his life. Freddy marvelled at the apparent nonchalance of these brave partisans, all of whom would be killed, quickly or very slowly, if this audacious mission went wrong. The vehicle drew up at a cluster of buildings to one side of the airstrip.

He reckoned that once, not very long ago, it had been a peaceful farm, far from anywhere, home to generations of hard-working people. Now they would be dead or scattered in prison camps around the country and their comfortable home had become the main command centre for this burgeoning Luftwaffe aerodrome.

There was a sense of extreme urgency about the place. Uniformed soldiers and airmen scurried around and vehicles whisked in and out of the gateways where, not so long ago, cows had been driven slowly by their herdsman. Freddy had to close his eyes. It was all so incongruous and heartbreaking.

He was jerked back to reality by the slight bounce of the vehicle as Leo dropped to the ground. He raised his hand to the rest of them and then, to Freddy's amazement, strolled languidly towards the main building! He returned a few salutes, threw up one or two for officers obviously more senior and disappeared through the entrance.

No one in the vehicle seemed to show any surprise at this extra-ordinary act of bravado. Whilst Freddy sat with sweaty palms and pounding heart they lit German cigarettes and were apparently totally relaxed. He was slightly relieved to see that close by each of them, hidden on the floor, was a selection of vicious looking machine guns and their hands were lolling very close to them.

"Leo is getting the flight plan" Johann whispered to him.

There was nothing he could do but try to look as bored as they did. The noise around them was jarring his brain; aircraft landing, taking off, revving their engines outside make-shift hangers as mechanics clambered all over them, lorries rushing in every direction, some pulling trailers laden with bombs and, squashed in amongst it all, the slave workers, a bedraggled army of the once so proud Polish people – *his* people.

They seemed hardly alive, shuffling, most of them bearing enormous loads from one place to the next, barely dodging the giant construction vehicles. One stumbled and a bull-necked soldier hit him with his rifle butt. Freddy saw one of the partisans drop his hand onto a machine gun. Johann gently eased it away. He realized that *all* these poor souls, not just this little group in the Personnel Carrier, were contributing their lives to enable him to escape and it made him very, very angry. He didn't want this, any of it. He wanted it to end – now. He did the only thing he could do: he shut his eyes again.

The sudden bounce of the vehicle made him jump. Leo was back. With swift commands in German they were off across the airfield. Leo was studying a sheaf of documents and spoke to the others about the flight plan and take-off procedure. No one took any notice of Freddy.

They approached a large three-engined transport plane being serviced by a ground crew. Salutes were exchanged, they dismounted and, again with studied nonchalance, opened their packs, put on the flying helmets and clipped the oxygen masks to them, leaving them hanging from one side ready to be fastened over their noses. They all knew exactly what to do.

Johann whispered, "Just do as we do. There is no problem."

The door in the fuselage was open with a ladder hanging down from it and they clambered aboard. Freddy was led to the cockpit and put in the right-hand seat. Johann strapped him in.

"Do not move from here or look around. Keep your head down and pretend to work the switches in front of you, but," he gave him a fleeting smile, "don't touch any of them." Then he was gone.

Freddy was only too willing to do what he was told. It suddenly struck him that he felt terrible. The stomach pains were back. He'd had no solid food for days, only the liquid nourishment fed into him by the doctors. Food had obviously not been part of the escape plan. Yet again he was required to sit still and say nothing and, staring at an array of dials and switches, he did just that!

*

SS General Streyer only had three moods, each distinct from the other with no gradation in between; he was nauseating and obsequiousness to his superiors, boorish and bullying to his subordinates and unspeakably evil to his enemies. To the Commandant of the air-base he had employed the middle mood. Although the man was only one rank junior to him he had received a blistering tirade bordering on hysteria from Streyer for his 'gentle' handling of the Polish slaves. These 'vermin', as he described them, were being fed, housed and transported to and from the prison camp as if they were almost human beings which was burdening the Third Reich totally unnecessarily. Streyer's orders were clear and supremely simple: work them to death. There were plenty more where they came from.

He left the office building still fuming but relaxed totally once he was back in the comfort of his staff car. None of his histrionics was anything more than a stage performance which he knew would be required to maintain his authority. It was the only way he could command any respect and, with the added advantage of the SS insignia on his uniform, he got it.

Now the car was leading him to the aircraft that would fly him to Oslo and the meeting with Reichsführer SS Heinrich Himmler. He would use the flight to prepare himself for a very different performance before his idol.

*

Freddy was startled awake by a bumping and clattering around him. How could he have slept? It amazed him. He felt the pain in his stomach again but by bending forward and holding his breath it eased slightly. Forgetting Johann's instructions he looked around and saw that a metal door was closed behind him; he was alone in the cramped cockpit.

Some printed papers – they looked like a sequence of instructions – told him that he was in a Junkers JU 52 transport plane and, reading through the document, it seemed that he was occupying the seat of the second pilot! Pity the passengers, he thought. And by the sound of it they were a noisy, ill-disciplined lot. The door opened and he automatically glanced round. One look from Leo and he averted his eyes back to the instrument panel.

The door closed and Leo settled into the pilot's seat.

The staff car reached the door of the aircraft assigned to General Streyer and he roughly returned the salutes of the ground staff and the crew who were lined up to receive him. He would send a note of high praise for the turn-out and bearing of his Luftwaffe personnel to their leader, Field Marshal Goering who, as his superior, he – of course – deeply respected. On board, his adjutant made sure that he was comfortably seated in the metal chair on one side of the narrow cabin and sat himself on the other side leaving a small passage-way between them. The General's valet settled behind them near the lavatory and small kitchen unit and two members of the crew hovered near him, the fifth was further back manning the machine guns in the turret on top of the fuselage.

They were all politely asked to brace themselves for the take-off. The General curtly acknowledged the request and put on yet another performance, this time showing calmness when in fact he was terrified.

Back in the cockpit Leo, with much twiddling of knobs and switches, fired up the three engines and the ground crew removed the wheel chocks, then he signalled to Freddy to put on his headphones and fasten on his oxygen mask. Thankfully the fetid atmosphere gave way to cool, clear air. The aircraft bumped its way through a labyrinth of obstacles to the end of the runway.

Leo grinned to himself. He hadn't been a crack fighter pilot for nothing – and he would be again. He, too, was on his way to freedom as were his comrades.

The plane bounced down the runway and climbed into the dull sky. Streyer opened his eyes and dared to look out through the small window. The desolate land fell away beneath them. A fighter plane – a Messerschmitt 109 – curved in and settled alongside the Junkers and out of the window on the other side the adjutant saw another Messerschmitt do the same. The General's aircraft, plus its fighter escort, set course for Occupied Norway, Oslo airport – and Reichsführer SS Heinrich Himmler.

Up in the cockpit the General's co-pilot – in seat occupation only – was totally unaware that on this next step towards freedom he was being accompanied by his erstwhile gaoler! Freddy had seen the fighters close in on them and had looked in panic at Leo who merely nodded. He spoke just one word through the microphone in his mask into Freddy's headphones, "Friends". To prove it he waved through the perspex cockpit window and to Freddy's amazement – and relief – the fighter pilots waved back!

"We cannot speak with them because ground control will pick up our messages but they know what to do."

Freddy nodded, not daring to speak. "It is alright, my friend. We are on our own internal frequency."

Freddy couldn't prevent himself asking "Where are we going?"

Leo adjusted the controls, "It is better you do not know yet. It is not too far. Sit back and rest."

The plane droned on. The altimeter indicated that they were

flying at twelve thousand feet and below them Freddy was grateful that the clouds, like a shroud, were covering his raped and dead homeland. He felt such overwhelmingly deep bitterness towards the inhuman monsters who, given no more right to exist than their victims, could perpetrate such atrocities.

Leo checked his watch and his map. So that three members of the crew could remain in the aft cabin on this flight he was his own navigator which, as a fighter pilot, he was well used to being. He clicked the switch on his mask and Freddy heard him breathing.

"Zero minus five. Acknowledge."

"Roger one,"

"Roger two,"

"Roger three."

Three whispered replies, calm and unconcerned. Leo turned to Freddy.

"We are now over the sea just north of Gdansk. It is, I believe, the right time to inform you, my friend, that you are not our only distinguished passenger today. I believe you have met the other one. SS General Friedrich Streyer?" He added airily, "We're relieving him of his command."

In the aft cabin General Streyer was making notes. His adjutant had prepared a mountain of briefing papers for the meeting with the Reichsführer SS but there was more, regarding his own achievement, that Streyer wished to modestly convey to Himmler. This mainly concerned his triumph in subjugating the wretched prisoner Crisciak to slavishly serving the Third Reich. Jotting this down reminded him to ask, as a very special favour, for the return of the Professor when the Reichsführer had finished with him so that he could dispose of him, slowly, in his own very special way.

Coffee and delicacies were served by the valet to the two of them. Streyer fastidiously dabbed his mouth with a silk handkerchief after each small sip or bite as he had seen Himmler do, a habit which privately infuriated his adjutant.

The three partisans heard the voice of Leo in their headphones, "Three, two, one, zero."

Neither the General nor his adjutant heard, over the roar of the engines, the gentle sigh as the faithful valet died. The cutting of his throat was carried out expertly and his body was laid down at the back of the cabin. Their first awareness of anything untoward happening was the simultaneous nudge of a gun muzzle into the nape of their necks.

"If either of you moves we will blow your heads off your shoulders."

It was the quiet, matter-of-fact voice of Johann. As he spoke the third partisan, now down from the mid fuselage gun turret removed their revolvers and slipped handcuffs over their wrists, fastening each to the side arms of their seats. Now that they were secure Johann and the other partisan removed the revolvers from their prisoners' necks and helped to tie ropes tightly over their hips and down under the base of the chairs.

Although the General and adjutant couldn't move their bodies, their tongues were in full spate. Oaths, orders, threats, the German vocabulary was stretched to its limit as they strained at their bonds but it soon stopped as, with thumbs and forefingers squeezed over each nose, their mouths stayed open to admit breath and were filled with wads of cotton followed by gags tied tightly at the back of their heads. It was tempting to continue holding their noses but their orders had been to keep the two of them alive.

Leo received a signal through the intercom from Johann and tipped the aircraft to starboard.

"We are making for neutral Sweden" he spoke in Polish to Freddy. "We arrive at Stockholm airport in just over one hour's time. You will then be free of the Third Reich."

He added as an afterthought, "And so will we."

Yet again Freddy was speechless with amazement at the turn of events. The slickness of the operation from the moment he had been lifted through the hotel window only eight or so hours before was literally breathtaking. Who planned it? Who trained these partisans?

"I shall continue to give false positions to flight control as if we are still on our way to Oslo. This will prevent any Luftwaffe interference. Perhaps you would like to go back and greet our fellow guest?" Leo's voice betrayed the irony of the situation, "It might cheer him up to see you – wait."

The last word was a command. Leo flicked switches and wrote quickly on a pad. A message was coming through on the ground-to-air frequency. When it was finished he handed it to Freddy. He had written it in German as he received it. Freddy read it and smiled.

"I will pass the message on to the Herr General," he said, undoing his harness and the wires and pipes connecting him to the plane.

Opening the metal door he saw before him a scene that he swore would stay with him until his dying day. The two SS Officers, resplendent in their 'meeting Himmler' uniforms were straining at their bonds, both leaning outwards trying to get their gagged faces against the windows on each side of the cabin. Their idea was obviously to attract the attention of the escorting fighter pilots but for what purpose would be hard to imagine. Even if they had been genuine Luftwaffe airmen they would hardly be able to do anything other than shoot the plane down.

One of the pilots now glanced across and radioed to his colleague. Simultaneously they waved at the grotesque images at the window and this caused even more apoplexy than before.

Freddy handed the message Leo had received to Johann who read it and laughed. He squatted between the two struggling officers turning the General's head physically and none too gently to face him. He had to shout to be heard above the roar of the engines.

"Herr General, a signal from your headquarters relayed by Pruszkow. It says 'Prisoner Crisciak escaped. Means unknown. Full search underway. Heil Hitler'." He chuckled. "I don't think the Führer will be doing much Heiling when he hears that, will he? He'll probably want a word with you personally."

The effect on the General – and his adjutant – was instant. Streyer's head drained from the colour of beetroot to white, matching the natural death-mask putty tones of his adjutant. It took a matter of seconds, as if a valve had been suddenly thrown open. He was no fool; he knew that high rank and even the protection of the SS counted for nothing within the Führer's inner circle. Unless the prisoner was quickly found his world had crumbled to nothing – not that it was in very good shape at this moment anyway...

"You look ill, General. Perhaps my fellow partisan can cheer you up." Johann moved back and signalled to Freddy to remove his helmet and flying mask and this he did, but not without a feeling of embarrassment and foolishness. He was not given to gloating or sensationalism and this, to him, merely added fuel to an already explosive situation.

The effect on Streyer did just that. Back came the beetroot complexion, saliva dribbled from his gag and the gasping and grunting noises rose in a crescendo of rage. His hands, straining to escape from the manacles, were as puce as his face. Freddy stared at Streyer and then into the cold cruel eyes of the adjutant who, unlike his master hadn't moved a muscle; he sat motionless, as white as a corpse.

Johann motioned Freddy to the back of the cabin.

"Alex will co-pilot now. He is keen to get back to flying."

Moving to a rear seat Freddy tripped over a body lying in the far corner of the cabin.

"The other German. He will be leaving us soon."

This cryptic remark of Johann's made no sense to Freddy until about thirty minutes later. Since leaving the flight-deck he had felt the plane slowly descending until, after bouncing down through the clouds, he saw through the window by his seat the sea below them and a fast-receding coast.

"Gotland," shouted Johann. "Leo will have radioed ahead and been told to descend below the cloud base. Shortly we shall have a Swedish escort."

He was listening through his headphones to Leo. "Roger."

He went to the fuselage door and to Freddy's amazement tugged it open. The cold wind flew in and engulfed them all. The adjutant turned his head. Now, at last, he looked frightened. Johann noticed this and gestured that he was about to throw him and the General out of the plane. In terror the adjutant shook his head. A trickle of liquid ran back from beneath his seat; his body had lost control of itself. Johann laughed. He signalled to Freddy to grab the dead valet's feet and help to drag him towards the door. Before he realized what he was doing the body disappeared, flying backwards and down, arms and legs waving as a final protest after death.

Freddy stared after the body until Johann had closed the doors and then he squeezed past the legs of the mid-turret gunner to the small lavatory in the tail. He vomited – and the lack of any solid food for so long made the pain even worse.

Freddy knew that he should, but he couldn't condone all this. An eye for an eye? Whatever horrors one side perpetrated on the other, it wasn't in his nature to be able to sink to the same level. Taking a person's life was totally abhorrent to him; he knew that he had no right, no justification to do so. And then he saw in his mind the hollow-eyed skeletons being literally worked to death at the airbase...

Johann touched his arm making him jump. He was pointing out of the window. Another fighter plane was now flying alongside the Messerschmitt 109 with what he presumed were Swedish airforce markings. Through the window on the other side he saw that a similar shepherd had arrived to guide them in to the airport. He could tell by the pitch of the engines and the dropping sensation that they were preparing to land. What would happen after that? A sudden stab of fear struck him. Perhaps they would send them back. For the first time for many a long hour he let his tongue touch the cyanide ampoule.

The Swedes, desperate to maintain their neutrality, were at their most efficient. As the Junkers JU 52 touched down police and army vehicles fell in alongside it on the runway and led the plane to the far side of the airport. Leo expertly brought the machine to a gentle halt and switched off the engines. Now the silence was only disturbed by the angry grunting of the demented General sitting, violently wriggling, in his seat. The adjutant was completely still and silent.

Johann opened the fuselage door. He and his companion, hands raised above their heads, jumped down to the tarmac. They each took one of Freddy's arms and helped him down. Leo and the co-pilot were close behind them. He slammed the door shut. In an instant they were surrounded by armed police and soldiers, guns pointing at them from all directions. A senior policeman approached.

"You will come this way, please. You have made an unauthorised landing. Until the matter is satisfactorily explained you are all under arrest." He spoke in German which, as they'd arrived in a Luftwaffe aircraft, was understandable.

Leo, also speaking German, replied calmly. "There are two wild animals still in the aircraft. You will need to find them a cage." The officer blanched and stared at the Junkers and then issued curt orders to a colleague who saluted and rushed away in one of the vehicles.

The group were led to an army truck and bundled into the back of it. Two young blonde Swedish soldiers piled in with them, machine guns at the ready. As the vehicle drove off Freddy saw the two Messerschmitts being herded alongside the Junkers.

Like so much of his confusing existence since he had seen Peggy off across the Baltic Sea the previous September the next event in Freddy's mad flight from the Gestapo took him completely by surprise. They were led into a sparsely furnished room which was obviously used to interrogate the stream of refugees seeking safety in this neutral country. Before he could really take in his surroundings his arm was taken and he was led to the back by an immaculately dressed British Naval Officer who saluted and took Freddy's hand. The grip was firm, the handshake brief.

"Professor Crisciak? I am Commander Richard Cook, Naval Attaché at the Embassy. Welcome to freedom."

No matter how much he wriggled General Streyer remained tightly fastened to his seat and would do so until such time as someone decided to release him. He tried to reach the window with his head but he couldn't get near enough to be seen by people on the ground. He stared at his adjutant expecting the man, as his servant, to find a way of extricating him from this mess. The adjutant remained impassive. He had spent the long hours of the flight perfecting the story he would tell the inevitable Court of Inquiry to ensure that they placed all the blame for this embarrassing fiasco on the head of his nasty little superior.

In the distance Streyer could see two airport vans approaching. He battered with his feet on the metal cabin floor. The noise was terrifying and the aircraft rocked and bounced. The detachment of soldiers around the Junkers JU52 blanched and fingers tightened on triggers. Word had quickly got around that wild animals were loose in the plane and occasionally they caught a glimpse of frenzied movements at one of the windows. By the volume of sound and the rocking of the machine they were obviously in a terrified state. The troops nervously raised their rifles and released the safety catches in case the fuselage door gave way. They were greatly relieved when they saw two vans from the airport veterinary service rushing towards them. This would mean either tranquilizers for the beasts or, if that didn't work, a bullet in their necks.

The vets were very efficient and considered themselves as well trained as the airport fire brigade. A temporary cage was quickly erected against the fuselage door. Still the frantic banging continued and, with some trepidation, one of them used a long metal pole to release the catch. The door fell open, guns were aimed, the tranquilizer darts were poised – and nothing appeared...

After some considerable time the senior vet, well protected in a padded overall, gingerly entered the cage. He tip-toed to the open door and paused. Eventually, wondering if he was literally putting his head into the lion's den, he peered inside. He couldn't believe what he saw. With a shout to his colleagues they all clambered aboard. A policeman was sent to find a pair of metal cutters and the vets set about the unpleasant task of ungagging the two men and restoring them to some sort of fit state to be seen in public.

Streyer and his adjutant were lowered to the ground with the cage, for some reason, still in place. Their faces were streaked with sweat and saliva and the General had joined his subordinate in wetting his trousers. A battery of flash bulbs and cinematograph lights greeted them and Streyer angrily waved them away – which made no difference whatsoever. A policeman who laid his hand on the General's arm was screamed at in such a way that he at first withdrew it, and then tightened his grip and led the protesting Streyer towards a lorry. The adjutant, without saying a word, followed behind.

Freddy couldn't believe the welcome. He stared at the Naval Attaché in amazement. Everything was happening too fast for him. How could he be recognised in a Luftwaffe flying suit? He smiled.

"You must forgive me, Commander. I was expecting a prison cell and here you are. I am very disorientated."

The Commander nodded briefly, almost impatiently. "We were told of your impending arrival by London. You are to be lodged at the British Embassy. A change of clothing is in the adjoining room."

Freddy went up to Leo and Johann and the other two whose names he would never know. From habit he started to speak to them in German but corrected himself into Polish.

"I have no sufficient words to thank you and your fellow partisans. Now it is my turn to do what I can for you."

Leo took his hand and shook it slowly. "It was a good mission. Now we make our way to England. The Polish Air Force was destroyed but not our spirits. We will join the RAF. Many of our comrades are there already. Goodbye, my friend. We'll meet in England."

He stood back and gave a smart Polish salute, copied by his three colleagues. They pulled off their Luftwaffe flying suits revealing uniforms of flying officers in the Polish Air Force and, with another salute, they were gone.

Freddy had no idea how they would satisfy the Swedish authorities who were jealous guardians of their neutrality, or how they would reach England but, compared with what they had all just come through, it would probably be the easiest part of their mission.

For him the danger was over – or so he thought. The relief had made him light-headed. At any other time he would have realized that there were still hundreds of miles of enemy occupied land and sea between him and his beloved Peggy – and that he was now further away from her than he had been in Warsaw!

*

"His Majesty the King."

They all stood, raised their glasses and drank the toast. The dinner had been delicious even though Freddy was only able to pick at it. The Embassy doctor had prescribed potions and rest but he had eagerly accepted the invitation to go down to dine with the Ambassador, his wife and other senior members of the

British Embassy staff.

Freddy was dazed at the sudden turn of events and, at the same time, appalled to realize how close to this scene of regal splendour were the unspeakable horrors of war being waged by the Nazis. The Embassy, he realized with a slight shudder, was almost identical in its decor and furnishings to the Hotel Bristol in Warsaw, and the bedroom given to him was frighteningly similar.

But here, on British territory, he was safe. The next major task, the Ambassador stressed at pre-dinner drinks, was to get him across the dangerous seas to England. Freddy, in light-hearted mood, missed the allusion to danger and went to bed for a night's sleep feeling, at long last, free of fear.

*

He was awakened by a knock on his door. Why hadn't he heard the key turning – and why would the SS knock? He was brought to his senses by the entry of a smartly uniformed footman bearing a bone china tea service on a silver tray which he set down by Freddy's bed together with two newspapers.

"Good morning, sir. The Ambassador looks forward to taking breakfast with you at nine o'clock. Meanwhile he suggests you may find this morning's newspapers worth reading." He bowed and left.

Freddy sat up, poured a cup of English tea and glanced at one of the papers – and then the other. There was no mistaking the distinctive shape of the Luftwaffe Junkers JU52 in the main picture on both front pages. In the foreground was the cage and in the cage were two very angry, very dirty men wearing stained and creased SS uniforms, one a General, the other a Major. Both papers gave the names of the officers, but it was the headline in the more popular daily paper that caught his eye:

HITLER'S ELITE SS PAY A COURTESY VISIT
TO SWEDEN

He lay back and roared with laughter. Something he hadn't done for a long, long time.

CHAPTER FIFTEEN

Sunday, 12th May 1940. *Belgian, British and French forces hold a line from Antwerp to Namur. The Germans plan to attack against little opposition to the South and clear the route to the Channel.*

Prime Minister Winston Churchill flies to Paris to confer with Premier Reynaud. He is told that the French army has no strategic reserve.

In Flaxton the first indication that Peggy was missing was that evening at supper time at Nell's house. As it was a Sunday there was no performance to alert the troupe, most of whom spent the morning having lie-ins to get over, in the case of the ladies, the exertions of the week's shows and, in the case of the men, their exertions in the Pier Head Tavern and The Anchor the previous evening.

Lunch-time came and went, as did the afternoon, but no-one at 34 Clarence Road worried about her absence; she was, after all, a free agent. Pat noticed that she wasn't around but knew that her friend needed space to handle the terrible situation she was in because only yesterday she had fretted at being crowded and hemmed in by them all.

So it wasn't until Nell's 'family' gathered in the kitchen for supper that they became concerned at her absence. Pat went upstairs to look in her room.

The first hint of something unusual was the empty space on top of the wardrobe where she kept her suitcase. With trembling hands she checked through the cupboard and drawers. It was difficult to be certain, but a number of clothes seemed to be missing. What finally confirmed her fears was the empty top of the little dressing table. No make-up, combs, brushes or washing-bag.

Pat rushed downstairs. "She's gone," she sobbed.

Everyone froze; Nell and Vi at the stove, Rita and Rena laying the table. They all stared at her.

"Just gone." She sank into a chair.

They all started talking at once.

"Are you sure"

"How do you know?"

"Hasn't she said where?"

"There must be a note."

Pat just shook her head. This is what she had always dreaded and somehow knew would happen. She put her head in her hands and burst into tears.

"It's all right, luvvie." Nell put her arm around Pat's shoulder and handed her one of Masters' large white handkerchiefs which were used to receiving a few tears and had always been a great comfort to her.

"Vi, check Peggy's room. Rita, Rena, I want all the troupe here, now, toot sweat. No excuses."

When Nell was like this no-one hesitated; the kitchen emptied.

"Switch off the pans, love. We'll eat later. When we've found her."

The confidence of the last sentence wasn't matched by Nell's inner thoughts. She was deeply worried. She too had feared that Peggy might go away, but why no note? Surely she would confide in her? She felt hurt and angry and chided herself for feeling so in these circumstances.

By eight-thirty her troupe was deployed. It was at times like this that the true spirit of people really emerged and the surprise for everyone that evening was none other than Tad Stevens. He borrowed Pat's bicycle and took Flaxton by storm. Gone was the cockiness and brashness and in its place was a very determined, if somewhat breathless hunter. Every one of his many contacts was found, questioned and put on the alert. Road-blocks, the bus depot and railway station, pubs, clubs, fishermen, the boat-yard – no-one escaped the incongruity of a visit by a stern, serious Tad, trousers stuffed into multi-coloured long socks, mounted on a wobbling ladies' bicycle!

Pru would have been proud of him if she'd known what he was up to but in fact she was very angry. Being her evening off all manner of delights awaited him; now both the meal and the hot water bottle grew cold, the effort of preparing them wasted.

Belvedere manned the control centre in Nell's kitchen. He'd drawn a rough map of the town on some wrapping paper and it was pinned above the fireplace. George and Elaine were sent to the theatre to check that Peggy wasn't there and Norman, Rita and Rena with Don and his back-stage crew toured the boarding houses to see if, for some reason, she'd moved away from them to be alone for a while.

Nell's mind came back to the absence of a note. In her heart of hearts she knew that something was very wrong and it was obvious to her that Bel and Tad felt the same but that none of them could share their dark thoughts; they were too terrible to contemplate.

As always, in times of great distress, Nell turned to her beloved Masters. She went outside and gazed at 'her' star.

"Help me, old fellow. Help me. Oh how I need you."

She turned back to her bomb-scarred house. Just looking at it made her sad. It had always been a happy home ever since she and Masters bought it so many years ago. Bright lights and laughter, parties and dancing, her troupe running through their routines around the grand piano in the front room, birthdays and anniversaries, such happiness and loving.

Now it was all gone, Masters was gone and her light had been extinguished; only a star in the sky was left. She looked up at it again and then back to the house. It appeared to be asleep, or dead. The garishly boarded windows gave it the appearance of a suddenly blinded person cut off from the world around. No light, no sound, dead. She was amazed to hear herself sob. To her it seemed very loud in the quiet evening.

This wouldn't do, Masters wouldn't have this. She bustled back up the path and literally barged her way through the front door to face, square on, the welter of problems engulfing her.

If outwardly number 34 seemed dead, inside it was a hive of activity. After their mission the troupe reported back to Belvedere and were de-briefed but none had any news of Peggy so, distressingly, his map was covered in red crosses. Tad returned from one of his sorties with a thick parcel of heavily rationed bacon from the butcher who'd felt it was the least he could do in the emergency and Rita and Rena quickly converted it into a large pile of sandwiches. They all ate in silence; there was nothing to say, the possibilities of what might have happened to Peggy were best left unsaid. Vi busied herself with kettles on the stove producing mugs of cocoa, horlicks or tea according to their choice whilst Belvedere busied himself with arrows and crosses on his improvised town map. No one wanted to leave. Such was the spirit of comradeship in the troupe that they all felt better and safer near each other so, when Belvedere was satisfied, Nell sent them either to their beds or to armchairs and sofas to rest. But, of course, sleep was impossible.

The next morning, amongst the letters through the letter box was an envelope with no stamp, just Nell's name scrawled on it in rough capital letters. Whoever had delivered it must have crept to the front door in the middle of the night. They all crammed into the kitchen and Nell tore the envelope open. Inside were two sheets of paper the first of which had a note on it clearly written by Peggy – Nell read it out in a shaking voice.

Dear Nell and everyone,

Sorry to frighten you. I have to be away for a while for Freddy's sake. I'm being well looked after and will be back soon.
I'm truly sorry for all the trouble I am causing.
Love to you all – and Mountjoy.

Peggy

Their relief was most noticeable in the way their bodies relaxed from the tautness of anxiety, as if a photograph had suddenly sprung into life. With it came murmurs and sighs but before anyone could actually speak Nell was holding up her hand so urgently that, again, they froze. She had scanned the second note and, not trusting her voice, handed it to Belvedere. This message, typed on a faded ribboned typewriter, was far less welcome. In an untypically quiet, small voice he read it to them.

Peggy will be safe if you co-operate. We require
the notebooks *now*. Put message in the Flaxton
Chronicle as to where and when.
Tell no-one. Her life depends on it.

For a moment there was shocked silence and they looked fearfully at each other. Elaine took George's hand and held it tightly, Rita put her arm around Rena. As if to help, Mountjoy circled everyone licking any hand within his range.

The typewritten note confirmed their worst fears. Peggy was in desperate trouble and, worse, her own brief message suggested that she didn't know it.

Pat whispered, "Poor Peg," and then they were all talking at once. Everyone had something to say. Ideas for Peggy's release ranged from calling in the army and police – even Winston Churchill if necessary – simply to handing over the note books.

It was Tad who made the latter suggestion and it stopped everyone in their tracks. This was obviously the old infuriating Tad again and, whilst they were disappointed that his reformation had been so short lived, they were hardly surprised. You can't, thought Vi, teach an old dog new tricks. They all turned on him with their usual forms of invective but Tad would have none of it. If Peggy's life was at stake then the notebooks, however valuable the contents might be, counted for nothing.

To everyone's surprise Belvedere immediately fell in with Tad's apparently simple solution. He stared bleakly at his rough interpretation of Flaxton's street plan now covered with thick red crosses showing where their searches had failed to find Peggy.

"We have no option. Peggy's safety comes first. Her husband – what's his name...?" He barked the question at Norman who flinched backwards. Why did Belvedere always thrust him back into his school classroom? All he could manage was "um..." before Pat saved him.

"Freddy."

Belvedere steam-rollered on. "Yes, well, her Freddy can write new notebooks. He can't create a new Peggy."

There was no arguing with that but the bluntness of the sentiment brought a loud sob from Rena who burst into tears. Rita comforted her. Everyone was on edge. Elaine, whose Welsh lilt always became more pronounced when she was riled, rounded on him.

"Very nice I'm sure, Bel. I expect your Shakespeare would find a kinder way of stating the obvious. And George agrees with me". George automatically nodded. Belvedere, hurt and surprised, drew himself up to his full height — almost twice Elaine's — and boomed with all his former gusto, "Dear Lady…" but he got no further.

"Don't you 'dear lady' me. I'm not your dear…"

Tad was in like a dart, "And she ain't no lady. Know what I mean?"

His finger licking coincided with yet another outbreak of Tad-induced bedlam. All the pent-up emotions stored through the drama of the fruitless search for Peggy culminating in the terrifying type-written note exploded as they turned angrily on him.

Nell viewed it all in disbelief. How could this close-knit, caring, group of people degenerate so spontaneously into such fury. She was quick to realize that the answer was, in a single word, Tad!

Order was restored by Vi who stood on a chair and belaboured the bottom of a saucepan with a wooden spoon. They subsided in varying degrees of embarrassment at having lost control of themselves — except Tad who, apparently unaware at what all the fuss had been about, carried on as if it had never happened.

"Bel, old cock, slight problem which I'm sure your big head…" there were dangerous murmurs, "…I mean enormous brain can easily overcome. Tricky to hand over the notebooks if we haven't got them to hand over. Know what I mean?"

They all looked at Belvedere wondering why on earth they hadn't thought of that. Then they were still again; it was all too frightening to contemplate. No notebooks, no Peggy. That's what the letter had said. As stark as that.

Belvedere fixed Tad with an expression that would have reduced Norman to jelly but was totally lost on his tormentor.

"I have them."

It was said quietly and long afterwards he would savour the effect it had on his audience; they stared at him in total silence.

George's mind went back to the special assignment he and Norman had been required to undertake with Belvedere. The package in the kennel perched on top of the rubble of the Post Office. The crafty devil! Now he understood. He winked at Norman who, surprised, returned the gesture – but didn't know why.

Belvedere continued quietly; quieter than they'd ever heard him speak before.

"Peggy entrusted the notebooks to me when she was in hospital. I have them in a safe place but, if you all agree – you particularly, Nell – I'll put a message in the Chronicle and we'll arrange the exchange. Peggy for the books."

Belvedere had never held an audience so completely in the palm of his hand – and with no help from the Bard!

The troupe drifted out of the cramped kitchen into the big front room of the house, the older members flopping exhausted onto chairs and sofas, and the younger ones curling up on the floor at their feet. The gathering now settled down to general chatter. Don and his team were in favour of more searching and George agreed with them – and Elaine, of course, agreed with George!

They felt that if the whole town was alerted to search for Peggy and if, as Tad assured them, she could not be spirited out of the area without the military road-blocks and his contacts at the railway and bus stations knowing, she was sure to be found. Belvedere cautioned them against antagonising her captors. Rita and Rena both closed their eyes and tried to shut out the noise. They just wanted it all never to have happened.

Tad couldn't resist doing a little more 'Bel-baiting' incurring loud declamations above the general volume of discussion such as "Poor venomous fool. Be angry and despatch," and the impressive, "Oh villain, villain, smiling, damned villain." The Bard would have been pleased but Tad grew weary of it all and felt that a lunchtime pint or two and a noonday glimpse of Pru's cleavage was essential if he was to avoid landing a well-aimed punch on one of Belvedere's many chins.

Nell's head was beginning to ache with all the chatter around her and the invasion of her home, albeit at her behest, was irking her. Having ordered Vi to silence them again with the pan and spoon in her own inimitable way she called a halt.

"Suspenders of activity," she declared firmly. Norman was appalled to hear himself, in the total silence that followed Nell's command, snigger like the schoolboy that forever lurked in the shadows of his mind. In fact it broke the awkward silence. Rita and Rena giggled, the men sighed with fond memories of suspenders they had known – and, in Tad's case, would know again very soon – and the women, not for the first time, wondered at the weird and sad state of the male brain.

Nell, as usual totally unaware of her malapropism, ploughed on with her instructions.

"It seems that everyone in Flaxton now knows about poor Peggy's disappearance and will tell us if they see her. Bel, Don and Pat, I want you to stay with Vi and me, there are plans to be made. The rest of you go and get some sleep, there's a show to put on tonight. No Baker girls so the rest of you will have to work harder than ever. Well done everyone. We'll find our lovely Peggy and get her back sound and safe. If I ever get my hands on the scoundrel who's taken her I'll kick him to Kumdon King." With that she subsided on the sofa, exhausted.

George led the very appropriate applause which theatricals tend to give each other when the moment's right and they all, less those ordered to remain, drifted off to their lodgings via, in the case of Tad, the Anchor – and Pru!

Nell and Vi, with Belvedere, Don and Pat settled down around the kitchen table, a large pot of tea in front of them, alone in their own thoughts. The house creaked as if to remind them how empty it was and how sad to have lost a loved one. No-one wanted to go upstairs and be near Peggy's room which was, to them, the scene of a heinous crime, a violation.

Vi broke the silence, startling them as she jumped to her feet and grabbed a tray.

"Clearing up to do." Nell sighed.

"Leave it, love. It'll be there later."

Vi shook her head, "Better now, luvvie. We don't want the mess."

Pat joined her; they both desperately needed something – anything – to do. Down the hall in the two front rooms where the troupe had spent the night, the wooden boards covering the windows made them more depressed than ever. As they loaded the tray neither knew that tears were rolling down the other's face until their glances happened to meet and then they fell into each other's arms and cried bitterly.

"What did the police say?"

Nell broke the silence in the kitchen. Don had spent a frustrating few minutes at the Police Station the previous evening.

"First I saw a stupid constable on the desk who said he'd already been called out on a wild goose chase a month ago to inspect Peggy's bedroom at the Post Office, and that the Police had more to do than search for a woman who'd probably nipped off for a good time in London. I nearly hit him but Constable Budd saved his – and my – neck by coming in and sending the idiot out to make tea. Budd took all the details and said he'd circulate them around the area." He added mournfully, "That was, of course, before we had the letters."

"You're very quiet, Bel dear. You've worked so hard you must be exhausted." Nell put her hand on Bel's which made him jump. People didn't put their hands on his. It was quite unnerving.

Nell tapped it lightly, which he rather liked. "Come on, dear. A penny for your thoughts. Unbutton yourself."

Vi was very quickly in with "Unburden."

Belvedere stood up, surprised to find he missed Nell's touch, and studied his street map. As he turned back to them Vi and Pat came into the kitchen with a laden tray of dirty plates, glasses and cups. A ray of sunlight through the window caught Pat's face as she passed and he saw how tear-stained and white it was. Peering at the others it struck him that everyone was the same. Their blood had somehow drained from them. The shock wasn't easing; it was getting worse.

It was his faithful Bard that saved him from blacker thoughts.

"Stiffen the sinews, summon up the blood." He was amazed to find himself roaring out part of 'Henry Five's' speech at Agincourt. The effect of his outburst was dramatic. Cups and plates clattered into the sink, Nell banged her fist on the table and Don, usually to the rear of Belvedere when he let forth at his audience, leapt up and retreated behind his chair.

"That's it," shouted Nell, "That's what we want. The old Bel. The old us. Peggy would expect it." She rose majestically from the table.

"Cry God for England, George and Saint Harry," she cried and planted a kiss on Belvedere's cheek.

Belvedere really couldn't understand his feelings. In the depths of despair his spirits soared. Such a state would be confusing for anybody but for this single, elderly, chauvinistic tragedian it was nearly all too much. He took a deep noisy breath, an enormous pinch of snuff, blew his nose and wiped his eyes with his handkerchief. Done in reverse order it might have been more effective – and, thought Vi, rather nicer.

"There's something that you four should know but it's so secret that no-one, absolutely no-one else must be told. I really believe that it spells the difference between life and death for Peggy."

They hardly recognised the man standing so solemnly before them. In time they'd realize that this was the real Belvedere and be rather more impressed by the very different persona he had created for his tragedian act, a persona that had drifted into the everyday Belvedere – except at times like these.

Don involuntarily got up and closed the kitchen door. Vi took his cue and pushed up the window to seal the room. Pat found herself stroking Mountjoy to calm her nerves and give her comfort. Nell did the same with Harriet, Alice's cat, who had jumped onto her knee in all the commotion.

Very quietly Belvedere told them…

*

That evening, with the show over, the takings from a good 'house' counted and the theatre all but empty, Nell sat in her office with Vi. The medicinal bottle of brandy was on the desk and each held a small glass which they were carefully sipping. Nell was dressed as usual in her 'post-show' outfit of dark blue evening frock, her husband's enormous overcoat and her hat with the ostrich feather. She hadn't been looking forward to this moment and had been putting it off for almost a month but the events of last night and today had decided her. And with the decision made, Vi must be the first person to be told.

"Vi, love. There's something I've got to tell you.'

Dear Lord, thought Vi, not more secrets. She really didn't know if she could take any more surprises, horrid or pleasant, on top of everything else. She drained the last dregs from her glass only to have it immediately topped up by Nell with, Vi noticed, a shaking hand. Poor love, thought Vi, this is all far too much for anyone to handle, even dear Nell.

"I'm going to retire."

It took a moment or two to sink in, then the shock hit Vi and she seemed to crumple before her friend's eyes. Nell quickly took her hand.

"It's alright, love. It's alright. Not right this moment. Not instinctly. We'll get Peggy back and reunified with her husband and the troupe booked with other shows. There are plenty of bigger ones around, and I've got contacts who owe me and Masters a flavour. We'll get everyone settled then call it a day. What do you think?"

To Nell's consternation Vi burst into tears. She knew it was stupid but she'd never thought of Nell retiring. Somehow she'd imagined the Pier Theatre Company going on forever as it was now, same troupe, same Don and his team, even the same acts! She knew it was Hitler's fault and would be delighted to have the opportunity to tell him so to his thin, ugly face.

All this went through her mind as she wiped her eyes on the proffered Masters handkerchief whose main use, it seemed these days, was to mop up his theatre troupe's tears.

The one question that had raced through Vi's head was what would *she* do? She was ashamed that she had thought so quickly about herself but at moments like this self-preservation tended to leap to the forefront of the mind. She had a little money put away but all her friends were here and if they left…

She drained her glass, stood up, smoothed her dress and made for the door. Why did she feel a little unsteady on her legs? Fatigue probably. She pushed her hair back and tightened the bun.

"Sorry, Nell. Stupid of me. Of course you must retire. You jolly well deserve to. As you say, we'll get this mess sorted out. With the news as it is I wonder if we've got much option anyway. That swine Hitler seems about to take it out of our hands."

"That's where I'm retiring to." Nell was disappointed that Vi hadn't asked. This was all going wrong. Vi turned at the door and saw that Nell was now standing up looking at the Highland scene on her calendar.

"To my sister's. She still runs the little shop – in her cottage. You'll love it."

Vi opened the door. She needed to be on her own and think. She smiled, "You should be safe there, luvvie – at least for the time being." She turned again to leave but then Nell's last words registered and she swung round, "*I'll* love it?"

"Of course." Nell settled down again at her desk and virtually disappeared into the giant overcoat. The ostrich feather seemed to turn and point directly at Vi. "You don't think I'd retire without you, do you?"

She saw no reaction on Vi's face and added anxiously, "You will come? Please?"

Vi came round the desk and took her hand. "Oh Nell, Oh Nell…"

Nell, who had never imagined it otherwise was surprised at this show of affection. She drained her glass. "We're a eunuch."

Bill Colbourn was the last to leave the Pier Theatre that night. He usually was because it took some time for his lamps and faders to cool down sufficiently for him to feel safe leaving them. Was it his imagination or were they getting hotter by the night? Old age probably, like him! One day they'd conflagrate the lot of them! As a Fire Watcher he'd have a fire to watch at last! His chuckle turned into a wheezing cough.

With an ever-present mug of scalding tea in easy reach he sat in his cubicle for about an hour after the show and twiddled the knob of his ancient wireless set between the Home Service and the newly introduced Forces Programme. The comedy shows were good – Happidrome, ITMA, Garrison Theatre and the like, but they were usually over by the time he switched on and anyway he'd just had a belly-full of comedy a few feet away from him.

It was the news bulletins that got his attention. Like his two mates, Reg Prentice and Don Preace, he'd gone through the last 'war to end all wars'. All three had been injured, Reg in the gut and Don now with a wooden leg. His was gas, hence the wheezing – and unless – or more probably until – the situation got desperate, they'd be fighting Hitler from their firesides. But Mr Churchill would, he was sure, soon change all that; there'd be a job for all of them.

He heard Alvar Lidell giving the nation the latest bad news of the war in Europe and, reading through a batch of petty domestic items, highlighting the lack of war here in Britain.

His mind was back on the Somme, that terrible stalemate that had taken so many lives; youngsters like he had been then. So many of his mates needlessly, pointlessly wiped out. It had been no use describing it when he got home. He didn't have the ability to paint a terrible enough picture of it to even touch on the fear, the squalor and the degradation. But then no-one had really wanted to hear anyway. In the twenty-two years since then he'd hardly ever spoken about it except, of course, in the privacy of the scene dock with Reg.

A dull voice in the news bulletin was now exhorting the nation to tighten its belts, dig up its lawns, plant vegetables, and report anything suspicious. What *have* we come to, he thought. He doubted whether anyone was really absorbing all these exhortations. History was repeating itself. No one would understand the gravity of it all until the battle reached *them* as he was sure, this time, it would. Here in Flaxton they had already experienced a foretaste of what was to come. He could imagine what it must be like in the overrun countries; the sudden snuffing out of an established, comfortable way of life; the snuffing out of lives themselves. Could there ever be anything so contrasting as the horror over there and the still cosy self-indulgent life in England? He took a loud, slurping sip of his hot tea.

On the wireless Alvar Lidell was back now with a final round-up of the day's news. The British Expeditionary Force was holding back the German advance but, Bill wondered, for how long? Countries over there just seemed to cave in rather than fight for every inch of their land, every ounce of their soil. That wouldn't happen here. This very day, according to Mr Lidell, Winston Churchill in a fine speech was offering blood, sweat and tears and he knew this country would be with him and do the same, like last time.

The news ended. Sandy Macpherson was now, as ever, churning out jolly songs on the theatre organ. Bill sighed and turned off the wireless. He checked his gold hunter watch, the only tangible memory he had of his father, and saw that it was nearly eleven. Later than usual. That's what thinking did for you. He drained his mug, ran the back of his hand over his mouth to wipe it – a habit that infuriated his wife – checked the dimmers for coolness and, satisfied, removed his woolly gloves and rose stiffly from his stool. Switching off the lights, by the low glow of the emergency bulb he made his way to the rear door.

The rain had stopped. He felt the cool, clean, Spring air on his face. Pity it didn't permeate into the theatre, he thought. In the pitch dark he fumbled with the key, locked up and made his way gingerly down the pier to the darkened promenade. He would dearly have loved to call into a pub – *any* of the many Flaxton pubs – for a beer and a chat but funds were low. He'd be in bed soon, asleep heaven knows when.

In the theatre the creaks and groans of the old, tired building were augmented by the staccato tapping of Morse code.

*   *   *

The following morning in the British Embassy in Stockholm Freddy found the mood to be very different from that of the previous evening. He wasn't to know that the Ambassador and his senior staff had never been as relaxed as they had appeared to be at dinner. Their working lives existed amidst the intricacies of diplomacy and protocol and they knew that the release of Freddy Crisciak to their custody was a very special favour, a touch of 'blind eye' from the Swedish Government, and would inevitably result in a violent protest from Germany. They wouldn't have been surprised to know that the German Ambassador had already sought a meeting with the Swedish Foreign Minister who, due to pressure of work – hastily conjured up – would not be able to see him until late afternoon.

Freddy was blissfully unaware of all this as, after a leisurely breakfast in his room, he bathed and dressed in clothes hastily purchased for him. He felt quite light-headed. As far as he was concerned he was now free from unlawful imprisonment by a foreign power and could exercise the right of every citizen of the world to do as he wished!

He had expected to meet the Ambassador that morning and was, indeed, shown into his sumptuous office – yet again to be startled at the uncanny resemblance to General Streyer's Grand Salon in

Warsaw's Hotel Bristol – but the man who greeted him somewhat curtly was not the Ambassador but his Naval Attaché, Commander Cook, now in civilian clothes.

"Professor Crisciak, please come and sit down. There are matters that need to be discussed urgently." The Commander motioned him to a chair at the large desk and, to Freddy's surprise, sat himself down in the Ambassador's chair.

For some reason which he couldn't quite fathom this man irritated him. Where he had expected warm, relaxed, cheerfulness that, to him, went with freedom, here was curtness and a cold precision in both manner and speech which unsettled him.

"There are three facts you must know before I explain to you what will happen next."

Well manicured hands were carefully placed, palm down, on the desk. Dear Lord, it reminded him of Streyer!

"First you are still in great danger, second your wife, Peggy, is safe and well and awaits you in England and third, my name is not Cook but Charles Turville of the British Secret Service, and my mission is to get you to England to continue your secret scientific work for His Majesty's Government."

He paused to allow Freddy to take all this in. Above all else was the confirmation of Peggy's safety. He was overwhelmed with relief and emotion, so much so that he felt himself about to cry, but the sight of this stern person opposite calmed him. The last fact, that he was now in the hands of an organisation which he reckoned to be equal to any trick the Gestapo might still try to play to recapture him, was the best news of all. That this man was someone other than he had claimed to be was of no interest to him whatsoever.

Turville, who relished subterfuge and acting a role – particularly a naval role – was disappointed that this revelation hadn't caused the slightest reaction from Freddy. How could someone not applaud such a masterly performance? He tried again.

"My true identity must only be known to you and the Ambassador."

Freddy nodded, "Of course."

His disinterest riled Turville. Didn't this man realize what was being done to save him from torture and a terrible death? It never struck him that of course he didn't.

Both men were now on edge with each other, one in a fit of pique, the other at being treated so arbitrarily. It seemed to Freddy that he should now have some say in what happened next. He was, after all, a free man in a free country and if it hadn't been for Peggy he might well have stood up, left this arrogant, vain man, walked out into the sunlight and offered his services to the Swedish government!

But there *was* Peggy, the only reason for his existence, and this man could – would – re-unite them. So, with an effort, he smiled.

"I understand the danger I am in … " he spoke gently, "and will do all that you require of me to help you succeed in this dangerous mission. I should like you to know how very grateful I am for what you are doing for me and my wife."

It was a masterly piece of psychology and worked perfectly. Both men relaxed and Turville, calmly and quietly, outlined the plan for his safe transit to England.

Whilst he was doing so, a Top Secret coded signal was being received in the Embassy Wireless Room. Later that day Turville deciphered it and read of Peggy's disappearance. This was a piece of information he had no intention of passing on to Freddy.

Roundly and loudly, and not for the first time, he cursed his colleague in this mission, Ludovic Henschel.

Only a short distance down the broad Stockholm avenue in the diplomatic quarter of the city a very much more volatile confrontation was taking place in the Ambassador's office in the German Embassy. General Streyer was rebuilding his shattered reputation using the weapons with which he was most familiar: fear, force and threat.

He wasted no time. As a start he convened the Court Marshal of his adjutant on a charge of 'endangering the life of his superior officer'. Streyer, as judge, prosecutor and jury, predictably found him guilty and the hapless man was summarily executed by the Embassy Protection Squad in the rear garden. Thus, at a stroke, the only witness to his master's ignominy was eliminated.

It was now the turn of the Ambassador, a proud and cultured product of the pre-Nazi era, to be harangued by the little General. He was made to stand in front of his own desk like an errant child whilst this evil product of an infamous regime sat in *his* chair and, in language embellished by every form of blasphemy and threat, offered him his life in exchange for the 'repatriation' of the prisoner Crisciak to German territory, in this instance the Embassy.

In this dark age into which his beloved Fatherland had precipitously descended the Ambassador wasn't sure whether he cared anymore. There was certainly no future for him or his kind in the Third Reich, and he was sure that it would only be a matter of time before he and his family would be eliminated and replaced by a man very similar, probably, to the animal now sitting at his desk. He looked at the framed photograph of Hitler on the wall above Streyer where, in the old days, had hung the splendid portrait of President Hindenburg in dress uniform. What an exchange: the corporal for the Field Marshal...

He was jerked back to the present by an impatient bark. "Well?"

Like most people faced with the prospect of life or death, he decided to put off the evil day for a while longer and do what he could to achieve the task set him by the General. It shouldn't be too difficult. He knew the British Ambassador and his staff well. Until nine months ago they had been close friends meeting regularly, almost daily, at receptions, government meetings and on the tennis courts. He was confident that the dear old chap wouldn't know how to spirit someone away from his Embassy and deliver him to far off England. He was sure that there wasn't an ounce of deviousness in him, neither, as was apparent during their frequent tennis matches in the past, did he incline towards the killer instinct. He almost felt he could invite this Professor to coffee and then, after a cup or two and slice of Sachertorte – flown in specially from Vienna in the diplomatic bags each week – hand him over to this evil little man.

"We will repatriate the Herr Professor, Herr General, fear not." His voice was icy calm, reflecting not an ounce of fear.

He strolled to a window and looked down on the peaceful, well manicured gardens below him which, yesterday, had provided the setting for an execution. This man, he felt, soiled his office, his Embassy, his country by his very presence.

"I shall be seeing the Swedish Foreign Minister later today and will make the strongest representations to him..."

Streyer started to speak – or rather, yell.

The Ambassador held up his hand and, amazingly, the General stopped dead, "…representations to summon my British coll…" he managed to correct himself, "…counterpart to attend the Minister where he will receive a demand for the Professor's release back into our custody. If he refuses to do so we will have to use other means."

He fixed Streyer with a steely eye and went on before the man could interrupt.

"Your colleagues in Berlin provided me three months ago with just the man." He turned back to the window not trusting himself to look at the General. "He has your – shall we say – style. Your command of our noble language. Your gift of persuasion. A man of action rather than mere diplomacy. Adolf Lunz, what a *splendid* Christian name, my – I think we call him – Information Officer, will succeed where…" now to the climax of his sardonic oration "…others, of all ranks and abilities, some of whom are still alive, have failed."

It was wasted effort. Irony was totally lost on Streyer who stood up and with little strides, marched to the door "Then do it," he barked. "I will brief this Lunz tomorrow morning."

*　　*　　*

That Tuesday morning in Flaxton-on-Sea the 'War Council' – Nell, Vi, Belvedere, Don and Pat – met in Nell's kitchen at eight-thirty, an unheard of early hour for thespians appearing in nightly shows. But this was an emergency and anyway, until Peggy was safely back with them no-one could sleep for long. There was only one item on the agenda: the message for the Flaxton Chronicle.

After much painstaking cerebral work resulting in pages of rejections – some long enough to fill a whole page of the newspaper – the masterpiece was agreed upon. It would appear under 'Classified' in a small box:

> CRISCIAK BOOKS FOR
> EXCHANGE
> The Stage – 11 p.m. – Wednesday 15 May

"Shouldn't we go to other papers as well?" Pat's voice was small and flat.

She jumped – they all jumped – as Belvedere pounded the table. "Well done, Pat. Of course. Under our very eyes. How could we have missed that?"

Nell let him subside a little. "What dear?"

Don chipped in. "We were told to put the message in the Flaxton Chronicle. So whoever's got her must live in the Chronicle's circulation area – or at least work in it. So she's not far away."

Belvedere was back at his town map. He drew a thick red oval around its perimeter.

"She's somewhere in here," he said, stabbing the map. Vi couldn't help herself. She hated deflating their newly built hopes.

"We knew that, though, didn't we? Tad found that out."

They were silent again. Nell summed it up.

"We know she's near us and alive and well. We must cling to that. Do the exchange and get her back." She looked at her watch. It was nearing mid-day.

Belvedere, extracting his gold pocket watch from his ample waistcoat, noted that it had taken three and a half hours to construct eleven words. Wordsworth would have composed at least one sublime poem – probably two – in the time...

"If it were done when 'tis done, then 'twere well it were done quickly." Unusually, the quotation was not boomed at them but said rather quietly and sadly. He put on his coat and set off for the offices of the Flaxton Chronicle.

The others sat quietly around the table deep in their own thoughts. Don broke the silence.

"Macbeth, Act One, Scene Seven," he said. "Fancy Bel forgetting to say that."

*   *   *

In Stockholm Adolf Lunz, masquerading as the German Ambassador's Information Officer but, in fact, Heinrich Himmler's 'SS Presence' in the Embassy, had received his orders from General Streyer that morning. He had enjoyed the half hour it had taken the General to provide him with the details he needed. This, he felt, was a man he could understand and relate to. *This* was the *new* Germany, an ocean apart from the old, doddering Empire represented by the Ambassador and his staff that it had replaced. Soon he was sure that he would be told to remove them all so that new products of the Third Reich could take their places.

Such satisfying thoughts were going through his mind for the umpteenth time as he sat at the wheel of a black Adler car in a side road nearly opposite the British Embassy. It was the second day of his surveillance. As yesterday the car was filled with thick smoke; he and his two companions, professional gunmen recruited for just such emergencies, were enjoying the luxury of the Ambassador's best cigars.

Information had been received through some careless talk in a bar frequented by the staff of many of the Embassies in Stockholm, that their quarry would be travelling today by car on the road towards Gothenburg on Sweden's west coast. Lunz, in his capacity as Information Officer, assumed that he would then be transferred to an aircraft at a remote airstrip on the route and flown out of the country and, on the strength of that brilliant piece of deduction, General Streyer had sent a signal to Berlin to alert the Luftwaffe who had total command of the air outside Sweden's territorial air-space.

Lunz was getting impatient. It was now three o'clock. They had been sitting in the car all yesterday and for nearly four hours today and the initial excitement of the mission had long evaporated – unlike the cigar smoke which, now stale, was making him feel unpleasantly sick.

He was beginning to feel the urgent need to stretch his legs, get some fresh air and relieve himself – in any order or all at once, he didn't care – when the first signs of action sent a familiar tingle down his spine. None too gently he nudged awake his companions. A large black car had drawn up to the steps of the British Embassy. Lunz drew in his breath. This was good. He'd be tailing nothing less than the British Ambassador's Rolls Royce!

Almost immediately two servants carried down heavy suitcases which the chauffeur stored in the boot and moments later two men appeared. They answered to the descriptions given to him at his briefing; a Naval Commander in uniform and a tall thin figure in an overcoat and trilby hat. They climbed into the rear of the car. The Ambassador himself stood at the main door of the

Embassy, and with a wave that was half a salute sent the Rolls on its way.

The black Adler pulled out into the traffic. They would keep a discreet distance between themselves and their quarry until they were well out of the city. The General's orders were that there was to be no brush with the Swedish authorities. Once had been quite enough!

*   *   *

It's doubtful whether many of the readers of the Flaxton Chronicle gave much thought to the small boxed message in Wednesday's classified section of the paper. Two people – other than the troupe – did, though, and both displayed, briefly, the hint of a smile. Most of the loyal readers of the daily journal were much more interested in and disgusted by the main story on the front page. It concerned a fire in Approach Road that had destroyed the home belonging to the late, unlamented, Chairman of the Town Council, Edward Bradley. His wife, Phyllis had been rescued just in time and was now in the town hospital critically ill suffering from smoke inhalation.

What angered the readers was not so much the suggestion by the police that arson was suspected, but rather that ex-councillor Ted had not yet arrived from his unknown hide-away to visit his suffering wife. Vernon kept his off-the-record confidence and didn't mention the auntie in Pontefract. The people of Flaxton were disgusted – but not surprised. It seemed par for the course.

But there was more. The story, spreading easily to page two, quoted a number of accounts given to the paper's Roving Reporter – Vernon Rogers wearing yet another hat – of at least two 'swarthy strangers' visiting clubs, pubs and shops enquiring about the whereabouts of the disappeared ex-Councillor. They used – the intrepid reporter reported – 'threatening language and gestures' much of which appeared to be bombast. Mrs Butterworth, who ran the newsagents, swept them out of her shop on the end of her broom!

This new outrage – for that is how Vernon Rogers, now back in his role as editor, described it – added to the strain of the already overworked and over-stretched Flaxton Police Force to whom the disappearance of a comedienne from the Pier Theatre Company ceased to attract any of their attention.

At another time this story in the Flaxton Chronicle would have been the subject of animated, non-stop discussion in every nook and cranny of the old groaning theatre. The troupe enjoyed a good gossip and these strange goings-on in the town would have created plenty of comment and opinion from them. But today was different. The mood was sombre. Everyone – even Belvedere – seemed to be speaking quietly, nervously smiling at each other as they passed, fussing over already ironed and darned costumes, fiddling with lighting, adjusting make-up into neat piles on their dressing-tables. The problem was that they really didn't know what to do.

Nell had called them for a two o'clock meeting. She didn't want them distracted by the Bradley incident nor questioned in any depth regarding Peggy so, she felt, they were better in the theatre than out of it. Both Monday's and Tuesday's performances had been understandably lack-lustre; the troupe had gone through the motions of their various acts professionally, but no more than that. Nell, of course, fully understood and, if it were possible, loved them all the more for keeping going. The strain for every one of them was almost unbearable.

Now they were all sitting in the auditorium in the dim emergency lighting. No-one wanted to be seen and Bill Colbourn's offer of the house lights was quickly turned down. Tad, who would normally take such a splendid opportunity to cuddle one of the girls, sat on his own; they all needed space. The stage curtains were closed. Nell, for some inexplicable reason, chose Fred Spriggs's chair in the orchestra to perch on which meant that she addressed them from behind his array of drums, cymbals and chimes.

"Tonight we get dear Peggy back amongst us." Her voice was tired and old, almost a whisper.

"On this stage tonight we shall exchange her for the note-books. She will be angry but we have no option. Her life is more important than anything. She must see that."

It was more as if she was justifying their decision than talking to them. Her eyes were far away. If ever she needed her beloved Masters it was now.

"I want the theatre cleared by half-past ten. The tabs open, Don. Only emergency lighting, Bill. Just me and Belvedere. The rest of you, if you want, can be at number 34. We'll bring Peggy back to you."

No-one moved. Tears falling down several cheeks were left unwiped. This was a Nell they had never seen. Tired and defeated. Exhausted.

The noise, when it came, was all the more alarming for following such a sombre interlude. Nell sat forward, grabbed Fred's drum sticks and crashed them down onto everything in sight. The cacophony was ear-splitting. They sat forward, some jumped up, someone let out a loud wail. It ended as suddenly as it had started but the silence was only for a moment.

"Buttock the lot of them," Nell shouted. "Come on. We've got a show to do. We'll welcome Peggy back with one of our finest performances. Let's show the swines who have done this that the Flaxton Pier Theatre Company is invisible."

She rose from the chair, the percussion instruments collapsed around her in a discordant fanfare of sound and she strode, walking-stickless, ostrich feather straining forward, towards the rear of the auditorium.

"Invincible, dear" said Vi as she passed.

"Indeed we are Vi," shouted Nell. Her eyes flickered upwards. That was odd, she thought. She was sure she'd seen a small movement in the dark recesses of the Dress Circle.

*   *   *

The two black cars, in viewing distance of each other, edged their way through Stockholm's suburbs and out on the Gothenburg road towards Nyköping. Soon the habitation thinned out and they were in open, rocky, country.

The Adler pulled back but Lunz had little fear of causing suspicion to the occupants of the Rolls; the Ambassador's car, of early thirties vintage, only had a very small rear window and no wing mirrors and the road constantly rose and dipped around bends that, more often than not, prevented visual contact between the two vehicles.

As yet espionage and surveillance were new skills to the young Lunz. Like his superiors in the SS he relied more on fear and pain to subdue his enemies so his plan was sketchy and haphazard to say the least. When he felt the conditions were right – a long stretch of straight road and no other vehicles in sight – he would speed up to within a few feet of the Rolls and his two colleagues, both sharpshooters, would lean out of the rear windows and empty the magazines of their pistols into the back tyres. Hardly subtle but undoubtedly effective.

The three men in the Rolls were tense. They knew only too well the dangers they were facing and were aware of the black car that had trailed them from the moment they left the Embassy. Knowing the mind of SS General Streyer they were surprised that there hadn't been an ambush in the main streets of Stockholm, but maybe even *he* was sensitive enough to realize that one highly embarrassing diplomatic incident, which had doubtless stretched Heinrich Himmler's faith in him to the limit, was already one too many!

Then, with a cough and a sigh, the giant Rolls Royce slowed to the side of the road and stopped. The engine was dead. The chauffeur opened his door and climbed down from the running board, unscrewed the two chromium catches on his side of the bonnet and lifted the lid.

Inside the engine gleamed – in silence. It was so very quiet, only a gentle breeze rustling the tall grasses of the shrubland clinging to the granite rock that surrounded them caused any movement or sound. There was no traffic – and no sign of their pursuing black car.

Lunz, in the Adler, saw the Rolls stop ahead of them, and it was only a dip in the road that maintained their cover as they, too, pulled to a halt. He was quickly out of the driver's seat and, edging to the top of the rise, he couldn't believe his luck. There was the car with one side of its bonnet open and the chauffeur, clearly identified even at a hundred metres by his uniform, bent over inside the engine. Lunz rushed back to the Adler realising that they must move quickly: Rolls Royces didn't break down for long.

He started the engine and barked over his shoulder, "No shooting. The Herr General wants these people alive and no, I repeat, no bodies to explain. Fear, not force."

The words sounded good — as they should; they were exactly those used to him by Streyer that morning and were now delivered with the same rasping coldness.

The car moved forward, the two gunmen eased out their pistols and released the safety catches. It was all very well to say 'no shooting' but there was every likelihood that the occupants of the Rolls would not feel bound by the same order and they had no intention of taking part in a one-sided gun battle.

The Adler pulled alongside the Rolls. Only now did it strike Lunz that he hadn't worked out what language to use. He had a smattering of Swedish and English but, at that moment, both totally deserted him.

In German he said to the chauffeur, "Good day, may we be of some assistance?"

The man jerked upright, "You startled me." He, too, used German. "You are kind. The engine is dead."

The two gunmen climbed out of the back of the car. Their attempt to appear as two law-abiding passengers was spoilt, not only by their total lack of ability as actors, but also by the fact that both were holding their guns! In a split second they had the rear doors of the Rolls open and their pistols pressed against the necks of the two passengers in the back. What they lacked as actors was more than compensated for by their skill as highwaymen!

The two passengers had obviously been asleep. Now startled into wakefulness they jerked forward. The civilian's hat fell over his face which apparently disorientated him. He raised his hands and felt steel enclose each wrist. With a mighty pull he was dragged from the car and dropped down onto the road on his knees. The pain shocked through his body, but before it could register he was jerked upright by his powerful assailant and leant against the car. It had all happened so quickly that there was no retaliation. He stood there, manacled, hands held in a vice-like grip as he was expertly searched for any hidden weapon.

On the far side of the car the Commander was not so lucky. He lunged at his attacker and received for his pains a cracking smash on his forehead from the butt of the man's pistol. He regained consciousness on the rear seat of the Adler, his blood pouring onto the polished leather.

"You fool." Lunz was not pleased as he held his pistol at the neck of the petrified chauffeur. "Now you will travel in the back with the man and dress his wound. Move."

The curt order was sullenly obeyed and the gunman found himself sitting between the two prisoners in the cramped rear seat of the car. For safety he used the men's ties to lash their handcuffs to the door handles. They were now helpless. Neither had spoken a word.

"Now my friend." Lunz searched the chauffeur as he spoke. "You are a very fortunate man. I would kill you now but it is not to be. Maybe some time another vehicle will come along. Until then..."

With a swift movement his fist cracked into the man's jaw and he crumpled to the ground. Lunz removed the Rolls's ignition key and settled himself back behind the wheel of the Adler. He looked at his watch; the whole action had taken four and a half minutes and had proved totally successful. It was, he felt, what Reichsführer Himmler would expect of a rising star in his elite SS. Well satisfied with himself he turned the car around and sped back to Stockholm.

Some five minutes later the chauffeur stirred. He had a severe pain in his head but, feeling over his body, everything else seemed to be functioning adequately. Gingerly touching his jaw he now knew where the knockout blow had struck him! He staggered to the driving seat and saw that the ignition key was gone but in the glove compartment, under a heavy automatic pistol, he knew there was a duplicate set.

The engine sprang into life: the smooth sound of six Rolls Royce pistons firing in perfect synchronisation. Closing the bonnet he eased the car back onto the road. It was too long to turn in the narrow width so he drove on into the village of Nyköping. It was eighty kilometres to Stockholm and he would take his time; the last thing he wanted to do was catch up the Adler. Slowly and sedately the British Ambassador's Rolls Royce purred its way back to the Embassy.

*

This Wednesday was not proving a good day for the German Ambassador in Stockholm. The dreadful, boorish, SS General had more or less completely taken over the Embassy. It was amazing how quickly the little man could incite such fear and loathing into a team of professional diplomats and their supporting staffs. At first they all, from the First Secretary downwards, tried to oblige the monster; they knew of the obscene power wielded by the SS and feared for their lives, but by lunchtime they had found it best to go to ground either in obscure corners of the building or out in the city's bars and restaurants.

Only the Ambassador and his small office team of secretaries stayed in the firing line of the despot. Try as he might he couldn't get Streyer to understand the intricacies of diplomacy; it was as well that he hadn't been told of the operation his Information Officer was engaged in on an open road in this neutral country! He would have to have tried to stop it but, apart from not succeeding, the consequences of the effort would undoubtedly have been dire.

Streyer had taken over the Ambassador's office. He had spoken by coded signal to Berlin and assured the Reichsführer's Chief of Staff that the operation to re-secure the prisoner Crisciak – whose escape, he reminded him, was due to the stupidity and treasonable actions of his erstwhile adjutant – was nearing a successful conclusion. This was due to the fact that he, himself, was commanding the operation. Now he awaited the return of his raiding party.

The Adler drew up to the rear entrance of the Embassy. Lunz climbed out and ordered the gunmen to lead the two prisoners, still handcuffed, into the building. The Commander, his Royal Naval Uniform splattered with blood and a crimson bloodied handkerchief tied roughly around his head, staggered slightly but then pulled himself erect and marched up the broad stairs to the Ambassador's office. His companion used his manacled hands to pull his mackintosh around him and adjust his wide-brimmed hat at an incongruously jaunty angle.

At the high double doors of the office Lunz curtly dismissed the gunmen. The coming glory was to be his and his alone. At their desks the secretaries cast furtive glances at the unfamiliar, very undiplomatic, scene unfolding around them. Lunz knocked. They heard the General's curt command.

"Enter."

Inside the office the Ambassador stood by the window. He would remember the scene that unfolded before him for a very long time to come. In disbelief he saw a British naval officer, in handcuffs, obviously wounded, and someone else whose face was somehow familiar, also manacled, being roughly pushed into the room by his Information Officer!

Streyer stood behind the Ambassador's desk with his back to them all. He gazed in awe at the portrait of the Führer. This was the moment he had been waiting for since that fool of an adjutant had allowed him to be taken prisoner in his own aeroplane. This was the moment to relish as his reputation was restored in the eyes of his leader, Heinrich Himmler. You did not outwit Friedrich Streyer, General, SS, more than once in your life…

"Ah, my dear Professor, welcome back…" Streyer's voice was quietly evil, "and, I believe, Herr Charles Turville of the British Intelligence Service." With a triumphant smile he turned to them.

Long afterwards, when the Third Secretary at the British Embassy, Christopher Lever, and his colleague, Richard Cook, the Naval Attaché told the story of their part in the rescue of Professor Crisciak, they tried to describe the look on the SS General's face when he turned to face them. Exultation, shock, disbelief, awareness, fear, despair, they all, and many more, were the ingredients that mixed themselves within the space of a few moments into the agony of total defeat.

Streyer shook, his small face, now white as a sheet and contorted into uncontrollable rage.

"Who are these people?" he screeched.

Very smoothly Christopher Lever, the Third Secretary at the British Embassy introduced himself and Richard Cook and then he turned to the Ambassador.

"You will be aware, Sir, I know, of the seriousness of this diplomatic incident. It will, of course, be reported by my Ambassador to the Swedish Government. Our representations will be made at the highest level. His Britannic Majesty's Representative in Sweden had his car and occupants, both accredited members of his Embassy, ambushed on the open, free highway, they were assaulted, manacled and conveyed against their wishes onto German territory. Kidnapped."

It was a splendid speech carefully crafted during the return journey to Stockholm. The Commander, not to be outdone, added his contribution:

"Piracy." It wasn't much, but it was said with appropriate outrage.

This extraordinary episode ended as any involving SS General Streyer would: in violence. He more or less staggered across the room and smashed the solid gold knob on the end of his baton into the mouth of Adolf Lunz.

*

At the same time that the British Ambassador on the Embassy steps was waving farewell to his Rolls Royce and its two passengers a small white van was being loaded with the Embassy dirty laundry at the rear service entrance. The two black overalled men lifted the large linen bags into the back and then, with the job done, one climbed in on top of the load and the other closed the rear doors and joined the driver in the front. The van pulled away into the traffic.

A man lolling against the wall some twenty yards away noted this uninteresting activity and would log it on his return to base. The SS General had said he wanted every coming and going reported.

Precisely according to Turville's plan the laden van pulled away thirty minutes after the Rolls Royce and Adler had started their journeys but to avoid any possibility of accidentally catching up with the Germans the van took the more northern route via Örebro.

In the rear of the vehicle Freddy Crisciak lay back in considerable comfort on the linen bags of laundry. He felt strangely safe in this metal box with only its one small window into the driving cab connecting him with the outside world. With his eyes closed he ruminated on this latest episode in his extraordinary escape from the Nazis. The problem was that he couldn't make up his mind what mood he should be in! Fearful again, now that he had left the safety of the Embassy? Relieved to be in the hands of such an obviously competent man as Turville? Apprehension at what lay ahead? Oh yes, certainly that!

Turville had outlined the plan to him the previous night and it had all seemed dangerously simple. They could not fly because of the danger of being shot down by the Luftwaffe, so the journey had to be by land and sea. Sure enough the 'careless talk' deliberately sprinkled around the bars known to be frequented by the German diplomats had worked and they had watched that morning from an Embassy window as the Adler dutifully took up position behind the Rolls.

Freddy marvelled, and not for the first time was humbled, at the risks people were taking to ensure his safety. The two Embassy staff, Lever and Cook, were undoubtedly endangering their lives by allowing themselves to be ambushed – and yet they had volunteered before they were asked!

When Turville, sitting next to the driver in the cab, checked through the small window into the rear of the van he saw that the Professor was gently bouncing up and down on his makeshift bed, fast asleep.

He looked at his watch, 5 p.m. They would be there by nightfall. To his right the placid water of the Vanern lake stretched into the distance. It reminded him that soon he and the Professor would be experiencing much rougher seas, mostly below the waves, as guests of the Royal Navy's Submarine Service.

CHAPTER SIXTEEN

Wednesday, 15th May. *Holland capitulates. Queen Wilhelmina and members of the Government flee to London on two British destroyers.*

The British Armed Forces, whilst seriously short of fighting men, have nine top ranking Commanders-in-Chief amongst the three Services defending the South of England with no-one to co-ordinate them!

Britain was in a sombre mood. The newspaper and wireless reports of the Dutch surrender and the German offensive sweeping ever closer to the Channel painted a picture of an unstoppable steam-roller flattening everything in its path. But maybe all was not lost; amongst the stark uncompromising comment of most newspaper editorials were some who spoke of the overwhelming resistance yet to come.

Hadn't France, caught napping once before, assembled one of the largest, best equipped armies in the world and was it not powerfully augmented by our own Expeditionary Force made up of over three hundred thousand of our finest soldiers commanded by the elite of the officer corps? That's what the optimists told their readers; 'the whole root and core and brain of the British Army' was how one eminent writer described it.

It's hardly surprising that two such opposing views – the unstoppable German steam-roller and the mighty armies blocking its path – would confuse and demoralise an already bewildered general public even more, probably, than being told nothing! What many women knew for a fact was that *their* men – sons, brothers, husbands – serving with the BEF in France were, at the very least, disquieted. They could tell from their letters that reached them in a slow trickle from the front line. Highly censored as they were, nothing could hide from their nearest and dearest the sense of impending disaster they all felt.

The mood of the people of Flaxton-on-Sea in mid May was much the same but accentuated by the knowledge that the enemy was now only some one hundred and twenty miles away from them – the same distance, as the crow flies, as London!

Some had spent their recent evenings at the theatre on the pier. A few of those who did so had seen the show before. They were the connoisseurs of 'Beside the Seaside' who came again and again for the escape from the real world and its troubles that a few laughs, sequinned tights and the shapely legs within them, some cheerful songs and, above all, the company of others, could give them.

But, to those connoisseurs, these last few nights had not been 'spectacular', as the bill boards suggested, not even very good; they'd been average, some felt below average. There were no major disasters – except the non-appearance of 'The Baker Girls' – but undoubtedly there was a listlessness that left the audience feeling no better leaving the theatre than when they had entered it.

Nell would have been appalled, distressed and deeply embarrassed had she realized this but, for the first time in her theatrical life, she was completely unaware of the disappointing performances her troupe was giving their audiences.

Had the people of Flaxton known of the nightmare the cast were all going through they would have been amazed that they managed to perform at all but Nell and Belvedere were insistent that, for Peggy's sake – and safety – everything should appear as normal as possible.

The 'War Council' spent most of the Wednesday afternoon in Nell's tiny office trying to decide how that evening's exchange of the notebooks for Peggy's safe return should be staged. The heady scent, which had quite a strange effect on Belvedere, and the rich draperies on the walls punctuated by sparkling stage jewellery were very much at odds with the prevailing pessimistic mood.

Being complete novices in the practices of the underworld into which they had been unwittingly pitched they found no answers to most of the imponderables. The vital question was the order of the handover; Peggy delivered safe and well and then hand over the books or vice versa? As Don said in his usual phlegmatic way it probably wouldn't be their decision anyway; the kidnapper held the advantage.

"We could do with an expert in this chic-canary." Nell, at her desk, was getting flustered and very frightened by it all. "Where's that Ludo man? He said he'd protect Peggy, keep an eye on her. It's too bad."

Pat put her arm around Nell's shoulders. It struck her that there'd been an awful lot of comforting to do, one to another, in the past few weeks, and each time the gesture had appeared more and more inadequate. We're not taught to comfort, we have to learn it the hard way, thought Pat as she helped Nell to find the big white Masters' handkerchief.

Belvedere, who, because of his girth, had been allowed the unique honour of filling the large armchair, stirred amidst the brocade cushions.

"I went to the camp to try and find the man. This morning. I insisted on seeing the Colonel who was most officious and unfriendly. The gist of his message was that it was bad enough having to play nanny to a bunch of foreigners without being expected to know where any of them were! He seemed very fidgety about Mr Henschel. I reminded him that I, too, had served in the last war and he said nastily that the fact that I had since sunk into such a worthless occupation offered him no comfort. I rose majestically from his desk and gave him a touch of Lady Macbeth. I think the point was made."

Belvedere's voice, at the best of times, was trained to fill a large theatre and in Nell's tiny office it deafened them. There was a noticeable echo when he'd finished accentuated by the fact that no-one said a word but despite the volume of sound they'd hardly heard him, wrapped up as they were in their own confused thoughts.

The office now became silent except for the sound of the North Sea a few feet under them lapping against the heavy wooden stanchions of the pier.

After a considerable pause Don pushed himself away from the rear wall against which he had been leaning.

"So he wasn't there?" There was no answer. This was getting them nowhere.

"Right," he said. Someone had to take charge. "The main foyer doors will be locked. We'll leave the Stage Door open and emergency lighting on the stage. You two will sit in darkness in the auditorium and play it as it comes. I shall be with the rest of the men waiting in the scene dock. Once the kidnapper is in the rear door will be guarded until I say he can go. And that won't be until Peggy is safely with us." He went to the door. It had been a fine, commanding little speech but now he turned to them half apologetically.

"Sorry to take over but we needed a plan. It's not safe for you and Bel alone, Nell. And anyway we wouldn't let you. We'll do this together. We'll get her back safely."

With that, he left. He wasn't sure why, but he'd worked on enough plays to know an exit line when it was delivered and, instinctively, he'd just delivered one. He made his way back to his cubby-hole well satisfied.

Nell and Pat looked at the closed door and Belvedere began the long, exhausting business of extricating himself from the deep confines of the armchair.

"Cometh the hour, cometh the man." But most of it was lost in heavy breathing.

Nell shook herself and, as she so often did these days, reverted in an instant to her old self.

"A lean border" she barked and, with a shake of her hat and its accompanying ostrich feather, swept out into the corridor.

Vi sighed her usual sigh. She tidied the desk. "A born leader."

Belvedere nodded and made his way to the small silver flask in his dressing-table drawer.

The evening's show was no better than recent performances had been. If anything it was more lack-lustre than ever. Norman – 'Over the Garden Wall'- got in a hopeless muddle.

"Ooh, there's Mrs Copplethwaite. Just had her operation.
How are you feeling, luv? Everything back where it should be?
(aside) A few bits still missing by the look of her ...
Did you get the you-know-what? (pause)
And put it you-know-where?
(aside) No wonder she's, um, sorry, um, what's-his-name ..."

With the punch line gone the audience was left unmoved and somewhat confused! Even Tad couldn't redeem the situation. It didn't help that he uncharacteristically told a noisy group of gunners to shut up, and from then on they barracked him unmercifully. Strangely, only Marvo really shone – but then he wasn't aware of the drama ahead. He gave a spirited performance which left Rita and Rena exhausted and a day of costume repair ahead of them.

Later, in the darkness of the empty auditorium, Nell looked at her fob watch. She could just make out the hands showing a quarter to eleven. The theatre was silent except for the never-changing sounds of the waves underneath the floor and the creaking timbers around them. The air was still thick with a mixture of tobacco smoke and stale sweat, the floors strewn with empty cigarette packets.

Nell and Belvedere sat in the middle of row G, seven back from the stage apron front and more or less in darkness. The stage, incongruously still set for the cheerful finale with the painted backdrop of the seafront and pier and at its centre the gate for entry and exit, was in half light from the two big unshaded emergency bulbs hanging over it. Without its stage coloured lighting it looked shabby and forlorn.

The two of them were motionless, hardly breathing, their eyes glued to that centre painted gate through which someone would enter, something would happen. Nell was now very glad that Don had insisted that he and the rest of the men would be hidden in the scene dock.

Belvedere was totally calm; he had experienced many lulls before storms, not least in the last conflict. Terrible memories of the trenches waiting for the order to go over the top into a hail of bullets. This, at least, was preferable to that – unless here there would also be gunfire...

Eleven o'clock came – and passed. Nothing. How long should they wait? All night? Nell was cross that they hadn't discussed this important point and unreasonably blamed it on Don. But everything *was* unreasonable, unreal.

The time passed. They were cold. Neither had thought to wear overcoats. Their bones stiffened with the chill and with it came despair, an utter hopelessness. It was all a cruel trick. They would never see Peggy again. More as a comfort that anything else they held hands and, despite the drama engulfing them, dropped into a troubled sleep.

Something woke them. A creaking board? An extra strong wave? Or maybe it was the subconscious knowledge of another presence? Then they heard a soft voice.

"Good evening."

The stage was empty, the painted gate still closed. Their gripped hands tightened painfully.

"Ah, the leaders of the pack if I'm not mistaken. Splendid."

They swivelled in their seats. The voice had come from behind. But how could that be? The foyer doors were locked. How had this man got in? They were both totally disorientated and tongue-tied and just stared as the man walked slowly down the aisle. And then Nell saw his face and stood up angrily.

"What are you doing creeping about like this? You could ruin everything."

*   *   *

Freddy Crisciak woke up feeling decidedly sick. The watch which one of the Embassy staff had generously given him showed half-past eight. He had been asleep, bouncing up and down in the back of the small laundry van for five hours. He knelt up at the small window and looked into the cab. Charles Turville was sitting bolt upright with a map on his knee scanning the road ahead of them. The driver, a chauffeur from the Embassy recruited for this mission, was slouched over the steering wheel looking tired and strained.

Freddy tapped on the glass. Turville glanced around not, apparently, in any way startled by the first noise he'd heard, other than the engine, since mid afternoon.

Turville smiled briefly at him and, by hand movements, suggested that Freddy should open the package of sandwiches thoughtfully provided by the Embassy and eat. He signalled that there was still at least another hour to go. Freddy nodded. It would be something to do. He saw a road sign flash past: Falköping; it meant nothing to him.

The scenery through the cab windows was dull and uninteresting, mainly granite outcrops of rock in scrub; very different from his beloved Poland and the rich agricultural lands on his estate.

Such a thought led him back yet again through the nightmare he had endured over the past nine months. Would it soon be over? Would his beloved Peggy be there at the end of it all, safe and well? The same questions; the same lack of answers.

He settled back and chewed. At least this well bolstered tin box was infinitely preferable to his other motorised escape vehicles; a fish lorry, a dustcart, and a German Junkers aircraft! Those, plus a British Navy submarine would be the bizarre set of conveyances that would, all being well, re-unite him with Project Omega. A strange mix. He bit off another untasted mouthful.

He was eating mechanically. What if his brain had gone; dried up as a result of its maltreatment? His moment of panic dissolved into a stupid giggle as he imagined having to tell the British Government, after all they'd done to rescue him, that he'd lost his memory! Perhaps they'd send him back! Was he going mad? Calm down.

Thank God for the notebooks, a glance through them would quickly re-ignite his brain into the sublime world of nuclear physics. He lay back onto his comfortable makeshift bed and gave himself up to scouring his memory for the formulae and equations that were carefully stored deep within it.

His brain was, as ever, his zone of comfort and security; he'd already proved that it couldn't be invaded or stolen against his wishes. He stretched out luxuriously on the linen bags and saw the figures and fractions, the hieroglyphics of his scientific world float before his eyes. For him, he mused, the dangers were over.

But of course they weren't...

The van had slowed down. Freddy dragged himself away from his luxurious deep dive into physical science and went to the cab window. Open country had given way to small clusters of wooden homesteads surrounded by fields of cattle. The evening was slipping into a clear night and though he couldn't see it the moon was obviously providing a strong light on the darkening countryside. He wondered if Charles Turville would find this helpful or harmful to their escape plans.

In the front of the van the mood was far more tense than was apparent to Freddy. Turville was under no illusion regarding the danger they were in. He'd easily picked out the man in the road at the rear of the Embassy when they were loading the bags. The idiot would need many lessons in surveillance before he fooled anyone.

To Turville the unknown factors were the length of time before the agent gave his report to his German master and what General Streyer, who was reported to still be in charge of the operation, would do about it. He would draw a blank at the airfield near Nyköping south of Stockholm and it wouldn't take too much intelligence to alert the German network of agents around southern Sweden to look out for a small white van. A salvo or two of automatic fire would quickly turn the little vehicle into a colander and its passengers into corpses. Turville wished he had a large can of paint; any colour but white!

But the damage may have already been done. Throughout the long drive he had at frequent intervals held a small hand mirror, borrowed from the Ambassador's wife, out of the side window to check the road behind them and had easily spotted a small unidentified civilian aircraft which had appeared to be far too interested in the little white speck speeding along the near-deserted roads. Twice it had flown unusually low, always behind them, as if it didn't want to be seen.

Why be so interested in a small innocuous van? Turville had no way of checking above them but he had an uncanny feeling that they were being kept in somebody's sights. It could, of course, be just the inquisitiveness of an amateur flyer but even if it were so he could well decide to talk about it to his friends on landing.

There was nothing to be done but plough on into the welcoming darkness and meet any trouble head on but it was not as his years of SIS training had taught him to do; he would rather have had time for some detailed planning.

According to his map there were a number of routes to the submarine rendezvous and one of them was presenting itself now. Seen or unseen it was time to leave the main road.

With a jerk, which sent Freddy hurtling against the left-hand wall in the back, the van turned sharp right. The road – more a track –

was unmade and the small vehicle bucked and juddered along the pot-holed surface. Freddy, literally brought back to reality with a bump, managed to clamber to the window but there was little to see. The headlights showed two furrows stretching way ahead with grass each side and between them. Turville was studying his map with a pencil torch and the driver was grasping the steering wheel as it tried to twist out of his hands. Freddy couldn't decide whether kneeling, sitting or lying down was best for absorbing the violent pitching of the vehicle but of one thing he was certain: he shouldn't have eaten the sandwiches!

For an hour they twisted and turned in the near darkness and at regular intervals Turville cursed the moon; the driver, on the other hand, blessed it. No-one had told him that volunteering for this assignment would entail driving a very basic, badly sprung van across the rock-strewn Swedish landscape; he'd only ever driven a small car through the streets of Stockholm. Anything for a bit of adventure, he had thought. Now he wasn't so sure.

Freddy was thrown around like a pebble in a bucket. With nothing to hold on to and no way of knowing what the van would do next he was unable to take any avoiding action. The only answer, he found, was to snuggle down with the linen bags around and below him forming a sort of trench. This meant they kept falling on top of him but anything was better than constantly being thrown at the metal sides.

Turville was much too preoccupied with his map-reading to give a thought for the comfort of his passenger. Such cosmetic matters never entered his mind; a bruised and battered Professor delivered to his masters was better than no Professor at all. He was far more concerned that he no longer was able to keep an eye on the road behind them. It was far too bumpy for the little vanity mirror to be of any use and the twists and turns of his route made it impossible anyway.

A sign to the right read Torslanda. It should; but even after all these years he still got satisfaction from the accuracy of his skills with a map, and a dark unknown landscape was a considerable challenge. A few kilometres and then the sea.

Still there would be danger; there were small islands for the boat to negotiate before they were safely on board the submarine. And how safe would *that* be? He smiled; this was an assignment he wouldn't have missed for the world…

The driver touched his arm and pointed to the fuel gauge. He'd glanced across and seen this extraordinary man smiling beside him when, as far as he could see, a smile was the very last expression this terrible experience warranted. He felt the near-empty gauge might wipe it off his face but Turville just nodded and returned to his map. Outwardly nothing seemed to trouble him.

The narrow track now dropped down slightly and swinging round a bend Turville saw, just where he knew it would be, the sea. The Kattegat.

"Lights out. Inch along."

The order was whispered and the driver instantly obeyed. The van crept along the track lit only by the pale light of the moon. For a short distance they drove alongside the water and then, apparently nowhere in particular, he ordered the driver to stop. "Switch off." Another whispered order.

It was eerie; silent except for the lapping of gentle waves on the shore. The driver shivered, Freddy in the back lay tense and still in his warm linen-bagged trench. They all felt total isolation in the sudden quietness as if their senses had been taken from them. After eight hours of incessant noise there was now nothing.

Freddy and the driver both jumped at the quietest of clicks as Turville let himself out of the van. It was amazing, one minute he was sitting in the cab, the next he'd disappeared. It struck the driver that maybe that's why the three of them had been issued with black overalls at the Embassy.

Turville pulled on a black balaclava and gloves and was now invisible to the naked eye as he silently climbed the small dune at the back of the foreshore. A thin breeze ruffled the tall grasses amongst the granite rocks. With trained stealth he lay still as if absorbed into the landscape, invisible to the naked eye.

The alertness of his senses told him that something was wrong. It couldn't be defined but it was there, and he knew he had to identify it quickly. One small, imperceptible move and a small, snub, automatic pistol was in his hand.

Below, to his left, was the van, its whiteness standing out starkly in the moonlight. The sight shocked him. He cursed himself for not having ordered the others out of it. Around the van he could just make out old fishing debris, ropes, cages, floats, piled haphazardly where their owners had left them for another time. Beyond, out to sea, he saw one or two lights on the cluster of small islands that lay off-shore between them and the submarine but inland there was nothing. Blackness.

And yet something was wrong. He knew it.

The fusillade of gun fire when it came startled even him. With the crack of each shot came the tearing of metal as the bullets penetrated the soft skin of the van and in horror he saw it rocking from the force of the impacts. Moving silently and at great speed he slid and crouched his way to behind the area of fire. It was easy to make out the three men who, believing all their quarry were in the vehicle, were standing up silhouetted against the sky.

"Like shooting ducks at a fair" shouted one, in German, to the others.

They laughed, but it was the last sound they ever made. Turville fired three deadly accurate shots into the back of their necks. They all died almost at the same moment.

Turville raced down the slope, kicking the dead men aside, and hurled himself at the van. He couldn't believe how careless he had been and how he had allowed the Professor, after all he had gone through, to be so easily wiped out.

The noise struck him suddenly. Violent banging – and the van was still rocking! He pulled open the rear doors and a very agitated Professor of Nuclear Sciences fell into his arms. The man was obviously injured, there was blood everywhere, but he was miraculously alive. He was gibbering, "the washing – destroyed – all around me – full of bullets – bags broken – terrible."

Turville half carried him to the seaward side of the van and sat him down against the rear wheel.

"Quiet as you can," he whispered. "There may be others."

"There may indeed, Herr Turville. For that's who I know you to be. Welcome back into my care Herr Professor. It is some days since we last met."

SS General Streyer levelled his Walther pistol at Turville's head, only a foot away from his right temple. "For killing my men you shall now pay the ultimate price."

Freddy Crisciak closed his eyes tightly as the shot blasted the silence. A moment later he heard the body fall heavily at his feet.

*　　*　　*

The tableaux in the auditorium of Flaxton's Pier Theatre was only held for a few seconds. Belvedere swivelled in his seat with a confused expression on his face and Nell stood alongside him, her ostrich feather pointing accusingly at Ludovic Henschel.

"What are you doing creeping about like this?" she said. "You could ruin everything."

Henschel made his way to the orchestra pit and, coincidentally, chose Fred Spriggs's percussion seat to settle onto. He laid his hat carefully on the cymbals.

"I think it rather more likely, dear Mrs Masters and, let me see, Mr Galbraith, tragedian..." he stressed the last word sarcastically, "that it is *you* who could ruin everything."

Nell, when confused, tended to shout a bit and have her usual trouble with words.

"Don't dally-dilly. We tried to reach you earlier at the camp place but you were out. We've got to hand over the boat-hooks"

Belvedere patted her shoulder.

"I'll handle this, Nell. It's all right my love." He frowned; had he really said 'my love'? How extraordinary. This would need thinking about – but this was not the moment.

"Then do so. Hand them over – NOW."

Ludovic Henschel couldn't contain his frustration. Could these two old fools be even more stupid than he had imagined?

"*I* have Peggy. I suggested she put herself in my care for a short while. To ensure her husband's safety. She, of course, agreed." His voice became careless as if he was throwing away unwanted information. "She had little option. I told her that he would probably die if she didn't."

"But there was another note. In with hers. Someone added a type-written threat, do you see?" Belvedere's voice was strained. He was thoroughly confused.

Henschel sighed. "You fool." His voice rose. "How can it be that such matters are in the hands of such imbeciles?"

Belvedere, angry now, buffeted his way along the row of tip-up seats and Nell, shouting in support, crashed her walking stick on the seat in front of her, the ostrich feather scything like a sword in battle.

"How dare you. DARE you. You insult us in my, MY theatre. You, sir, are a startup."

As if on cue and far more slickly and disciplined than at any performance the stage filled with the male reinforcements, led by Tad who bounded to the front of the stage with such menace that Henschel actually flinched! Behind him Don, Reg and Bill strode on purposefully. This man was nothing compared with some of the actors they'd had to deal with in their time. At the rear, but looking – well at least *looking* – belligerent, came George and Norman who, being actors, attempted to take up threatening poses, but not very successfully. It was fortunate that they were at the back and therefore relatively unseen.

None of this show of strength had the desired effect – in fact any effect at all. Henschel merely shrugged his shoulders. He stood up and put on his hat. The cymbal clanged as if he'd just concluded a spectacular stage trick.

"No books. No Peggy. The situation has not changed. The British Government requires the notebooks for safe keeping. It would make sense to do the same with our subject's wife. Keep her hidden away. I am, however, instructed to be accommodating. She will be returned to you fit and well – WHEN..." he barked out the word, "WHEN you hand the notebooks to me."

Belvedere sank, defeated, into a front row seat. He looked up at Henschel; his voice was thin and old.

"How will it be done?"

Tad knelt down on the stage apron and tapped Henschel's shoulder making him, maybe for the first time in his career, jump in alarm.

"No Peggy, no books, old cock. Know what I mean?"

Henschel shrugged off the hand that was now aggravatingly tapping him. He'd seen this loathsome man on the stage. The Pole-abuser. He directed his comments to Belvedere.

"We will go to your telephone. Just you and Mrs Masters. I shall 'phone a number and arrange for Peggy to be delivered to your house. When she is there she will 'phone you. Your woman Vi, who I know to be there, will verify it is a genuine call. If I then have the notebooks my men will leave her there. If not, she will be removed to a new location. Somewhere she will *not* enjoy. Understood?"

Belvedere looked back at Nell. She just nodded. There was nothing more she could do. The three of them threaded their way through the men on the stage to her office.

Henschel, shielding his dialling with his body, was almost immediately through to his accomplice. "Take her to Clarence Road. As agreed. Number 34. Now."

Although they supposed it would be so they were shocked that he knew of Nell's home address.

"How long will it be?" Belvedere was suddenly feeling very tired.

Henschel turned to them. "About ten minutes. Sit down please."

It was almost an order. He ushered Nell to the armchair and Belvedere to the desk and leaned nonchalantly against the door. They did as they were told, as if they too were prisoners.

On stage the men looked at each other. No-one knew what to do next. Bill Colbourn stuffed his hands into his pockets.

"We should have broken his fingers until he told us where Peggy is."

Reg nodded mournfully. "And then pulled out his fingernails."

"Better to do that before we broke his fingers." Bill was warming to the subject.

George, remembering the ritual dismembering of the roast chicken every Sunday lunchtime felt unwell. "Stop it you two. We couldn't do that. Horrible."

There was a stirring from Norman in the back row. "My auntie did."

They all turned and looked at him. He was immediately flustered. Why had he joined in?

"Broke her toe." They relaxed. "Tripped over the cat" a pause. "the cat wasn't hurt though."

It broke the tension and they laughed, quietly.

Norman looked around him. They had laughed – at something he'd said. It was a warm feeling. He'd raised a laugh without that absurd

345

brassière and terrible frock and it was a revelation to him. In his next show he reckoned he'd do away with props altogether. Just him.

Tad said bitterly "Do anything to him and we've lost Peggy. And that means for good. Know what I mean?" He'd like to have knocked the man down – or at least helped others to.

Don now moved. He jumped down the steps into the auditorium.

"Right. George, Bill and Norman to Nell's house. Tell the girls what's happening and to expect Peggy and an escort – and make sure the 'phone's working. No rough stuff. Say nothing about the notebooks. Nothing. Clear? Tad, Reg and I will stay here to support Nell and Bel."

It was just what was needed. No-one queried Don's authority, they jumped to it.

In the little office Belvedere sat at Nell's desk as ordered to by Henschel. No, he thought, he was damned if he would. He stood up and moved to the outer back wall and, copying Henschel's position, leant against it.

"Ten minutes you say?" He boomed.

Henschel nodded.

Belvedere knitted his brow. His mind was on the roughly made street map covered in the red crosses in Nell's kitchen. Ten minutes. So she had been that close all the time. They'd missed her. Where? His concentration was broken by the sound of distant laughter. What on earth were the men on stage finding to laugh about? Most inopportune.

Henschel heard the laughter too and half turned towards the sound. He assumed that they were laughing behind his back and it aggravated him. Could these idiots still not see the gravity of this whole business; that the outcome of this war depended on the notebooks and this damned Professor and his stupid wife?

God, how he despised these absurd theatre people with whom he'd been made to become entangled. He wanted them to apologise for wasting his time. He thought of telling them about his demeaning activities in Flaxton; tailing the girl, and her escorts, searching bedrooms, picking locks and, worst of all, sitting for hours in the gloom of the Dress Circle watching their foolish antics; the sheer unadulterated boredom of protecting them, often against themselves; a Secret Service agent of his calibre. But why bother?

They weren't worth the effort and the big fat idiot would undoubtedly have a clever riposte, some stupid quotation. He fixed Belvedere with a malevolent stare and was surprised to receive one back of even greater intensity.

Nell sat deep in her armchair. Her thoughts were of Peggy. What had she gone through at the hands of this obnoxious man? If any harm – ANY harm – had befallen her she would see that he suffered. She had her troupe around and she knew she could depend on a large part of the population of Flaxton to support her. Councillor Winifred, worth a whole army, Vernon Rogers wielding the 'power of the Press' to name but two, and a host of others. Just let him have laid one finger on her…

They were all startled from their very different thoughts by the shrill ringing of the telephone. Nell and Belvedere felt their hearts thumping in their throats as Henschel sauntered to the desk and picked up the handset.

"Yes?" His voice was quiet, almost conversational. He thrust the instrument at Nell. "For you. It's your woman."

At any other time Nell would have struck him with her stick; broken it over him. Now she just took the 'phone from him.

"Yes?" her voice was almost a whisper. Then she broke down, "Oh Vi. Vi love. Let me speak to her."

She closed her eyes for a little prayer and then suddenly sat forward.

"Oh Peggy my love, dear Peggy. Are you alright, luvvie? Unhurt? You mean it? You're sure?" – a pause – "they're there?"

She sounded surprised. "Good for them. They'll protect you. We'll be back soon." She thrust – almost threw – the 'phone back to Henschel.

He spoke into it in an oily sarcastic voice. "So glad you're safe and well, Peggy." His voice hardened, "Put my man on."

After a moment they could hear a male voice. "Stay on the 'phone until your next orders."

He put the handset on the desk and looked at Belvedere. "The notebooks now, if you please."

Nell handed Belvedere the safe key and he rummaged inside amongst the ledgers and boxes bringing out from the back a well-wrapped parcel done up with thick string.

"Open it."

The command was curt but Belvedere noted a tiny tremor in the voice, rather like first night nerves. Was this *so* important to this man who appeared to be totally unemotional? Belvedere, with some difficulty, undid the parcel. Five small, identical notebooks, all scuffed and scratched with wear and age, fell out onto Nell's desk.

The male voice was shouting through the telephone earpiece. Henschel grabbed it from the desk.

"Wait, man. Until I say," he barked, throwing it down again.

Despite himself he couldn't prevent a tiny shaking of his hands as he thumbed through each book. None of it meant anything; a maze of data that was a foreign language to him. But what he *did* know was that he had in his possession five priceless artefacts.

There was complete silence in the small cluttered room and no-one moved. It was, thought Belvedere, like a stage set, a tableau, with the lighting provided by the sun casting a solid dusty beam through the narrow window onto Nell's desk illuminating the central characters of the plot: the notebooks.

Henschel, as silent and unmoving as the rest, stared in awe at them. Such was his confusion of thoughts at that moment that suddenly his actions became fast, almost frenzied, making them jump at the sudden movement. He wrapped the brown paper around the books, thrust the package into his mackintosh pocket and picked up the 'phone.

"You will leave the woman there. Report back to base". Without waiting for any acknowledgement he flung the handset back onto the desk and opened the door. Seeing ranged against the far wall of the narrow corridor Don, Tad and Reg, he faltered, but only for a brief moment, then he strode past them and out through the rear stage door.

"Good riddance," shouted Reg who felt somebody had to say something.

Nell was very, very tired. Belvedere helped her to her feet and into her overcoat. He always felt the garment helped to take the attention away from her awful hat and ostrich feather. Don locked the stage door.

"We'll use the main entrance. I want to make sure it's firmly locked. How did that man get through it?"

He led the shell-shocked party across the stage, through the auditorium, then out into the night.

The relief gun crew found the prostrate body of Ludovic Henschel as they came on duty at midnight. He was lying in the passageway between the side of the hall and the railings of the pier almost exactly where Norman had been thrown into the sea a month before.

The back of his head was badly bruised and a nasty cut was oozing blood. As they none-too-gently moved him he groaned and they dropped him back onto the planks.

"Bleeding drunk," said one gunner with great authority.

"Takes one to know one," said his mate.

They went to their command post beside the gun and 'phoned for an ambulance and by half-past midnight Henschel was tucked up in a hospital bed, bandaged and sedated. Severe lacerations and concussion was the verdict. One nurse searched his suit for evidence of identity and found what was needed. Another went through the two pockets of his mackintosh – both were empty.

*

"But I could come and go as I liked. I wasn't a prisoner."

Peggy smiled at them all. It was good to be home even if they were treating her as if she'd just been released from prison! She was trying to explain it all to them and couldn't work out why something so obvious was confusing them. There was tut-tutting and head-shaking. She tried again.

"Ludo was helping, you see. He came to the house when you were out. He told me that the only way that Freddy could be safely rescued was if I was in a secret, guarded, place in case the Germans tried to abduct me."

There was still no response. "There was no other way." She was defiant now. "So I left you the note. Well, I didn't actually. I was so flustered I took it with me and he kindly brought it to you straight away."

No he didn't, thought Don, the blighter gained valuable time by keeping it until the next morning whilst we all despaired and feared the worst. But he didn't say anything. Now wasn't the time.

They were in their now almost familiar places in Nell's front room, the older actors on the big chairs and settee and the twins cross-legged on the carpet. Don, Bill and Reg stood by the door on guard. Peggy was back with them and nothing, no-one – other than Freddy of course – would prise her from them again.

"Yes, but..." Norman, as ever determined to say something, wanted to clear up the business of the second note, the threat.

"Ssh dear," Nell was quick to butt in. "Let Peg go on. She's centre stage. In the lime-lamp-lit-light. Go on luvvie."

"So he took me to the camp." Damn, thought Belvedere. Why in Hades didn't we think of that?

"I was to be a refugee. I used the smattering of Polish Freddy had taught me but the others in my hut were told that I was in a state of shock and could hardly speak so they left me alone. They were so kind though..." her voice trailed off. She had actually enjoyed her few days there, acting a role again. It had been some time since she'd done that. The Palace Theatre. 'Careless Rapture'. Freddy...

The troupe sat quietly and patiently. They could see that Peggy was far away, her mind in a different place at a different time. They'd seen her like this before. They'd witnessed the torment of her escape from Poland and her struggle as she had sat in this very room only a few weeks ago and told them her story. Now, they felt, by letting her experience this sequel to it they had failed her; they had vowed to protect her, and they hadn't. But this time her story just didn't seem to make sense; she was telling them she had *volunteered* to disappear completely unaware that she was being duped by Ludovic Henschel.

"Worst thing was letting you all down. Poor Pat." She looked at her friend. "No 'Baker Girls'. I bet you were much better without me."

She hardly heard the protests from around the room. "But you see I had to. For Freddy."

She looked around the room at their friendly, caring, concerned faces.

"You *do* see, don't you?"

They were all embarrassed now. The more they let her go on the worse it was. Who would tell her about the notebooks – and when? Henschel had carried out an unforgivable deceit and played on her vulnerability regarding her husband's safety. They shuffled and shifted their eyes away from her; they couldn't look her in the face.

Peggy received the wrong signals from their discomfort and jumped up.

"I couldn't do anything else. I'm sorry." She was defiant now, her eyes blazing as she rushed from the room pushing through Don, Bill and Reg.

Nell got up. "Go and comfort her, Vi. Bel and I will be with you in a jiffy. The rest of you home to bed. Boys see the girls to their doors – and not a word of this, not a single word to anyone. Our lips are scaled."

She bustled out and made for the kitchen where she heard the kettle boiling and Belvedere, feeling he was far too old for all this, followed her.

Tad stood in for Vi as interpreter. "She meant sealed. Know what I mean?" He wondered how Pru would react to the sound of the key in her front door at this hour in the morning. It seemed the best thing to do. Take his mind off the problem for a while.

They all left quietly, almost tip-toeing along Clarence Road. Norman found himself yet again having the last word.

"It was good of that Ludo chap to look after her so well."

The others said nothing, grateful that Tad had set off in the other direction and Belvedere was still at Nell's house. Neither would have let such a remark go – not even from Norman!

The five of them, Nell, Belvedere, Vi, Pat and Peggy, sat around the table in the kitchen. Vi had poured the ever-necessary tea and they were all holding the mugs up to their chins, elbows on the table, enjoying the scent of Ceylon and the warmth of the china.

Nell had been sorely tempted to send them all to bed. It was nearly two o'clock and on any normal day they would be exhausted, but after what they'd been through they were almost beyond sleep. Anyway, Nell was sure that putting off the moment of truth for

Peggy – how Henschel had used her – was wrong. She must know now. Then they could plan the next move.

Peggy looked around the table and felt their deep distress. Dear Nell and Vi were obviously so troubled and Belvedere appeared to have all his considerable stuffing knocked out of him. And all because of her, the interloper who had turned their simple, innocent lives upside down. She knew, for the thousandth time, that she should never have come here. But why were they so uneasy now? She was back with them, Freddy was evidently safe and, please God, on his way to England and soon they'd be free of her. Why were they behaving like this? Everything was going wrong. She'd never had a problem communicating with them all before. She decided to plough on hoping more explanation would help but in her distress the words seemed to gush out faster and faster.

"Ludo told me that tonight Freddy would be safe and well in England somewhere and as soon as he knew for certain I could come back here. I waited in the Colonel's office with this man who works for Ludo and then we got the 'phone call. He seemed to act very strangely. He wasn't at all nice. He bundled me into a little car and brought me back and here – most of you – were. What kept you so late? Vi was very jittery, she said you were still at the theatre."

Belvedere lowered his mug of tea and took her hands in his across the table. This wasn't going to be easy.

"Peggy, my dear. There are things you don't know..."

Poor Belvedere. Had he first told her of the hours he had spent, day and night for a week, creating five notebooks full of similar but totally irrelevant formulae and calculations carefully copied from science books borrowed from the library, and *then* told her about the typewritten threat and the handing over of the substitute nonsense books to Henschel in return for her, all would have been well.

But he got it all the wrong way round. He started with the recent scene in the theatre and Nell's office and Henschel leaving with the books – and all hell broke loose! Peggy went berserk. So much so that she woke Rita and Rena in their room at the top of the house and they came rushing down in their nighties. Belvedere quickly averted his eyes and was grateful, as he so often was, that Tad was not here to see their undressed state.

Nell restored order and sent the twins back to bed so that Belvedere could stop intently studying his map of Flaxton on the mantelpiece and start calming Peggy regarding the notebooks.

When he had done so she threw her arms around his neck and gave him a large, noisy, plonking kiss right on his lips. There was that strange, warm feeling again! Things were happening to Belvedere that he really didn't understand. And he was only in his late sixties...

Nell then sent everyone to bed. Belvedere was allocated the settee in the front room and provided with armfuls of blankets, pillows and, despite it being late May, a stone hot-water bottle. He feared that he'd have an awful lot of explaining to do to Mrs Chumley, his landlady, tomorrow.

As it was his un-slept-in bed only served to fuel her suspicions; she'd noticed the little photograph of Nell Masters which was now on his bedside table...

*   *   *

Freddy, sitting against the rear wheel of the bullet-ridden laundry van, didn't want to open his eyes, there seemed nothing to open them for. Everything, literally everything, was lost. And here, only a couple of feet in front of him, was the sea connecting him with England and safety.

Ironic? Dear God, there wasn't a word in the English language to describe it. He was startled by a noise, and even more confused to realise that it was himself – groaning. It was some time since he'd felt with his tongue for the cyanide capsule.

"Just got the blighter. Good shot Stevens. Second Lieutenant Anthony Firth, Royal Marines. How do you do. You'll be Professor Crisciak."

It was all said calmly and in perfect rhythm. Freddy opened his eyes and looked up at three men in heavy protective clothing one of whom was squatting down in front of him, smiling.

As if that wasn't confusing enough he saw at his feet the very dead body of General Freidrich Streyer, a large patch of blood spreading through his thick coat from the area of his heart. His face, noted Freddy, registered nothing, no surprise, hatred or pain; just, it seemed, total disinterest.

All this had happened in the course of less than a minute. Turville had disappeared but now returned as silently as he had gone.

"That's the lot." He spoke totally unemotionally. "Our driver's dead. Burial at sea, I think. Rocks for ballast. Field dressing for the Professor. He caught the final moments of a bullet or two. Let's move."

Still Freddy had said nothing; he was literally dumbstruck. He chided himself; why did he so often want to cry these days?

The soldiers expertly patched him up. To his surprise, he'd forgotten about the wounds he'd received in the van. They were only grazes, he was assured, the bullets had lost all their force in breaking through the van wall and shredding the dirty washing in the linen bags. Freddy's deep trench in the centre of the vehicle had saved his life.

In his highly strung state his mood easily switched from bewilderment to anger at the impersonal attitude of them all. The poor innocent driver dead; people shot as nonchalantly as they would shake hands. He wondered if Turville would ever thank the man who saved his life!

"The boat's a hundred yards south. We heard the shots and felt it best to investigate rather than run straight in here."

Turville grunted acknowledgement as they moved along the shore. One marine carried the dead driver, the other supported Freddy. A 'well done' to the young officer might have been in order but it obviously wasn't in Turville's vocabulary. Taciturn, thought Freddy, that was the word to describe him, taciturn – and a few other things besides...

The small boat's motor sprung into life making a deafening noise but no-one seemed to care; this was, after all, a neutral country and boats could come and go as they pleased at any hour of the day or night.

Freddy saw that they were getting into something similar to a large rowing boat obviously used for fishing judging by the bits and pieces of gear rolling around the duckboards. Its owner, dressed in waterproofs, helped him aboard and appeared quite unconcerned with the drama going on around him. Freddy wasn't to know that this fisherman had been only too happy to be bribed with a handful of krona to undertake this unusual trip but had been less than pleased to be ordered to *row* the boat to the shore, oars muffled to maintain silence.

Now, with no need for stealth, the engine pushed them out around the islands and towards the open sea.

Above the noise of the engine Freddy became aware of raised voices. In the dark he could see Turville, using his limited knowledge of the Swedish language, having what appeared to be a flaming row with the boat owner who, to the detriment of the direction in which they were heading, kept on taking his hand off the tiller to help his wild gesticulations. Turville came up to the centre of the boat and flopped down on the cross bench obviously defeated.

"He won't stop for us to tip over the dead man," he said testily to the officer. "He wants to take him back to shore and 'phone the Embassy to collect him. Goes on about his family or whatever."

The Second Lieutenant nodded. "Much the kindest thing."

Freddy was delighted – particularly at seeing Turville's look of surprise and confusion. The boat chugged on into choppier seas as they lost the protection of the islands. They were now in a vast emptiness. Freddy shivered; would this nightmare never end?

The marine in the bows called out. "Ahead, two o'clock."

They could see it now, a flashing pin-prick of light which the marine answered with a powerful torch. To Freddy it seemed to be many miles away but, in fact, it was quite close. He watched the light, mesmerised by it, seeing it as the final link between him and Peggy. It was his first contact with Britain since all this started and represented, as far as he could believe, safety. He willed it to enfold them and, as if answering him, in no time the pinprick became a small hand-held lantern which, as they approached, rose up high above them.

Then he saw the black outline of the submarine, huge and menacing, with the tiny guiding light at the top of its conning tower. Involuntarily he shivered.

The boat pulled alongside and eager hands pulled them up the sloping side onto a narrow deck. Freddy never saw the boatman to thank him and he doubted whether Turville had done so but before he could gather his wits he was manhandled through a hatch cover and down into the warm dimly lit belly of the submarine. A hand grasped his.

"Welcome to His Majesty's Submarine Torness, Professor. You are now in the care of the Royal Navy. I'm the Captain, Lieutenant Commander Toby Mallory. You'll have my cabin of course. Prepare to dive." The last comment was shouted over his shoulder.

No time wasted and a dangerous passage ahead. Five hundred feet below the North Sea Freddy Crisciak was on the last stage of his journey to Peggy and, he fervently hoped, safety.

*   *   *

In Berlin and Stockholm the repercussions of the Crisciak incident were proving exceedingly uncomfortable for quite a number of people, some of very high rank. The Führer was enquiring politely when the eminent Herr Professor, now fully indoctrinated into the glorious Third Reich, would be at the Kaiser Wilhelm Institute in Berlin to share his unique knowledge regarding nuclear fission with his German colleagues? He was uncharacteristically polite because his enquiries were levelled at the SS Reichsführer Heinrich Himmler; one of his few subordinates who warranted such treatment.

The SS Reichsführer, far less polite but none-the-less oily and smooth in his tones, was asking his subordinates for the latest information from his accident-prone colleague in Warsaw – who, for some reason, was in Stockholm – SS General Friedrich Streyer. He was not best pleased to be informed by the aggravating Ambassador to Sweden that the Herr General was unable to answer the question because he was at that very moment rounding up the Herr Professor for repatriation to the Fatherland.

The last the Ambassador had been told was that Streyer was in pursuit of a white vehicle that had been reported by a vigilant amateur flyer – a member of a Stockholm flying club which had been asked to report any such sighting – to be travelling towards Gothenburg on the northern route. That was all the Information Officer, Adolf Lunz, could tell him and even *that* was somewhat garbled through a mouth with few teeth and very swollen lips!

The Ambassador had been only too grateful that something – anything – had taken the revolting little General away from the Embassy – and Lunz, for all his Gestapo fervour, thoroughly agreed with him!

*

The next day, Thursday 16th May, two fisherman discovered the bodies of four men on the coast near the town of Torslanda. Three had been shot in the back of their necks, the fourth, a senior officer, through the heart. The fishermen informed the police who, from identities found on the bodies, alerted their colleagues in Stockholm regarding three of them and the German Embassy regarding the fourth.

Thus it was that the body of SS General Friedrich Streyer was borne to Berlin where, with full military honours, and in the presence of the SS Reichsführer Heinrich Himmler himself, it was laid to rest amongst the great and the good.

CHAPTER SEVENTEEN

Late May 1940. German Armoured Divisions are within twenty miles of Dunkirk. For some inexplicable reason Hitler has ordered them to stop.

The British Admiralty is rounding up shipping of every size and nature to prepare for an evacuation of the B.E.F. from the French port of Dunkirk.

Outwardly, the week following the late-night drama in the Pier Theatre passed quietly. The troupe returned to its long-established routines spending the days in slow preparation for the journey to their dressing-rooms and, when there, their own particular and, in some cases, peculiar transformation into the characters they would be portraying on stage.

This preparation ranged through muttering, declaiming small snatches of out-loud dialogue, a bit of bickering, quickly executed dance steps and, for those who preferred silence, a little quiet reading. Tad, of course, did none of these things; there were knick-knacks to be sold through the long days before a last-minute dash to the theatre.

So it appeared that everything was back to normal but, of course it wasn't – nor ever would be again. The Germans were getting nearer by the day and everyone knew that the previous six or seven weeks had only been a slow build-up of pressure towards the eruption that was about to engulf them all. And they were frightened; every one of them was very frightened.

They weren't alone. The whole nation was gripped by fear, some people expressing it, but the majority being 'British' and containing it whilst giving an outward appearance of cheerfulness. "We can take it," they assured each other with a smile, then retreated back into their private fearful worlds.

The people of Flaxton were no exception. The radio news bulletins couldn't hide the stark fact that the enemy was nearly at the gates – and they, on the east coast, knew only too well that they were occupying one of the most convenient gateways into the country. As a result, nerves were frayed and people behaved irrationally and untypically. Vernon Rogers splashed the front page of the Chronicle – as Sports Reporter – with the news that the Womens' Institute only narrowly voted against marching on the Bowls Club and digging up their sacred patch to plant potatoes! These formidable ladies said they considered it improper that such a sport should be continuing in these grave times. Vernon, in his editorial column, wondered what Francis Drake would have said!

For Nell Masters all was confusion. The events of a week before in her theatre and her house were very nearly the last straw. She ached for the Highlands and retirement. Her sister had expressed her delight at the idea and had pointedly assured her in her most recent letter that a small, delightful cottage was for sale at the other end of the village. Ideal, she said, for Nell and Vi. On reflection Nell saw that it was by far the best idea; sisterly affection was one thing, but they'd each enjoyed their independence for far too long to lose it now.

'The Baker Girls' had been back in the show for a week and the takings reflected their popularity. It was also obvious that Peggy's return had lifted the cast back to its high level of performance but Nell and Vi kept to themselves the embarrassing fact that the cinema audiences had far outnumbered those for 'Beside the Seaside' for the past fortnight!

"Unperceptable", Nell said sweeping the daily returns sheets, carefully and neatly drawn up by Vi, into the waste-paper basket.

"Acceptable dear", she corrected as she rearranged the papers.

"No it isn't" retorted Nell testily and Vi decided to leave it at that.

Whilst all the rest of the troupe did well to cover their personal anxieties with a veneer of light-heartedness Peggy rose above them all. She threw herself back into the act with Pat and the audiences loved it. And yet there were so many unanswered and, it seemed, unanswerable questions churning through her mind that sleep at night was almost impossible and no one thought could be pursued to a logical conclusion before being overtaken by another.

Where was Freddy? Everything paled into insignificance against that. The last she'd heard of him was from Ludo when he'd tricked her into going to the camp. He'd said Freddy was safe and on the way to her but he'd been lying all along so he couldn't be trusted to tell the truth about anything. It was then, usually in the dark loneliness of the night, that she would break down into silent tears. She realized that she really knew nothing regarding Freddy's fate since that terrible moment last year when he'd put her and Anya onto the small fishing boat en route for Norway. The images, all with question marks, flashed through her mind; Anya? – Freddy? – fighting? – captured? – tortured? – dead? Sheer exhaustion would send her into a troubled sleep in the early hours of the morning.

Belvedere, on the other hand, was more concerned than troubled, although he would have seen only a very hazy line separating the two incapacitating conditions. *His* sleep, however, was not affected; the nightly intake in the Pier Head Tavern ensured that and, as Mrs Chumley, his landlady, would verify – from a safe distance – he slept heavily and noisily, his snoring interrupted by the occasional cry of 'Raze out the written troubles of the brain' or similar quotes from the Bard's Scottish King.

It was the whole business of the notebooks that was concerning him, for a number of reasons. First, once a scientist of any calibre examined the fake versions Henschel would be told that he'd been duped; second, a ridiculed Henschel would be a very dangerous adversary, and third, that led to an even worse imponderable: did the terrible man have control over Peggy's husband's destiny? He seemed to be closely linked with those who were supposedly rescuing the Professor and he could therefore wreak terrible revenge. Belvedere agonised. Should he have handed over the *real* books – and by *not* doing so had he jeopardised the chances of Crisciak's safe return to this country? And, anyway, was the man still alive?

He tossed and turned, grunted and snored. Mrs Chumley felt that something would have to be said...

Apart from these three – Nell, Peggy and Belvedere – the rest of the troupe somehow felt that the whole terrible episode was over, that all would now be well and Peg and her husband soon reunited. They, of course, didn't know about the substitution of the notebooks but anyway their attention was then diverted to another mystery which caused all manner of speculation in the dressing rooms.

Nell and Vi were off to London and would be away overnight. Belvedere would be in charge – but he didn't know that Nell had had a word with Don regarding 'sublime authority' if a drama occurred in their absence.

"Supreme," Vi whispered to Don who, whether sublime or supreme, doubted that Belvedere would, in the event, warm to any interference from him.

Tad, of course, had the most lurid explanation; Nell and Vi had been invited to London by a couple of well-heeled 'officer types' for a wild fling. Elaine, her Welsh accent stronger than usual, rebuked him doubting that at their age and with mounting rheumatism either would be willing to be flung anywhere...

*

Flaxton General Hospital had already forgotten about the man who had been admitted a week ago and had discharged himself early the next morning. Identity papers in his suit pocket showed him to be a refugee, Ludovic Henschel, and the cut on the back of his head was assumed to be have been caused by a fall on the pier. That he had the ingratitude to leave without notifying anyone was put down to the disorientation they were all suffering from due to the traumas they had recently experienced. The camp was informed and the hospital was somewhat surprised at the disinterest shown by the Commandant's clerk regarding the said refugee Henschel.

Henschel, however, had not forgotten the episode. Far from it. In the nearest state to panic that he had ever experienced he had left the hospital, dizzy and with a splitting headache, and returned to the theatre. He didn't know why he went there but he needed to start a search for the notebooks somewhere. The building was locked but he let himself in with his lock-picking tool, climbed up to the Dress Circle and sat in his usual seat at the rear.

The dark quietness soothed his pain and he felt able to think. His most likely assailant would have been a member of the troupe. Only they knew about the notebooks and that he would be walking down the passageway beside the theatre at that time. He had seen a man –

he assumed it was a man – emerge from the shadows just ahead of him so it couldn't have been any of the people he'd just left in the theatre. And the person had spoken as he hit him – the last sound he'd heard – so that ruled out at least another of the idiotic actors...

He went down to the foyer and angrily ripped a playbill from the wall. Climbing the stairs he saw that underneath the large print listing the artistes the back stage team were also shown in much smaller type. He crossed off Belvedere and Nell who were with him in the room and Don, Tad and Reg who had been standing in the corridor when he came out of the office. That left a large number of people it might have been. He studied the playbill again; Norman Jackson, no guts: Elaine Price and George Noble, midgets – this man was tall and very strong: The Great Marvo, dumb, this person had spoken: Rita and Rena, wouldn't be able to part his hair let alone cut his head open. There was one other stage man, the electrician, Bill something. No, so full of First War gas his wheezing would have given him away.

But *someone* had the notebooks and he had a vague idea who it might be. It would be a pleasure to retrieve them. A grim smile made him wince with pain.

The message he had received from Headquarters in London before this nonsense with the books suggested that this coming weekend would see this wretched assignment successfully completed. Then, he was sure, the books would resurface. Slowly he made his way back to the camp, had his wound dressed in the Medical Centre and, well drugged with pain-killing pills, sank into a deep sleep.

*

At six o'clock on the evening of Thursday, May 23rd, on the BBC's Home Service, Alvar Lidell announced in sombre tones the terrible news that His Majesty's Submarine 'Torness' had been lost in the North Sea with all hands. It was one of the navy's first major losses of the war and it shocked the whole nation. Later, such a news item would raise little more than an extra jolt to the embattled population but these were early days. Some were surprised that information of this kind was announced at all; wouldn't it cause unnecessary grief to relatives of the crew and, maybe worse, joy to our enemies?

It was, of course, only a momentary shock to the general public; a topic of conversation and conjecture in homes, shops and pubs, but it was quickly followed in the BBC bulletin with an item much nearer listeners' everyday lives – the shortage of food due to the loss of shipping sunk by enemy action. This would mean a likely reduction in the weekly allowances of essential items. The nation's housewives fretted; they'd have to rethink their menus for the two big meals a day they provided for their husbands and children.

It was good that 'Sandy Macpherson at the Theatre Organ' immediately followed the news programme and soothed their agitations with a selection of their favourite tunes...

*

That evening Nell returned from London with Vi. She was comforted that the visit had gone well. It had been pleasant to see her dear friend Beresford Clarke again and watch his new production of 'Glamorous Night' from the Palace Theatre wings. He had been pleased to see her and was particularly relieved to hear that Peggy was well and had slipped comfortably into her role as comedienne.

And then they had got down to business and, after a little hard bargaining – Beresford found himself negotiating with Masters rather than with Nell – a deal was struck!

The next morning she sat in her office and knew that this period of her life would have to end very soon. Her alarm clock said 10 a.m., her Highland calendar, Friday May 24th.

In any other age there would be a light, happy mood in the soft warm Spring air as the town got into its stride for the summer season but now, thought Nell, it was one bit of bad news piled on top of another – and then more on top of that! She opened her desk drawer and helped herself to a little nip of medicinal brandy. At midday, before the cinema audience invaded them, she'd reveal the details to the troupe.

The frantic ring of the telephone startled her. These days she associated the 'internal instrument', as she frequently described it, with bad news and with a sigh she put it to her ear. On the other end of the line was an unusually flustered and embarrassed Councillor Winifred Ledbury.

"I'll have to come straight to the point, Nell. No beating about the bush."

And then she couldn't bring herself to do so! She ranged around a multitude of topics concerning her unenviable job of holding the town together in 'these dark days' – like so many others she was inhaling Churchillian rhetoric into her vocabulary – and Nell only started to pay attention when she mentioned a visit she'd made that morning to the parents of one of the lost submarine's crewmen.

It brought the war so close to them all; the second time in the past few weeks that Flaxton had been projected into the front line. The Navy had evidently done what it could, sending an officer and a civilian within hours of the terrible telegram being received but now, said the Councillor, the family seemed numb, almost complacent at the loss of their only child. It was, she felt, almost too early for grief and tears to overwhelm them.

Even with such sad news Nell enjoyed talking to Councillor Winifred who had rather taken the place of her dear friend Alice Banbury as her confidante away from theatre life. But time was getting on and there was preparation to be done for the impending troupe meeting. In a momentary pause she cleared her throat.

"What bush aren't you beating about, Winifred?"

It took the Councillor a moment or two to understand the question and then, in an unusually dull voice, she said simply, "They want you out, dear. Tomorrow."

Nell froze. There was no other word to describe it. She just seized up because, stark though the statement was, she somehow knew exactly what it meant. Rather than a month or two to slowly effect the so recently planned transfer of the show from the dangers of the East Coast to Beresford Clarke's newly leased theatre in London and then her ordered withdrawal into retirement, 'they', whoever they were, had decreed that it should all end in the next twenty-four hours.

'They', of course, could. The war, or Hitler, or whoever, had seen to that. And there would be no appeal, no acceptance of the impossibility of it all; of the total upheaval of so many lives. As all this raced through her brain Nell had a sudden vivid image of the parents receiving news of their sailor son's death and she knew that none of *this* mattered a jot.

Councillor Winifred had got up steam again and was well into various outrages concerning that element of the town's population who wouldn't accept the strict disciplines now being imposed on them, but it was all a cover for her embarrassment at what she was required to pass on to her friend by that amorphous body 'The War Department'.

"You see, dear, THEY" – she spoke the word in capital letters – "require the pier theatre as a, let me look at what they say..." there was a paper rummaging sound, "...ah yes, a strategic command centre for the defence of the coastal stretch between..." there was another pause, "...I evidently wasn't meant to tell you, dear. It says it's for 'my eyes only'."

Nell wanted to help.

"It still is, Winifred. I haven't seen it, have I? But *tomorrow*?"

There was a sigh on the end of the 'phone. "They also say that in the light of the present situation they consider it unsafe for you and your people to be so exposed. And I wasn't supposed to tell you that either, but as the BBC tells us all this at least four or five times a day it's hardly top secret is it?"

They were both silent now, Winifred in embarrassment and Nell in total mental confusion.

"Can we do tomorrow night – Saturday – as our final show?"

There was more sound of papers being shuffled.

"It says 'from midnight Saturday.' You'll have to clear all your belongings during the day and then," a pause before she resumed with a breaking voice – an unknown affliction for Councillor Winifred – "that will be it." She could think of no other way of putting it.

"And the cinema...?" Nell's brain was back in working order.

There was a sigh at the end of the 'phone.

"I don't think the War Department rates entertainment as a very high priority just now." Winifred's days were spent as the butt of their bullying tactics. "Dear old dreamy Flaxton-on-Sea is taking on a new role according to the War Ministry..." there was more paper rustling "...as part of the Front Line of Defence."

Heaven knows what the creators of the 'Careless Talk Costs Lives' campaign would have made of the telephone call but, in fact, everything that was said was common knowledge and the main source of discussion in every one of Flaxton's drinking establishments. And, anyway, thought Nell, prosecuting Councillor Winifred Ledbury would have been an uphill task even for the Lord Chancellor!

She sat for some while looking at the telephone seeing it as the villain of the piece, the messenger of every disaster that had befallen them in the previous weeks. She had a good mind to rip its wire from the wall, cart it outside and hurl it to a watery grave as near Hitler and his wretched henchmen as her throw could carry it!

With a shake of her head she struggled painfully to her feet. Now there was work to be done. This latest and, it seemed, final disaster was something for her 'War Council' to sort out. It was all *definitely* too much just for her.

*

The 'War Council' meeting didn't go well and Nell became more confused than ever – if that were possible. It seemed that the more uncertain her people became regarding their future, the more independent were their thoughts. The team was breaking up and they were looking to their own survival. She told them about the arrangement she had made with Beresford Clarke to move the troupe to London and revamp the show and to her surprise that upset rather than relieved them.

Belvedere annoyed her with yet another quotation, this time deserting the Bard for Wordsworth: "Our destiny, our being's heart and home, is with infinitude."

What did he mean? How did he store them all – and remember them – when he often forgot to do up his fly buttons and had to be checked by Vi before he went on stage?

Pat dropped the biggest bombshell by suggesting that maybe some of the troupe might want to do something more tangible for the 'War Effort'; munitions, work on the land or, for the younger men, which really only meant Norman, join the Forces.

Nell was dumbfounded. She realized that she had become so overwhelmed by the dramas of the past few months – Peggy, poor Alice, the bombs and the ever-present money problems – that any thought of the war taking her troupe apart had never entered her head! It made her fretful, and without considering whether it was the right moment – which it certainly wasn't – she told them of her decision to retire a month after the move and, as if all that wasn't more than enough, take Vi with her!

Pat and Belvedere simultaneously started protesting and it was Don, who had sat quietly through it all, who brought some sense to the discussion. First, he said very firmly, Nell could and should do what she liked because she owned the Theatre Company; second, there was a war on out there and that took precedence over everything; third, Pat had already suggested that at least some of the troupe felt they should be doing more to help win it and, lastly, Nell jolly well deserved to retire! Quite a speech from the usually taciturn Stage Manager.

Then, of course, everyone apologised to each other and Belvedere insisted, with no recourse to quotations, that they break the rules just for once and retire to the Pier Head Tavern to toast a happy retirement for Nell and Vi. The landlord was unnerved to see the bulk of the great tragedian sweeping through the door into the bar at lunchtime and even more so by his insistence on buying a round, with cash, for four people!

There would be few amongst the British population who could argue that the main story in the lunch-time BBC news bulletin on that Friday actually came to their aid but so it was with Nell. The bar in the Pier Head Tavern had gone silent as the six pips from the wireless on the counter led to a sombre Bruce Belfrage announcing the plight of the British Expeditionary Force clinging to the French coast as the mighty German army and airforce pummelled it towards extinction.

Hitler's war machine was obviously unstoppable and a few miles of water was going to be nothing more than an inconvenient ditch to jump. The apparently informed commentators predicted that the cunning Führer wouldn't put all his eggs in one basket and therefore the invasions would be launched on a broad front from France and Holland onto the British south and east coasts.

Allowing for spirited rear-guard actions by the BEF and the need for the Germans to re-group and assemble an armada of landing-craft it would, the pundits assured the frightened population, happen in the next two or, at the most, three weeks. Possibility had gone out of their reckoning: it was now considered a certainty. Churchill's fine rhetoric had inspired everyone for a while but many doubted whether even his 'victory at all costs' was now a viable option.

Nell looked around her. It was like a silent film; a bar filled with people but absolutely no sound; more, maybe, like a photograph because neither was there any movement. This was it. People finished their drinks quietly and drifted out into the warm Spring air. A gentle breeze riffled in from the sea. It was all so calm and gentle, like waking from a bad dream into a comfortable reality. What made it all so frightening was that it was, in fact, the reverse; they were walking away *from* reality and *into* a fearful future.

Nell was far too much of a straightforward person to realise the advantage the news gave her that afternoon and, frankly, wouldn't have wanted to. Everyone was assembled in the auditorium seats. Don had put a chair on stage for her and wearily she climbed the steps to it. No-one spoke; there was no banter. Like the rest of the nation the breath had been knocked out of them. Even the taps of Nell's walking-stick seemed muffled as she shuffled, bent from the pain of her arthritis, to the chair.

She told them the news with no preamble or embellishments. The loss of the theatre, the offer of a London venue, now probably too late, and her and Vi's impending retirement. They all were, of course, deeply shocked but not really surprised. As with grief everyone's mind was quickly tuning to a new wavelength made up of doubts and fears, anger and uncertainty. Nell's latest information would slot comfortably into that format and the fatalistic 'we can take it', 'stiff upper lip', 'business as usual', culture would from now on govern all their actions.

Individually they were planning their futures even as Nell was giving them the news. For Peggy it was, of course, particularly hard. If the troupe disbanded how would Freddy find her if he really *was* free and Ludovic Henschel kept his word now he had the diaries? Would she have to rely on the odious man, even, she shuddered, even put herself under his protective custody again?

Nell sensed that she had lost them all – in more senses than one. She could see that their thoughts were all miles away. George and Elaine were whispering to each other and so were Rita and Rena. Marvo was busily scribbling notes, Tad was fiddling with the catches on his knick-knack suitcase, Norman could almost feel a khaki uniform enveloping him and was fingering his tight collar, Belvedere seemed to be in communion with his precious Bard and Pat was gently stroking Peggy's shaking hand.

Don and his team kept quiet as befitted the back-stage crew. Nell's stick banging on the floor galvanised them into rapt attention as she exhorted them to give all that they had this evening and tomorrow evening, the last night. Tomorrow would be clear-out day and then after the final Show that night she would need to know their decision: London – or disband.

"Let's give Flaxton everything we've got. We won't let that pottin Hitler defeat us." She stood up. "We'll go out with our hands held high…"

Vi quickly scotched this inadvertent reference to surrender.'

"Heads, dear."

Nell was into her stride now, her voice was strong, she was standing to her full five foot three inches brandishing her stick above her head, the ostrich feather on her hat waving like a conductor's baton.

"Heads it is Vi, and always will be."

Her audience was now beginning to lose the thread which she had already lost but she was not deterred.

"The Flaxton Pier Theatre Pier Company will go into suspendered amination for the durexion of this terrible war."

They were all spellbound. It was a bigger performance than even Belvedere had ever dared. The theatre, in all its long years, had never seen or heard anything like it. She ended almost in a screech.

"Britain never, ever, never – ever – shall be Slavs."

With a wobbly about-turn she strode off the stage to a stunned silence.

She was back in her office in floods of tears, clutching the photograph of her beloved Masters, when she heard a distant sound, rising to a great pounding that seemed to make all the paraphernalia in the room shake and dance.

Tad had started it. With a feeling of emotion that he had never experienced before he stood up and clapped. In no time the whole troupe joined in and then, almost frantically, they were stamping their feet. If the theatre had never witnessed such a stage performance, neither had it experienced such spontaneous love and affection welling up from the stalls for one small, very determined Scottish lady. At that moment Masters would have been – probably was – brimming over with pride.

A 'phone call from Vi, and Vernon Rogers in dual roles as Editor and Arts Reporter of the Flaxton Chronicle quickly went into action. If tomorrow was to be the last ever performance of 'Beside the Seaside' then he would give it the maximum possible publicity to ensure it was packed out. Above a front page story full of a heady mixture of pathos and praise he ran a banner headline –

THE END OF THE PIER SHOW

It was undoubtedly his finest moment and, as it turned out, nearly his last as the one-man editorial and newsroom team of 'East Anglia's Oldest Provincial Newspaper'; a proud boast slashed above the title on each edition.

Within a month he would be a member of the Armed Forces and, six months on from that, the one-man editorial and newsroom team of the army's own Eastern Command newspaper aptly titled 'On Parade'. Vernon Rogers would be doing his bit for King and Country.

*

Nell went through that Friday evening's performance in a dream – but then, so did everyone else. By tradition the theatre had always been a close-knit community and, in fairness, it was regularly punctuated by the sadness of the end of a run; a family flying the nest.

But this time it was different; security – if anything in the theatre could be labelled as such – was giving way to uncertainty, new lives, new disciplines. As Belvedere had put it, 'strangers in a strange world'. He couldn't ascribe the quotation to anyone and it gave him a warm sense of achievement to realize that it was his own!

Nell, sitting on her chair in the wings with Vi standing behind her, heard the stage acts as an echo but, as if tranquillised, a very pleasant one. Pat and Peggy were doing their first spot in their charladies outfits each side of the dummy bomb…

PAT   "Before the war the park keeper would never put up with a thing like this in his flowerbeds.

PEGGY   Before the war we had a park keeper.

PAT   True. I heard Alvar Lidell this morning on the news saying that Mr Churchill wants to send all our old metal for munitions.

PEGGY   *(kicking the bomb)* Kind of Adolf to join in. Perhaps he'll send us his saucepans next…

PAT   *(kicking the bomb)* My cousin Fred's in bomb disposal.

PEGGY   I thought he was a bomb aimer in the RAF.

PAT   He is. He disposes of them over Germany."

There were hoots of laughter from the audience, particularly the soldiers who assumed that any reference to the 'boys in blue' was an insult. The airmen were happy to wait their turn to get their own back.

Vi's mind slipped back to the afternoon. She had found Nell in a terrible state after the meeting, sobbing her heart out. Her hat with the ostrich feather was lying in a corner of the room where she'd thrown it and she was sitting with her head resting on the photograph of Masters who looked up at her benignly from the desk blotter. In a word, thought Vi, she was distraught.

After she'd heard all Nell's self-recriminations and self-accusations, and there'd been the banging of fists on the desk top mixed with pointless cries of 'if only' they settled in a form of cuddle, Vi kneeling beside her, soothing her as she would the baby she'd never had.

Nell promised her that she would concentrate on the happy future they would have in the peace of the Highlands. They both knew that such a life was, at this time, highly unlikely but they agreed to fantasise if only to see themselves through the next few days.

A slightly embarrassed wave of laughter brought Vi, standing just behind Nell's chair in the stage wings, back to the present. Tad, in his terrible blazer, yellow trousers and 'co-respondent' shoes, was stroking the microphone stand as if it was Pru's backbone, his bald head shining in Bill's strong lights...

"My missus cheered me up last night.
'Did you know', she said, 'that if you lose your hair at the front it means you're a great thinker. And if you lose it at the back, you're a great lover. That means,' she said, 'you *think* you're a great lover.'
I turned the other cheek. She did too, and we went to sleep back to back.
(*licks fingers*) – know what I mean?
I asked her the other day what she'd like on her tombstone. She was quick, I'll give her that. 'Wife of the above,' she said."

The audience erupted. It wasn't rude – there'd been plenty of that already and, if they knew their Tad Stevens, there'd be more to come. Nell smiled. She drifted back to the Highland glens of her youth with their cool, clear burns. She felt the bubbling water through her fingers and heard the childhood laughter...

But it was real laughter. Norman, in his grotesque brassière and frock was slouched against the stage-prop wall, his huge bosoms resting on its top...

"What about her over there? Taken in a lodger.
Oh, he's been taken in alright...
She says he's in a 'reserved occupation'...
Nothing reserved about hers...
He came out of the garden shelter yesterday morning shell-shocked.
And we hadn't even had a raid last night..."

There was absolutely nothing that set Norman off at a gallop like laughter, and tonight the audience were loving him. He got faster and faster...

"I've been under the doctor, you know. Could hardly breathe...
It was me legs you see. I got a pain every time I kicked the kids.
The doctor said I had water on the knee.
I said to him, with only four inches allowed in the bath, I was lucky if it covered me confusion, never mind me knee."

Adjusting the mammoth bra straps he half fell off the wall leaving the bosoms anchored now at ear level. It had happened before but tonight it brought the house down. Norman looked with glazed eyes into the noisy darkness of the auditorium and seriously considered whether he'd be helping the war effort more usefully by keeping the troops happy this way rather than cowering in the bottom of a trench...

When Norman finally left the stage – he almost had to be tugged off by Vi – Elaine and George sang beautifully and received the respectful applause they felt was in keeping with their art, and Rita and Rena did all they could to inspire a rather listless Marvo to achieve at least some reasonable level of illusion in his act.

Nell was pleased for them all. They'd rallied to the call and performed like the seasoned troupers they were. But reality tripped back the moment the final curtain dissected the make-believe world of the theatre from the grim reality of their private lives. There was hardly any talk in the dressing rooms. Everyone felt strangely embarrassed to say anything that might expose selfish feelings and attitudes to the others. Before today they'd been a group; now, for a host of reasons, they were individuals thrown too intimately together.

This metamorphosis was even more graphically illustrated later by the three empty seats in the Pier Head Tavern. Not one of their regular late evening occupants could bring himself to occupy them realising that that lifestyle had gone for the foreseeable future, probably forever. Everyone said quiet goodnights and went to their beds. Tad, of course, oblivious to the need for such sacrifice, chose Pru's after a few jars at the Anchor.

Some time later, in the closed, quiet theatre, the sound of creaking timbers was punctuated by the urgent tapping of Morse code.

*

No-one slept for long that night. Before first light deep heavy rumblings and vibrations dragged the people of Flaxton out of their beds to their windows, many fearing that the invasion had already started! In fact they weren't far out because the town *was* being invaded – not yet, though, by the Germans but rather by their own troops. Convoys of heavy military traffic were trundling through the streets. The country's 'First Line of Defence' was being strengthened. It was as if a vast khaki blanket was being spread along the coast, smothering the scattered towns and villages in its wake.

Instead of being grateful for this added protection the townsfolk grumbled, partly because in absolutely no way did they want to be a 'First Line of Defence', but also because Saturday usually started with a bit of a lie-in and their sleep had already been curtailed by late night chatter about the seriousness of the war situation. Should they move inland, or at least the children, maybe the womenfolk as well?

But the noisy traffic was only a part of it. The greatest surprise was reserved for the proprietor of the Station Hotel on the outskirts of the town who was given five hours to vacate his premises! Family, guests, and their personal belongings were bundled out of the building which was then encircled with barbed wire and guarded by a platoon of the elite Royal Marines.

As the morning progressed keen eyes behind neighbouring net curtains saw occasional bursts of activity as large black saloon cars drew up at the hotel entrance and important-looking people were quickly hustled past saluting guards.

At 34 Clarence Road, Nell, already virtually sleepless, had not taken kindly to being awakened from her first real period of unconsciousness by a lengthy ring on the front-door bell. It was, she noted disgustedly, only eight o'clock!

Certain that it was Belvedere – only *he* rang so forcibly – she threw caution to the winds and opened the door in her dressing gown. An army Colonel stood on the step resplendent in immaculately pressed uniform, Sam Browne and highly polished shoes. He saluted her and then removed his cap.

They made an odd couple in the front room. Full Dress army uniform and dressing-gown. Nell was pleased that she'd removed her hairnet and curlers as she came downstairs.

The Colonel spoke to her very quietly and what he had to tell her lifted a fair proportion of the gloom that had engulfed her in the past few days. She was sworn to secrecy and given her orders.

Vi, having heard Nell pounding down the stairs was now up and fully dressed. She brought them both a cup of tea and made a mental note to remind Nell that it would be more proper to entertain a gentleman – particularly a high-ranking gentleman – fully clothed and without one curler perched on top of her head. She would, she thought, pick her moment.

*

Charles Turville and Freddy Crisciak were finding the rear seat of the small Austin motor car very cramped but after a week in a crowded, claustrophobic submarine they were well used to confined spaces. Stowed away in the wardroom the dangers encountered on the voyage and the skill of the Captain in avoiding the ever-close enemy had been deliberately kept from Freddy and he knew little of what was happening until he was told to prepare to disembark. Neither did he know that, officially, HM Submarine Torness had been lost with all hands!

He had felt the submarine surfacing and wondered where on earth they could be. The old fear had gripped him. He had felt completely safe surrounded by the quiet, cheerful efficiency of the Royal Navy but now, as he re-entered the real world, he felt vulnerable again.

The smell and feel of fresh air when he climbed the ladder onto the tiny sloping deck made him stagger and it took two burly sailors to steady him and help him into the small canoe. He saw a flat, deserted shoreline some way off but Turville, alongside him, didn't think to tell him it was England! He assumed he'd know.

*

HM Submarine Torness slipped silently below the surface on its way to the Royal Naval base in Gibraltar to take on a new identity. Only the Secret Service, the crew and their next-of-kin – who were now obliged to say nothing under the Official Secrets Act – knew of the subterfuge.

More deliberate 'careless talk' in certain Stockholm bars had let slip that the escape vessel was the Torness. The deception worked perfectly and now, as far as the Third Reich was concerned, Professor Freddy Crisciak was dead, at the bottom of the North Sea.

*

Ludovic Henschel was, as usual, in a bad mood, partly because he was sitting uncomfortably in one of the armchairs in the guests' sitting room at the Anchor Hotel – he preferred a position from which he could move quickly in defence or attack – but his bad mood was mainly because, having been summoned to appear here by a secretary at Headquarters he wasn't expecting to be interrogated and searched by armed Marines, have his gun removed, and then virtually marched into this dreadful room and told to sit.

He was angry – and confused. Why had this quiet, drab hotel been transformed into a fortified stronghold? He felt the hand of Charles Turville in all this. He hadn't seen or heard from him for a few days but it would be typical of the man to invade his territory and arrange a stunt like this without telling him. He was about to fly into one of his more spectacular rages when the breath was knocked out of him by the arrival in the room of no less a person than the Chief of the British Secret Service himself, Sir Philip Southern!

He struggled to his feet, received a curt nod for his efforts and an inclination of the head to resume his seat. The atmosphere was tense and, ever thinking first of himself, he feared he had been brought here for a showdown regarding his handling – bungling – of the notebooks fiasco.

It was Henschel's look of discomfort which Turville saw first as he entered the sitting room and, quite unjustifiably, it gave him instant satisfaction. Now back in civilian clothes he was as immaculate as ever, the ravages of the week on the submarine having been quickly washed away. Sir Philip's smile and cheery wave to an armchair was, in its friendliness, in stark contrast to his greeting for Henschel. He drew heavily on his pipe.

"So you're back amongst us, then laddie. And with your extra piece of luggage. Not, I hear, without a skirmish or two."

This gross under-statement was followed by a deep chuckle, the reason for which was totally lost on Henschel who was becoming increasingly agitated as one inexplicable event led to another. Sir Philip dragged him away from the brink of a violent explosion of wrath – which would have done his career no good at all – by banging his pipe out on a large brass ashtray. He leant forward, motioned his two agents to do the same and then, in a quiet voice, outlined to them the plan for the re-uniting of the Professor with his wife, Peggy.

It was now Turville's turn to frown.

"Why the theatre?"

Sir Philip re-filled his pipe and smiled.

"Our Leader is a very sentimental man. Winston Churchill sees this episode almost as much as the reuniting of sweethearts as the saving of the world. I think that he would love to have watched the reunion himself from the stalls – and directed the lighting and music. Perhaps the two of them moving towards each other from opposite sides of the stage…" His voice drifted away and then, with energy, he swung round to Henschel.

"The Prime Minister has followed every stage of this assignment. Remember, Henschel, even if *we* go under it matters not a jot. Our task is to protect this man Crisciak who can, in the right hands, we are assured, save the rest of the world."

Henschel sat further forward and was about to speak but a warning glance from Turville set him angrily back into the depths of the armchair. He couldn't believe all this rubbish about sentimentality. What an unnecessary nonsense it all was. It could have been so simple. Intern the wife and use her as a lever to force the scientist to do as he was told. No work, no wife. He couldn't understand the British mentality, but nothing really surprised him now that the strange, unpredictable Churchill was in charge. Anyway, none of it would matter soon.

Sir Philip levered himself out of the armchair and towered over him.

"I'll leave Charles to give you your orders Henschel. This afternoon. Fifteen hundred hours. Everything clear?"

Henschel nodded wearily. The next question from Sir Philip was the tricky one.

"And the notebooks?"

He had prepared his answer.

"With the actors, C. When the two are back together they'll be handed to the package – the Professor."

As far as Henschel could tell, this would be so, but which member of the troupe had hit him and retrieved them from his mackintosh pocket was still a mystery. It hardly mattered. He'd get his revenge later. Few people managed to injure him and those that did never had the chance to do it again.

"How is the Professor, Charles?" Sir Philip seemed relieved to turn away from Henschel to Turville.

"Tired and confused, as he has been for a very long time. He doesn't know why he's here and speaks all the time of his wife."

Henschel grunted and the other two glanced at him. He sat forward, "I hope he will be quickly forced to get his mind back onto nuclear physics and off this stupid wife fixation. Or punished."

The last two words were the final straw but no verbal rebuke was needed; the stare they both gave him was quite enough.

*

Down the road, the Pier Theatre was the scene of more intemperate words. Nell Masters was berating a Royal Marine sergeant, twice her height, who, despite years of action repelling many of His Majesty's most violent enemies, was none-the-less flinching at the near proximity of her gyrating walking-stick.

"We are as one," she shouted, "my troupe." She indicated the full might of her Theatre Company ranged behind her.

"And so are we, madam, a troop," he felt he should try to calm this frightening lady by going into a bit more detail regarding the structure of the Royal Marines. "Except that we call ourselves a platoon."

Nell, had that morning been told by the smartly dressed Colonel to parade – just her and Peggy – at the theatre at 3 p.m. precisely, and had carried out her orders nearly to the letter but, having confided in her War Council, she'd been persuaded by Belvedere to repeat the deployment used when they handed over the notebooks to Henschel the week before.

He, as usual, reinforced his message by calling upon the Bard. "A victory is twice itself when the achiever brings home full numbers," he had boomed and then, slapping Don on the back, had added, "A Midsummer Night's Dream."

All of this had led to Nell marching at the head of her troupe down the steps to the theatre. There she was met by two Royal Marine sentries guarding the pier gates from which coils of barbed wire now stretched, apparently, all around the theatre. As the determined group approached, one of the sentries had hurriedly summoned the sergeant and that had led to this angry confrontation.

"Remove your pantaloons immediately."

Nell's command was clearly heard by several passers-by, now gathered in small groups, and most of the lunch-time drinkers at the Pier Head Tavern who had drifted outside to watch the fun. The command triggered a bout of ragged cheering from them and some foolishly audible sniggering from the sentries who would live to regret both their lack of discipline and the misfortune of being present when their sergeant was being considerably embarrassed.

"Platoon, madam, and my orders are that you and a woman to be identified as one Peggy Baker are to be the only, I say again, only people to be admitted through this gate. The others must disperse NOW." His voice had moved from quiet conversational to loud command in the course of the one sentence.

Norman and the twins flinched, the rest of the troupe looked and felt awkward and none of it was helped by a familiar bellow from Belvedere. "This fell sergeant, death, is strict in his arrest."

The sergeant, unfamiliar with Belvedere or, for that matter, the Bard, slipped automatically into 'action stations' procedure.

"Stand to, the Guard." His bellow was almost as powerful as Belvedere's and certainly had more effect. Fully armed marines rushed from around and inside the theatre and formed up in three ranks just inside the gate.

"Hamlet, dear boy," crooned Belvedere.

"Sergeant Cummins to you, mate, and clear off the lot of you. NOW." The sergeant seemed to enjoy that last word and it had the desired effect. With a nod from Nell they fell back strategically towards The Tavern leaving her and Peggy at the pier entrance.

The whole silly episode had taken only a couple of minutes but had, unhappily, achieved exactly what the SIS had set out to avoid: close attention from passers-by to the forthcoming event in Flaxton-on-Sea's Pier Theatre.

*

At ten minutes to three the net-curtained watchers living around the Station Hotel saw a burst of activity as a large black Wolseley motor-car drew up at the entrance and three people were quickly ushered into it. It pulled away into what the army would describe as a convoy; a car, an army truck ahead of it, and another behind. To the onlookers it seemed that an awful lot of precious petrol was being wasted...

The car was full; over full. Freddy Crisciak sat between Sir Philip and Charles Turville and an SIS marksman sat next to the driver.

Freddy couldn't help dredging from his mind the fearful journey in the Mercedes to Warsaw flanked by the SS Colonel and Captain. Then it was a rougher road – but a smoother engine! Why, oh why did the brain play such silly, pointless tricks...

He was fretting. For some ludicrous reason he'd almost expected Peggy would be on the shingle shore waving to him as the small canoe brought him to the land from the submarine; a reverse of their terrible parting. He still had been told nothing other than that she was fit and well and they'd meet soon. He decided that if it hadn't happened by tonight there would be a show-down; the pain had gone on long enough; far too long.

Looking out of the side windows he saw a scene that suggested that, despite the carnage on the continent, England had changed hardly at all since his pre-war visits. The car drove past line upon line of small, neat, bungalows. People were tending their gardens, walking along the pavements, some pushing prams, others chatting and most of them seemed to be cheerful!

Did these people have no idea of what was about to hit them; rounding-up – segregation – reprisals – babies heads battered against walls – humiliation? And so his mind sped downwards, in a spiral.

He shifted his thoughts. Why was he here? The nearest town to the landing point. Yes, but why had they made him stay? Surely he could be in London by now – and with Peggy. With the staccato action of a machine gun his mind rattled through endless questions to which he had no answers. Very much the pattern these days.

They were jolting to a stop and his eyes focussed again out of the windows. He saw that they'd reached the sea. Dear Lord, surely they weren't going to subject him to another voyage; he'd had quite enough of submarines to last him a lifetime. He realized that his hands were clammy and he was shaking. Why, when it seemed that against all odds it was all about to end successfully, was he experiencing such fear?

The car drew up at the pier and Turville got out and went to the gates. At last Freddy saw something associated with war: an ever-growing ring of soldiers forming around the perimeter of the structure. Behind them was a large, rather dilapidated wedding-cake of a building that looked as if it might, at any moment, slide into the sea. Wedding? Peggy?

He saw a group of people, holding drinking glasses, standing outside a nearby pub and had a sudden urge to be one of them. He jumped as the door handle was turned and Sir Philip rested a hand gently on his arm.

"It's alright, dear boy. Be calm." He was patted again.

It struck him that he hadn't been patted for a very long time.

Turville helped him out of the car and, as much a prisoner as he had been in Warsaw, he found himself being almost frog-marched through the sentries and on into the foyer of the theatre. Unbelievably the two senior Secret Service men brushed him down and tidied him and, even more unbelievable, he allowed them to do so.

He would never in his long life to come ever forget the next few moments.

He was gently propelled into the auditorium – and on the stage stood Peggy…

Freddy just stood there.

It was as he had first seen her on stage. But then, in that other age, she had been singing a song from 'Careless Rapture', now she looked apprehensive and frightened, peering into the darkness of the auditorium.

To her left, near the rear scenery which, he noted, was a rather rough imitation of the pier he'd just entered, was a very small, bent lady leaning on a walking stick wearing a heavy overcoat and a ridiculous hat with a feather wobbling above it. It was a tableau similar to paintings he'd seen long ago in fairy-tale stories.

Peggy could just make out a tall thin figure flanked by two others. She knew it must be Freddy, Nell hadn't been able to resist dropping broad hints, but this man was so old and gaunt and, whereas her Freddy stood erect, here were bent shoulders.

But all that was over in a flash; as she stared into the gloom, holding her breath, he moved at great speed down the aisle and up onto the stage. Then they were in each other's arms.

Sir Philip Southern dropped into a seat in the front row. He would note every detail should the Prime Minister demand a detailed account of the reunion, as he doubtless would. Turville followed Freddy onto the stage, for once thoroughly agreeing with his absent subordinate, Henschel, that the plan for the reunion was embarrassingly sentimental nonsense.

He and Nell advanced cautiously on the embracing couple. He was nervous at the vulnerability of the Professor caught in bright lights with, at Sir Philip's insistence, all the armed soldiers excluded from inside the theatre. True they had thoroughly searched the place and then guarded every entrance, but still...

As the two of them reached Peggy and Freddy they were joined by another person from the wings of the stage behind Turville. Nell, only partially aware of the extreme security that was supposed to be in operation, was more annoyed than surprised.

"Marvo," she said, "you gave me quite a turn. You're meant to be extruded with the others."

"It will be wise for you to all remain perfectly still."

When Sir Philip Southern came to write his somewhat delayed official report on the mission he found it difficult, even with his considerable experience, to separate the events of the next few minutes. For a start he had no idea who would be surprised by whom, and it would have helped him to know how each person reacted at the time. This, however, was not the way of the Secret Service.

For a start, whilst Sir Philip and Turville were amazed that someone had either got through the army cordon or evaded discovery during the search of the theatre, only Nell and Peggy were startled by the fact that Marvo, dumb Marvo, had spoken to them! But it was the strong Germanic accent that caused Turville to reach for his pistol.

Whilst priding himself on being faster on the draw than most, even he couldn't match a man already holding a gun. Marvo now brought his right hand from behind his back in which was a vicious looking Walther automatic, the barrel of which he stuck with some force into Freddy's neck.

"So, Professor, it was all in vain, huh? Marvo's next trick will be to perform the full circle, huh? Back to Berlin and your new friends at the Kaiser Wilhelm Institute? When we have disposed of these we will walk out slowly. Your journey will start tonight, huh?" He had an infuriating way of making each sentence sound like a question.

Everyone stood stock still except Sir Philip who, with remarkable agility for such a large man, had leapt up from his stalls seat as the man approached the group, and now, using the darkness of the auditorium, was slowly feeling for the gun in his shoulder holster.

Almost lazily Marvo raised his silenced automatic and a bullet plopped into Sir Philip's arm muscle throwing him backwards into the second row of seats where he lay semi-conscious. Both women involuntarily screamed and clutched each other.

"So, enough of the heroics I think, huh? You..." he looked at Turville, "bring your fat friend on stage and please remember, I will pull this trigger even as, if you are foolish enough, you fire at me. I have orders; the Professor alive – or dead. Which it is to be matters little to me, huh?"

Turville went into the stalls and, as gently as he could, eased Sir Philip up into his arms and half dragged him up onto the stage. The pain must have been excruciating but the injured man made no sound except a hoarse whisper, "Take no risks."

Nell now found a quiet voice. "You have been cheating us all along. It's pisdicable."

Marvo smiled at her. "Dear Nell, I enjoyed it, huh? You make me welcome. My little transmitter? Up there?" He pointed up into the lighting gantry. "Every night. Good messages I send to my control. Your searchers didn't look upwards, huh? Careless. So, enough." Tonight they collect us..." he pointed at Freddy and Peggy, then looked back to Nell, "but you three will know nothing, huh?"

His voice, heavily accented as it was, was devoid of any compassion. He seemed to feel a need to explain his role to them more through arrogance than a wish to apologise for his deceit. He now fixed Peggy with a cold stare.

"For weeks I follow you – and your followers. It was a pity our dear Norman could swim, huh? It would have saved our audiences more pain, huh?" The chuckle was as cold as the voice. "Now I take you, Peggy, with the Herr Professor. Orders, huh? A waste of space but the Third Reich will find work for you or..." the next word was accompanied by a cheerless smile, "death, huh?"

There was silence. No-one moved. The gulls cried and the waves lapped as the theatre staged a performance unique in its long, chequered history.

Freddy now found his voice. "I cannot work without my note-books and I fear they are lost." He was surprised at how calm his voice was. Maybe he was getting used to being on the point of death!

"Do not fret, Professor. I have them. They will travel with us to the Institute in Berlin." Nell and Peggy caught each other's eye. Should they tell him that the books were a load of rubbish? Would it save them all or mean instant death now? Peggy found Freddy's confused eyes looking at her. She tried to give him a reassuring look but it didn't work.

"So, we will start with you, Herr Turville. The honour of our Secret Services demands that it should be quick – as it was meant to be when that foolish train guard stood in the way. I then used your army's service revolver as disguise. Not good. A poor weapon. This though, huh?"

He tapped the pistol pressed into Freddy's neck. Turville braced himself. His mind was racing. He needed time.

"Would it not be wise..." but as he started the sentence the small gun lifted from Freddy's neck and he saw down the black hole of the muzzle.

The shot resounded around the theatre accompanied by another scream from Nell and Peggy.

Marvo crumpled to the floor without a word, a small round hole drilled into his forehead precisely equidistant between his eyes.

"I told you it was a bad idea."

In the murk of the auditorium they could just make out Ludovic Henschel leaning over the rail of the Dress Circle. He was putting his gun back into its shoulder holster.

Before the echo from Henschel's gun had disappeared amidst the flaking plaster of the auditorium's dome the theatre was full of soldiers. As their training demanded they instantly took up crouching postures in every doorway and corner ensuring that their combined arcs of fire covered all parts of the building. And they did it in almost total silence.

With the area now 'secure', in military language, the central characters were quickly evacuated with dire warnings regarding the need for total security. Freddy and Peggy were hustled into the Wolseley and driven at alarming speed with armed escort back to the Station Hotel during which time, to his great relief, she told him the story of the substitute notebooks.

Nell was delivered to her troupe in the Pier Tavern where she downed a large brandy in one long series of gulps.

"It was putrefying," she assured them – but would say no more.

Sir Philip was rushed to the hospital, and the body of Marvo – or whatever his real name was – was spirited away in good SIS fashion. No one would ever know its final resting place.

There were some strong words at the Station Hotel when the two cars had deposited their occupants. Charles Turville would not hear of Freddy or Peggy leaving the building and intended to keep them cooped up until he was ready to deliver them to London. Freddy, by now a seasoned campaigner in matters regarding his own safety, simply threatened to refuse to co-operate with the Government on Project Omega unless they had their freedom and that led to a compromise whereby they could do as they wished provided he knew where they were at all times and they allowed Henschel to act as their bodyguard.

So it was that the three of them arrived at the theatre for the evening performance and Freddy stood in the wings to watch Peggy on stage as he had done almost exactly two years before in London.

That evening, the very last performance of 'Beside the Seaside', was a tremendous success. Vernon Rogers, via his two-page spread in the Chronicle, had spurred on the town to descend on the theatre in force and show their appreciation for what the troupe had achieved in its time in Flaxton.

Throwing caution to the winds Nell opened the Dress Circle, and the old building creaked and groaned as if it knew that, for its proper use, it was experiencing its final fling perhaps for ever, certainly for a long, long time. No-one could see much point in the ring of Royal Marines surrounding the building when it was filled to overflowing.

As Norman confusingly put it, "Who are they guarding what from who?"

Everyone performed well – it hardly mattered, they would have been cheered even if they hadn't! To the complete surprise of all the troupe Don, in an uncharacteristic act of bravado, offered to be 'The Great Marvo' so that the twins could take part in the Show. Dressed in the fez and kaftan of his late-lamented predecessor he played the role of illusionist that he had so often watched from back-stage. Rita and Rena revelled in it and reckoned that he was much more fun to work with than the other one!

The curtain calls went on and on, bouquets were presented by Councillor Ledbury and her team to all the cast – the men were suitably embarrassed – and she and Nell made short, moving speeches. There were no dry eyes on the stage and few in the auditorium. Everyone who was there knew that the evening marked so much more than the end of a theatre run; another bit of their familiar, comfortable lives was being chipped away leaving more room for doubt and uncertainty – and fear.

They stood and sang the National Anthem and then the band, of their own accord, struck up Jerusalem and Rule Britannia. Alf, Claude, Geoff and Fred had obviously rehearsed the pieces privately because they were, more or less, recognizable. It hardly mattered anyway; they were drowned by the singing and foot stamping.

And then it was all over. The audience drifted reluctantly back to homes, military camps and the refugee camp, aware that the late night BBC news would bring them all down to earth with a bump. The troupe cleared their remaining few belongings from their dressing rooms and dragged themselves silently to Nell's house. No-one wanted to experience their usual routine; they needed to be together for as long as it might be.

Don suggested that Nell might like to have one last tour of the place but she declined. It was done now; the chapter – in fact the entire book – was closed.

The last man to leave the theatre was, as usual, Bill Colbourn. He was still listening to his wireless whilst the stage lights cooled when the army arrived in the form of a lance corporal and two privates. For this, he thought, we were made to close down! Whilst one of them was detailed to look-out duty, the other two, now joined by the stood-down members of the gun crew, made themselves comfortable on the stage. Soon a brew was bubbling away and yet more cigarette smoke added to the already fetid air.

As soon as he felt his lights were safe Bill took off his singed woolly gloves and placed them with the utmost care on the now-cooled fader boxes. He arranged them neatly; they'd be needed no more. He saw it as the last, almost reverential, act of the Flaxton-on-Sea Pier Theatre Company.

The clatter of a mess-tin reminded him that, for once, he wasn't alone at this late hour. The soldiers were strewn around the stage in untidy heaps and as he wove a way through them he raised a weary hand in salute.

"Look after the place, boys. She deserves it."

He was out of the stage door before they could think of a suitable reply. He leant on the balustrade by the silent gun. The air was cool and a breeze was blowing in from the sea. Before very long, he reckoned, it would be joined by an armada of German landing craft.

*

The gathering at 34 Clarence Road after the final Show was a sombre affair. They were tearful enough without the need to tell Nell that they all had decided to go their own ways rather than transfer as a troupe to London. It seemed so unfair to abandon her after all that she had done for them but she reminded them that she really did have to retire however much she loved them all and therefore she and Vi would have only been able to stay for a month even if they had transferred. None-the-less their future worried her. Where would they go? What would they do?

Over a heady mix of beer, cocoa, brandy, tea, whisky, gin and horlicks they discussed their future plans and, helped by the alcohol, the tensions eased and the mood relaxed. George and Elaine had been offered a spot on the BBC's popular 'Workers Playtime' programme, and the *Welsh Nightingales* would take it from there.

Tad, needless to say, had no problems regarding his future. His range of contacts in most of the vast number of pubs in East Anglia was legendary and now, thanks to the war, he could add all the military camps dotted around the area to his client list. His type of stage act went down well wherever men were gathered together, his knick-knack suitcase was always full and there was a whole range of 'Prus' of various shapes and sizes dotted around to fill his leisure hours.

Rita and Rena had already got work in an Ipswich army clothing factory and Norman, spurred on by the Bofors gun crew, would enlist into the Royal Artillery the next day. Tad couldn't resist telling him he'd probably soon be wearing 'drawers cellular, short' – army underpants – lovingly made by the twins. All three of them blushed scarlet and Tad, almost for the last time, was rebuked by Nell.

"Don't be smutty," she said. "The girls don't know about such things as male undermentionables"

Reg, Bob and Bill had decided to retire to their allotments to 'dig for victory' but Don had been appointed stage-manager at Beresford Clarke's new London theatre which was a giant leap up the ladder for him.

That left Pat and Belvedere. The great tragedian, untypically, would divulge nothing – well, virtually nothing. He could spare them – or, rather, didn't spare them – a typically apt quotation: "The past and the future are nothing in the face of the stern today," but he couldn't for the life of him ascribe it to anyone!

"Adelaide Ann Proctor," said Peggy. "We had to do her at school." Belvedere was decidedly miffed...

Pat didn't feel like making any firm plans yet. She'd been so close to Peggy through all her torment and she felt absolutely exhausted. She was going to miss her friend terribly and any stage role would be unsatisfactory – unthinkable without her. She wanted to do something useful, perhaps join the women's services or volunteer for ambulance driving, but Nell was insisting that first she must join her and Vi in the Highland cottage for a while – "to reciprocate, dear."

In the early hours of Sunday morning they all drifted to their beds – except, of course, Tad...

*

At the Station Hotel Peggy and Freddy passed a gentle night together in a heady mixture of love, passion, relief and a fair portion of shyness. They heard their 'minders', Turville and Henschel, moving around and the murmur of their voices downstairs, but apart from that and the clumping of the sentries outside they were allowed to remain undisturbed. It seemed that the whole dramatic episode involving the rescue of Professor Freddy Crisciak, thereby securing the future of Project Omega for Britain, was over.

It nearly was; but there were still three incidents of varying degrees of importance to experience before the file could be finally closed...

CHAPTER EIGHTEEN

Sunday, 26th May 1940. The French port of Calais
fell to the Germans today. Only Dunkirk remains as a
link between the British Expeditionary Force and Britain.
An armada of boats of every shape and size is sailing to
France to bring out as many of the BEF as is possible.

Britain is bracing itself for an impending invasion which
now seems to be inevitable.

Belvedere Galbraith smiled and gave one of his slighter bows
reserved for those who had not yet applauded him.

"I wish an audience of your master," his voice boomed into the
ferret face of the Marine on duty at the main entrance of the Station
Hotel.

The guard, at attention in the presence of such an overpowering
spectacle as Belvedere in his best-and-only dark blue suit, long coat
and wide-brimmed hat, was totally lost. He could think of only one
thing to say.

"Halt, who goes there?"

Belvedere sighed. He was already at halt and had been so for some
time. He decided to go on the offensive by taking an enormous pinch
of snuff followed by the obligatory sneeze. The Marine, despite
himself, winced and yelled for the Corporal. Belvedere was glad
that he had chosen 'wish' instead of his more usual 'crave' because
he guessed that it would have been an even longer battle to see the
man called Turville than it would now doubtless prove to be!

Twenty minutes later he was wedged in one of the inadequate
armchairs in the Residents' Lounge.

He struggled to stand up as Turville came in but was waved back
into its dusty depths. His mission was tricky and it was really
Freddy that he needed to see but, having been sworn to secrecy,
the deed, as the Bard would undoubtedly call it, would have to be
done this way.

It was strange that when he had been involved in any of this drama as it unfolded all pretence in his manner automatically dropped away; the flamboyant, extrovert tragedian was replaced by a quiet, calm and obviously deeply sincere man.

So it was now as he told, with no call on the Bard, the story of the notebooks, their rescue from the roof of the kennel perched on top of the ruins of the post office, his week of frenzied work creating the substitute bogus ones filled with similar looking calculations, the staged reluctance to exchange them for Peggy when threatened by Ludovic Henschel – Turville was appalled to hear of this not-reported episode – and the lodging of the real ones in a Bank vault in town. Now, with no flourish, he produced the brown paper parcel tied with thick string and liberally smothered at the joins in thick red sealing-wax.

"You will understand that it is to Peggy that I have to deliver them?" It was said as a question, almost pleadingly, but he was ready to be determined about this; he hadn't gone through this nightmare to be bullied at the last moment. He was surprised by Turville's response.

"My dear chap, of course you shall – and must."

The fact was that Turville, maybe somewhat to his own surprise, liked this man who couldn't have been more opposite to him in every facet of human existance. The notebook switch had been a master-stroke made sweeter, he mischievously thought, by so thoroughly deceiving Henschel, and his organisation of Peggy's protection had been skilful if somewhat over-zealous. To cap it all his behaviour on the stage when faced with the German spy and his gun was exemplary. He only wondered how the man could allow himself, when acting, to appear as such a buffoon!

Turville sent for Freddy and Peggy and, with a little bit of the old tragedian poking through, the notebooks were handed over via, Belvedere insisted, Peggy's hands to Freddy.

"You will find my next request rather a strange one." Turville stood with his back to the closed door which rather suggested that they wouldn't leave until they had agreed to it. They were further alerted to expect some highly confidential instruction by the unusual quietness of his voice.

"This whole business of the real and bogus notebooks. Please keep this information to yourselves. I will choose the right moment to inform my master *and* my subordinate, Henschel." He added as if it explained everything but, to them, certainly didn't, "this is for strategic reasons."

The three of them saw Belvedere off at the hotel entrance, their praise – even Turville joined in – ringing in his ears. He allowed the Bard just one quote as he left. With mock modesty he doffed his wide-brimmed hat to them and, bowing deeply, declaimed "This comes too near the praising of myself."

With a light heart, he went joyously on his way bellowing over his shoulder "The Merchant of Venice." Then he was off at a surprisingly fast speed for such a large man. He had a plan – and now was just the time to put it into action...

*

Turville stood at the window in his hotel bedroom so deep in thought that he took in no detail of the view outside. Having felt last night that, with the German spy's death, the assignment was over he was now aware that this was not, in fact, the case. First, he was confused by the untypical behaviour of his SIS colleagues. It hadn't surprised him that Sir Philip had discharged himself from hospital the previous evening and was now settled in an upstairs bedroom but he was concerned to see a 'do not disturb' sign on his bedroom door at a time when, despite his bullet wound, he would be expected to take active command of the last phase of the operation.

Secondly there was Henschel who was wandering around the hotel in an infuriatingly cheerful frame of mind! And now, somewhere, there was a set of bogus notebooks that could cause considerable complications when and if they ever surfaced.

He was pulled out of his frustrating reverie by a knock on his door and an orderly informing him that Sir Philip wished to see him in his room after lunch.

Turville picked at his food in a confused frame of mind. He knew, just knew, that something was wrong but try as he might he couldn't identify it. All the major objectives of the assignment had been achieved at little final cost – although allowing your chief to be shot, was considered by many in high places to be somewhat careless!

392

But that wasn't it. He'd been in this dangerous business long enough to know, through untypical behaviour, or a word dropped out of character, maybe just a look or inflection from others, when things were not as they appeared to be. Call it an innate sixth sense, whatever, *something* was undoubtedly out of place.

He made his way up the grimy stairs and along the corridor to room eight. For some reason he was relieved that Sir Philip's room was two along from his; it didn't seem right to have only a thin partition wall between their respective bed headboards!

"It's Charles, C" he half whispered at the peeling paint which somehow still clung to the cheap deal planks. He heard the key turning in the lock and then a puffy watery eye looked him up and down before the door fully opened and he was admitted to a room as grimy and unwelcoming as his.

As Sir Philip pulled the door open to let him in a number of sensations struck him.

First, the bulk of the occupant was totally out of proportion with the size of the room which, whilst bigger than his and sporting a double bed, which Sir Philip would more than fill, would have fitted into a small corner of his palatial London office. Turville realised that in the ten years he had known his chief he had only ever met him in his large office and this had disguised from him the true size of the man.

The second point was more interesting: the bedroom was immaculately tidy and a slight hint of perfume which he associated with Sir Philip was hanging on the dusty air mingling unsatisfactorily with the antiseptic smell of the wound dressing around his chief's right upper arm.

It was the tidiness which confused Turville. Sir Philip was renowned for his unkempt appearance, much to Miss Gilbert's chagrin who, try as she might, had never been able to make an impact on the dishevelled state of his clothes. They hung haphazardly on him from his shoulders – the only two bits of his body that were more or less horizontal – and now, with the wound, every garment seemed to be on the point of falling off.

Yet, by contrast, here in this sordid room his few possessions were carefully laid out, his clothes obviously put away neatly. It took Turville another moment to notice that, unlike any other room in the hotel, this one had obviously been dusted: all the surfaces were clean.

"Sit you down, Charles."

Because of his earlier gut feelings it somehow didn't surprise Turville that Sir Philip obviously wasn't at ease and yet, on the face of it, he should be. Despite the near disaster at the reunion in the theatre, the assignment *had* been successfully concluded and the old man would undoubtedly receive great credit for it from Winston Churchill himself.

Turville was motioned to the only chair whilst Sir Philip lowered himself heavily onto his bed causing a discordant squeal from the springs.

"Your man Henschel."

Turville wished he wouldn't call him 'his' man; he was far more Sir Philip's than his but he saw that his chief was in obvious discomfort, gently feeling his wounded arm and roughly adjusting the wide sling, and decided to let the comment pass. Sir Philip picked up his pipe from the bedside table and, with his one good hand, relit it, adding to the airlessness of the room. He was uncharacteristically on edge and it was such a rare condition for him that he had no experience of how to hide it.

"I have been deceiving you, Charles." The familiar Lothian lilt to his voice had flattened into dullness.

Ah, so this was it. Yet again the gut feeling hadn't let him down.

"I said to you the last time we met that such was the scale of this operation, greater than anything we had previously experienced, or would again, that there would inevitably be irrational behaviour and I, more than any other, have been guilty of it with you."

As if to scourge himself he violently knocked the stale tobacco from his pipe into the ashtray.

"You'll have to refill it for me, laddie. Too much for one hand," he said distractedly as he handed the pipe and tobacco pouch to Turville. He hauled himself upright with some difficulty and went to the window. There was a long pause. Neither man moved until at last Sir Philip turned and, with an effort, fixed his eyes on Turville.

"Henschel is an agent with the Central Intelligence Agency."
Turville froze.

"I beg your pardon, C?" He knew it was a stupid thing to say but that's what came out.

Sir Philip came forward and looked down at him.

"Yes, an American CIA agent. Has been for some time. We discovered that he was working for both countries and were about to take appropriate action when I was summoned to Whitehall and told to leave things as they were. It was then that I was briefed by Churchill on the Project Omega operation and told to use Henschel on it."

Sir Philip had been talking urgently, almost willing Turville to accept the deception, and now he sat again on the bed leaning forward towards him. He held out his hand and Turville automatically gave him the filled pipe, lit a match, and passed it to his chief.

"The Professor is off to America tomorrow." Sir Philip seemed determined to use shock tactics to explain this strange twist to the tail of the operation. "With Henschel, of course."

Turville just stared.

"Of course," he said with a fair degree of sarcasm.

Sir Philip ploughed on. "Some time ago it was decided that Britain would not be able to guarantee long-term protection to the Omega team whereas America, which Churchill is determined to have as an ally in this war, is sufficiently distanced from any likely hostilities. They are already well advanced in this nuclear business so it makes sense to concentrate the scientific work over there."

With the latest news showing the Germans on the brink of an invasion Turville had to agree that it all made sound sense but it didn't prevent him from being very angry at the deception.

"And you couldn't tell me this?" He felt hurt that Sir Philip of all people would deceive him. Expecting an apology he was surprised at the retort.

"No. It was deemed inadvisable. Your relations with Henschel would have been impossible. I doubt you would have accepted the assignment." Then he added, gently, "And it had to be you, laddie."

Turville couldn't argue with any of that. But there was one more point to be made.

"Will the Professor agree to go? All along he's said he'll only work where his wife is. That's been the main problem."

Sir Philip didn't meet his eyes. "They're going together. They've agreed. Well, I gave them no choice really – but they fully understood. The Professor has had quite enough fear for one lifetime and it seems there will be an abundance of that commodity over here for some time to come."

There was another silence in the room.

"When did you tell them?" Turville couldn't work out when he would have had time to do so.

"Last night." Sir Philip was relaxed now. The worst was over and the question suggested that the deceit had been accepted. He added quite jauntily, "I went to their room when I got here from the hospital. About midnight. They seemed surprised to see me but I soon put them at ease."

"You went to their room? At midnight? Are you sure that was wise, C? All things considered." Turville marvelled at the innocence of the man.

Sir Philip drew heavily on his pipe and blew out a perfect smoke ring, his eyes following it to the ceiling.

"Why on earth not? I don't think they'd been asleep so I didn't have to wake them up."

With a smile and a shake of his head Turville opened the door.

"A last point, Charles." Turville turned and was signalled by Sir Philip to close it again.

"The notebooks. Your man Henschel has them I believe?"

Turville gritted his teeth and then couldn't resist himself. "*Your* man I think you mean, C."

To his relief Sir Philip smiled.

"A fair point laddie. You'll see that the Professor has them today?" Turville matched the smile.

"Everything is in hand. Please don't give it another thought." For reasons of his own he very much hoped that Sir Philip wouldn't...

Turville left the room on the understanding that they'd go into more detail regarding this extraordinary development later in the day. He would have stayed and hammered it all out then but he could feel that Sir Philip had had enough for the time being.

Walking along the corridor his mind was confused by a plethora of contradicting emotions ranging between anger and understanding at the deceit by Sir Philip and increased loathing for Ludovic Henschel.

As he neared his room a door on the left opened and a small, trim figure blocked his way. He looked up – and stared into the startled eyes of Miss Gilbert. She was dressed in a long dressing gown and held a towel and a sponge bag. With a quiet yelp she scuttled back into her room and closed the door.

"Well, well, well. The old rogue." Turville chuckled to himself as he let himself into his room.

He sat on his bed and a number of mischievous thoughts struck him; Sir Philip's tidy, dusted room, the smell of perfume – of course, it was Miss Gilbert's, always evident in her office – and the pipe. Who had filled his pipe before *he* had been asked to do so at the meeting just now? All totally innocent he was sure. But why was she here? If there was a good reason, why hadn't Sir Philip mentioned she was with him? But then, thought Turville with a rare grin, there really was no good reason. No good reason at all. Unless, of course…

*

The final scenes of the drama on that Sunday were not restricted to the Station Hotel. At 34 Clarence Road Nell Masters had a visitor. She had invited Belvedere to call in at teatime to thank him for all his help and support during the past months. He had become, she said, a 'relevation' to her, a real friend and advisor. He showed suitable humility and embarrassment – but then he was an actor of long, very long standing and had he not performed alongside Larry and John, and dear Donald? Nell, of course, saw through it all but she smiled and patted his arm.

"My strength and stays," she murmured.

And then it happened.

They were alone in the house and sitting at the table in the kitchen. Suddenly with surprising speed, Belvedere fell over! Well that's how Nell described it later to Vi over a strong cup of tea.

One moment he was sitting across from her quite normally and a moment later, with a crash of furniture and cups and saucers he had pushed the heavy table to one side and was pawing at her. It took her a moment to realize he was seeking her hand which, somewhat roughly, he grasped in his.

"Fair Nell, and most fair. Will you vouchsafe to teach a soldier terms such as will enter at a lady's ear, and plead his love-suit to her gentle heart?"

Nell patted his hand. "Alright luvvie? Did you hurt your knees?"

She was confused by the explosive collapse of Belvedere and his apparent suggestion that she should take up teaching soldiers. Shakespeare's Henry V and, particularly, the good King's plighting of his troth to the fair Katherine, suitably adapted for the occasion by the tragedian – Belvedere, not the Bard – was somewhat lost on her.

Belvedere staggered to his feet in extreme embarrassment and, making more noise than ever, dragged the table back to its central place as they both skilfully caught cups and saucers rolling towards the edges.

"Oh Nell. Sorry. Sorry. Sorry" was the best he could manage. "So stupid. So de trop."

Nell had been running her mind back through Belvedere's rather pretty speech. She thought she might know what he was after.

"Were you asking me to marry you, Bel?" Better to get it out into the open, she thought.

"The gist, dear Nell, the gist indeed." He looked so mournful, like a naughty little boy who had done something rather unpleasant in front of an indignant aunt!

"Better not, luvvie. Bless you. I love you dearly, I really do. But you see…" she leant across the table and took his hands in hers, "it really wouldn't work. It really wouldn't. I have Masters you see, pet. I couldn't manage the two of you. It would be polly…polly…"

She pushed herself up and went to the stove. With her back to him her eyes filled and spilled over with tears. She lit a match and put the kettle over the burner then leant forward, bowing her head, as her tears splashed onto the flames and sizzled.

Belvedere was very confused. He assumed that his plight – or his troth – he couldn't decide which, had been rejected. Perhaps he'd try again later.

*

Back at the Station Hotel there was a further confrontation that Sunday. Ludovic Henschel had now moved into there from the refugee camp and had received an angry summons from Turville to attend a meeting between the two of them. Under normal circumstances such a command would have been met with characteristic petulance but, on this occasion, he descended the stairs with an air of grim satisfaction.

Somewhat incongruously, they stood at the bar in the Residents' Lounge and, to all appearances, could have been two businessmen meeting for a drink after a successful day's work. But a closer look would have shown that, whilst one was seemingly relaxed, the other was obviously extremely angry.

"We shall not discuss your defection except for me to express my utter repugnance that you should have done such a thing. You are under my command until midnight tonight with the formal ending of this assignment. This will be your debriefing session."

Turville's manner was haughty and autocratic and he expected an angry reply but here, as so often in the past, he had misjudged his subordinate.

This was a meeting that Henschel had been savouring. It would have been in keeping with his nature to pour out a stream of uncoordinated invective expressing every aspect of his disdain for Charles Turville and all that he stood for but, instead, he followed a well-rehearsed route.

The truth was that indeed he had, whilst an agent in the British Secret Service, approached a 'Foreign Power', albeit the United States of America, and offered his services to them and so, technically, was a traitor. It was only the extraordinary circumstances – the perilous position of Great Britain and its need for help, even rescue, by the USA – that had caused a blind eye to be put on his totally selfish actions.

Henschel, the Government felt, could be useful and he would by no means be the first or only rogue to be harnessed to the war effort.

Henschel leant back against the bar with well-rehearsed nonchalance.

"I don't intend to discuss any matters relating to my CIA status, Turville. I am under their orders which are to accompany the package and his wife to America where he, I presume voluntarily, will continue his scientific work. Then I expect to be assigned to other duties."

That was all he had intended to say but, despite all his effort and resolve, he found himself, with relish, adding "whilst you become a guest of the Gestapo in German occupied Britain."

Turville shook his head. There was so much he wanted to say to this traitorous man but now was not the time. He would have left the room had it not been for one piece of information that he required, and he didn't feel it would be long before a dose of bragging would volunteer it to him. He moved away and sat in a corner chair, shadowed from Henschel. He felt some bait was needed to move things on.

"So while a Hungarian magician was secretly working for the Germans, a naturalised Englishman of Polish descent was doing the same for the Americans?"

Such was Henschel's euphoria at his changed status with Turville that, for once, he didn't rise but, instead, smiled and chuckled – two reactions that somehow didn't work satisfactorily so rarely were they used.

"I had, of course, suspected the ridiculous Marvo for some time but could prove nothing. His belongings in the camp were clean and a CIA search showed that he had indeed been an illusionist in the Hungarian theatre and had – it would seem to mark him out from others – acted as though he was dumb. I had seen him following the girl but always assumed it was as part of those damned patrols the fat idiot organised. He did, however, seem to volunteer often. He also threw me off the scent by making some sounds when he hit me. He was a fool, he should have killed me. He must have been disturbed."

Turville had to marvel at the man. He was even more dispassionate than himself! This needed to be brought to an end. He tried more bait.

"So in the end *you personally* achieved nothing. The *British* Secret Service brought the Professor to his wife and the politicians are sending them to America…"

Henschel again uncharacteristically didn't rise to this but he did try another unsuccessful smile.

"My daily reports to my American Control in London have painted a somewhat different picture. Whilst you acted the hero escorting him back – I believe a Navy submarine actually did the work – I kept the girl safe – you'll remember impressing upon me that that was the key to the success of the mission – and then *I* shot the spy. Having not been invited to the handover I decided to be there anyway. I knew there'd be trouble."

Henschel went on apparently quite calmly to stupefy Turville.

"I had to decide in an instant whether I should let him kill all of you first but reckoned, I believe correctly, that Control would prefer your lives to be spared if possible. I find the Americans almost as squeamish regarding such matters as the weak British."

Turville's knuckles were white on the arms of his chair. This was proving harder than he'd imagined. But then, at last, came the moment. Henschel turned and looked down at him and the grotesque smile appeared again on his gaunt, grey face.

"And then, of course, there is the matter of the five notebooks. The CIA are almost as – what is your word? – paranoid regarding them as you, my friend. They see them as the key to the scientist's full co-operation in America. You know my feelings regarding force and pain, maybe on the wife, to get what they want from him but, as I said, they are as stupid as you in these matters."

He came forward now and, towering over Turville, looked down at him. "I returned to the theatre after the performance last night. The notebooks were with Marvo's transmitter up above the stage where I guessed they'd be. They are at this moment on an aeroplane bound for America, eagerly awaited by the CIA who will examine them in great detail. What was it you kept saying to me? They are a vital part of the man's future work? They will let him have them when he agrees to all their demands."

Turville didn't dare look up at Henschel; he feared the satisfaction, a mixture of triumph and amusement would show however hard he tried to mask it. He was also aware that games like this, with such high stakes, were wrong, unprofessional, but the man *was* a traitor and, as such, it was right that he should be deceived. He wished he could justify breaking his neck. Instead he shot up out of his chair having the limited satisfaction of causing Henschel to fall back against the bar.

"So you will be judged by your new masters on your success in obtaining the notebooks? So be it. I'm sure even you will be surprised at the magnitude of their reaction. I am told that you will now be taken by our – *my* – colleagues for a thorough decommissioning; an ignominious procedure that rightly befalls all those who are dismissed from our organisation."

He turned at the door. "I never wanted you, Henschel. I fought against having you and I was proved right. I never wish to meet you again."

Henschel stood alone in the room. He knew that something was wrong but it would be some time later, and three thousand miles away, before he was forcibly – very forcibly – told what it was.

*

Monday evening – and in the Pier Theatre the men of the Look-Out picket were bored. Like the rest of the British population they had spent much of the day hearing on the wireless the news bulletins reporting the incredible rescue that was taking place in the English Channel; the armada of ships from destroyers to cabin cruisers braving bombardment from the land and strafing from the air as they brought off the survivors of the British Expeditionary Force from the beaches of Dunkirk.

There is nothing that demoralises Servicemen more than the spotlight, depicting acts of great heroism, being pointed at their comrades whilst they idle away their days in parades, fatigues, spit and polish, pressing, darning, painting, scrubbing and anything else their officers can think of to keep their minds off the less wholesome things of life. And being a Look-Out picket is only one small step better than all that!

There were now eight of them under the command of a Corporal and already, only a day into this new duty, they had made themselves very much at home.

To cut out draughts and the forbidding blackness of the auditorium they found the electric switch that drew together the splendid burgundy velvet curtains and had turned the stage into a mess hall with various tables and chairs brought from the dressing-rooms. The dressing-rooms themselves, each with cold running water – the boiler was not permitted to be lit – made splendid bedrooms with two camp-beds apiece and plenty of room for all their personal and military belongings. So they were comfortable – but bored.

At nine that evening – twenty-one hundred hours – the gun detachment, relieved by their comrades from a four-hour watch, came onto the stage to join the off-duty Look-Outs. After steaming mugs of tea and thick doorstep spam sandwiches they settled down to a serious game of football. The tables and chairs became goal posts and corner flags and, in the dim emergency lighting, 'Guns versus Eyeballs' got underway.

The trouble was that no-one could see the ball very clearly so, through experimentation at the knobs, switches and faders in Bill Colbourn's cubby-hole, probably the first flood-lit game of football in the British Isles took place.

No-one remembered the score; it really wasn't important, but after forty minutes or so they'd all had enough and in the splendid lighting which also helped to keep the place warm they settled down to reading, smoking and chatting until, one by one, they sloped off to their camp-beds. The Corporal switched off the stage lights checked on the two men on duty outside who would, at the appropriate time, waken their reliefs, and went to his bed.

*

Bill Colbourn's old woolly gloves couldn't take the punishment any longer. They had rested on the lighting faders as the metal became hotter and hotter, had singed, smoked and then, just after midnight, burst into flames. Everything around them was tinder dry and, as fire will, it explored various substances – rope, cloth, wood, even dust, before bursting into a sudden sheet of flame.

Instantly the stage curtains were alight, flames running at incredible speed up to the top of the proscenium and exploding sideways to quickly engulf the whole arched area of velvet. Within minutes the whole stage was an inferno.

It was exploding lamp bulbs that woke the sleepers in the dressing rooms. Grabbing what they could, they rushed through the already smoke-filled passageway and out of the stage door. The Corporal, not a two-stripe Non-Commissioned Officer for nothing, gathered them together, counted them and then ordered them to keep their mouths shut! The Bofors gun sergeant did the same to his men.

"Act of God, boys. That's what it is. An Act of God," he declaimed in his deep Rhondda voice. It might have been more convincing if he'd believed there *was* a God, but it would have to do and orders, particularly from an NCO, were orders.

*

Nell heard the sound of fire-engine bells in her sleep. She had been dreaming of Belvedere and was rather relieved when he turned into her old school mistress ringing the bell to bring them in from play-time.

Then she was awake. The noise of motors and bells took her to the window. She opened the curtains and blackout and was soon joined by Vi, Pat, Rita and Rena who crowded around her. They said nothing, just held hands tightly, hushed by their own thoughts. There could be no doubt about the location of the fire, flames were already shooting into the sky from the domed roof of the theatre.

Nell was thinking of Alice and the bomb; the same noise of bells and similar billowing smoke. Then she had a terrible thought: had Belvedere done it in a fit of rage – or despair?

They threw on some clothes and hurried down the town steps towards the doomed theatre. Forcing a way through the growing crowd of onlookers they found the rest of the troupe pressed against barriers hastily put up by the police.

The fire-crews had no chance. Wood, thick layers of paint and furnishings, all old, brittle and dry, made fine tinder for the flames.

At first they thought all would not be lost; the front facade appeared to be untouched. The main portico flanked by its two big towers was now framed by smoke and flames above and to each side but the large board above the main doors still suggested to the on-lookers that **The Nell Masters Concert Party presents BY THE SEASIDE** and there, on the flanking panels, were all the troupe's names in red and black on the bill-boards.

Then, like the burning of a sheet of paper in a fireplace, the front of the building was almost lazily consumed. First they saw flames through the glass panels of the doors; the fire had broken into the foyer, then the oriel windows in the towers shattered funnelling out thick plumes of smoke.

With a mighty crash the door glass exploded, the flames licked at the outside wall and slowly, from one edge to the other, the Company's identity was obliterated; **BY THE SEASIDE** was consumed. Nell, mesmerised, noted with strange satisfaction that the last word to go was 'Masters'. He would have been pleased...

Almost as a final gesture of defiance the flames licked up the two flagpoles and, in perfect unison, sent sharp needles of fire up into the night sky. Within forty minutes the building was gone.

The Flaxton fire-crew had been joined by a fleet of army and RAF fire tenders but, even with hoses drawing water directly from the sea, they were no match for the speed of the flames. It was all they could do to save the Bofors gun on the pier head, and there was subsequent praise for the sergeant and his men who hurled all the stored ammunition into the water.

Slowly the crowd dispersed. As happens when people witness a drama over which they have no control they had viewed it in complete silence cuddling each other in the cool night air and holding hands as a sign of comfort. There was really nothing to say; to most of them it was the destruction of a landmark that they had grown to take for granted but for the troupe it was the ultimate final curtain. Somehow it didn't matter anymore, they'd already moved on; the building was nothing more than a husk. Now it was not even that...

And yet the troupe felt they couldn't leave. Turning their backs and walking away would undoubtedly be the final gesture and none of them wanted to be the first to do so. As dawn broke they were still at the make-shift barrier, now joined by Councillor Winifred and Vernon Rogers who, as the Observer's Picture Editor, was busily taking photographs. Smoke and steam were still rising from the wreckage as the remaining fire-crews damped down what little was left. And it *was* little because, where the once proud, mighty theatre had stood, there now was a large gaping hole!

Beyond it, its barrel stuck defiantly into the air, stood the Bofors gun marooned on its small surviving area of decking.

Tad nudged Vernon – just as he was clicking the shutter on his camera.

"There you are, old fruit…" he winked, "prophetic, that's what you are. Bloomin' genius. You said it would happen and it has."

Vernon, as so many people had over the years, looked at Tad nonplussed.

Tad tried again. "Your headline. The other day. The fire's done it for you, know what I mean?"

They were all now staring at him.

"Get on with it, man" bellowed Belvedere back to his normal self.

Tad winked at him. "The fire. Don't you get it?"

There was silence. None of them did!

"It's let the end of the pier show. Know what I mean?"

*   *   *

The mood in the small control room at the airfield in the flat Cambridgeshire countryside was a mixture of sad and sullen. Ludovic Henschel couldn't understand the animosity which had been directed at him by everyone since the revelation of his 'dual allegiance' as he liked to call it. His SIS colleagues had immediately distanced themselves from him and Sir Philip had gruffly reminded him of the Official Secrets Act which forbade him to divulge any known information about the British Secret Service to any person outside its domain.

He and Charles Turville acknowledged that such a constraint was unlikely to be adhered to once Henschel was in America and, anyway, he'd had a point in suggesting that it probably wouldn't matter to the British in a few weeks' time…

Freddy and Peggy were slightly warmer to him. Both saw the sense of continuing work on Project Omega in the safety of the United States – Freddy had experienced quite enough Nazi hospitality to last him several lifetimes – but Peggy still rankled at Henschel's deception in imprisoning her and then trading her for the notebooks. It was, however, delicious that he wouldn't know about the real books until after he had admitted his incompetence in losing the fake ones to his CIA masters.

Under considerable protest from the SIS who were paranoid about secrecy, five troupe members were there at the airfield to see them off; Nell, Pat, Vi, Belvedere and, somewhat amazingly, Tad. Freddy, at Peggy's insistence, had said that if their friends weren't allowed to attend the two of them wouldn't go! As simple as that.

Tad, as might be expected, quickly lifted the gloom that had settled on them all – other than Henschel who sat away from them reading The Times – by providing them with some startling news.

"You'll never guess. Never. Know what I mean?"

Belvedere shifted uncomfortably on his chair and wished he, too, had a newspaper.

"Bel and I. Joining up."

Nell patted Belvedere's knee. "He's far too old, Tad. In the wylight of his tears."

Belvedere humphed a subdued protest but was overwhelmed by Tad.

"Not the armed forces, love. Of course Bel's too old – and I'm too frail. Brittle bones, you see, know what I mean?"

He rode with ease, and from long experience, through the howls of outrage from the others.

"The stage, you see. On the stage." He was excited now and stood up behind the uncomfortable Belvedere, his hands on the poor man's shoulders.

"Bel does his pompous act. You know, the poems and speeches..." Another humph, "and I interrupt with my witty repartee making fun of him. It can't fail. Easy. We've done it since we first met. Works a treat. The audience will love it."

They were all now staring at Tad and Belvedere in turn.

The Great Tragedian squirmed on his seat. "Got to keep up with the times, do you see?" His voice was gruff, almost pleading. "They laugh at me now. So I'd rather it was at scripted jokes, well, that's what Tad calls them, than at my poor efforts to educate them..." His voice trailed off. He might have added that with no stage work on offer and the need to keep a large body and soul together he had really no option but to move with the times.

"Bubble and Squeak." Their eyes swivelled back to Tad. "Bel looks and sounds like a big bursting bubble and I've been told my

407

quick-fire delivery sounds like a squeak. Ideal names for us, know what I mean?"

With grating teeth, Belvedere interjected, "Prospero and Trinculo. The Duke and the jester do you see? The Tempest." Again it was said as a plea. He needed, he felt, all the help he could get.

"Well, luvvies", said Nell. "I must say you've gabberflasted me. I think you'll be a huge success." As usual, she had her finger on the pulse of the theatre world. "Why not try 'Galbraith and Stevens'? It might work better."

*

On the concrete runway a large American airliner revved its four supercharged engines. In the spacious cabin were just three people, Freddy and Peggy tightly holding each other's hands and, alone some distance from them, Ludovic Henschel. It had been a strained farewell; many tears and hugs but no ability to say to each other the things they wanted to.

The last to embrace were Pat and Peggy. Nell had gently pulled the others back. These two had shared every intimate moment of this drama for so many months. It was, thought Nell, as a mother must feel as she hands over her daughter to the care of her husband. Loving pride coupled with total emptiness.

They all stood outside the hut and waved furiously. From the plane Peggy could just make out Nell's hat with the feather being swung above their heads by Belvedere. And then they were airborne. As a neutral country they would have safe passage to the States so, at last, the tension was over; they could relax.

Each sat, still tightly clasping the other, immersed in their own thoughts, Freddy already programming his brain back into the world of nuclear physics, Peggy wondering when, if ever, she would see her friends again.

EPILOGUE

6th August, 1945. An atomic bomb explodes at 8.16 in the morning 1900 feet above the courtyard of the Shima Hospital in Hiroshima, Japan. It has the equivalent yield of 12,500 tons of TNT.

It would take just over five years for Peggy's question to be answered. They *would* meet again, all of them, but their reunion is another story.

Freddy and Peggy were flown in to a military air base near Washington and then, in time, on to Los Alimos in the wilds of New Mexico. There Project Omega was merged into the Manhattan Project and the atomic bomb was created.

In different parts of the British Isles all those who had been part of the drama, whether principals or bit players, had added reason to pause and reflect on the news of the first atomic explosion over Japan.

Their minds drifted back in vivid detail to the extraordinary events that had invaded their lives in that small seaside town on the East Anglian coast in the early months of 1940 when Britain had stood on the brink of defeat. It would be a story to tell their children and grandchildren. Or maybe write down as a book...

Also by Jeremy Carrad

Stage Plays

HIDDEN WEALTH
THE END OF THE PIER SHOW
TEAM SPIRIT
ON THE LINE